Praise for the novels of Sop
and the Toil and Trouble Series

"*De-Witched* is a perfect example of grumpy/sunshine goodness. With mystery, witchcraft, and a bit of adventure—this cozy enemies to lovers is a charming read!"

—Lana Ferguson, author of *The Fake Mate* and *The Nanny*

"A magical romance filled with heart, humor, and sizzling heat... This is grumpy-sunshine perfection, featuring a forbidden romance and a deliciously restrained hero who snaps in the most satisfying ways."

—Sarah Hawley, author of *A Witch's Guide to Fake Dating a Demon*, on *De-Witched*

"*De-Witched* features everything I should ever want in a witchy romance: grumpy book boyfriend excellence; some of the steamiest smut scenes I've ever read; and an opposites-attract romance to cheer for. PLUS! A whole lot of adorable dogs. This book is pure magic."

—Jenna Levine, *USA TODAY* bestselling author of *My Roommate is a Vampire*, on *De-Witched*

"With a sweet and sexy romance, complicated family dynamics, and a few twists along the way, *The Witch is Back* makes for a fun, enjoyable read to pick up this spooky season!"

—Hazel Beck, author of *Small Town, Big Magic*, on *The Witch is Back*

"With this tongue-in-cheek paranormal rom-com, Morgan draws readers into a world of magical mayhem... Watching the endearingly awkward protagonists navigate witchy high society is a joy. This is sure to win Morgan some new fans."

—*Publishers Weekly* on *The Witch is Back*

"The high-stakes secrets and reveals lead to satisfying moments that make the plot sweet and magical.... Morgan distinguishes her steamy witch rom-com with impressive twists on romance tropes that will bewitch fans of the genre."

—*Library Journal* on *The Witch is Back*

SEASON OF THE WITCH

SOPHIE H. MORGAN

Recycling programs for this product may not exist in your area.

ISBN-13: 978-1-335-01638-6

Season of the Witch

For questions and comments about the quality of this book, please contact us at CustomerService@Harlequin.com.

Harlequin Enterprises ULC
22 Adelaide St. West, 41st Floor
Toronto, Ontario M5H 4E3, Canada
www.Harlequin.com

HarperCollins Publishers
Macken House, 39/40 Mayor Street Upper,
Dublin 1, D01 C9W8, Ireland
www.HarperCollins.com

Printed in U.S.A.

To Christmas, because you make the impossible seem inevitable

one

There were so many ways a witch could murder her ex.

Tia Hightower stared hard at her computer screen. The report on potion distribution was one she'd been waiting for all morning, but the black type and colorful charts were obscured by the incessant tapping coming from the desk across the room.

Tap. Tap. Tap.

A muscle beat in her jaw and she blinked a few times to bring the report into focus. Maybe murder was going too far. Maiming, though... That had real possibilities. Witches were cutthroat, especially Higher society ones like her. *Legacies* like her. It would be encouraged—no, expected. Nobody insulted or pissed off a Hightower and got away without at least a dick rash.

Amusement ghosted through her at the idea, even as the tapping picked up pace.

Taptap. Taptap. Taptap.

She blew a thin stream of breath out her nose, clinging to her poker face with a glance at the open door and the glass walls surrounding her. Her cage for the past month, thanks to her family—and *his*.

The stack of crystals piled in her in-tray with its shiny new logo caught her seething attention. *PH Inc.* A new name for the merger of two powerful witch families. The coming together of potion-making excellence and a company that evolved other companies. The business that would take potions to new heights.

If she and its other next-gen warlock didn't kill each other first.

With her mom's warning buzzing in her mind, Tia chose the path least likely to land her in trouble. She braced her hands on the desk and pushed to stand, slow and easy. The tapping paused.

Tia didn't need to look to know people were watching. Waiting. Tia Hightower and Henry Pearlmatter, together, in an enclosed space? *Boom* goes the dynamite. Even when they'd been dating—nope. No way she was going there.

She applied a tight smile to her face, like the bold red lipstick she preferred. "I'm getting coffee."

She hurried away without offering to get him one. It was for his own good, honestly. An open container, potion ingredients lying around... Temptation was hard to resist for a reason. And it'd be so sweet to see him bark like a dog for a few hours. Be *her* little bitch.

But then she'd really be fucked, and her parents had made her promise not to embarrass them.

The reminder made a flush rise to her skin, hot and uncomfortable, stilettos stalling halfway through the outer office. It wasn't like she *tried* to disappoint her parents, but being herself hadn't exactly won her "daughter of the year." Normal childhood rebellion turned into one lecture after another, lasting through her teens, into her twenties.

Why would you play with the shy witch who's barely society?

Why do you have to wear such bright lipstick and tight dresses?

Why can't you be social at parties like (insert perfect Higher witch name here)?

Why open a bar with the shy witch and a human when your family legacy is more appropriate?

And of course, the kicker: Why did you let Henry Pearlmatter, shining Legacy warlock, get away?

Get away. Like she was supposed to chase after him when he'd left her first, in all the ways that mattered.

Fuck opening herself up to anyone again. She'd take easy sex and no messy emotions, thanks so much.

She ignored the curious looks as she moved forward, wishing she could hide from everyone waiting on the latest spectacle from the Hightower misfit. Fuck them, too. Pride alone powered her into the kitchen. There, mostly out of sight, she splayed her hands on the counter and let her head hang.

And *fuck him* if he thought she'd let him edge her out of this company. He must want to; after all, until the merger, he'd had a direct line to CEO, and he'd sacrificed everything for that goal. Everything.

Now the whispers circulated and the gossips placed their bets on who'd be made *the heir*—and she refused to believe it would be anyone but her. Yes, she'd played at other careers, even opening the bar Toil and Trouble with her friends, but taking over her family's thriving potion business had always been her plan. A career she could make her own, be good at, love. And make her parents proud. Finally.

"Coffee sounded too good to pass up."

At least until this fucker and his family had stuck their brooms in.

Henry's deep voice, with its hint of New Orleans drawl, dragged up her spine and she squared her shoulders against it, curling her hands around the counter until white bone pushed against her brown skin. She flicked him a cool look. Today he wore a tailored navy suit. The color was vivid against his pale skin and short platinum hair and followed his muscular frame faithfully.

She hated it.

His tall body blocked most of the doorway, but past him, she saw no fewer than three workers ogling.

Don't lose your shit.

"There's the instant stuff," she said in as even a tone as she could manage. "Or I was about to grind the new beans Jorge brought back from Brazil, if you want in on that."

"You know what I want."

She didn't respond, didn't trust herself to, as she measured out the beans and added them to the grinder. He stopped close by, a wisp of his scent teasing her senses. Memories stroked along her nerves and she gritted her teeth as she flicked the switch. The air came alive with the sound of beans being run through the mill. She knew how they felt.

"Tia," Henry murmured, half-behind her.

"No," she bit out, eyes forward.

"I thought we'd agreed to be civil."

"Do you *see* that pen sticking out of your jugular?"

She caught his smirk out of the corner of her eye. Asshole. She'd known he was doing it on purpose.

He moved closer. "You can't ignore me forever."

"Watch me."

"All that animosity...someone might think you were still hung up on me."

Her head whipped around, a retort ready until she caught the glint of triumph in his face. Reining it in, all she did was scoff. "I'm not the one who can't leave the other alone. Why are you so obsessed with me?"

"If you call trying to form a functional working relationship *obsessed*..."

"We agreed to be civil," she countered, realizing her voice had lifted and hushing it again. "We didn't agree to hold hands and skip."

He ran his tongue around his teeth. "My dad thinks—"

"Ah, yes," she cut him off. "Dear old Dick. I hope he's doing well."

"Real nice."

Considering Richard Pearlmatter was a large part of why Henry had left her, she felt her bitterness was justified.

"I never understood why you two didn't get along. Maybe now—"

"No chance in hell," she interrupted again. "One of the many, many benefits of not having you in my bed anymore is that I don't have to put up with him watching me like I'm not good enough to wipe his boots. But I guess he doesn't need me to, now he has you licking them."

Tia flicked the grinder off as Henry opened his mouth.

He glared at her.

"Careful," she chided as she set the coffeemaker going. The bubbling merged with her voice, hiding the unforgivably raw note. "Daddy wouldn't want his little robot to show anything but team spirit, right?"

A muscle jumped in his jaw and victory sang in her blood.

"I don't see you fighting against Gloria's decree, either," he pointed out, low and tight.

Like it was the same. While Henry had been busy asking his dad how high, she'd been juggling her mom's lectures with living her own life. But this time, she had to toe the line. This was her future, her family.

She only needed one chance.

So if biting her tongue helped her parents see she could do this, she'd leave it a ragged, bleeding stump before she screwed this up.

They stood in silence until the coffeemaker switched off. She reached into the open cupboards above their heads and picked out her mug, red with a gold T, then an obscenely pink one with a unicorn riding the handle. She offered him the latter with her lips curled.

Henry's eyes, palest green, narrowed. A light fizzing sensation tickled her fingers before her mug disappeared from her hand and reappeared in his.

Mindful of their audience, she kept her smile in place. Barely. "Give me back my mug, jackass."

"Say please and I'll give it to you."

Her smirk grew. "You'd have to beg me to ask you to *give it to me* ever again."

Something invisible sizzled across the air as his head dipped toward her. "We both know I could have you on your knees if I wanted it."

"You're delusional."

"You're blushing."

Goddess, she was *not.*

Fuck it. She'd sooner order coffee in than stay here with him one more second. "Screw you, Pearlmatter," she hissed between her teeth.

Without looking back, she moved past him, smoothing her hands down her tight violet dress so nobody would see them fist. Or shake.

Henry didn't watch Tia go. Instead, he carefully placed her mug on the counter and stared at the floor.

Fuck, he was such an idiot.

Civil, he'd told her. Told himself. Like he had every morning for the past month, resigned to working in close vicinity with his ex. An ex who still had the power to get under his skin. An ex he still…

Outside, a bush that was part of the newly landscaped PH Inc. grounds caught fire, quickly smoldering to ash. He didn't worry about the mess; a groundskeeper would find it soon. The chatter on the lower floors was that there was some weird fire warlock getting their kicks from burning shrubbery. If only.

Henry's focus had always had one particular target, and eight years had done nothing to quench it. Even when their relationship was as much ash as that innocent bush outside.

He always had every intention that this day would be the one that would start them on a new path. But Tia was just so…

Tia. Aggravating, provocative, unreasonable. And still so goddamn gorgeous she stopped his heart.

Pushing both hands into his hair, Henry concentrated on cooling the simmering emotions Tia always stirred. His dad had tasked him with ensuring the seamless integration of both companies, making sure the puzzle pieces slotted together to create a stronger whole. He'd asked Henry if Tia would be a problem for him. It wasn't like Henry could've said yes. Weakness in front of Richard Pearlmatter wasn't acceptable.

He'd figure it out. *They* would. She couldn't hate him forever.

He only needed one chance.

The past mocked him as he filled a new mug with the coffee she'd made, before he braced himself and headed back to their office.

two

Tia drummed her nails on the couch arm. Once. Twice. Bored of that, she knocked her feet together on the expensive Aubusson rug, faded from age and sunlight. She smacked her lips, running her tongue along her teeth in a lipstick check, then cracked her neck. The noise echoed through the large, tastefully decorated room that many witches would die to be in. Idiots.

When she began to bounce her knees, Emma, her best friend and business partner at the bar, elbowed her. "Quit it. You're making me nervous."

"Sorry." Tia tried to sit still, curling and uncurling her toes to get rid of the excess energy. Late-afternoon sunlight shone through the high arched windows, casting golden puddles on the carpet. "I've only got an hour."

Leah, the third in their trio, glanced over from a cushioned ivory armchair. "You didn't need to be here."

Tia gave her a get-real look.

The pretty blonde human sighed. "You know, I've officially been *out* in witch society for more than half a year. I don't think Isabella's going to come after me with a hex bag." She said it like Tia was the one being ridiculous. Fact: humans weren't supposed to know witches existed. It didn't mean squat that, thanks to her warlock boyfriend, Leah had managed to wrangle probation into their society. Tia was here to ensure nothing bad happened to her friend if her welcome ever wore out. Even if these social visits were going to be the death of her.

She tapped her cell to illuminate the screen. *Four oh three.* She could practically hear Henry's snide thoughts about taking time off in the middle of a workday. He probably had a crystal logging every second she was gone, citing it as lack of commitment. Bastard.

"I know that look." Leah tipped her Cubs cap back as she leaned against the cushions, her fuchsia nail polish standing out against her fair skin. "What's he done now?"

"Breathe," Emma said drily to Tia's left. "Exist."

Tia transferred her glare from her phone to her friend. The brunette smiled, unrepentant.

Unwilling to prove them right, Tia lifted her chin. "Actually, it's my mom," she lied, or half lied, since the mirror message that'd come through four hours ago still stirred unease in the pit of her stomach. "She's summoned me. Tomorrow, eight sharp."

"Ah, so, it's not what *he's* done," Leah mused. "It's what *you've* done. Which is...?"

"Nothing." Tia drilled her red nails on the couch arm again, a little harder. Right? She'd done nothing to deserve getting chewed out. At their doubtful looks, she added, "Seriously. I haven't done anything to the jackass."

"Hex bags?"

"Haven't used any."

"How many have you made up?"

Silence.

Emma snorted, shifting in place. "Pretty sure Henry could defuse them anyway."

"Shit. You said his name." Tia conjured a canister and thrust it at her friend. "Quick, salt a line before he's summoned."

"Ha ha."

"Hey, it worked for the Winchesters."

"Salt doesn't stop a summoning, it stops ghosts," Leah put in.

"As long as it stops *him*, I'll buy stock in salt mines."

"Wait, are there actually ghosts around?" Leah peered at both of them, blue eyes wide. "How have I not asked this before? Does Casper exist?"

Emma poked Tia before she stirred the pot. "Don't freak her out. Goddess, mention Henry and you turn into a five-year-old."

Because she recognized the partial truth, Tia grew sullen. "I don't know why you don't hate him as much as me." She set the canister down on the table harder than necessary. "He turned away from you with everyone else."

A Higher witch clinging to the lowest rung of the social ladder, Emma had been jilted by her childhood fiancé eight years ago and all of Higher society had blamed her for it. That was how their sucky society worked.

Bastian Truenote was a golden Truenote.

Ergo, it must have been Emma's fault he'd run like a little bitch.

Henry, Bastian's friend, was equal in status and could have helped Emma, if he'd stepped up. If.

Instead, Emma had ended up fleeing to Chicago, leaving witch society completely.

Emma shrugged as if that time hadn't left scars only Bastian's return had healed, though some color touched her pale cheeks. "Henry wasn't one of the ones that shunned me. He didn't do anything."

"Exactly."

Emma gave her a look, but Tia refused to back down.

Realistically, if it was just about him not standing up for her friend, Tia could have gotten over it, or at least not been mortal enemies with the guy. It was the catalyst that had forced them apart, an easy excuse Tia could cling to and keep her pride in public, but deep down, below the shields and walls she'd built, she knew the real reason she couldn't let it go.

Put simply, that night had been the final time he'd shown, once and for all, that she hadn't been enough. He'd run from their relationship, chasing his dad's approval, instead of even trying to make her a priority. She hadn't been worth the effort, she guessed. Found wanting, yet again. The Hightower misfit who always strove for acceptance but never managed it.

And now he was in her face every day.

She dragged her hands through her hair, magic collecting under her skin like iron shavings to a magnet. "I swear, I can't take much more of him," she muttered. "Him and his endless staring and unspoken words and his smug, stupid face. Arrogant warlock asshole."

"Maybe..." Emma hesitated, then went for it. "I mean, wouldn't it be easier just to let things go? You know, forgive him?"

Her eye twitched. "I will never be that weak." *Again.* Before her friends could nag, she said flatly, "Let's just change the subject."

It wasn't the time to get into it, not when they were sitting in one of the parlors at High House, waiting for their hostess to arrive. If she ever did.

Four oh seven.

Ever since Leah's initiation into witch society, the three of them had been coming to New Orleans once a month to have tea with Isabella Castello, one of the High daughters. The High Family was the witch equivalent of royalty, or at least, an overseer family that governed all North American witches. All of the siblings, the main ruling body, were beyond powerful. They brooked no opposition, took no prisoners—well, unless laws were broken, and then she imagined they did—and were scary-ass mothers to deal with.

Which was why Leah's insistence on coming alone to the monthly afternoon teas was laughable. Especially since the High daughter had some kind of fascination with Leah. Whether it was because she was human or because she'd snared Gabriel

Goodnight, the so-called Warlock of Contempt, who knew. Luckily, the fascination was on the innocent side. So far.

The teas had been…fine. Gossipy, light, frivolous. But the High Family never did anything without reason. So here Tia sat, when she should be staring Henry down from the desk across from his.

Four ten.

"Maybe she forgot," Emma posed, half-hopeful, her social anxiety probably playing the xylophone on her ribs.

Tia opened her mouth to respond when the door swung open.

"Ladies." A stunning brown-skinned witch spoke, her voice a touch Southern. Dressed in a mint summer dress, matching cardigan and with a hair ribbon tying her heavy white curls back, all Isabella Castello needed to round out her picture of innocence was a coterie of doting woodland creatures. But not even that would've concealed the magic that pulsed in the air around her. The first moment it hit was the worst, breaking over Tia like thrashing waves against a cliff face. Thankfully, the effects lessened with time.

The witch waved her manicured hands, conjuring a groaning tea trolley. Swiftly, four gilded side plates appeared on the coffee table, along with a cake tower stacked with French fancies. A teapot materialized next to them, steam lazily wafting from the spout.

Isabella took her seat, saying over her shoulder, "We're fine, Bianca."

The door shut on the butler, leaving the four of them alone.

"We'll leave the tea to steep," Isabella said, smoothing her skirts out. "Emma, how is the wedding planning going?"

Emma's throat bobbed but she managed a smile. "G-good, thank you. We've decided to get married at Bastian's parents' mansion. His parents offered and I don't mind where we do it, so it makes sense."

Isabella clapped once. "I do love a wedding. And the Truenote mansion is so charming. I assume you hired a wedding planner?"

Emma nodded, fingers curling into her jeans. Tia laid her hand on Emma's and answered for her tongue-tied friend. "Tamsin White."

Isabella hummed. "Tamsin is a treasure. You couldn't have better in charge."

Emma nodded again, then ventured, "She's great. I feel so much better knowing she's handling it all."

"As you should. It's your job to enjoy all the lead-up to the ceremony, not get bogged down with details."

As minutes passed, Isabella continued to pry answers out of her nervous friend, only pausing to pour them all lemon verbena and to pass out the tiny cakes.

Emma slumped in relief when the High daughter turned her laser focus onto Leah. "And how is darling Gabriel?"

"He got angry at the microwave last night." Leah, who, at most, had a passing acquaintanceship with fear, shot Isabella a delighted grin. "He'd accidentally pressed defrost and yelled for a minute straight about how it was out to sabotage his attempts to make dinner."

"Why didn't he just use magic?" Tia asked, genuinely baffled.

"Male pride?" Leah shrugged. "Those three months living as a human made him think he could master everything. Spoiler: he can't. You don't want to know how many times I've had toast for dinner in the last month."

Isabella's laugh joined Leah's, and even Tia smiled. She wouldn't have believed serious Gabriel could hook up with her sunshine friend but that was the power of Leah. And love, Leah would say, but she was mushy like that.

As if Isabella could sense her thoughts wandering, she pounced on her. "And how is work, Tia? Other than the bar."

"Fine."

"That's what you said last month."

Her smile stretched tighter, plaster covering the cracks. "And it's still the case."

Isabella hummed. "I would never have pictured the Hightowers and Pearlmatters merging. Then again, you and Henry Pearlmatter...you were involved, yes?"

Tia would sooner gargle with bat dung than talk about this but you didn't exactly refuse the High Family. She gave Isabella a clipped nod.

Amber eyes gleamed. "Not an easy breakup?"

"You could say that."

"I think *you* said it. Earlier when you said he was a—what was it? Arrogant warlock asshole?"

Emma choked on her tea.

Isabella's smile broadened. "Walls have ears in this place. I'd never have guessed you and Henry are so at odds. Such... passion." She considered Tia's face, which she knew had gone sour. "Are you still in love with him?"

Tia's jaw tightened. "No."

"He's very handsome," the other witch murmured, sly. Searching.

"You date him, then," Tia muttered before remembering who she was talking to.

It wasn't that Isabella was cruel. In fact, she had a reputation as the most compassionate High Family member, but considering the family, that wasn't saying much.

Isabella only laughed, a husky peal that relaxed even Emma's shoulders. "I don't think we would be a suitable match," she said, amusement dancing in her voice. "I doubt I'm his type, and I like a different kind of warlock."

"What *is* your type?"

All eyes swung to Leah, who turned bright red at the obvious social faux pas.

As if the personal question had flummoxed her, Isabella sipped her tea, watching them over the rim. "Is this girl talk?" she finally said.

The frankly shy question took Tia aback.

The few seconds of awkward silence were broken by Emma. "Talking about men is pretty standard for that, yeah. But you don't h-have to..." Nerves tangled her tongue, as they sometimes did, when the witch's stare moved to her.

Expression still faintly baffled, Isabella let out a considering noise. She drank more tea, eyebrows threading as she thought about it.

Tia snuck a look at her cell.

Four thirty-seven.

"I don't suppose it matters," the High daughter concluded, setting her teacup aside. "I will most likely marry for reasons other than love."

Leah opened her mouth, then caught Tia's glare and shut it. The diehard romantic looked inches from bursting at the unfairness. Tia, though, wasn't surprised. A lot of witch society marriages were for power or magic; the High Family couldn't be any different. It sucked.

It was why her family insisted on keeping a candle of hope alive for her and Henry. As her mom and nana said with great passion and frequency, his Legacy line was equal to the Hightower's. Legacies were the pedigree dogs of the witch world, and to a society where breeding mattered, the idea of throwing away such an influential and powerful bond... Inconceivable. They should be a match in every way—except that Tia would like to take that match and set fire to his dick.

"Obligation ties us all," Isabella murmured, and when Tia raised her gaze, the woman was staring at her. "But smart witches make their own rules in the game."

Unsure if she was trying to comfort, help, or mock her, Tia settled for a wary nod. As Isabella tactfully changed topics to books, she brooded into what was left of her tea.

Smart witches might make their own rules, but she also bet they never got entangled with Henry Pearlmatter in the first place.

three

Gloria Hightower's office was as practical as the rest of her, but like the woman, it also had touches of softness. The desk was metal and modern, the bookcases white and stark under the sun that struggled to poke through the gray clouds of New Orleans October. But a lush rug of navy spread across the expanse of dark hardwood, pots in mixed colors sat on varying levels around the space, and the curtains hung across the wide windows were crushed velvet. A silver frame displayed photos on a loop, sat at a right angle to the sleek modern phone she insisted on using when dealing with human suppliers. And her office chair was supple leather with soft curves in dove gray, the guest chairs similar in style and ideal for comfort.

"Sit up straight, Tia."

In theory, anyway.

Tia restrained her eye roll and stiffened her spine as a good little witch did. She swore her mom, sitting across from her, read her mind as she gave her a warning look.

While Tia most closely resembled her nana, she saw her features hinted at in her mother's no-bullshit eyes, the slope of nose, the stubborn chin. Gloria still looked to be in her late forties, magic slowing the aging process. A suggestion of wrinkles, of laugh lines, were all that showed in her dark skin. Those laugh lines sure as shit weren't visible now as she leaned back and stared at her daughter. "Did you write down a curse to transmogrify Henry into a pig last week and leave it on his desk?"

Tia opened her mouth. Closed it. Like she was seven again instead of twenty-nine, she felt the urge to shift in her seat. "It was a joke," she muttered.

"Wasting company time?" Gloria hiked an eyebrow. "Not to mention the immaturity of the act. Not exactly behavior I'd like to see from someone potentially inheriting our company one day."

Tia ran her tongue around her teeth. It was hard to argue. Though if she *was* going to argue, she'd point out she'd only resorted to it because Henry had been repeatedly staring at her. Even after she'd asked him to stop in every way possible. She'd been particularly proud of her mime. Not many ways to mime "fuck off," but judging by his thundercloud expression, she'd managed.

"Did you see the tweaks to the Prima potion I sent over?" she asked instead. Part of their hobbies range, the potion coordinated the drinker's limbs to dance a ballet routine for the space of one number. Tia's team had worked through the night polishing it, and Xia, her secondary alchemist, had performed a dance from *The Nutcracker* to perfection last week.

Gloria's face softened a fraction. "I did. Your solution to the chemical delay was genius."

Pride glowed inside her as she allowed herself a smile. She knew she was one of the best; alchemy was her specialty as a witch after all. It wasn't a big surprise that the other business she'd started with her friends was a bar famous for witchy cocktails, and what were cocktails if not human potions? But direct praise from her mom was harder to get than blood out of a stone. There was almost always a "but."

You look beautiful, but maybe you should wear something more elegant, like a true Hightower.

Your ideas are interesting, but there are too many of them and you need to think logically, like a Hightower should.

"But," her mom added on cue, crushing the glow, "a Hightower doesn't resort to childish tactics. Especially not with a warlock of Henry's caliber. I don't know what he must have thought of you."

"He tattled, didn't he? Little snitch."

Gloria flicked her a look.

Tia ground her hands in her lap, using her magic to twist part of the curtain tighter and tighter. Pretending it was Henry's neck.

"Don't crush my curtains," Gloria warned, a flicker of humor washing the sternness from her face. "You knew you would be working in close proximity. You could have raised any arguments then."

"I *did*." Through the first conversation, the negotiations, the signing, Tia had made her feelings clearer than a crystal cauldron. Which was to say it was a fucking mistake.

"Your breakup was years ago. Surely it's time to bury the hatchet."

"In his head," Tia mumbled. "Let me guess: a Hightower would let it go?"

"Don't be petulant. You have so many wonderful qualities but this blind spot with Henry is affecting your judgment. You used to be so good at working together—when you taught him how to master his fire magic into shapes? And when he helped you perfect your first anthology of potions?"

Tia felt her blood pressure rise. "Mom…"

"Henry has no problem working with you."

"Of course not. Daddy's perfect boy would never say no."

"Tia."

"Come on, Richard says kiss my boots and Henry hits the dirt."

Eyebrows winged up at that. "It's not a sin to respect your parents."

Tia slumped, resigned to the tut of disapproval. "Trust me, if I didn't respect you, I'd have already walked."

"You're too stubborn for that, which is a blessing here, I suppose."

Tia snorted at that coming from her mom. Her dad claimed the only reason they'd broken up for six months before they'd married was because he'd refused to give in on an argument. Family legend had it that Gloria made him crawl before she took him back.

Stubborn bred stubborn, was all she was saying.

As if she'd heard the silent sass, her mom's lips pinched. "There was a time when all you wanted was to be with Henry."

"I also wanted to be a scuba diver and thought money grew on trees. Then I grew up." Tia's tone soured. "And you can tell Nana to stop dropping hints, too. No matchmaking."

"Nobody tells your nana what to do." That humor surfaced again as Gloria twisted her wedding band. "She still has her sights set on a wedding."

Tia stared her down, unamused.

Gloria huffed a quiet laugh and stood, graceful in a citrine pantsuit. Her black hair was coiled in her usual bun, leaving her face open to interpretation. Tia needed no interpretation to know her mom had shifted from mom to matriarch.

Sure enough, Gloria's tone was sterner as she picked a clear quartz crystal from the desk and passed it from hand to hand. "We've been approached by a potential new client from Europe."

Tia's brows rose. Their potion research and development company was well respected but on the smaller side, meaning a lot of European business slipped through their fingers.

Had been on the smaller side, she corrected herself. And with all the press swirling around the merger—some around Henry and Tia, to her disgruntlement—there was no reason why the company couldn't have gained attention from the international crowd.

"Who?" was all she asked.

Gloria passed the crystal across as she perched on the edge of her desk. Tia spoke the access word and an image projected onto the far wall.

She'd place the man around sixty, though if he was a witch, he could've been older. His face had the lines of aristocracy, softened with age, a pair of joyous blue eyes and thick brown eyebrows over a straight nose. Broad grin. Fair skin with a ruddy undertone. His hair was brown shot through with silver and shaggy under a tweed flat cap. The crystal didn't show from the neck down, but if Tia had to guess, she'd go for a lot of tweed and maybe some galoshes.

"Lord Archibald Siddeley." Gloria's fingers curled around the lip of the desk. "One of the richest warlocks in Europe, though he makes his primary home outside London in a town he presides over. His assistant contacted us last week, saying he'd love to meet when he was in New Orleans."

"He wants to check us out."

A nod. "Siddeley is an investor with pockets so deep, you'd need equipment and a day's worth of food before you hit bottom. His last three projects have gone international within two years, to great success."

Now her mom's clutching fingers made sense. It had forever been her ambition to grow the company, sometimes to desperate ends—cough, *merger*, cough—and her eyes had always been on international business.

Tia sat forward, eyes trained on Siddeley's image. "The witch who persuades Siddeley to invest would have a lot of sway in the company. A lot of respect." Maybe even…approval?

Gloria's gaze connected with hers, meaning in every sweep of her lashes. "Indeed." Even as Tia's lips spread into a grin, her mom warned, "This is your first big test under the new structure." She watched her daughter closely. "Don't let your emotions cloud your abilities. Be the Hightower I know you can be. Get us that warlock."

***

Henry grinned at his mom over the teacup he held. "And then what did she say?"

Maybelline Pearlmatter lifted her nose, the feather she wore quivering in her blond hair. "She had the audacity to claim I didn't know a Lobbitin spell from a Pyrotyke," she declared in an accent straight out of *Gone with the Wind*. "I told her, honey, my family's been dealing with Pyrotyke spells longer than you've been dabbling with eternal youth potions. I know one when I see it."

"Brutal." Henry swallowed another disgusting sip of the chamomile tea his mom had served.

"Brutal is as brutal does."

"What does that even mean?"

"It means don't dish it if you can't take it." Maybelline smiled in satisfaction as she selected a small lemon cake from the platter between their easy chairs.

Henry couldn't disagree. That was witch society: polite but vicious. Small cruelties with a smile. He'd never understand it.

The clock on the polished mantel struck two. It meant he'd already been here an hour and needed to get back to his desk, but he lingered anyway. The tradition of taking tea with his mom had started when he'd been a boy, after one of the many times his dad had brushed him off. Always in his mom's parlor, so welcoming with its plush feminine furnishings, they'd have cake and tea and talk. About anything. No judgments. It was one of the many reasons he adored his mom, even if others found her a little eccentric and gossipy. Here was his safe haven, complete with the tang of lemon polish and the notes of his mom's French perfume.

If only she'd let him have coffee. He sighed and forced himself to finish the chamomile, setting the cup in its saucer on the coffee table with a click.

"Are you leaving?"

"Work won't do itself," he said lightly.

Before he even stood, she crossed arms clad in pale green cashmere. *You work too much*, he mouthed in time with her, and grinned again.

She huffed, even as a smile tugged on the corner of her mouth. "Think you're smart, do you?"

"I'm your son."

"Don't flatter me." But she preened anyway. "You're your father's son, through and through. Work this, work that." She sighed, missing the tightening of his expression. "Life is for living, Henry. When was the last time you brought a witch home? When am I gonna have my grandbabies?"

Heat funneled up the back of his neck. He refused to react, knowing that was half her plan. "Dad doesn't complain about my work ethic." It was near enough one of the only things that earned him praise from the old man. He still remembered the glow of finally being invited into his dad's private study to discuss business, the relief of having something in common.

"Oh, don't get me started on your father." Frustration stole over his mom's sharp, pretty features. "Does the man ever take a day off to be with his wife? An hour? No, he has to drive himself and our son into the ground, and for what?" She sniffed, shaking back long, loose hair the same color as his own, undeniably striking against skin so pale, it had blue undertones. "A company."

"A legacy."

"Honey, you spit out that Kool-Aid before it rots your brain." The prim words made him laugh. She clutched her hands together, despairing. "Love is what you should dedicate yourself to. And for once, your dad has done right by pairing you with Tia again."

Abruptly, his humor shut off, a lid closing a box with finality. "Don't," he warned, his voice flat. Harsh.

She ignored him. "Why can't you make it work? You two were so beautiful together."

He gave her a half-incredulous stare. "We argued constantly."

Except when they'd been in bed, and even then, every time had been a challenge, neither willing to give in.

Crisp sheets under hot skin, mouths roving, hands gripping hard enough to bruise.

The memories made lust coil tightly in his gut.

"Heat is essential."

"Mom."

"Boy, how do you think your dad and I made you? We burned up the sheets plenty, still do when the man looks up from his computer and his crystals to remember he has a wife."

"Hey, far as I'm concerned, all you guys do is kiss. The Goddess must've floated me down on a cloud."

His attempt at humor failed as she peered at him from suddenly soft eyes. "You don't have to work so hard for him, honey," she said, equally gentle.

It made him tense. "I don't. I work hard for me."

She clicked her tongue, doubtful, and like that, all Tia's past accusations about being a lapdog rose from where he'd tried to bury them. He stood quickly, disturbed. "I have to go."

Far from put off, his mom crossed her arms again. "Henry Charles Pearlmatter, did I raise you to run out on your mother?"

"You raised me to know when to flee a losing battle." He stooped, kissed her cheek. "Nobody ever wins an argument with you."

"Think you're charming, huh?" But she smiled a little. "At least think about it. About what's important."

He knew what was important, but he also knew his mom and he would never agree on that.

Before he could leave, his dad strode in. Though he'd been working from home, he still wore suit trousers and a shirt. His hair was neatly brushed ebony, framing the angles of a lightly tanned face more likely to be called distinguished than handsome. Pale green eyes, exactly like Henry's, examined the teacups.

Henry stood taller, fighting not to shift in place. "I was just taking a small break."

"Hello, dear." His mom waved before his dad could respond. "Remember me, your wife?"

His expression cracked as he turned from his son. "I thought you looked familiar. Divining tattoos, veil, full moon ceremony?"

"I was the one in sage green," his mom confirmed. "Come kiss me, husband, before you drag our progeny off to the labor camp."

His dad chuckled and did as ordered by his wife, his love for her a subtle constant all of Henry's life. The only time the man ever unbent was with her.

Sure enough, any affection drifted away from those eyes as they shifted to Henry. "I need to speak with you."

Henry nodded and left without a backward glance.

Ten minutes later, he masked the challenge racing in his blood. "I can get him."

"I have no doubts." Seated, Richard placed his hands on his antique desk, the surface well-ordered and well maintained. It was dark wood, much like the bookcases that lined the walls, the only relief the plants his mom insisted he have in here. The sun didn't touch this part of the manor, so lamps were always burning on the dark furniture. The rug beneath Henry's feet had barely faded with age, although it should have with the amount of times he'd anchored in this spot. Richard Pearlmatter didn't have "guest" chairs. And that was what Henry still felt like here—a guest.

But if he managed to convince Archibald Siddeley to invest, if he was the one who secured international business for PH Inc.…

Maybe, his mind whispered.

Richard tapped a file folder twice before it appeared in Henry's hand. "This is the dossier we've put together on him. He's to attend a company party we're hosting in three weeks. I want you to memorize that."

"Yes, sir."

"Be ready, Henry." The words were stressed. "I have no doubts that Gloria and Peter will similarly equip Tia Hightower." A small amount of distaste crept into his voice. "If we could keep her away from Siddeley, it would be better, but that idea was naysayed."

Meaning his dad had gone toe-to-toe with the Hightower women and lost. Henry sympathized.

His dad let out a short, aggravated breath. "I understand they're Legacies, but why they persist in this pretense that Tia be involved in the company… It's sheer stubbornness. They'd be better trying to marry her off."

A Legacy family, much like his own, was the cream of the society crop. Every generation added to the next by sacrificing a small amount of their magic to make the line stronger. Not as strong as the High Family, but definitely a desirable match.

Henry forced away the image of Tia walking down the aisle to a no-faced warlock, his skin feeling too tight over his bones. "Tia would never go for that."

Richard harrumphed. "Likely you're right. But we need someone calm, efficient, who listens to others. Her hotheadedness is too much of a hazard."

The disparaging words burned in Henry's chest. His jaw worked side to side as he forced a nod. It wasn't like his dad was wrong. He might have been the fire warlock but Tia had a quicker temper.

Well. Most of the time.

These days, it was hard to remember that he'd ever had a reputation for being the calm, charming Pearlmatter. Shove Tia and him in a corner office for five weeks and all that had been shot to shit. From the day they met to the day they exploded, they'd worked against each other like flint and stone, and now after eight years, they'd picked up their swords like no time had passed.

Every day she trained a look on him that dripped condescension, every time she scoffed when he mentioned his dad, every time she pushed just to push him, his resolve weakened like toffee held under a flame. There was only so much he was willing to take before he snapped. And then…

He'd see those red lips part with desire, not insults. The breathy catch she used to make would bleed into the air when he bent her over the desk, her body shuddering under his roaming hands. As she writhed, he'd flip up the skirt of those dresses she swanned around in and he'd—

Fuck.

Savagely, he snapped the thought off. Not because he couldn't face the truth—he'd long ago accepted he'd never find a woman who made his blood run as hot, or his head as dizzy, as Tia Hightower. But Tia didn't change; she was as stubborn as ever. He'd loved her for it, as much as he despised what it meant—there was no future for them. And fantasies where he could relearn how to make her moan, or hell, even just laugh with her, were pointless.

"Just remember," his dad warned, bringing Henry back, "Siddeley is English. Breeding and etiquette will matter to him. Manners." The look Richard leveled on his son was pointed. "No matter how Tia tries to provoke you, I don't want any scenes."

Henry stiffened his spine. "No scenes," he agreed, ignoring the unease that flipped in his stomach. He could handle his feelings around Tia for one night. For his dad's sake.

Right.

Somewhere, he just knew the Goddess was grinning and rubbing her hands in anticipation.

four

When Tia saw the dress her nana had laid out—like she was twelve—she balked. "Absolutely not," she'd stressed and then hissed as she was forced into it.

Now she stood in the large event space of one of the Hightower buildings, gritting her teeth against the cold that swept in from the open doors. They led out to a large balcony where all guests would be invited to watch the fireworks at midnight, a few taking advantage of the fresh air—and shadows—early. The party was a celebration of two new products being launched, but Tia knew it had been cobbled together for Lord Archibald Siddeley. If he ever showed.

"You sure this man's coming?" she said out the side of her mouth.

Her nana, four feet with hair as white as her skin was dark, knocked Tia's leg with her cane. And not gently. "Bite your tongue."

Tia refused to rub the smarting ankle, well used to thwacks from that cane—and worse. When she'd been fourteen, she'd made the mistake of comparing her nana to Gandalf the White. She'd narrowly escaped being hit with a hex bag that would've cursed her for fifty years.

"It's almost ten," she said, hearing the sulk in her own voice.

"You got somewhere you need to be?"

Tia thought of her bar, the one she hadn't had time to work at in months. She could be mixing cocktails, flirting with human men, joking with her best friends. Her escape from being "Tia Hightower."

Instead, she was here, wrapped like a present with nipples so cold, they could cut glass. She'd conjure heat if her nana wouldn't whack her again for being "a weakling."

When the old witch eyed her for a response, she sighed. "No."

None of the other guests seemed to mind the temperature, all in their finery and gossiping in buzzing groups. This was where Higher witches thrived: parties, socializing, gossiping.

A feather bobbing across the crowd caught her eye. She shifted, immediately on edge. Maybelline, Richard and Henry had arrived two hours ago, the former dressed in peridot silk, the feather she always wore braided into her hair like some twenties flapper. Henry's mom's eccentricity was well known, what with the habitual feather and the fact that she refused to wear anything but shades of green. She'd never said why, but as powerful a family as the Pearlmatters were, she didn't need to. Tia had always loved it, figuring she'd probably turn out the same. No excuses, no apologies.

So far, Tia had managed to avoid her, though she knew it couldn't last. The woman was a crocodile: she didn't let go of her prey. And she'd never lost hope that one day Henry and Tia would get over their differences. Fat chance.

Tia didn't slouch—she wasn't about to get whacked again—but she badly wanted to. "You know, some grandmas cuddle their granddaughters."

"You want a hug, get a dog," was the no-nonsense, slightly bewildering answer. "Eyes on the prize, Celestia."

Tia inwardly gagged at the name only her nana used. "Sir, yes, sir."

The cane prodded her again.

Another half hour crawled by. Her mom and dad were in the thick of the crowd, dancing and schmoozing, but Tia wasn't allowed to so much as get a glass of champagne. A year ago, she'd have defied the lot of them, refusing to let anyone tell her what to do. Now she ground her teeth and waited it out.

After another fifteen minutes, though, she gave in. "I'm going to the bathroom."

Her nana mulled—actually *mulled*—this over before giving a curt nod. "Don't be long."

Tia bit back a retort and stalked for the hall, which led to the bathrooms. Her skirts swished around her legs, the long slit that exposed her thigh allowing her to move quicker, meaning she reached the blessedly empty hall in seconds. With a look behind her, she headed toward the front steps of the old Southern building. She just needed some quiet. One minute to clear out the noise.

With a thought and a word, she created a bubble of warmth around herself so that when she stepped out, it was with a degree of comfort.

That vanished as soon as someone moved from where they'd been leaning against the balustrade. The twinkle lights draped around the porch railings bounced off platinum hair, and her stomach soured.

Henry tipped his head in greeting, one hand loosely clasping a glass of champagne. "Hightower."

She didn't say anything.

He chuckled, and the sound raised every hackle.

She went on the attack. "Why aren't you inside?"

He shrugged. "Why aren't you?"

"I asked you first."

"I asked you second."

Steam whistled out her ears. She bit off an even more childish response, lapsing into frigid silence.

He leaned back, one elbow on the railing, trailing his gaze

down her body. She refused to feel heat burn in its wake, standing stiffly under his inspection.

Finally, he drawled, "Hell of a dress."

Tia bared her teeth in a facsimile of a grin. She drew a hand down the curve of her hip, triumphant when he watched. "Nana's going fishing."

"With you as the lure?" She could've sworn his jaw tightened as he saw the slit, her thigh. "Siddeley might cut bait and run as soon as you open your mouth."

Although she was surprised at the bite in his voice, all she did was smirk. "I've never had complaints from men about my mouth."

His gaze sharpened. "Ah. So, your escort for the evening is…?" He looked past her, knowing already, the bastard, that the warlocks around here were too spineless to date her. She hadn't had a date—at least a magical one—since him. Thank the Goddess for human men.

She clamped down on her snarl. "What simpering witch has the bad fortune to be *your* date tonight?"

An easy shrug. "Came alone."

"Don't tell me your charms aren't working anymore?" She made a moue. "Are all the Higher witches finally bored with Daddy's little boy?"

"*Little* isn't something I've ever heard from women," he parried, turning her own words around.

And she hated herself for the flash of jealousy. For the fact that it made her step into his space, chin lifted. Also hating that no matter how high the heel she wore, he'd always look down on her. "You're not winning this one, Pearlmatter. I'm taking you down."

All she got was a slow smile. "In that dress, I might let you." Something darkened in his eyes. "You know I like you in red, little moth."

She did. She did, dammit, which was why she hadn't wanted to wear the stupid thing. A long wash of red silk crisscrossed around her breasts and tied behind her neck. The fabric parted to showcase the gentle rise of Tia's full breasts, her warm brown skin glowing against the red silk, catching the eye of every man there. Designed to catch one eye in particular.

The bait wasn't for Siddeley; it was for Henry.

And he knew it.

Worse was that nickname on his lips. *Little moth.* Once used as he'd kissed her, teasing about her playing moth to his fire magic.

She didn't have time to snap at him before he sighed dramatically. "Sadly, I'm on my best behavior tonight so I'd better leave before you throw any more insults."

"Me?" she managed, watching him smoothly move around her and toward the doors. "After that escort crack?" And the old nickname that dragged up baggage she already felt weighing heavily around her neck.

He tossed a grin over his shoulder before leaving her alone.

She scowled down at the ground, tempted to release some of her frustration in a burst of magic, but she wouldn't give Henry the satisfaction.

Good thing, too, because seconds later, a portal opened without warning and the man they'd all been waiting for stepped out.

He was dressed up, clad in a three-piece evening suit with tails, and carried a decorative cane he twirled idly as he looked around. A plump white cat coiled around his legs as four people exited after him, three women and one man, all matching Siddeley's formalwear.

As he caught sight of her, Archibald Siddeley clapped his hands with boisterous cheer. "A welcome party? How brilliant. I say, am I late? There was a spot of bother with the cravat and then we somehow ended up in the desert of all places. Portal-mapping's not our strong suit, eh, Nige?" He slapped the man on the back, sand falling from the latter's hair at the blow. "Nige" offered a thin-lipped smile, still clearly sore from what had presumably been Siddeley's incompetence.

Tia hid her grin and walked forward, her steps light. If Henry hadn't tucked tail and run—*again*—she'd have had to share the first impression. Maybe this would teach him to hold his ground in future. Then again, she couldn't expect the impossible.

"Lord Siddeley," she greeted him as she came down the stairs, offering her hand when he lifted his, only slightly bemused when he bowed over it. "Welcome to Hightower Seven. I'm Tia Hightower."

"Pleasure, pleasure. Let me escort you inside, Lady Hightower, bit nippy out here after all!" Missing her jolt at the honorific she barely claimed, he squeezed her hand, threading it through his arm as he continued to chatter about their journey. Tia led him inside with an encouraging smile, tasting the sweetness of victory when Henry's eyes narrowed on her.

She winked as she steered Siddeley away from the Pearlmatters and over to her parents.

That dress.

Flames licked under his skin, his fire magic a torrent of heat Henry struggled to control even as he showed the world ease and charm. Even as wrath stirred with every warlock's face that went slack as she swished by, curves and red silk. Sadly, there were no handy bushes around to destroy tonight.

She'd been told to curb her temper; that much was obvious. He and his parents joined the Hightowers and all Tia did was smile thinly before introducing Archibald Siddeley to "Lord Henry Pearlmatter." He bet she choked on that. He couldn't deny a small part of him loved it. Even as he found his gaze on her for the tenth time.

That fucking dress.

The warlock was nothing like he'd expected, contradicting the cold, stiff-upper-lip British stereotype. Instead, he was warm, loud and excessively enthusiastic. About everything.

His familiar had joined him, a snowy white cat that was outrageously plump and bared its teeth at anyone who dared go near it. His opposite, Siddeley explained with a booming laugh.

He was currently listening to Tia as she told him about Toil and Trouble, the bar she'd opened with her friends. It was strategic of her to downplay the rebellion it represented, the whispers from society she'd provoked—not that Tia ever cared what others thought of her. She always went her own way. No matter who she left behind.

"*Love* a good pub," Siddeley enthused as she paused, nodding vigorously as he looked to his associates, who all dutifully nodded back. "A real sense of community in a pub. Shoulder to shoulder with the common man. That's what matters—people. Witches and humans alike. I find humans fascinating, don't you?" He didn't stop to let her answer. "And to name it with a nod to witchkind. Droll, very droll, Lady Hightower. Most amusing!" He tilted his head back, letting out another bellow of laughter.

Tia watched him like he belonged in a straitjacket. Henry coughed to hide his amusement, turning Siddeley's attention to him.

"And the young Lord Pearlmatter," he was addressed, much to his chagrin since it made Tia snigger. "What do you do in your spare time?"

Static filled his brain as he faltered. "Well, I..." He glanced at his dad, who silently urged him to answer. "I..." *Fuck*. He couldn't think of anything.

The truth was work consumed his life, and he doubted the English Lord wanted to hear about his movie tastes or how he preferred buttered popcorn over sweet.

Tia cleared her throat. "The young Lord Pearlmatter runs," she crooned, the pointed jab unsubtle enough to have others in their group shifting.

Henry's eyes narrowed to dangerous slits.

Siddeley nodded sagely. "Physical exercise, so important. Capital, Pearlmatter! How far do you run?"

"As far as he can go while still being in earshot of his daddy." Tia's smile was poisoned sweetness until she flinched, gaze cutting down. Henry followed it to her nana's cane. As he watched, it poked her in the leg again before retreating.

Henry intercepted before anyone else could. "She's just joking, Lord Siddeley. Tia rarely takes anything seriously." *There*, he thought, baring his teeth at her. *We're even.*

Or not.

"I might joke around some," she admitted to Siddeley, leaning in like they were friends sharing secrets, "but once I give my word, I commit. You'll never see me change my mind on a whim. Henry, on the other hand…"

"Funny, I've seen you change your mind very quickly," he retorted, their last fight flickering to life like an electrical storm, gathering heat under his skin. "And for pointless reasons."

Her cheeks flushed. "Just because I have a spine and stand by my own convictions—"

"Stand by them?" He snorted. "You build walls out of them. Shrines. You might as well be failing people before they even try."

"Did you try? All I remember was a whole lot of *giving up*."

His stinging retort died on his tongue as his dad gave a pointed—and irritated—cough.

Shit. Shit, shit, SHIT. He recoiled, falling back from where he'd edged closer to Tia, dread making his skin clammy.

Siddeley was glancing between them, a smudge of confusion on his brow. "Is…something wrong?" he asked, hesitation between the words.

Henry plastered on a tight smile. "Of course not. We…bet on a football game and she lost. Sore loser."

Tia's eyes drilled daggers into him but she said nothing, clearly realizing she—both of them—had stepped over the line.

He didn't dare look at his dad. Instead, he wrapped a hand around Tia's upper arm. "Excuse us a minute."

She waited approximately ten seconds before muttering, "If you don't get your paws off me right now, I swear I'll hex bag you."

"Easy, you alley cat," he said under his breath, steering them out of the event space. He towed her complaining ass into the hall before shoving her into the first vacant room. One long bench stacked with various potions and bottles, burners and lab equipment stretched the length of the room. A pile of data crystals was neatly organized under the lip in a hidden shelf, metal stools tucked in.

Warning, a sign on the white wall above read. Atmosphere Could Be Volatile.

They got that right. He released Tia and took a large step back, away from her scent, the feel of her skin, before it imprinted on him. He flexed his hand by his side as he faced her.

She brushed the bare skin he'd touched, eyebrows drawn tight. "Don't ever go caveman on me again."

"It was your fault. What the hell was that?"

She didn't play dumb, instead crossing her arms under her chest. He tried not to watch as the globes of her breasts plumped under that teasing crisscross of fabric. "We fucked up," she stated baldly.

It was automatic to say, "You started it."

"Are you kidding me right now?"

He knew it was childish. He *knew* it. But Goddess help him, Tia always could set him off. He used to crave the challenge until he realized that catching her was like catching smoke. Even with his fire magic, nobody could hold what didn't want to be held. She called it giving up. He called it recognizing the inevitable.

He shrugged in response, knowing it would start her eye twitching.

She blew out a breath, stalking up and down the length of

the lab bench. Her body moved under the silk and he felt desire twist his spine.

She spun back. "I am *not* losing this investor because you're a rash I can't get rid of. You need to back off."

He choked. *"Me?"*

"It's obvious we can't work together, so you need to let me reel him in. He likes me."

His gaze dipped to her breasts.

"Don't you dare."

He smirked.

"Pig. All I'm saying is I'm charming *and* I've got the knowledge to land this account."

His hands left his pockets as he took a challenging step forward. "You might know a little about potion research, but I've been in the business of growing companies half my life."

"Bully for you."

He ignored her. "I should be the one to talk to him. I know about our plans, our base and how our business is primed for investment."

"And how're you going to do that if you don't know the product?" she exclaimed triumphantly. "I know our potions like the back of my grimoire. I get down and dirty while you keep clean. When's the last time you did anything with your own two hands?"

"What, you want her number?"

Danger sparked in those hazel irises. "Real men don't brag. They don't have to. And we're not talking about sex."

He really wished he hadn't seen her red lips curl around that word. "You think you know our business better than me? I share an office with you, Tia. I've seen you work on a curse for two hours instead of looking at any growth charts, or marketing plans, or budgets..." Damn unnerving that curse had been, too, especially how detailed it had been, down to its inflections. And the less said about the doodle of him as a pig, the better. "I should be the one to pitch him."

"He's investing in our potions. In how they can go global. He's interested in people. Not robots."

He clapped a hand to his chest. "What a hit."

"I bet you can't even remember what goes into a simple Aphrodite mix." With the name of the beginner's-level potion on her lips, she pressed her hands against the bench, tipping forward in challenge. "How're you going to convince him of product knowledge and the market for it if you don't *know* it?"

"I know it."

"Yeah?"

"Yeah." He braced his hands on the other side, matching her so they were almost nose to nose. The air was thick between them. "What's more, any potion I created would be more effective than any one you made."

"Okay," she said, humoring him. "Let's get you back to your dad. You're malfunctioning without him here to put words in your mouth."

Blunt annoyance shoved under his skin. "Let's do it."

"Do what?"

He held her stare. Restraint was long gone and he was making a stand. "We both brew a potion. Whoever's is the most effective gets to make the pitch to Siddeley. Winner takes all." He heard a warning go off in his brain, how stupid this was, but couldn't stop the challenge as he purred, "Or are you chicken, Tia?"

five

She never could resist a dare.

As they set their brewed Dionysus potions on the lab bench—making an Aphrodite potion was out for obvious reasons—Tia couldn't decide if accepting this one had been really, really stupid or really, really smart. She liked to think it was the second but had a horrible suspicion it was the first.

"Last chance to back out," Henry challenged in that low, smooth purr he'd used to throw down the gauntlet. Knowing damn well she'd pounce on it, especially after bickering like a child in front of a huge investor. She needed a win.

Although her stomach jumped, she thrust up her chin. "Don't even try it. Just be glad we didn't set a side bet."

"We could do it now," he challenged with a sweep of his hand. Cocky as hell, like he'd always been before he'd tried to act above it all for the company. Gloves were off, then.

She sneered. "Don't think I won't."

"You sure?"

"Set the terms."

There was only the murmur of background noise as he studied her intently, the party still in full swing even after the forty minutes they'd been absent. Goddess knew what her family was thinking. Maybe that she'd finally killed him and was trying to figure out where to dump the body. There was always that active volcano Emma had shown her photos of last week. Her friend liked to travel and would know all the best burial places.

A gleam appeared in Henry's eyes that was downright unsettling. "All right. Loser has to compliment the winner in front of the entire office."

Tia snorted, cocking a hip, her dress parting to expose a thigh. "Amateur. Always thinking small."

He gestured in invitation. "Have at it."

He wished. "Loser," she drawled after a moment to think, "has to attend a society ball in their underwear."

He blanched. "What are you, twelve? No way."

"Always so worried about other people."

"Or common sense?"

She shrugged. "Overrated."

"How much have you drunk tonight?"

"Just enough to stomach the sight of you."

He glowered. "Pick something else. Private."

"The days of private showings are well over, babe. Move on."

He ignored that. "Maybe loser should stop making hex bags and hiding them around our office."

Ha. She knew that'd get to him.

She crossed her arms, rocking back on one foot. He was so concerned with reputation and what his dad would think. He hadn't cared so much when they were younger. Now, though… it'd take a bulb up his butt to get him to lighten up.

Speaking of…

She tilted her head to the side in consideration. "How about…when I win you have to wear a cap that says 'Daddy's little boy'?"

He choked.

She trapped the laugh bubbling up her throat. "Scared to lose, Pearlmatter?"

His narrow-eyed stare was expected. His slow, "All right," was not.

Surprise turned into a thousand butterflies in her belly. "All right," she confirmed, half disbelieving, turning to the potions. "Shall we…?"

"But when I win," he interrupted, mirroring her again by crossing his arms, "you have to wear a T-shirt that says 'Daddy's girl.'" His eyes glinted. "And I'll wear one that says 'Daddy.'"

It was her turn to choke. He couldn't be serious.

Oh, but he was. And daring her again.

Her fingers twitched for a hex bag at his smug expression. He thought she'd throw in the towel. Run scared. *Puh-lease.*

Why was she even worried? It might have been a few years since she'd made Dionysus—a fun potion that caused a drunk-like rush for a short time—but she had alchemy in her blood. She had this.

"Game on." She thrust out her hand and he extended his. Something jolted down her spine at the contact, the first they'd made in years. It hit low and deep, twisting and uncurling as they shook. Magic sparked.

His eyes were dark when he let go. "Ladies first."

Surreptitiously, she wiped her palm down her thigh before picking up her potion to uncap.

"Wait."

She slid him a sideways look. "What now?"

He made a motion. "Drink mine."

"Yeah, right."

"I'm serious."

"And that's what makes it so funny."

Her words made his jaw tighten. "It's only fair if we judge the effects of each other's potion. Otherwise, we could fake it."

She batted her lashes. "But you can't tell when I—"

His growl cut her off and she tamped down a grin. He'd left himself wide open for that one.

She measured his logic, reluctantly accepting it. Acting giddy wouldn't be hard but picking a winner would be if neither admitted their potion didn't work—which neither of them ever would.

"Fine," she choked out.

He grinned. "You mean, I'm right."

"I mean, I don't trust you to be honorable."

He clutched his chest, expression not dimming. "Ouch."

She exchanged her bottle for his and shook it, examining the bubbles that fizzed. After waiting a few seconds for the mixture to calm, she pulled the stopper out and inhaled. Rose and juniper. All signs pointed to it being brewed properly so far. Damn it.

She kept that to herself as she toasted him with the bottle. "Just so you know, if this kills me, I'm coming back as a spirit to eternally haunt your ass."

"Where's the difference? Can't get rid of you anyway."

Her chest pinched as she glowered. Jerk.

She might've been faking the fear for his benefit but as she tilted the bottle, unease chased the liquid down her throat.

One beat passed. Then two. "Well, I'm alive at least," she mused.

"Damn." He snapped his fingers. "Another plan foiled."

A wide grin split her lips. It took over her face as her head lolled to the side. A short laugh bubbled up and she pressed the empty bottle to her lips, licking at another drop. "Funny. Always…so…funny. Won't be so funny when I best you, oh, no, no, no."

He was watching her when she looked up, humor darting around the face she hated to admit was gorgeous.

His smile broadened. "Thanks."

She frowned. Had she said that aloud?

"Yes," he replied. He crossed his arms and the muscles in them flexed beneath his shirt, his jacket discarded earlier. Her fingers curled at the sight. "Safe to say my potion worked."

"Nuh-uh," Tia heard herself say. She thought about it. "Well, maybe a teensy bit."

"The temptation to be bad right now," he murmured, a lock of pale hair brushing his forehead. It was so quiet she wondered if he'd said it to her or himself.

"Right here?" She waggled her eyebrows as she patted the bench before boosting herself up. The split in her dress fell open to display her thigh, smooth brown skin in the overhead lights.

His gaze went there like it was magnetized. "I was...kidding."

Her sigh was gusty and she leaned back on her hands, tilting her head up to the ceiling. "Talk, talk, talk. Same old Henry."

"What's that mean?"

When her head came up, he was closer. Something caught her eye. "You have a small scar." She brushed his chin with her finger. "I never noticed."

A muscle feathered in his jaw. "Experiment went wrong. Two years ago. Flying glass."

She continued to stroke it.

"Tia."

"Mmm."

"Stop touching me."

She stole a look from under her lashes. His expression was closed but his eyes were full of flame. It had been years since she'd seen him look at her like that.

Wrong, her inner self murmured. They didn't acknowledge it, but sometimes, when he wasn't expecting it, she'd catch him staring at her. Just. Like. That.

A twinge hit low, her thighs tightening on reflex. She grazed her lip with her teeth as she watched him.

"Tia," he said, whispered really. A long gap, the space of four heartbeats. His hands bracketed her as his body swayed closer. He took a breath. "Do you ever wish...?"

Something shifted inside. "Yes?"

"If we could go back." Under her fingers, his jaw hardened. "Do you think…?"

Her thumb touched the corner of his mouth where his smile used to spread. She loved his smile. "Yes?"

He gazed at her, and it was like a curtain briefly pulling away. Longing and desire spilled out, burned into her for one bright second, before his eyes shuttered again.

Swearing, he stepped back. Tia let her hand fall away, fingertips tingling with the feel of his stubble rasping her skin. Her heart confused with the words unsaid. With what she'd seen. The potion softened the edges until that slipped away, a cloud floating to the sky.

"It'll be done soon," he said, arms crossed, chin tucked to avoid eye contact. His body was taut. "Five minutes at most."

Tia didn't care; she felt too good. She kicked her legs as they waited, but the delight finally drained away, leaving her sick and off balance.

She speared him with a glare, hands tight around the bench's lip. "It wasn't supposed to have any Aphrodite elements to it."

His smirk was by rote, as if he'd forced it. "It didn't."

Her face burned, humiliation and insecurity twisting incessantly inside her until they resembled a braided bit of rope. She couldn't think about what he'd almost confessed, or her response to it. They weren't supposed to say it aloud. Better to bury that shit deep.

She swallowed hard. "Whatever was said…it was the damn potion."

"Fine." He plucked her bottle from the bench. "My turn." He shook it. "Think I'll go all giddy, too?"

"I hope you choke on it," she said sweetly.

He toasted her with the bottle, unstoppering it and tossing it back.

She waited in silence. It had taken her less than a minute to feel the effects. But all he did was stand there.

Shit. It had been a few years since she'd made this one but she'd been pretty sure she'd remembered it right. When it came to potions, it was all about focus. You had to keep your intention pure. Okay, *maybe* she'd had a stray second of desire to wipe any thoughts of her "inferiority" from his mind. But that was neither here nor there. It should still work.

If it didn't—she didn't even want to think about it. She wasn't made for being on the lam; neither were her heels. But damn if she'd be sticking around to hear him gloat.

As she planned her escape by portal, his gaze gradually unfocused. Her shoulders fell from around her ears and she loosed a breath. Thank the Goddess. It was work—

His eyes rolled back in his head. He toppled, hitting the floor with a thud hard enough to make her flinch.

"Very funny," she scoffed after a few seconds, hoping he didn't hear the thread of nerves circling the words.

He didn't move.

She hopped off the bench and stalked to him, nudging his leg with her foot. "Pearlmatter."

When he still didn't react, her stomach flip-flopped. She kicked him again, harder this time. "Pearlmatter."

She wasn't even sure he breathed. His lashes made dark crescent shadows on his face, and his skin seemed extra white against the crispness of his tuxedo. The room was silent as the grave.

All the blood in her head drained. "Henry?"

A roaring sounded in her ears and she collapsed to her knees, barely feeling the sting. She took hold of his shoulders. "Henry. Damn it. Don't die. Fuck you if you think you're having the last word." She shook him, fighting for air as her lungs squeezed. "This isn't how it's meant to go. Please. Open those stupid eyes." Was he even breathing?

As she went to lay her head on his chest, he shot up with a loud, ragged breath. His forehead clipped her chin painfully, but she didn't even care as Henry stared at her, dazed.

"Thank fuck," she breathed. Adrenaline rushed her, dizzying

with the relief that he was alive, that she hadn't killed him, and she didn't think. She just went to throw her arms around him.

Except he apparently thought she had a different motive. For the second time, as her head came down, his lifted.

Their lips collided.

Her breath stuttered.

It should have been a second, a shocked blip before she pulled away to yell at him. Except his mouth was warm and soft, a memory she'd never been able to sweat out of her system no matter what she tried.

His hand came up to cradle her nape, his lips brushing hers. Tentative. Strange for Henry, this gentle coaxing, but her body was amped up and he felt so solid and strong and *right*…

Her fingers curled deeper into his tuxedo jacket as she kissed him back. Again. And again. And—

"Tia."

Tia's eyes flashed open on the heels of her mom's gasp. She broke the connection but didn't go far, chest rising unsteadily as she stared at Henry. He was just as unsteady, his eyes burning with thousands of questions, none of which she could answer.

The moment stretched between them, his breath whispering over her skin, until he finally released her neck. Reality slapped her in the face and she reared back, cheeks burning in embarrassment.

Any explanation she might've made died on her lips as she jerked around to face her mom.

No. Not her mom. At least, not *just* her mom.

Gloria.

Richard.

And Lord Siddeley.

FUCK.

"Um," she said inelegantly. "I can explain."

She was saved from having to try by a boom of laughter. All heads turned to the English lord, who wagged a finger at Tia and Henry playfully.

"I knew it," he crowed, beaming. He patted his lean stomach. "The gut always knows."

She stared, as uncomprehending as a human without a translation spell.

"I *knew* there was something between you and Lord Pearlmatter," he continued, one finger rubbing his bottom lip. "Like the air before a thunderstorm hits." He gave her a broad wink. "Don't worry. I was young, too, once upon a time. I remember sneaking away for a passionate interlude."

Aghast, Tia barely held back a *passionate* denial. He thought they…that she and Henry had…that they'd snuck away to…?

Half-baked alternatives washed away like sand on a beach. And the truth wasn't much better. No way could she say, "Actually, we were competing for who could pitch to you by each brewing a potion and mine knocked him out." That wouldn't exactly win the investor's confidence. Besides, for all she knew, Henry had been faking. Probably had been. Jackass.

She slid him a look that should've left only a black charred mark behind. He blinked back, usual smirk wiped clean.

She knew why. That kiss…

Goose bumps brushed the surface of her skin and she inwardly cursed.

When she dared a glance at her mom, the withering one she got in return had her wincing.

A true Hightower, Gloria betrayed nothing as she said, "I do apologize, Lord Siddeley, for their inappropriate timing."

"Seems to me like we had the inappropriate timing," he joked, and Tia fought the urge to close her eyes. "No need to apologize. I suppose youth gets the better of us all."

Behind Siddeley, Richard didn't bother hiding a seething expression, staring at his silent son as if willing him to come up with a better explanation. But Henry wouldn't even look at him.

A hint of worry fluttered into her chest as she noticed for

the first time how pale he still was. She gauged the distance between his height and the floor, remembering that fleshy thud he'd made, and more worry reluctantly unspooled. He needed to be checked out.

With the three in the doorway still watching, she lurched to her feet, balancing easily on her spiked heels. She hesitated before holding out a hand to Henry. He swayed as he boosted himself up and she flung herself forward to keep him from tottering.

Siddeley beamed as Henry's arm settled around her waist. "Young love in the next generation of the company. No wonder you merged! I imagine you'll only be stronger for it."

Tia tried to concentrate but Henry was breathing hard against her ear, his frame wilting like it was a challenge to stay upright. And the bastard was heavy. She pinched his waist and he straightened, shooting her a bewildered look.

It was starting to freak her out. No, scratch that. It freaked her the hell out and she wasn't sure how to handle the wings brushing anxiety into her system with each beat.

"Maybe we should let them get presentable." Richard's voice was toneless. "They can join us on the tour in a few minutes." The order came through loud and clear, and she had no doubt they'd both be raked over the coals for this later.

Siddeley, amenable to the end, agreed and they left the room, Gloria shooting one last dark look at her daughter before the door shut.

Immediately, Tia let go and whirled on Henry. It backfired as he swayed and she had to lunge to catch him. His hands landed on her shoulders and his weight dragged her a few steps before they steadied.

"Shit," she said, breathless. "What the hell was that? Did you knock your head?"

He stared down at her.

"What?" Embarrassment coated the edges of her voice. "If

this is about the kiss, don't even start. It was…relief that I hadn't killed you. Don't make a thing of it." When he still didn't speak, she poked a knuckle into his side. "You lost your voice or something?"

He glanced around as if he was checking out the room. "Or something."

She stared at him, unnerved. "This isn't funny. If you don't knock it off, I swear I'm going to hex bag the shit out of you. Remember the last time, when we were seventeen? You squawked like a crow for three days."

He frowned, like it was news to him. "We know each other?"

A chill flashed from the top of her spine downward. She tightened her grip as a stupid possibility swirled into her mind. "Henry…you know who you are, right?"

He rolled his eyes, a hint of arrogance in it. "Well, yeah. I'm not an idiot." She didn't have time for relief before he caught her with a look that was eight parts confusion and two parts interest. "Why did you kiss me?"

"*You* kissed *me*," she shot back, habit setting in.

A lazy smile kicked up his lips and he leaned in. "You could kiss me now," he suggested, deep and smoky.

Dread dropkicked any relief from her system. She searched his face, scanning for anything familiar. All she saw was openness, a tremor of amusement and that interest. No tension, no shadows, no flashes of passion. Nothing.

Bile churned up her throat. "What's my name?" she whispered. She wanted to scream it but forced her tone even. "Henry, tell me you know who I am."

His forehead crimped and he drew back. Hesitation flickered before he blinked. The answer was written across his blank expression.

Panic ballooned in her chest, making it difficult to breathe. Her heart raced, faster and faster, as she shifted. Her foot knocked something, the echo of glass rolling over the floor drawing her eye.

The small bottle came to stop against the legs of the workbench, a drop of liquid easing onto the floor. Realization torpedoed through her remaining calm as she watched the potion droplet fall.

Oh, fuck.

six

"Fuck, fuck, *fuck*."

Henry watched the woman pace up and down the room he'd been hustled into an hour ago. It was a nice enough room, two couches in soft gray with a teak table between, and a large fireplace with a wooden mantel in the same finish. Bookcases with hardbacks lined all the walls except for the tall window that offered a view of the darkness beyond.

He caught his reflection in it. Sharp jaw, long nose, high cheekbones, white-blond hair cut short and shaggy. All familiar. Attractive, if you listened to any of the girlfriends he'd had over the years. Except—when he tried to think back over the women in his past, there was a black haze he couldn't penetrate. The last one he could remember in detail was Missy Greentower when he'd been sixteen, and then there was…

He concentrated hard, frustrated at the blank spaces.

Annoyingly, it wasn't the only gap.

When he'd admitted he didn't know who the woman—Tia—was, she'd full-on freaked out and herded him from the laboratory or wherever the hell they'd been, past some kind of party and into this room before leaving him with instructions to stay put. She'd returned with a small group, among them his parents and the woman who'd interrupted that kiss. One of the group was a warlock who'd examined Henry with a crystal wand as he and the rest fired questions at him.

Did he know his name? Yes, Henry Charles Pearlmatter. Born April twenty-fifth.

Did he know where he was? The land of Oz (turned out, joking wasn't appreciated).

Did he recognize anyone in the room? His parents—whose faces cracked with relief at that—but the tall Black woman with striking features was a mystery; so was the older woman with a cane who glared at him the entire time, and Tia remained a huge blank. A blank but one he'd kissed by instinct when he'd first woken up. He found that interesting. As was the way her eyes skittered away from his whenever they met. It made him want to catch her attention.

"Tia," the woman from the doorway chided at the string of swear words. Tia's mom, maybe.

"No, let her curse," the short crone who also resembled Tia snapped. "Girl's got a right to. She fucked up." She thumped her cane on the carpet. "You're saying this fool's lost his memory?"

Henry snorted softly.

The warlock only nodded, placing the crystal wand back in a black leather case. "From what Lady Hightower said and from the tests I've performed, the potion Lord Pearlmatter drank stripped away his memories, but only ones where..." He hesitated, throwing Tia a glance.

She folded her arms beneath her breasts. Her eyes were not green or brown, but a mix of both, and full of passion as they glowered. That look was vaguely familiar but when he tried to catch the memory, it remained elusive as a butterfly.

The warlock sighed. "It seems any memory connected to Lady Hightower has been veiled." He hesitated. "What *did* you put into the potion?"

Potion? Henry's head throbbed with confusion as they continued to talk around him. Had Tia hexed him? She'd mentioned something about that back in the lab but he'd been pretty focused on getting her mouth back on his. Probably should've paid more attention.

Ingredients were listed, arguments raised, dismissed, blame tossed, voices rising.

His mom sat next to him, hand resting on his shoulder. She masked her concern behind a bright smile, a common habit. "How do we fix it?" she interrupted, her Southern accent smooth like honey.

The arguments stopped.

His mom settled her skirts around her with one hand, rubbing his shoulder with the other. "If it's magical, surely there's a cure?"

The warlock brightened. "Of course. For every magical malady, there is an antidote." He grimaced. "It may just take some time."

"How much?" The clipped voice belonged to his dad. He was hard to read—like always—tall and intimidating as he faced off against the women with a scowl. Clearly, there was some beef there.

"Well, I... The potion Lady Hightower brewed isn't known, so..."

Henry didn't miss Tia's jaw flexing, the hot color in her cheeks.

"Then we've lost this investment." His dad paced, cutting a glare at Tia. "This is all your fault."

"It was your son's idea," she shot back.

"Which you led him to, I have no doubt."

Henry frowned.

"Keep your broom parked, Richard," the old woman snapped, pointing her cane at him like a javelin. "Celestia knows what she did. Not everything is lost. Siddeley loved the idea of the two of them together. Peter's showing him off the property now and he'll steer him to come back."

Before his dad could retort, Tia's mom put up her hands.

"Enough. Maybelline's right. We can cure this but until we do, this disaster stays in this room." She tossed her daughter a meaningful look. "The last thing we need is for it to get out that one of our potions gave Henry amnesia."

His mom's hand squeezed his shoulder once more before falling away. "Exactly. We'll fix this. We just need to stay calm and keep Henry out of the office for a few days until his memory returns." She brushed back the hair that swept over his forehead. "You can move home until this is sorted, honey. We'll help you remember what you're missing." She winked as if she wasn't worried at all.

It seemed as good a plan as any. His mind was like a book with the odd page ripped out. Kind of hard to get the full story, and from the animosity in the room, it seemed like there was a good one here. He smiled at her, patting her knee to erase the hint of anxiety he sensed. It'd all be fine. He refused to think otherwise.

"I'll work with Lionel," Tia muttered, scuffing her heel on the carpet.

The warlock—Lionel—nodded gratefully. "Your assistance would be most welcome."

The door opened on the heels of that comment and a man stepped in, dressed as the rest in a tuxedo. Tia's dad.

He pressed his back to the door to close it, gaze on Henry. "Diagnosis?"

"Magical amnesia," his wife returned, just as the old lady said, "Boy's gone potty."

"Only memories connected to Tia," Maybelline explained, the feather in her hair flopping as she gestured at the woman in question. "But unfortunately, that includes a lot."

"Like the merger." Tia's dad nodded, slipping a hand in his pocket. He looked to Tia. "You'll help fix this."

Tia didn't point out she'd already volunteered, only dipped her head.

"Siddeley's sorted," the man continued, the calm in a storm. "For now. He loves that our children are…together."

His dad scoffed. "And what, we just let him believe that?"

"Yes." Tia's dad shrugged. "What he doesn't know won't hurt him. Better he believe in a fake relationship than we lose this investment."

"What if he tells someone?" Tia asked, gripping her sides so hard, the blood bleached out her skin. Henry watched, wondering why everyone was so hard-up for this man.

"He's leaving for England in a couple of days. He won't have the time. In the meantime, Richard and your mom will make the pitch."

"But—" Tia cut off at his steady look.

"You've done enough," Richard snapped.

Nobody stepped up to Tia's defense. Henry might have, if he'd known what the hell had happened. It was strange having his memory but not at the same time. Like the morning after the night before, a hangover that obliterated the best and worst bits. Maybe he should've been freaking out, but that was a life with magic. Expect the unexpected. And this was definitely the unexpected. He'd get his memories back sooner or later. Why dwell?

So he didn't. Instead, he focused on the woman everyone was ganging up on. Okay, it was kind of a clusterfuck, but he still thought it was pretty shitty of Tia's parents not to back her up, like family should. Across the room, separate from everyone, she looked very…alone.

His chest seized and he rubbed it with the heel of his hand, frowning slightly.

"Then, we're agreed?" Tia's dad stepped away from the door, attention on all of them. "We keep this between us until Henry regains his full memory?"

They all nodded. Henry didn't bother; nobody was looking at him.

His mom leaned over and pecked him on the cheek, tweaking it like she'd done when he was five. "Don't worry, honey. We'll have you back to your old self in no time."

Whoever that was, he thought, eyes lingering on Tia.

Tia sat, spine straight, on the antique couch in Maybelline's parlor. The clock on the mantel chimed and sunlight swirled across the floor through the window. For November, it was a gorgeous day, but she couldn't relax enough to enjoy it.

Two weeks. It had been two weeks and from all reports, Henry still hadn't regained his memories.

She refused to let guilt nibble at her. It wasn't like amnesia had ever killed anyone. He just…got a vacation from remembering her for a while. Sounded nice, actually. There were definitely days with him she'd like to forget.

She picked at the skin around her fire-red thumbnail, jittery at this out-of-the-blue summons to the Pearlmatter mansion. Even without the whole screwed-up situation, she didn't like being here. The past haunted every corner: her laughing up at Henry as he leaned over her in dark spaces, his breath hot in her ear as she teased him after dinner, his hand in hers as he led her out to the gardens. She'd taught him how to make creatures with his fire magic in those gardens, had pored over old textbooks for weeks mastering the words and hand gestures, all so he would be in awe of her. He had been: chasing her down, flinging her over his shoulder to her laughing protests and spinning around, shouting to the world how amazing his witch was.

Tia pushed the memory away. He'd get better soon. He had to. She was working on the antidote with Lionel, their best potion analyst, every day. Not that she wanted the smirking jackass back, but she admitted her accidental "intention" to wipe away any thoughts of her being unworthy had gone a little… awry. Her bad.

Gloria hadn't swept it aside so easily. "I won't be able to protect you if you don't control your worst self," she'd full-on shrieked, pacing in her office. "When will you settle down and be the Hightower I know you can be? You *will* keep your head down about this, Tia. I swear to the Goddess, if you tell Emmaline or Leah, you're out of this company."

"I'm disappointed in you," her dad had said, the impact of those four words somehow more of a blow. And her nana had just shaken her head.

Yet again, she'd let them down by being herself.

Tia nibbled at the corner of her thumb, shoulders high around her ears. The clock continued to count time away, a soft mockery.

Two weeks wasn't long, not really. Even Bastian, Henry's friend and Emma's fiancé, had only asked about him once, jokingly wondering if she'd killed him since he hadn't been able to track him down. Apparently, any memory of Bastian was too tangled up with Tia for Henry to remember him. She thought she'd played it off well, even if her palms had gone slick. The lie tasted like ass but for once, she wasn't going to make everything worse.

Her knee bobbed as she waited for someone, anyone, to walk in. All the summons had said was that this had to do with Siddeley. If they'd lost the investment, she knew she'd be blamed. She'd deserve it. First with the argument, then the potion, capping off with the kiss.

No. She closed her eyes. She wasn't thinking about that again.

The door opened and she leaped up, grateful for the distraction. She wasn't sure how to feel when Henry walked in, looking every inch the gorgeous warlock and not some stray with holes in his memory. He blinked, as if surprised, then the corner of his mouth tugged up in greeting. A stranger's smile, polite but absent of any connection.

She told herself it was guilt and not anxiety that burned in the pit of her stomach at the sight. He was closely followed by Maybelline, dressed in dark green with her hair pulled back, and his dad. While Richard wore a shirt and trousers, Henry wore soft jeans and a fisherman's sweater with the sleeves rolled up. He hesitated a moment before heading to Tia.

"Hi," he said when he got close. He held out his hand. She looked at it, baffled, as he continued. "I'm Henry Pearlmatter. I'm thirty years old, a warlock with fire magic mastery, and I've been told we're exes." Laughter glinted in his eyes. "Nice to meet you."

Since it was awkward leaving his hand outstretched, Tia grasped it and pumped twice, quickly letting go. "Hi."

He watched her as he tucked his hand into his jeans pocket. "You're Tia Hightower. Twenty-nine. An alchemist—"

"Not a good one," his father put in, dropping into an armchair with a glower.

"Richard," Maybelline warned, as only Maybelline could.

Henry ignored them both, searching her face as though he could read their past on it. She hoped he couldn't. He wouldn't like what he found.

Her parents walked in at that moment, her dad shutting the door behind him. "Tia," he greeted her with a small smile. She'd take it. Her mom still couldn't look at her without huffing.

"Does anyone want tea?" Maybelline waved at the tea service that appeared in the corner. Her ever-present feather bobbed as she headed over. "I have a lovely lavender tea for calming nerves."

Henry caught Tia's eye and shook his head.

"Let's just get to business," Richard snapped, then slumped as Maybelline glared at him. "Fine. But none of that lavender stuff."

"You'll have what I give you, Richard Pearlmatter."

Their interplay always used to amuse Tia but today she couldn't focus. She hovered in place until Maybelline gestured. "Take a seat, Tia."

Tia did as ordered, relieved Maybelline hadn't turned on her as well. She wouldn't have blamed her; she *had* stripped away her son's memories after all. Her stomach knotted as Henry chose to lean on the wall instead of sitting next to her.

Richard was given tea, to his consternation, and the other cups were distributed before Maybelline took her seat. She set her cup on the table with the spoon continuing to stir idly. "Okay," she told her husband.

He cast her a half smile before shifting to the edge of his chair. As his attention moved to Tia, the smile wiped clean. "We've heard from Siddeley."

Tia clutched her own tea. "And?"

"It's good news," Gloria said, picking up the reins. "He's interested in further talks."

Tia wanted to slump, maybe slide out of her chair to lie prostrate on the ground. A second chance to fix this. "That's great."

A shared look.

Her spine snapped straight. "Isn't it?"

"There's…a little hitch." Gloria sipped her tea, taking a moment as if to organize her thoughts. She studied her daughter, expression veiled. "Apparently, you and Henry made a real impression on him at the party."

Although her cheeks burned at the dark look from Richard, Tia held her chin high. "Well, that's good, isn't it?"

"Under other circumstances."

Her dad crossed to her mom's side and sank down next to her. Like always, he didn't pussyfoot around. "Siddeley wants to discuss the investment further in his home. He's invited you and Henry to stay with him throughout December."

She couldn't have heard that right.

"Us?" Tia pointed at herself, then the warlock against the wall. "Him and me?"

Peter nodded. Gloria sighed. "He thought you were *utterly charming*."

Maybelline beamed at them. "He's not wrong. Henry, honey, you sure you don't want some tea?"

Tia didn't let him answer. "We can't go. Henry's..." She struggled for the words.

"We're aware of the situation," Richard retorted. He sipped his tea, made a face and hastily put the dainty china down. "Unfortunately, the man is set on it being you two and you two alone. If we're going to secure this investment, this is how it has to be."

"I could go alone," she suggested, inspired. Or was it desperate? "We could say Henry's sick."

"We can't risk he won't be put off by that." Gloria shook her head. "He was adamant it be next month and be you two."

"Going would be a bigger risk," Tia argued. She had no idea what to feel, but the churning was making her nauseated. "If he slips up, we'd have to admit he's lost his memories, and why." She winced at the sea of unimpressed faces. "Yes, I get it, my fault. Which is why I should be the one to fix it."

"And you can," Peter agreed. "But not alone."

"We'll keep working on the antidote in the meantime," Gloria assured her. "But we're counting on you to help us with this. You just need to fill in the gaps for him."

Tia's lips opened and shut without words. This had *mistake* written all over it. So many things could go wrong; one tiny slipup and they were outed.

But...she could fix it. Her heart beat faster at the idea. She could prove her mistake was a one-time thing and she still had what it took to be a leader. She could run the pitch; she'd wanted to do that anyway. Any lines Henry had to say, she could feed them to him.

It *could* work.

Her guts were still in knots, but she gave them all a tight nod. "All right. I'll do it."

Gloria looked relieved. "Good. Henry?"

Before he could speak, Maybelline picked up her teacup and held it to her mouth. "You're forgetting something," she said brightly, before taking a sip.

Tia looked at her blankly.

She swore Maybelline's eyes glittered. "The kiss, honey. Siddeley thinks you and my Henry are together."

Tia didn't move. Didn't breathe.

"A couple," Maybelline prompted. "Sweethearts. Lovers."

Richard grunted. "Maybelline."

"I'm just making sure she understands. She doesn't seem to be getting it."

Tia hoped she wasn't. Because it sounded like Maybelline was implying…

"It's not like you don't have experience being in a relationship with each other," the other woman mused, barely disguising her satisfaction. "And you were so good at it, too."

"Didn't we break up?" Henry spoke from his position against the wall.

Tia felt like her back was to one, too. "Yes. Yes, we did."

Maybelline lifted one shoulder. "Things change. And for this to work, Siddeley has to believe that what he saw that night was the truth." Her smile was coy. "Maybe it will be."

"*Maybelline.*"

She rolled her eyes at her husband's gritted statement.

Tia thrust a hand into her hair, dragging it back as a ridiculous urge to laugh hit her. They had to pretend to be a couple? The past month and change had been hard enough and they'd been trying to be civil. For this to be believable, she'd have to touch him. Smile at him. Share his space. All while pretending that she didn't loathe his existence.

Except—this Henry wasn't the one who battled with her on a daily basis, who made her aware of every mistake and every flaw. With their past hidden, he had no reason to be anything but helpful.

Maybe she could still do this. Maybe.

Did she really have a choice?

Shaky, she directed a small amount of telekinesis into the rug on the floor, twisting the threads of the tassels together.

It helped keep her calm as she turned to the man in question. "You think you can do this?"

His thoughts were veiled as he considered her question, braced against the wall. "Can *you*?" His eyebrows rose in soft challenge. "I hear you still hate me."

Surprise made her eyes widen before she caught the movement. "Gossip's already made the rounds, then."

He shrugged, intent on her face. "Is it a lie?"

Yeah, not about to go into this in front of their parents. "I can be professional if you can."

She caught a glint of mischief as he dipped his head. "Well, then. I'm in your hands."

She hated her body's reaction, the strings he plucked so easily, even without his memories. But he would get those back, she reminded herself fiercely. And when he did, everything she said now would be mocked or torn over.

Her gloves wouldn't lower; they weren't out of the ring.

And, apparently, jerk was his factory setting. Awesome.

She didn't get a chance to counter before he sealed their fate. "I'm in."

seven

"Do you think you'll have sex?"

Tia choked at the out-of-the-blue question and poked her head out of her walk-in closet to gawk at her friend. Leah sprawled across the queen-size bed, one arm behind her head. She flashed a grin.

"What?" Tia managed, clutching the underwear she'd been about to pack like pearls. "Sex? What?"

Leah shifted, curls strewn around her pretty face. "A foreign country, Christmastime. It practically screams sex."

"Except she's going alone," Emma pointed out without looking up. She sipped coffee as she perched on the window seat, scrolling through baking recipes on her phone.

"Exactly." Leah rolled to her front and propped her head on her hands. She kicked her legs like a teenager. "A holiday romance."

Tia avoided their eyes as she backed up and dumped the underwear into her suitcase. Guilt at the omission gurgled in her belly like bad shrimp. "It's a business trip."

Leah raised her voice. "You're staying in an English manor over the most romantic time of the year."

"Tia has no romance in her soul."

That made her smirk and she shoved her suitcase back into the bedroom, puffing hair out of her face. "She's right. I'm dead inside."

Leah peered down. "Pretty fancy underwear for someone not planning on having sex."

Tia slammed the lid shut and Leah grinned. "Just think," her friend pushed on, the definition of bullheaded, "after all the tension you've been feeling lately, wouldn't it be good to unwind a little? Speaking of..." She cleared her throat, as subtle as a rock through a window. "How's Henry?"

Tia barely controlled the telling flinch. "Don't even."

"I don't know why you don't just bang and get it over with."

Emma snickered.

Tia grabbed a pillow and bashed her laughing friend on the head. "Seriously, how does Gabriel put up with you?"

Leah sprang up, a ball of energy in human skin. "He loves it." She grabbed Tia's hand and towed her back into the walk-in closet.

When Tia had rented a place in Chicago, the city they'd picked to open the bar, she'd gone for quality. Admittedly, Chicago apartments were on the small side, but with a TARDIS spell, everything could be more than it appeared. Rows for shoes upon shoes, and racks of gowns, sweaters and shirts slotted between multiple drawers. A marble island in the center held her jewelry and underwear in cleverly hidden nooks and crannies. The entire far wall was a mirror, bookended by velvet chairs in Tia's signature red. Leah dropped into one to try on the Louboutins she'd grabbed.

She rubbed one on her cheek. "Oh, to have these in every color."

Tia flipped through some suit jackets. "I love you, Leah, but you'll find a hex bag in your purse if you try and steal them."

"It might be worth it."

Uh-huh. She knew her friend, and while Leah loved pretty

things, she was much more the Cubs cap and jeans type, especially with four dogs to walk.

"Emma," Leah called, selecting another pair with ice-pick heels. "Come and try these shoes. They might work for your wedding."

Emma wandered in. "Pass."

"Because they're violet?"

"Because they look like they double as a murder weapon."

"Fine, fine, but you need to start thinking seriously about these things."

"Why? I have you two." Emma batted her lashes as Tia snorted.

Leah stroked a covetous hand down a swath of silk. "Seriously, T, your closet's like a boutique. Oh, this one's pretty. You taking any of these?"

"Maybe one?" Tia straightened from where she'd dumped a bunch of jackets and skirts. She expelled a tight breath. "Honestly, I don't even know what to take. What kind of businessman invites you to spend a month with him in his home?"

"Very old world," Emma agreed, holding a cashmere sweater against herself.

Leah's eyebrows waggled. "Is he good-looking?"

"He's older than my dad."

"Age gaps are hot."

Tia flicked her fingers and magic nudged Leah in the ribs. Leah just grinned and repeated the gesture.

It was weak, baby magic, but it sent a frisson of nerves down Tia's spine. "You know you're not meant to do that. Not until you and Gabriel get bound officially."

When a human and a witch chose to be together, they bonded. The human took on a sliver of power from their partner to boost their health, slow their aging, essentially ensuring the human could live as long as their love.

The High Family had final say on this—*usually*—but Gabriel had accidentally gifted Leah some power without permission.

They were all keeping it on the DL until it was made official by the High Family, which would only happen when either Leah or Gabriel made their relationship permanent.

Blasé as always, Leah waved that off. "Aren't I getting good? I'm practicing on Gabriel."

Emma cleared her throat. "Are you gone over Christmas?" The pointed subject change had Leah rolling her eyes, but tough. They were both a little overprotective of the human.

"That's the plan." Tia grimaced. "Sorry to miss out on Christmas Eve cocktails."

"It's okay. Bastian and I were thinking of taking Sloane to Paris to see the lights anyway." Emma smiled as she mentioned her younger half sister. "Kole might even join us since we're definitely not visiting the rest of my family." She made a face.

Yeah, Emma's mom and brothers—other than Kole, who they were all friendly with—were pretty much the worst people ever.

Leah bounced. "And Melly and I have this big family thing planned for Gabriel. Since they haven't really had a big celebration since their parents died, we wanted to make it special."

"Gabriel must rue the day you and his sister became close."

Leah stuck her tongue out at Emma.

"Well. Good." Tia pressed her lips into a smile. "We all have plans, then." She should've expected they'd have plans, she told herself, listening with one ear as Leah asked Emma about Paris. They had partners now, families. It wasn't just the three of them anymore.

Maybe she *could* have a holiday romance with an English warlock. It wasn't like any of the American ones were interested. Much too polite and deferential. She deserved someone who would drag her out of a room, push her against a wall and just go to town. It had been too long since someone had been to town. She was starting to worry she'd never have a visitor again.

Except this was a business trip. A business trip where she was fake dating her ex who wasn't her ex. Not exactly rife with chances to meet someone and *unwind.*

She had an investment to secure anyway. Better to focus and not let sex distract her.

I'm in your hands.

The whisper slunk into her mind, all curling vowels and suggestive consonants.

She resolutely shoved it right the fuck out.

Henry waited in the foyer of the Pearlmatter mansion, two bags at his feet. He'd been ready to go with one but his mom had thrown up her hands at the idea of a person surviving on a single suitcase. She'd handed him a second packed bag over an hour later. He felt like a kid about to go on a school trip. He allowed it because he knew, despite her assurances, she was feeling the nerves. She wasn't the only one.

He'd been ready for half an hour and everything inside him coiled tight in anticipation of Tia arriving. He was pretty sure the feeling wasn't returned. He *was* her ex, he supposed, but still. He had his work cut out for him on this trip—professional and personal.

Normally, they'd portal to England, but they'd decided two weeks ago, with everything Tia and Henry needed to go over, to charter a jet instead. Figuring to spend as much time with her as possible, Henry had requested to ride with her to the hangar; she'd agreed with gritted teeth and he'd thanked her with a chuck under her chin. He was positive he'd been inches from losing his fingers.

Why did that amuse him so much?

The memory master he'd seen had urged Henry to go with his instincts, that his mind would follow paths it knew were there, like a man who'd gone blind but knew his environment.

Apparently, his instinct was to challenge Tia. He didn't know what that said about them, but he noted it down with his other observations, like the way her eyes turned stormy and her skin flushed at every subtle innuendo. She hadn't lost her shit—yet—but he figured it wouldn't be long. Maybe when she shed the stiff politeness, something would shift in the black haze.

Heavy footsteps sounded on the marble behind him and his grin faltered. His dad moved into view, a manila folder in his hands.

"You ready?" Richard said, sliding his free hand into his pants pocket. Above, the whirr of the ceiling fan rustled his hair and the nearby leaves of a giant potted palm.

"I think so. I'm just waiting for Tia."

"Mmm." Disapproval lurked in eyes that matched his. "You want to watch yourself with her."

Henry cocked his head with a quizzical frown.

"She's quicksand. You got out once before. Don't make the mistake again."

"You don't like her."

His dad pursed his lips, shadows dipping behind his watchful gaze. "She's just not a good influence." As if to avoid more questions, he offered the folder. "I made you this. A cheat sheet of the pitch. It, ah, should help."

Henry took it, lifting it in acknowledgment. "Great, thanks."

They stood there awkwardly for a few more seconds. It had always been this way, from the moment Henry became aware that other dads were different than his. He'd worked twice as hard as his friends to get half the attention. It wasn't that his dad was cold, he was just...distant. He'd never figured out if that was worse.

"You need anything, just call," Richard said finally, clumsily patting Henry's shoulder. "I'm sure your mom will want you to anyway. You can always use the mirror. Or, you know, your cell."

Henry nodded.

Another silence.

Shit, this was painful. He was wondering if he should go wait outside when—

"You are *not* sneaking off without saying goodbye!" came a very welcome Southern trill and the *tip-tap* of heels on marble. Henry didn't know who was more relieved.

Maybelline barreled into him and wrapped her arms tight, making an *mmm* sound. "Don't forget to have fun."

"It's business," her husband reminded her.

She scoffed as she drew back, a flick of her eyes telling him what she thought of that. "Can't have business without some pleasure." Her smile was sly. She'd made no secret of her ambitions for Tia and Henry to bond on this trip.

Maybe if he had his memories, he'd have been embarrassed or annoyed, but he just found it amusing.

A horn honked outside.

"That'll be Tia." Maybelline put her hands on his cheeks. "You sure you have everything?"

He nodded dutifully, feeling like that child again.

She beamed. "You'll be fine. Pearlmatters breed tough. But we also love with all our hearts, so if I don't hear from you at least once every few days, I'll be portaling over to check you're still alive." She clapped him lightly on his cheeks as he snorted. "Now, go have fun and charm their pants off."

"Whose pants?"

She winked. "I was thinking Lord Siddeley's, but Tia's would be good practice."

A second, elongated honk made his eyebrows skim up. "You could be right about that."

They'd been flying for over an hour when Tia started fidgeting.

Across the table from her in the jet's cabin, Henry looked up from the papers she'd ordered him to read, his attention going to the fire-red nails she tapped on the tabletop. Catching him, she stopped, sliding the hand into her lap.

"Nervous?" he asked casually, finishing the page and placing it facedown on the stack of other reports she'd made for him.

He'd already read the information—Richard had been working with him for weeks—but it'd seemed easier to agree than argue over a seven-hour flight.

She made a noise somewhere between a scoff and a hum. "What do I have to be nervous about?"

"That I'll lose control and set the plane on fire, sending us crashing into the ocean?"

She paused. "Okay. Now I'm nervous."

He smiled to himself, pretending to read the report. He opted not to tell her that his control over his fire magic was shaky at best. Magic was often linked to their emotional state, and Tia obviously made him emotional in some way. Another mystery to solve.

She left it another few seconds before clearing her throat. "We need to talk. About things."

"We have been talking. Well," he corrected, still skimming his eyes across the page, "you've been talking. *Grilling* might be a better word."

He sensed more than saw her raise her chin. "I need to know you can answer basic questions."

She hadn't even waited until the wheels were up before launching those "basic questions" at him, like he should be sitting under a white light with bamboo shoots under his nails—*who is our CEO? What is our bestselling potion? What recent businesses has PH Inc. taken on?*

"I didn't even get a lollipop for getting all the answers right," he commented.

"You don't like lollipops."

Interesting how confident she was. "Maybe you don't know me as well as you think."

"You're saying your tastes have changed?"

He took in the woman sitting across from him, haughty and hot as hell in her soft sweater and ripped jeans. She was lithe and lovely, touchable light brown skin with curves in all the places a man wanted them. "Not every taste," he murmured.

Catching the intent, she folded her arms, glaring. "Don't even."

"Don't even what?"

"Try charming me. Save it for the English, buddy."

"I'll do that," he said, amused. He put the papers down and sat back, watching her closely. "Is that why you're nervous?"

"I'm not nervous." Her eyes pulsed with annoyance, green, then brown.

He bit back his smile. "Okay. You wanted to talk."

"Yeah." She let out a breath, shifting in her seat. Threading her hands together, she set them on the table. "We should get our story straight."

Interest snared, Henry extended his long legs so they brushed hers. "It would help to know how our story ended."

She snarled at him, yanking her legs back. "Get out of my space, Pearlmatter."

"You don't like me," he observed, the fact an itch he couldn't scratch. "Which means I must have done something."

"It doesn't matter."

"It does to me."

"Then that's a you problem," she shot back. "All they need to know is we got back together."

Stubborn, he thought. So fucking stubborn. But funny thing—so was he.

He'd circle back. "How long has it been?"

She paused. "Since we were together?" At his nod, she said, "Eight years."

"And how long were we dating?"

"About four."

They'd dated young. First loves, maybe. The realization made something like smugness pulse through him. You never forgot your first.

The irony hit and he almost laughed. Unless you were him, apparently.

Instead of going that route, he chose a different question. "Have we seen each other a lot since?"

"Not really. We keep out of each other's way." She spoke firmly over his next question. "We've been working in the same office for the past couple of months. We'll just say the *flame*—" she grimaced like the word tasted bad "—was rekindled."

Somewhat enjoying her discomfort, Henry tapped his flat belly. "When I kissed you after hours?"

She gaped.

"Or did you throw me onto a desk?" he mused. "You seem like you're a take-charge kind of woman. I might've enjoyed that."

Her mouth closed. Opened. Closed. Then, "Stop. Talking."

He pressed his lips together to keep back a smile. Already, her polite façade had disappeared. All right, he was a bit of a dick to make her uncomfortable, but he knew, on a gut level, rolling over for Tia wouldn't get her respect in the long run.

Besides. He kind of liked winding her up.

She went back to the matter in hand. "They won't ask details. All they need to know is we're a couple."

He doubted that but let it go. "So, how long have we been back together?"

"I don't know." She relaxed in her seat but stiffened when her legs brushed his. She pulled away. "A few weeks."

"Honeymoon phase," he ruminated with wicked intent.

It earned him a curse.

He lifted his hands innocently. "I'm just saying, people who've only been hooked up a few weeks are all over each other."

"Like you're an expert?"

Shrugging idly, he tapped his finger to his lips. "Just so you know… I'm willing to go method on this. Feel free to touch me anywhere."

A muscle feathered in her jaw. "You're not taking this seriously."

"I'm trying to figure out the ground rules," he replied, keeping his amusement bottled. "You're the one who won't set them."

"Fine." She tossed him a filthy look. "No touching."

He made a noise.

"*What?*" she snapped.

"Siddeley picked us because we're the next-gen couple—who had to sneak away to get our hands on each other." He enjoyed the hint of growl that came from her throat. "He's clearly a romantic. He'll want to see us coo a bit."

"It's business," she said stubbornly.

"You won't even hold my hand?"

"No."

"Scared?"

Her mouth dropped before she blustered, "Fuck you."

"Language, Celestia."

Hazel eyes boiled. "Don't you call me that."

He held his hand out, palm up. "I dare you."

"Oh, for the Goddess's sake."

"It's a show," he told her. "Holding hands is bare minimum. I'm not saying all day but sometimes you might have to take one for the team." He wiggled his fingers. "Unless touching me is too much temptation."

Her palm slapped his with so much force, it stung. And yet, it felt like victory.

He weaved their fingers together, unable to hide a grin. Her skin was warm, soft. The opposite of her expression.

He rubbed his thumb along her palm, enjoying her hitch of breath. The way his own heart thrummed a bit faster as if in recognition. "See? Easy."

"For you." She stared at their hands as if it was surprising. It probably was, if they'd barely been around each other for eight years.

"Did we used to hold hands?" He couldn't stop that question, didn't want to, intrigued by what kind of couple they'd been. Tia didn't strike him as the PDA type but the way she was staring, as if memories were blinding her, had him wondering.

Her eyes rose and she blinked before tugging her hand out of his. She made a production of wiping hers down the front of her sweater and he chuckled.

She tucked her arms around herself and sat straighter, gaze shuttered. "We've been back together a few weeks. We keep the PDA to a minimum and are taking things one day at a time. That's all they need to know."

If she thought she had final say on that, she was deluded, but for now, he inclined his head. "Luckily," he drawled, encroaching on her space under the table a little more, "one day at a time is my current specialty."

eight

It was well past eight p.m. GMT by the time they escaped Heathrow airport. According to Siddeley's directions, he lived in the county of Surrey, presiding over the small town of Westhollow, an hour or so from London. That was if you didn't hit traffic from hell, where it took twenty minutes to inch a mile. When they turned off the "motorway," as the English called it, and hit countryside, Tia could've wept.

All she wanted was a bed, a pillow and a space that didn't have Henry in it. After almost twelve hours with her ex, she could cheerfully pour a mute potion down his throat.

He *talked*. All. The. Time. And not only that, he asked questions. About them, about the company, about her life in Chicago and her friends. Cheeky bastard even had the nerve to ask about her lovers. She'd taken great delight in describing one of her sexual encounters, embellishing it so much that had it been real, she would've still been walking bowlegged.

Yeah, he'd shut up then.

For about ten minutes.

She'd claimed the driver's role and even though she was on the wrong side of the road on the wrong side of the car and so tired her eye was twitching, part of her thrilled at being in

England. She couldn't even remember the last time she'd been out of the country. She and her friends had talked idly of doing a girls' trip somewhere but things kept cropping up and then Emma had gotten engaged and now Leah was deep in love with her warlock. Life was just more complicated now.

Pushing aside the uncomfortable emotion that inspired, Tia focused on the road. It curved and dropped abruptly, the only light the beam of her headlights as she concentrated on *not* testing the car's capacity for off-roading.

"Goddess," she muttered, sharply twisting the wheel to the right as another corner leaped out of nowhere. "How is the death rate not higher around here?"

"Maybe they don't all drive like they're in Formula One."

Tia would've thrown Henry a glare but she was genuinely concerned she'd crash if she took her eyes off the road. "What can I say?" She cursed as another corner shot up and noticed Henry grab at the *oh shit* handle above the door. A smirk turned her mouth. "Just eager to get away from you."

His chuckle in the dark cab raised goose bumps that had no business whispering over her skin.

She checked the navigation, relieved to see their destination was about two minutes away. Her palms were slick on the steering wheel as she slowed her pace, watching for the gates Siddeley had said indicated the entrance of his property.

Henry shifted, his tall body attempting to arrange itself comfortably in the confines of the passenger seat. Tia *might* have spelled the seat when he wasn't looking so it would only move so far back. Yeah, it had been fucking petty but he was so unbothered by her—and *yes,* she knew he couldn't remember why he should be bothered, but it was still exasperating. Exhausting. Harder than she'd thought to only see humor and interest in eyes that had once burned for her.

She figured she'd earned some petty, especially as he was taking every opportunity to poke at her sore spots. If he wasn't careful, she'd move from petty to pissed and the hex bags would come out.

Finally, the high beams caught on twinkle lights wrapped around wrought iron. Tia crept up to the gates, lowering her window as she approached the intercom box. It had no buttons on it and she stared dumbly.

"What?" Henry asked, his breath tickling her ear.

She almost leaped out of her skin. "Christ. Back the hell off, Pearlmatter."

"What're you staring at?" he asked, ignoring her. Naturally.

He was too close. She could *smell* him and for someone who'd traveled for half a day, he had no right smelling of citrus and something darkly masculine.

She held herself flush to the seat so they didn't touch. "There's no button."

"Huh." He leaned even closer to see and she held her breath like a child. "There is," he said, not sounding at all affected by how his chest was millimeters from hers. "It's just on the underside." He rubbed his fingers together, blowing out a breath. "Let's see if it's just fire…"

On that somewhat perplexing statement, he flicked those long fingers and twirled his wrist. Something pinged on the box and a crackle sounded.

He aimed a cocky grin her way.

"You've always had a talent for pushing buttons," was all she said before shooing him with a hand. "Back in your seat."

He stayed where he was, eyes full of mischief. "Am I disturbing you?"

"You're disturbed in the head," she shot at him before her brain caught up with her mouth. She winced.

His chin lowered so he could whisper in her ear. "And whose fault is that, Celestia?"

The feel of his hot breath coasting over her skin sent a shiver down to her toes. Thank the good Goddess she didn't have to come up with a reply as a voice sounded from the box.

"Yes?" A flat British voice drew the word out so it was two syllables.

Tia craned her head out the window, relieved when Henry retreated to his seat. "Tia Hightower and Henry Pearlmatter to see Lord Siddeley. He should be expecting us."

"Of course. Please follow the drive and park next to the reindeer."

Tia paused. "The what?"

"The reindeer, my lady."

Maybe she was even more tired than she thought. But the gates were opening and it made more sense to follow the path than ask for a third time.

She eased through, happy to see the road stretched out with no twisting corners. She tapped her fingers on the wheel, her stomach jumping as lights shone in the distance.

She kept her eyes peeled for any animals willing to play chicken with a car. "Well," she said after a minute. "See any reindeer?"

"No, dear."

It took her a moment. "Hilarious."

She didn't have to look at him to know his lips would be twitching. Without their past a scar between them, he found it—her—amusing.

It might be worse.

They drove for another thirty seconds. The lights from the manor got brighter as they neared, excessively so considering it was close to midnight thanks to their traffic snarl. Maybe everyone here was a night owl.

They reached the end of the drive where it curved in a circle and she gaped through the windscreen. Her foot slid off the gas pedal, landing on the mat with a thump. The car slowed as it crunched over gravel.

"Holy…" Henry cut himself off with a whistle.

It wasn't that it was sprawling, a Georgian building almost

as tall as it was wide, with a circular drive and central fountain as idyllic as any spa brochure. She'd expected that.

What she hadn't expected were the Christmas lights. And Christmas mechanical toys. And Christmas trees. And an actual reindeer chilling to the right of the wide stone steps that led up to the front doors.

"Did we take a wrong turn and end up at Santa's village?" she couldn't help but ask, belatedly hitting the brake.

"It looks like Christmas threw up," Henry observed.

Something caught Tia's eye and she gaped. "Tell me that's not a camel."

"How many lights do you think that is? Two thousand?"

"Probably more." Realizing with some relief that the camel was mechanical, Tia tore her gaze away. "It's..."

"Intense."

Out of principle, she couldn't agree with him, but ho-ho-holy hell. *Intense* was the word for it.

Christmas lights of all designs—from signs to people to simple twinkle lights—trailed over every inch of the building and grounds. There were at least three Christmas trees she could see, one large by the fountain and two standing sentry by the doors, all done up perfectly with baubles and tinsel and a giant gold star atop each. The effect was near blinding.

"Is it putting you in the mood?"

She startled, whipping her head to Henry. "*What*?"

"For Christmas." His oh-so-innocent eyes trailed her face. "What did you think I meant?"

Tia rolled her eyes. "You lose your memories and I gain a comedian. Perfect." She gripped her door handle and stepped out. She stopped as she crunched something that wasn't gravel and looked down. A blanket of white spread underneath her.

Her mind reeled. "Snow," she breathed.

She heard Henry's footsteps crunch around the car to join her. "Magic, you think?" he asked. Since there'd been no hint of snow anywhere else on the journey, it was the logical assumption.

She nodded, despite herself slightly enchanted with the lights and the snow and even the reindeer, who grunted a greeting. Honestly, Christmas had been the last thing on her mind, especially since she wouldn't be spending it with her girls or her family. Even Leah decorating the bar hadn't made a dent in her lack of spirit.

But she couldn't help but feel giddy, like a child, at the exuberance here. The obvious joy in it.

The doors flew open, snapping her out of the Hallmark moment. Noise spilled out as a man dressed in black-and-white filled the gap.

"Don't tell me," Henry murmured. "It's the innkeeper."

"If I see a barn, I'm out of here."

"Good evening, Lady Hightower, Lord Pearlmatter." The man inclined his head, his bearing every inch aristocratic as he gestured for them to approach. "Your bags will be retrieved and stored in your room. Please. Come in."

Tia jumped when she felt Henry's hand close around hers. Immediately, she tugged away, hating the trip in her pulse at the familiar touch.

He held firm. "Showtime, Tia," he said under his breath. "Game face on."

She grimaced before applying a bright smile. "Just don't get any ideas, Pearlmatter."

As she gingerly picked her way through the snow, she pretended not to hear his low, "Too late for that."

They were left cooling their heels in a parlor decorated in frills and fuss, all low, hard couches in material that looked hundreds of years old, chairs with spindly legs and arms, dark sideboards with dust catchers on their tops, and yet another Christmas tree done up in black and gold. A fire roared in the stone hearth and Tia watched as Henry drifted toward it.

"What did you mean when you said *if it's only fire*?" she asked.

She didn't want to talk to him, but they were stuck waiting here anyway. The man who'd opened the door—"Call me Primm"—had gone to fetch Siddeley five minutes ago and if she didn't speak, she'd fall asleep. Not even the rock posing as a couch was helping.

Henry huffed a sound which might have been a laugh. "My fire magic is...not reacting well to the holes in my memory. My control is pretty much shit. But at least basic stuff—like telekinesis—seems to be working okay."

Hence the button-pushing test. "You can't summon fire?"

"Summon it, yes. Control it, not so much. The other day, I tried to light a candle." He pushed his hands into his jeans pockets. "I melted the wax."

She didn't know what to react to first. The fact that his fire magic was on the blink or that he'd just admitted failure to her.

It threw her off. Normally, she'd attack, make a sarcastic remark and he'd retaliate in kind. But he was like this because of her.

"Huh," was what she came out with.

He turned so the fire cast shadows on half his face and leaned an elbow on the mantel. His hair fell over his forehead, styled softer than normal. "What's your talent?"

She shifted on the couch, freezing when it creaked alarmingly loud. "I have many." Telling him her mastery was in alchemy was just setting herself up for a joke.

"Can you juggle?"

"Only my men," she said airily, which was such a big, fat lie, she could've laughed. Not like she was sought after in their society, though she wasn't sure why not. She might be strong and opinionated, but Higher society witches were all acquired tastes.

"How does a man make the cut?"

"Not being my ex would help."

His fingers tapped the mantel. Long, lean fingers. He'd always had good hands. "Does it help that I don't remember being your ex?"

"You are, though." *She* had to remember that.

"What if—"

"Lady Hightower!" boomed Siddeley as he strode in, interrupting whatever Henry had been about to say. "Lord Pearlmatter!"

Tia popped up from the couch in relief. "Lord Siddeley. Sorry we're so late. We hit traffic."

"Ah! It can be so dreadful around here. I always portal, but I suppose one must have a picture of where they're portaling, mustn't they?" He grasped her outstretched hand and squeezed. "Mindless of me, I do apologize. But you're here now." He shook Henry's hand, beaming at them both. "How do you like Silkwood Hall?"

"The Christmas display is..." Garish. Obscene. Something they could see from space. "...impressive."

That earned her an even wider smile. "Mother and I just adore Christmas. Best time of the year! It's why we were so keen on you staying now, so you can appreciate everything Westhollow has to offer in the winter season. But where are my manners." He smoothed his hand over a waistcoat embroidered with dancing snowmen. "You must be exhausted. I'll get Primm to show you your accommodations and we can start fresh tomorrow morning. How does that sound?"

Heaven; it sounded like heaven to Tia.

Until she found herself staring down at a queen-size bed covered in a lavender plush duvet.

The *one* queen size bed in the *one* room they'd been shown to.

"Lord Siddeley trusts you both will find this comfortable," Primm intoned. He was a beanpole of a man, white, around six foot four, thin and dressed in a pressed suit like any good English butler. He had a trimmed mustache that was gray like his neat, short hair. His wolf-blue eyes moved between Henry's and Tia's blank faces.

"One room," Henry murmured, and she could've sworn his gaze darted to the bed and then her. His throat bobbed. "It looks, ah, great." He put his suitcase on the side of the bed nearest the door.

Tia was still stuck on the *one*-ness of it all. "We're not married," she said to the butler, her voice sounding off even to her own ears. Her heart kicked into a new gear, one she worried would end in a heart attack. "Lord Siddeley doesn't mind us sharing a room?"

"We English are not so stuffy," the butler told her. Stuffily. "Breakfast is served at six a.m. until nine. You can follow the locator cloud. It will be outside your door whenever you're ready. Complimentary candy canes are on the dresser."

With that, he was gone, closing the door behind him with a click that slammed into Tia's knees, weakening them.

"Guess we should've expected it," Henry said after a minute of awkward silence. His hands lay on his suitcase and tapped restlessly as he stared at the confines of the room. For once, not so cocky.

It wasn't that the room wasn't nice. It was, dominated by the wooden four-poster bed that could fit a harem of witches, two end tables on either side, two armoires—his and hers—and a giant mirror that faced the bed.

Normally, Tia might have made a joke about that but all she could focus on was the size. It could've been a shoebox for how much breathing space it gave her.

There was a door on the opposite wall and she headed for it, twisting the old-fashioned knob to reveal an en suite almost as big as the bedroom. Unlike the bedroom, the bathroom was modern, white marble, with a sunken claw-foot tub and a shower that boasted five showerheads and a small bench seat. Her eyes lingered, brain taking that in all sorts of directions before she squashed it. She turned back to the bedroom and emotion fluttered inside her. It wasn't panic, but it wasn't far off.

How was she supposed to stay in one room with Henry?

Scratch that. How was she supposed to share a bed with him?

Her lungs constricted and she put a hand to her chest. Great. Now she was going to hyperventilate.

"Which, ah, side do you want?" Henry gestured. His expression was tight, the flirty comedian nowhere to be found as he avoided looking at her.

"I always take the right," she said.

He stilled. "Not going to argue about sharing a bed with me?"

That baby panic spread. "I'm an adult," she returned, forcing herself to saunter toward her suitcases, which had been left at the door. "Not like anything's going to happen that I don't want to happen."

One eyebrow winged up.

And she realized how that sounded. "I mean, I don't *want* anything to happen," she blustered and snagged the smaller bag that held her night stuff. "And if you come anywhere near me, you'll lose more than your memory."

"Uh-huh." With that annoying sound, Henry unzipped his suitcase. "Sounds like someone protests too much."

"I broke up with *you*," she pointed out with vicious relish.

"And no one's going to say anything if you change your mind." He grinned as the suitcase flipped open.

Tia's eyes zeroed in on the five—*five*—boxes of condoms that sat on top of his neatly folded clothes. Everything stilled before her heart leaped into a gallop.

Henry stared down at the boxes.

"Well." Tia cleared her thick throat, tightening her hold on her suitcase. "You think a lot of your stamina."

"I'm...they're not..." He blinked rapidly, color spreading up his face. She couldn't remember a single time Henry had ever blushed. She lingered on the sight as he took a breath. "Mom must've snuck them in."

Even though it was probably true—and what level of hell was she in that her ex-boyfriend's mom was throwing condoms at them?—Tia ran her tongue over her teeth. "Convenient."

"I mean it."

Tia made herself move to the bathroom, away from those condoms and the warlock standing near them. "Sounds like someone protests too much."

The bathroom door snapped closed on his continuing objections.

nine

The curse of partial memory loss, aside from the obvious, was that when Henry said it was the hardest night of his life, it didn't really mean much.

The condoms had been only the start—and thank you, Mom, for that surprise. He doubted sleeping in the same bed with an attractive woman would've ever been easy, but Tia apparently preferred sleeping in shorts and silky tops that barely covered her breasts and showed off acres of touchable, lickable skin. He was pretty sure he'd stopped breathing when she'd stepped out of the bathroom, her scowl warning him not to joke. He hadn't been able to think, let alone speak as she'd slipped in next to him. But not before she'd summoned a shimmering energy wall down the center of the bed.

"So you don't get any ideas if you get scared in the night," she'd said with a smirk before using telekinesis to switch off the light.

Like that helped stop his fantasies. It was a big bed. Lots of mattress. And Tia, she'd be wild. He didn't need his memories to know that.

That thought hadn't helped him sleep.

Which was why he used his morning shower to take care of

it, gripping his cock while picturing her delicate fingers, her red lips whispering in his ear all the dirty things she wanted to do to him. His groan was drowned out by the showerheads and he felt like a lust-soaked teenager as he toweled himself afterward. Maybe it was always like this between them. He made a note to ask and grinned as he imagined her expression.

Steam curled out after him as he emerged from the bathroom to find her sitting cross-legged on the bed with her phone in her hand.

"You shower like a girl," she grumbled, not taking her eyes off the screen. "What are you even doing in there that takes that long?"

Ridiculously, he felt his ears heat. He hadn't even known that was a thing.

He hid the embarrassment behind a wall of confidence, sauntering to the bed and flopping down backward so his head was in her lap. She squawked as he grinned up at her. "I could always use company."

She shoved him off her lap so hard his head bounced. "You have two hands."

Ah. Irony.

He crossed those hands behind his head. "What're you looking at?"

Her gaze flicked up, then to his arms where they lingered before she fixed her eyes down again. "Just checking in."

"Right. Guess I should, too."

A smirk lifted her lips. "Maybelline will want to know how it's going."

He cringed. "I swear I had no idea."

"Mmm." She lowered her phone to her jean-covered lap. Her sweater was plunging, a blue-green color that brought out the flecks in her eyes. "Well, it's only a month and you'll be back with your harem. You can put them to good use then."

"My harem?" News to him. He'd asked around and nobody remembered anyone significant since Tia.

"All the witches that parade around on your arm like they've caught a prize fish." She wrinkled her nose and slid off the bed. "The bonus of being part of a Legacy family, I guess. For you anyway."

"Not you?" He watched as she inspected her hair in the mirror. Watched and didn't lower his gaze to her perfect curved ass. Not for more than a second anyway. "Warlocks don't parade you around? Is your family not as big a deal?"

Her body stiffened and she whirled on him with clenched fists. "We're just as good as the Pearlmatters."

He blinked. "I didn't mean—"

"Hightowers go back generations, producing top-tier witches and warlocks. We've always been first pick when society is looking for a match. Any warlock would be thrilled to have me."

He sensed he'd stepped on sensitive ground. "I know."

"Just because my family has a hard-on for your bloodline doesn't mean we're desperate."

"I know."

"My mom is just really intense about it all. But hooking me up with you is only one of the options we have. You would be so lucky to have another shot."

He'd started to sweat. "I know."

She didn't look like she believed him.

"My dad wouldn't merge with any old family," he added, grasping at straws to make that expression disappear. "And my mom wouldn't be throwing condoms like confetti if she didn't approve."

That got him a twitch of the lips, like she badly wanted to smile and refused to.

It cheered him. "And if I spent years with you passionately lusting after me, I obviously thought you were worth it."

He'd meant to make her roll her eyes. Instead, a shadow crossed them.

Before he could push, she tucked her cell into her back pocket. "So, breakfast," she said, as if the conversation hadn't happened. "I figured we'd go down, hand in hand, make with the nice and then hit him with the business."

After a drawn-out beat of hesitation, he decided to let it be. He'd think about that shadow later. "All right."

"Let me take point. I know more about the potions side, especially since you, you know, forgot it all."

"All right."

"And don't go overboard on the touching." She narrowed her eyes at his sudden grin. "I mean it. We are not that honeymoon couple who get down and dirty in an elevator. Be professional."

He tucked his tongue in his cheek. "But what if I don't remember how to be?" When her expression tightened, he smothered a laugh. "All right, all right. Minimal touching. That it?"

She folded her arms beneath her breasts. The neckline shifted and it was a struggle not to let his eyes drift. "You're being damn agreeable."

"Yep."

"Why?"

This woman. He let the laugh roll out this time and sat up, moving off the bed toward the door. He didn't bother to grab his cell since he had no idea what to say to some of the friends messaging him anyway. "Guess you'll learn of my dastardly plans later." He reached for the door and managed to open it about two inches before a blast of pressure slammed it closed.

When he turned, Tia was storming up to him, a finger out and jabbing into his chest. "You will take this seriously, Pearlmatter," she warned. This close, her perfume whirled around him, notes of some kind of spice and, oddly, vanilla. "A lot is riding on this."

"Damn, it is? 'Cause you only told me five thousand times." He closed his hand around her finger. "I get it, okay. Trust me."

She was relatively tall, her silver heels lifting her close enough he saw the doubt that flickered in her eyes. He was surprised that it pinched.

"Let's just do this," she muttered, pulling her finger free and reaching for the door.

As Primm had promised, a locator cloud hovered outside, whirling lazily in a puff of petal-pink smoke. Locator clouds were potion-based creations with one function, generally only coded with a few phrases. When Tia asked for the breakfast room, it drifted down the hall immediately.

Henry fell into step beside Tia as they trudged down corridors lined with paintings decorated with tinsel and strings of baubles. The runner was ancient and thin, covering creaking floorboards, other doors shut tight as they passed. It was quiet; the only sounds those of the morning outside.

"What do you think Lady Siddeley's like?" he murmured to Tia as they navigated downstairs to the main foyer he recognized from last night. The eight-foot Christmas tree covered in sparkling lights was a giveaway.

"I did some research." She shrugged as they turned left. "Less on the London society scene for the last twenty years but a grande dame for sure. Gossip pages say she can make or break a witch with a few words, and her opinion is sought after. In a word, she's Maybelline. But English."

"Then we shouldn't have anything to worry about." Unless she, too, passed condoms around like party favors.

The cloud crossed through an open door. Sound filtered out, the clink of cutlery and the quiet hum of conversation.

He offered his hand. "Showtime?"

He caught the small hesitation before she nodded. "Curtain up."

Palm to palm, they entered the breakfast room—and halted.

The room was long, dominated by a dark table that could easily seat twenty, a chandelier arching above while breakfast trays lined tables set against the wall. The Christmas decorations, at this point, were predictable, bordering on garish as they wound their way toward two French doors. Weak sunlight danced across the multiple heads that turned their way.

He'd expected Siddeley, maybe his mom. He hadn't expected the five others around the table, or the man at the buffet holding silver tongs.

Siddeley sat at the head of the table, but rose as he caught sight of them. "Finally!" he rumbled with excitement, dressed in beige pants, a shirt, an ascot and a muted green padded vest. "I was beginning to wonder if you lovebirds were ever going to emerge from your room."

From the corner of his eye, he saw Tia blanch.

But Siddeley wasn't done. "No matter, no matter," he continued as he strode around the table. "It's a holiday, after all! But now you're here, our party is complete and we can get started."

"Party?" Tia asked, her smile forced.

"The house party."

"Oh." She looked a little lost for words. "I didn't realize... Are these your family?"

A laugh spilled from Siddeley and he clapped a hand on the back of a chair. "While I think of guests as family, these are just my victims for the winter extravaganza, same as you, Lady Hightower."

A man lounging in a chair, an empty plate in front of him and a coffee cup in hand, drawled, "Hardly unwilling victims, Archie." His accent was polished elegance. Another Brit.

Siddeley's smile was broad. "True, true. And it's my hope you all have such a marvelous time that you'll forgive me for making you trek out here."

Maybe it was the memory loss, the time difference, or that he was operating on very little sleep, but Henry was lost. "These are...other guests?" he posed.

"Quite so, Lord Pearlmatter. Let me introduce you." Siddeley indicated the lounging man first. "Theodore Sawyer, a warlock who works in magical confectionary."

"Pleasure," the blue-eyed blond murmured, a dimple creasing his tanned cheek. Siddeley hadn't added a *Lord* in his introduction, which meant the warlock wasn't Higher society. That he'd been invited meant his business must be booming.

Henry nodded at him.

Siddeley waved at the Black man next to Sawyer. "Kingsley Chrichton."

Tia started. "As in Chrichton cauldrons?"

The warlock's smile was slow. "That's right." He was British, too, and, like Sawyer, dressed in tailored pants and a sweater.

Siddeley turned to the other side of the table. "Lady Annaliese Fairweather. Her family has patented a few hundred spells."

"Hi." The redhead nodded, light gleaming over the dozen barely-visible freckles splattered across her fair skin.

Henry was getting the kind of feeling that begged for a life preserver as Siddeley indicated the next witch. "Lady Romina Lopez, inventor extraordinaire."

"You flatter me, Archie. And please, call me Mina," the gorgeous woman with tan skin and brown eyes invited, a hint of a Spanish accent curling around the words.

All eyes turned to the final man by the buffet. Siddeley beamed. "And the warlock unable to separate from his bacon is Lord Griffith Zhang."

Unrepentant, the man selected a slice from his plate and bit in. "You can't blame me, Archie," he joked in an Upper East Side accent after he'd swallowed. "And to finish his spiel, my company works in potion research. But you already know that." His gaze was amused as it shifted to their joined hands. "Not only the companies merging, I see."

Dread came at Henry like a pillow intent on suffocation. Griffith Zhang knew them. Knew them well enough to make Tia's color rise. Henry tightened his hand on hers as she tensed.

She gave Griffith a sickly sweet smile. "You want to watch the bacon, Griffith. Wouldn't want you to choke and die."

The warlock grinned.

Siddeley faltered, but soldiered on. "Good, well, no need for introductions for you, then, but to the rest, this is Lord Henry

Pearlmatter and Lady Tia Hightower, whose family companies have just merged. They work on potions and numerous other projects. And that concludes our party!" He smoothed a hand down his ascot, which Henry noted was Christmas green and stitched with snowflakes. "And Mother, of course, but she, ah, wanted to take tea in her own suite today." He looked shamefaced for a minute before clapping his hands. "Anyway, sit, sit. Or fetch some breakfast and then sit. I have so much planned and you'll need your strength."

No kidding. Henry met Tia's eyes. This wasn't a party. There were five other businessmen and women in the room, all who'd kill for an investment of Siddeley's magnitude. He was Santa Claus and they were all desperate to get on the nice list.

Tia's chin jutted up and danger glowed in her eyes as she locked on to her targets.

No, this wasn't a party. This was war.

ten

Tia barely got through breakfast. Only Henry's prodding had her eating any of the pastries he put on her plate, her focus on the English warlock at the end of the table laughing with another of his *guests*.

Her competitors.

She'd wanted to immediately drag Siddeley to another room, bind his hands and run through their sales pitch over and over until he gave in. Since she was pretty sure the family would frown on a hostage situation, instead she'd stiffly parked herself in the nearest empty chair. She was nothing if not a swan.

Calm on the surface, thrashing like hell underneath.

With that in mind, she passed thirty minutes making small talk with the confectionary warlock and pretending the sweat on her face was a natural glow.

But hell. Thinking of everyone counting on her made swallowing difficult, until finally she refused to eat anything else. When her leg started to bounce, she realized the second cup of coffee had probably been a mistake as well. She cradled the china in her hands, bobbling it when Siddeley cleared his throat.

His smile was eager as he stroked the fat white cat in his lap, making it purr. It looked fluffy as hell and twice as adorable, until its gaze fell on Kingsley Chrichton. Fangs extended past its lips as its eyes narrowed, a long hiss erupting from its throat.

Funny how fast a warlock could scoot a chair when properly motivated.

Siddeley tickled the beast's chin with no fear for his fingers. "I want to thank you all again for coming to this little shindig, which, I promise, you'll enjoy tremendously. With that in mind, I've arranged a few activities for us over the coming weeks." A small flourish and six cream-colored cards appeared in front of them, one split between Tia's and Henry's place settings. Elegant script at the top read: *Winter in Westhollow: Itinerary.*

Forced socializing.

FML, Tia thought, grimly keeping her smile as she read down the list.

Christmas baking... Mulled wine tasting... Snowman building... Christmas caroling... Starlight carnival... Snowflake Ball...

"Ugh," she said under her breath.

"What?" Henry murmured, yet again too close as he read over her shoulder. His lashes were long and tipped with gold, and she hated that she'd noticed. Just as she hated that her body was on high alert, screaming that only two inches separated their arms.

She pitched her voice low, nose wrinkling. "Snowflake Ball. I mean, come on."

His eyes flicked up, beautifully green in the daylight. "You don't like balls?" As the words fell between them, a beat of childish glee resonated in her chest. To her surprise, a flush spread across his cheeks.

Since big ears were everywhere, she just smirked.

He gave her a faint smile in response. Rueful. Cute. A smile she hadn't seen since they'd been seventeen and starting to circle each other.

"I'm all for the wine tasting," commented Mina from across the table, jarring her from the eye contact.

Sawyer snorted. "Tasting, Mina. Meaning you have to spit more than you swallow."

Up the table, Chrichton choked on his coffee. Tia almost did the same.

Mina smiled coolly even as her brown eyes flared in warning.

Siddeley was either oblivious to the innuendo or determined to ignore it. "We might even convince the witch who's holding the tasting to let us make a batch," he enthused. "Wouldn't that be fun?"

More fun than a stupid Snowflake Ball. And what was a *Christmas light walk-through*? Tia sighed.

"I know some of you are on different time zones so please take the morning to settle in, wander the grounds, maybe have a nap." Here he paused to wink at Henry and Tia, and she wanted to dive under the table. It was a good reminder to set up a soundproof barrier around their room, though.

For their secrets. Not for…anything else.

She fanned herself with the card as Siddeley continued. "Lunch will be cold and self-served on the sideboard here, so help yourselves. If you want anything specific, please ask Primm. If you call his name three times into a mirror, wherever he is on the estate, he will hear you. Our first activity will be at two p.m. and we'll meet in the main drive to walk into Westhollow."

"Walk?" Annaliese queried, wrinkling her freckled nose. The statuesque redhead looked like she thought her legs were for fashion, not function.

Siddeley nodded as he scratched behind his familiar's ears. "Westhollow has many witches living in its bounds but there are also humans, so we must keep ourselves discreet."

Tia wondered at how snow that kept only to the Silkwood estate was discreet, but *discreetly* chose to keep that to herself.

By noon, she was dragging. Her body screamed for a soft surface to lie down on and her eyes were gritty and sore. Henry didn't look much better on the other side of Siddeley as the three strolled in the gardens.

She'd ambushed him; she was witch enough to admit it. Before any of the other *guests* had finished breakfast, she'd asked Siddeley if he could show her and Henry his favorite walk on the estate and of course, the jolly warlock was happy to oblige.

Unfortunately, everyone had piled on—Sawyer seemed confident enough with "Archie" to leave him to the masses, but Chrichton, Griffith and Mina kept pace behind them. Tia actually felt Griffith breathing down her neck at one point. Thankfully, Annaliese had drifted back to the manor ten minutes in. Maybe the walk had been too much for her.

From the first step into the rolling snowy lawns, down the slope to the enclosed wooded area strung with lights and baubles, Tia chattered about the company and what they were working on, how their latest potion was selling and what types of containers they were looking at.

Siddeley nodded absently as the words kept coming, pointing out a favorite ornament in the spaces between her sentences, delighting in a robin halfway through a potion shop layout, clapping his hands when he triggered a mechanical Santa to sing "Santa Claus is Coming to Town." Tia smiled weakly at Siddeley and lifted her voice above the noise.

"...and I think if I showed you some of the figures—"

"Later." Siddeley waved a hand, attention on something else.

Stung, she searched for what to do next. Her mom had stressed again that morning how important it was for the company to expand into foreign markets. Short of hogtying the man and going back to Hostage Plan A, Tia was running out of ideas.

Henry cleared his throat in the interim. "The gardens, Lord Siddeley, they're...great."

She mouthed the word *great* at him with wide eyes. He shrugged, adding, "Very Christmassy."

Siddeley clapped Henry on the back, making the younger warlock stagger. "Quite so! We go all out here."

"Are you a weather warlock, Lord Siddeley?" Chrichton piped up in a rumbling voice. He'd tucked his hands into his pockets, though a telltale shimmer around his body indicated he'd summoned a heat barrier to block the chill.

Siddeley nodded. "Parlor tricks, mostly."

"I love the snow," Mina sighed, outfitted in a furred hat and beige trench coat Tia envied. "Christmas just isn't the same without it."

This brought a beaming smile from their host.

Tia narrowed her eyes.

"Does it run in the family?" Chrichton asked.

"Father was very adept." Siddeley brushed some frost off a tree branch and rubbed his fingers together as if relishing the bite of cold.

"And Lady Siddeley?"

"My mother has particular skill in glamour—which makes her very popular with her society set," he joked.

A laugh circled the group, all of them polite.

Tia set her jaw. "Well, we're launching a new potion for those nips and tucks soon—"

"So are we." Griffith, the son of Hightower's biggest rival, sneered. "So are all the other potion researchers. Didn't the merger come up with any fresh ideas?"

Her temper bubbled like a cauldron left on the boil.

Henry intercepted. "You can't expect us to give away our secret projects. But anytime Lord Siddeley would like to hear them, we'd be happy to give a rundown."

Tia kept pace with Siddeley as they turned a corner, sliding on a dip the snow had covered. Henry grabbed her by the back of her coat and yanked her back on track. She barely blinked. "How about tonight after dinner? I have some figures I could pull—"

"Not tonight," Siddeley deterred, and Tia ground her teeth. "Maybe later."

"Tomorrow?"

Siddeley laughed. "Work, work, work. You're here to enjoy yourself, Lady Hightower."

Desperate, Tia smiled at him. Or she hoped she did. Otherwise, she'd just bared her teeth. "Call me Tia, please."

Delight filled his features. "And you must call me Archie." But the ground she'd gained fell away as he continued, "Let's see how the days pass, shall we? Enjoy the season."

Sensing weakness, Mina put in, "Christmas is my favorite time of year."

Siddeley turned with sparkling eyes and took her arm. "Tell me what your most favorite thing about it is."

Triumphant, Mina drew him off with her arm linked in his. "Well, family is all-important to me..."

Tia drifted to a stop as the group continued. Griffith threw a smirk at her as he sauntered ahead. She hoped he tripped and fell on his face.

Looking back, Henry reversed his steps. "What's up?" The hat he'd pulled on drooped over one side of his forehead.

It shouldn't have been adorable and she was crabby enough to contemplate yanking it off him. "He won't let me talk."

Henry gave her a good-natured look, pushing his hands into his pockets. "Maybe he couldn't get a word in."

"I paused."

"When?"

"To breathe."

He snorted.

She kicked at the snow and let her head fall back. Puffs of white curled from her mouth as she let out an annoyed growl. "How the hell am I meant to convince him to pick us if he won't let me tell him about the business?"

"That's the problem. You're telling him stuff instead of showing him."

She scoffed. "What, you want me to act out a potion experiment? Mime our profit margins?"

"Are you ever not a smartass?"

"Too bad you don't remember."

"Very nice." He nudged her with his hip. Too close. Again. "He's invited us all here to *enjoy the season*, right?"

"Ho freaking ho."

"*Maybe* what he wants isn't a business pitch." He tipped his head to the side. "You want to know what an amnesiac is really good at?"

She had some ideas.

His smile upped another notch as if he'd heard the traitorous thought. "Observing," he answered for her. "The guy isn't a typical businessman."

"Okay, Lord Amnesia, I could've told you that."

He tugged on her hair and she batted his hand away.

"He's like…a puppy," Henry decided. "He wants to bond with us. He'll make decisions with his heart."

Tia let her eyes travel over the many, many whimsical decorations scattered around the estate. And sighed. "We're going to have to up our game."

eleven

Tia skipped lunch in favor of brewing a jet-lag potion, summoning Primm to find the ingredients. The stoic butler did as requested, setting Tia and Henry up in a room decorated in green-and-red tinsel. He even sent over a lunch tray of mystery meat sandwiches, which Tia designated as Henry's job to taste test. The first bite confirmed the bastard still couldn't be trusted.

He was still chuckling as they headed through the foyer for their first "activity," her clipped steps followed by his lazy stroll.

"You're an ass," she told him over her shoulder.

"You're the one who wouldn't share the potion."

"Yeah, because you're an ass."

A small pause. "But that's why you love me."

"I *don't*—"

He grabbed her hand, spinning her up against the wall. Shocked silent, she gaped as he bent to her ear. "Annaliese is in the next room."

His breath tickled the sensitive patch of skin behind her ear and she shivered. "How much can she see?" she murmured, hands hovering over his hips before fisting at her sides. Her heart had picked up as soon as he'd entered her space, thumping double time as he continued to lean against her.

"My face and your back."

She tried to think past his smell, the way his energy vibrated against hers. "Drop a kiss on my head."

His eyebrows shot up. "What?"

"C'mon. It'll be freaking adorable. It'll sell it." When he hesitated, she pinched his nipple.

His hand clamped down on hers. "Don't threaten me with a good time, Celestia."

I hate you, she mouthed.

He grinned and leaned left to press a soft kiss to her forehead. She breathed him in as he lingered, a touch of smoke, of citrus, of Henry, the combination fluttering in her chest. The moment he should've drawn back passed and neither of them moved.

Instead, his lips drifted to her temple, brushing another kiss there. She stood still, knowing she should protest or back away.

She didn't.

Encouraged, he eased down, slow and soft, until he was tracing the fine edge of her jaw with his mouth. His hands slid over her hips.

A traitorous melting was happening inside her, hands curling against his chest as she fought not to tip her head to the side, offer him access to her neck. To her lips.

He grazed his teeth over the spot between her jaw and her ear and a moan rose to her throat.

A freaking *moan*.

She shoved him harder than was necessary.

"Henry." Her scold was playful even as her gaze should've melted his eyeballs. "Wait until we're in our room, you animal."

He snorted, his cheeks flushed. He followed her to the door, pausing when his phone chimed. He fished it out of his back pocket. "It's my mom. Gimme two secs."

"I'll be outside." She didn't wait for his answer, hurrying the last few feet. Cold slapped her cheeks as she stepped out, heeled boots sinking deep into Siddeley's snow. That didn't bother her; she could outrun a deranged psychopath in heels. And even if she couldn't, she'd take the risk to put a little space between her and her ex right now.

She watched the icy plume exhale from her mouth. Her body felt tight and she rolled her shoulders back, mentally adding bricks to the wall she needed between her and Henry. They'd agreed they'd have to be more touchy-feely, more obviously affectionate. She just hadn't been prepared for the impact.

She set off down the steps toward the fountain, breathing in the cold until she could feel it in her throat. It was refreshing—not like Chicago, where one step out the door froze your tits off. She smiled with a tinge of homesickness just as something in the fountain caught her eye.

At first, she wasn't sure what she was seeing. Big and bulky, covered in gray-and-white fur, it…no, it didn't float but kind of hunkered down. Four legs, a tail…

"*Shit.*" She bolted forward like a bullet from a gun. A dog, a fucking dog, was in the fountain with its head under water. "Hey, boy," she shouted as she ran. "Hey, dog!"

It didn't budge.

Vaguely, she heard Henry's muffled call through the blood pounding in her ears, but she didn't pay him any attention. Instead, she thumbed through the catalog of spells she knew, coming up blank on something to help. As she reached the lip of the fountain, she didn't hesitate, swinging her legs over and splashing across to the animal.

The water was freezing, spray from the spouts misting her face and hair, but she was all about the dog as she sank her hands into its fur. "Hey—"

It *moved.* No, it reared up, like a wild stallion or a beast from hell, sending her lurching back in instinctive panic. Her foot slipped from under her and she shrieked as she toppled, ass breaking the surface with a splash. Before she could move, the beast leaped forward, practically waterboarding her as it pushed her under.

She floundered, choking on the water before getting her

hands under her, pushing the dog back—or trying as it began delivering kisses of the slobbery wet tongue variety. "*Blegh!*" she managed, turning her face as much as she could. "Get off me, you big idiot!"

Henry drew up short at the fountain. His mouth twitched.

Her eyes narrowed as she successfully held the dog off. "Make a joke. I dare you."

His lips trembled as he flattened them. "Never." He cleared his throat, the edge of a laugh trapped there. "You love dogs, huh?"

"I thought it was drowning."

"In a fountain?"

"You can drown in six inches of water."

"So you thought he was drowning…voluntarily?"

She succeeded in forcing the big oaf away and pushed to her feet. Water streamed off her, everything sopping. *Everything*. Her ass was so chilled, it had goose bumps. With all the dignity of a High daughter, she waded to where Henry stood, his eyes dancing.

"If you'd been in here, I'd have strolled past, cackling," she told him, slicking back her hair.

He pressed a hand against his chest with a mock wounded expression. Then held it out for her. "Allow me, hero."

Her jaw ticked. She should rise above. That was the sensible, logical, mature…

Screw it.

She slid her hand into his, smiled sweetly—and yanked. Even when the water drenched her a second time, it was worth it. The dog woofed in delight and repeated his trick, putting paws all over the spluttering warlock as she hooted out a laugh.

She'd managed to wring out her hair by the time he surfaced. Using both hands, he wiped his face, flinging water everywhere as he shook. He gave her an arch, unreadable look. "You think that's funny?"

The dog splashed in the background as she eyed Henry's

damp hair, the drops clinging to his eyelashes, the soaked jeans that would be a bitch to take off, especially since his magic was on the fritz and he couldn't use a blow-dry spell. "Yeah," she said, taunting him with a smile. "I do."

"Hmm." He didn't give any warning as he shot forward and yanked her off balance.

She squealed as she went down, landing on top of him and getting a mouthful of water in the process. She spat it out, digging an elbow into his side as she fought to lever herself up. "*Asshole!*"

He laughed. His arms were loosely roped around her waist, he was soaked to the skin, his balls were probably literally blue…but he tipped his head back and he laughed. The kind of laugh she hadn't heard from him in years.

She wanted to hold on to her annoyance, but it slipped from her grasp. A strange aching filled her chest, ballooning outward until she gave in. And smiled back.

Just a small one.

When the dog came to sit next to her, she switched to a scowl. "You're an idiot," she told the animal, resisting the urge to scratch its head. "So are you," she added.

"And you're adorable wet." Henry tucked a hank of hair behind her ear. "Anyone ever tell you that?"

When his hand dawdled on the shell of her ear, she stilled, the heart that had slowed pumping harder, faster again. Thankfully, the dog chose that moment to bark and launch out of the fountain.

"Rudy!" a familiar English voice exclaimed, shifting to confusion as he added, "Lord—uh, Henry? Lady Tia?"

Tia closed her eyes momentarily. "Lord Siddeley." She pushed upward and, after a beat, held out her hand to Henry. He eyed it with some humor before allowing her to help him up.

Both saturated, they turned to the group. The dog, an Old English sheepdog, Tia realized, danced around his master before doing a full body shake. Each witch threw up an air shield instinctively. Everyone was staring.

"We can explain," Tia said somewhat awkwardly.

The small town of Westhollow was exactly the kind of place Henry would expect a warlock like Siddeley to live in. Clusters of cottages on streets with names like Buttercup Drive, Blossom Hill and Daisy Lane gave way to the town square, covered with grass tipped with ice and a wooden gazebo painted fresh white. Around the square were various businesses, all brightly colored and in good condition, with large glass windows that displayed attractive goods. Children rode bikes around in packs, and couples walked their dogs or pushed their babies, hand in hand. Everyone was smiling.

"Stepford central," Tia muttered from where she strode at his side.

He stifled a laugh.

Siddeley brought the group to a stop in front of a navy storefront where gold lettering spelled out "Pie Hard." A navy-and-white-striped awning shaded the glass window, where cake stands of varying sizes displayed cakes, cookies, muffins and more.

"Pie Hard is an institution in this town," Siddeley shared with a grin and a pat of his flat belly. "Damon's lemon cake has been fueling the local gym's business for years."

"Damon?" Tia asked. She'd changed into a pair of thick leggings and a violet tunic covered by her coat, all leg and heeled boots. It made Henry's mouth water. More than any lemon cake, that was for damn sure.

At Tia's question, Siddeley's smile dimmed. "Pie Hard's proprietor. He's...a character."

Henry looked past him, intrigued. Anyone Siddeley—a man who wore Christmas ascots—called a character was someone he wanted to meet.

"Damon has generously agreed to host us for our first winter activity." Siddeley glanced at the door, then back. "He does like to be a tad…grumpy, but don't take it to heart. He's all bark and no bite, I assure you!"

Henry nudged Tia. "Just like you."

She slid him a look. "Who says I don't bite?"

He swallowed a groan. He didn't want to push his luck, not after the fountain. When she'd finally smiled at him, he'd felt it: a flicker of old and familiar adoration. It still buzzed in his system as he followed her into the bakery, a happy little hum flirting with his mind.

The space was large, with a long navy counter on one side, half with a chiller cabinet underneath, and matching navy stools tucked beneath the other half. The rest of the room was taken up by white tables and navy chairs, and vintage posters from restaurants were framed in odd sizes over the white brick walls. The smell of sugar and coffee hit, making his stomach gurgle.

A man, tall, white, with dark hair and dark eyebrows drawn low, wiped the counter and didn't look up at Siddeley's approach.

"Damon," Siddeley greeted him.

The man grunted.

"We're here!"

"I got eyes."

Henry's eyebrows winged up.

Siddeley floundered for a second. "Shall I introduce you to everyone? This is—"

"Yeah, yeah." Damon flung the towel over his shoulder and looked up. Steely gray eyes glowered out from under a flop of black hair. His mouth was a slash to match his scowl and he folded bulky arms displayed by a white tee.

Henry noted Mina perk up and glanced at Tia. She didn't react, not looking at him, though she must have felt his gaze.

"I'm Damon," the man said, his accent sharp and British. "This is my business, one I take considerable pride in and will not be happy about you wrecking. So some rules. One, cut the pastry, not your skin, and if you're stupid enough to forget that, don't get blood all over the place. Two, this isn't a free lunch and what you eat, you pay for. Three, the ovens are big enough to kill a witch so don't annoy me and I won't stuff you inside one."

Siddeley's laugh was buoyant, trying to rise in a stormy sea. "Didn't I tell you? Such a joker. Now, everyone," he said, missing Damon's snort, "for our first winter activity, Damon is going to give us a masterclass in mince pies!"

"Mince pies?" Annaliese wrinkled her pert nose. "Like, meat?"

Damon eyed her. "Are you stupid?"

As Annaliese bristled, Siddeley hurriedly said, "I can see why you'd think that, Lady Annaliese, but these are a classic English staple of the Christmas diet. Small sweet pies filled with mincemeat, a mixture of sugar, raisins, currants, some brandy and other delicious items. You will love them! Now, has anyone baked before?"

Nobody lifted a hand.

Damon muttered something and stalked out the back through a swinging door.

"I like him," Tia decided.

Henry side-eyed her. "Of course you do. Must be like looking in a mirror."

She scratched her cheek with her middle finger and he grinned.

Siddeley didn't miss a beat. "Excellent, we're all on a level playing field, then!" He gestured around at the tables. "Damon has already set out the ingredients you'll need. I thought it would be most fun to be in teams, get to know each other a little."

Tia perked up. "I'd be happy to bake with you, Lord Archie."

He preened. "How kind, but I know you'd prefer to be with your young man. I'll always bend the rules for young love."

"Don't look too happy," Henry whispered as the others duked it out to be Siddeley's partner. He bumped her with his elbow. "Besides, you got points for saving his dog."

After hearing their story, Siddeley had all but gotten down on his knees to apologize for Rudy, who apparently liked to blow bubbles in the fountain. Like that was normal.

Tia crossed her arms. "Right. I just looked like an idiot."

"But a very cute idiot."

"Shut up." She watched as Annaliese was paired with Chrichton, Mina with Siddeley, and Griffith with Sawyer. "We need to get closer to him."

"Stick to the plan. Slow and steady." *Slow and steady*, he reminded himself as his gaze moved over her face. He had to admit, though, he kind of liked the prickliness, the hints of softness underneath. Made him feel like each small smile was won and his alone.

"I don't like going slow."

"I'll remember that."

The look she shot him was irritated. "Would you concentrate?"

"I'm playing into the stereotype of the obsessed lover." He gave her an exaggerated leer. "I need to distract myself before I lose all control and throw you down in the flour."

Victory fireworked inside when he saw her lips twitch. "You're an idiot."

"Then we're a matching pair." He patted her on the head and dodged her swipe. His grin in place, he caught Griffith staring before the other man snorted and looked away.

Damon returned from the back with a large jar of what Henry had to assume was mincemeat. He plonked it down on the counter next to a bowl and ingredients. "I'm not going slow, so get over here and keep up."

"Think that's what he says to his lovers?" he heard Mina murmur to Annaliese, who giggled.

Damon scowled at them. "You want to shut up back there? I have bread rising so we're making this quick and no stupid questions. Here's what you do."

twelve

If the object of the activity was *fun*, Henry didn't think Tia succeeded. He wasn't sure if she knew the meaning of the word.

"Relax," he'd had to tell her at least four times in the two hours they'd been at Pie Hard, but she might as well have had pastry stuck in her ears. Hell, it'd been everywhere else.

"Breadcrumbs," Damon had snapped at their station, peering into the bowl. "You think that looks like breadcrumbs? You've *seen* breadcrumbs before, right?"

Henry had manhandled the rolling pin off her before the warlock wore the indent of it in his forehead.

It hadn't helped that Griffith had made perfect pastry, earning the least amount of insults from Damon and the most praise from Siddeley, who looked as happy as a child in a sandpit. The two warlocks bent their heads together, chatting amiably as Damon shoved their pies into the ovens.

Tia had begun to look desperate, and she'd snarled at Henry when he suggested she was adding too much filling. He'd wisely kept his mouth shut when the contents leaked out into the oven.

In the end, Damon had grimaced at the pies they'd produced, all shriveled and dark. "Congratulations," he'd said, poking at the pastry. "You've managed to underbake and burn them at the same time. That takes a special kind of ignorance."

"Still like him?" Henry had murmured, and been glad he had possession of the rolling pin.

"So much for teamwork," Griffith had snickered, leaning over from his table. "Looks like you two are still incompatible."

Tia's eyes had swung to Siddeley before she'd pounced on Henry, wrapping her arm around his waist so tight he'd wheezed. "I don't know what you mean," she'd declared loudly. "We make an excellent team. Don't we, baby?"

Safe to say, Tia was as good an actress as she was a baker.

"Did everyone have fun?" Siddeley asked as they all filed out, Damon locking the door behind them without any attempt at subtlety.

"So much fun," Tia enthused, a spot of flour behind her ear. She looked rumpled and a little wild and Henry's fingers curled with the need to touch her.

Oblivious, Tia charged ahead to Siddeley, hip-bumping Mina out of the way, earning herself an arch look. "It reminds me of this holiday party we had at Hightower Seven once," she gushed. "We'd just launched our Hair Growth potion—you've probably seen it. It's one of our top-grossing products, earning a good five hundred thousand in profit for the company last year alone."

Siddeley hummed in response, turning to speak to Chrichton on the other side of him.

Henry rolled his eyes to the sky. So much for slow and steady.

"They made me bake," Tia said as soon as Emma answered.

"What?" Something clinked in the background. "No, put the boxes on the other side," Emma said to someone else. "Who made you bake?"

"Siddeley." Tia flopped backward onto the bed, staring up at the ceiling. She'd come upstairs, ostensibly to cast a soundproofing spell, but really just to wallow. "I am not a baker, Emma."

"I could've told you that."

"I don't enjoy things I'm not good at."

"Does anyone?"

"Yes."

"Who?"

Henry, Tia wanted to say. Rolling out dough with careless strokes, throwing flour into the air like a performance piece, laughing at his own misshapen efforts. It was weird. BP—before potion—Henry would've never given her a reason to make fun of him.

She bit her lip. No, that wasn't true. He would've, when they'd been together and it had been good between them. He used to drive her mad, teasing her, doing stupid things to make her smile. It was only after…

Well, they'd both raised walls, she guessed. She'd never really thought about it before, how he'd closed off to her as much as she had to him.

So this reversal to before was weird. Weird, but…

Nice.

She grimaced. "Other people in the house party," she sidestepped, not wanting to get into it. Especially since she hadn't told Emma or Leah about her tagalong.

"I'm sure you made a good impression," Emma soothed. "You said the plan was to show you're having fun, right?"

"I…might have let competitive Tia out."

Emma snort-laughed. "Not the way to win friends and influence people, T."

"I know," she wailed, covering her face with her hand. "Help me. How do you let go and have fun but also show off your best side?"

"I think you meant to call Leah. Social anxiety here, remember?"

"Leah didn't pick up."

"Wow."

Tia's lips curved. "You gotta have some advice. Or if not you, Bastian. Is he still attached to your hip?"

"Abstinence is making you bitter."

"Please." She scoffed but her eyes went to the door, teeth grazing her bottom lip. "I can have sex whenever I want."

"Any prospects? Leah will want a full report."

Pale green eyes lit with humor. A grin that made her want to smile back. Long fingers that…

"No," she said forcefully. "This is about work."

"I thought it was about fun?"

"Oh, screw off."

Emma's laugh floated down the phone. "C'mon. Just…forget it's business."

"Forget that my family is depending on me to win this investment? Okay, let me just do that." She kicked out her feet, making the mattress bounce. "I can't help it, Em. I need this to go well." If she ever wanted her parents to forgive her.

"It will. And, hey, at least Henry isn't there," her friend said, trying to go for the bright side and fumbling the ball. "You get some space from him."

Tia stared at the ceiling light until black spots appeared. "You're right. Henry isn't here." Not the closed-off Henry.

But flashes of the boy she'd loved. And a man who intrigued the hell out of her.

"I just have to remember what's at stake," she said, to both Emma and herself.

Emma blew a noisy breath down the phone. "Leah's right. You're wound way too tight. You need some way to destress or you're never going to relax."

"That's just—it's not even the point," Tia protested, switching ears and sitting up. She played with the duvet cover, doodling with a finger. "The point is to make a good impression."

"Yeah, and until you loosen up, that isn't going to happen." Emma clicked her tongue. "You just need to find a way to blow off some steam."

★★★

"The first Lord Siddeley was an extremely impressive weather warlock," Lady Mildred Siddeley intoned from the foot of the dinner table that evening. She brandished her fork like a weapon, chin-length gray hair quivering as she fixed her sharp brown eyes on Chrichton, who paused mid-chew to give her an uneasy nod.

She narrowed those eyes. "A *Legacy* warlock," she emphasized. She sniffed. "Back then, we didn't let just anyone dine with us."

"It's a wonderful choice of meat, Mother," Siddeley jumped in from the opposite end of the table. His smile was awkward as he indicated his plate. "Venison this time of year always hits the right spot."

"Good hunting meat," she agreed. Her gaze slid to Sawyer, the other unfortunate guest not to hold a title. "Siddeleys have always been hunters and landowners," she told him loftily. "Generous to our *less fortunate*."

Sawyer smiled blandly. "Charity's great, but you've got to look out for number one."

She looked like she'd sucked a lemon.

Tia hid a smile behind her napkin. It had been like this the entire dinner, the snobby old broad firing insults and Sawyer letting them roll off him with lazy confidence. Chrichton seemed content to settle for his meal, every so often speaking softly to Annaliese on his right.

Sawyer, though, was just cocky as hell. Tia didn't blame him. If she'd built a candy empire from the ground up, she'd have all the Willy Wonka swagger, too. It made it hard not to like him, even though she did her best. Competitor and all.

Mildred droned on about the Siddeleys, spearing peas on her plate with terrifying precision. Tia tried to nod in the right places, but honestly, her mind was elsewhere. Specifically, back in her bedroom a few hours ago.

Blow off some steam.

Henry smiled at something Sawyer said, drawing her attention to his profile. Strong, aristocratic, arrogant. Sexy.

No, she scolded herself, redirecting her gaze back to her plate, where the venison sat bloody on a bed of mashed potatoes. She hated him. Loathed, despised, pitied. He'd walked away from her, after he'd made her beg. He'd made *her* weak. Made her feel worthless. She'd sworn never to forgive him.

Except…it was hard to remember that. When he *didn't* remember. When things felt almost like they used to.

Beneath the table, something bumped her leg and a wet patch formed on her dress. Lips turning down, Tia nudged Rudy with her foot but the stubborn dog just licked her again.

Sighing, she cut a piece of venison and, when nobody was looking, threw it under the table. She heard the snaffle, the happy panting.

When she looked up, she caught Henry's smirk. She bristled. "What?" she said, too aggressively.

"Nothing."

She glowered, spearing another bite defiantly and tossing that under the table, too. "I don't like venison," she muttered, taking some green beans for herself.

"And you're a softie."

"I am *not*."

He didn't say anything but his mouth curved. That damn smile. She needed to focus on that, on how he infuriated her. Not on how much he reminded her of *her* Henry. Or how good he'd felt against her, his body broader, heavier, than the boy she'd loved. Or what his lips had felt like on the underside of her jaw, as if buried deep in his bones was the knowledge of how that made her tingle, right down in her—

Her knife scraped abruptly against the fine china, bringing everyone's attention squarely to her.

"Ah, Lady Hightower," Mildred said, lifting her goblet and taking a sip. "I knew your nana in my youth, you know. Excellent family, the Hightowers. How is she doing?"

"Good." Tia ignored the wet nose pressed to her bare calf. "Still causing trouble for the company part-time."

"As she should! Family companies demand family input. Why, I still pride myself on taking an interest in Archibald's work." Her gaze switched to Henry. "But I hear it's not a family company anymore."

If she hadn't been close, Tia might have missed how he hesitated before answering. "Actually," he said, "we're still a family company. It's just two families now."

"And Archibald says you two are intent on making that one?"

Tia almost blanched. "We're…taking it slow."

Beady eyes shifted between them. "Hmm."

The doubtful noise clanged every alarm bell. "And very happy," she added with emphasis. "*So* happy."

Henry let out a noise as she dug telekinetic fingers into his side. "So, so happy," he wheezed.

"Weren't you two engaged when you were younger?" the older witch demanded.

The knife slid into its familiar place. Tia dropped her gaze to her plate. "Not engaged. But we dated for a while."

"And why is it you broke things off?"

"Um, well…" Tia swallowed the bitter taste and stole some time by patting her lips with her napkin. "We were young."

"It's true. Young people never know what they want. That is why they need experienced adults to guide them." Mildred nodded to punctuate that condescending statement. "And you, Lord Pearlmatter. I hear you're quite proficient in fire magic."

He inclined his head.

"Such a rare gift," she congratulated. "I should like a demonstration."

"A demonstration?"

"Of your magic."

Tia watched Henry's throat bob as he placed his knife and fork exactly together on his plate. His hands went to his lap where they wound together to form a fist. "Of course," he said, betraying none of the nerves. "I can light the candles for you, if you like."

"That's a parlor trick," Mildred dismissed with a wave before Tia could panic. "I should like to see some of the pyrotechnics I've heard others gossip about."

Dread solidified into a fist that jammed down her throat. *She'd* taught him those. Which meant the knowledge of how—even if he could control his magic—would be lost.

He hesitated.

Griffith, the bastard, leaped on it. "Having stage fright, Pearlmatter?" he drawled, slouching in his chair, wineglass in hand. "I heard you took any opportunity to show off."

"That would be you," Tia retorted, trying to divert attention to her.

It didn't work. "When did you learn the art of casting creatures out of fire? Remind me of the spell?"

Henry faltered. "I, uh, I'm not..." Something flickered in his eyes, something that made her heart unexpectedly twist. "I think it was..."

That ache intensified as color spread into his cheeks.

So she snorted loudly. "Who cares? Remind me of *your* special talent, Griffith?"

"Pretty fast to jump in." Griffith tilted his glass to Henry. "Good luck putting up with that for an eternity, my friend."

Her cheeks went hot and she opened her mouth to counter.

"I don't need luck," Henry stated firmly. He covered Tia's hand where it curled on the table. "And you should rethink how you talk about my girlfriend in the future, *my friend*."

"Can you taste the testosterone?" Mina murmured across the table. Even with everything, amusement made Tia's lips twitch. She rolled her eyes at the witch, pretending that the phrase *my girlfriend* hadn't tripped her pulse like an alarm.

"I think we may have got a little off track." Siddeley hurried to cover the tension. "An exciting day has overtired us all. Perhaps a demonstration another time, Mother."

She harrumphed. “Very well. But you must tell me how you learned, Lord Pearlmatter. I am quite proficient with rain and wonder if I could apply the same techniques.”

Henry’s hand tightened on Tia’s momentarily. “Sure. But I… I need some time to…go over it. To make it clear for you.”

“Good. Good. I look forward to the lesson.” Her smile was all teeth. “Shall we say tomorrow?”

“Oh, but we have the mulled wine tasting tomorrow,” Lord Siddeley said in dismay.

“Pish posh. Surely Lord Pearlmatter can squeeze in a lesson.” She turned expectant eyes on him.

His skin went sickly white under the dim lighting. “I…”

Apologizing silently to Rudy—though part of her thought he deserved it after the fountain—Tia sent a well-aimed dart of telekinesis his way. It was gentle, but unexpected, and the sheepdog howled, bumping his head on the underside of the table, knocking over glasses and clattering cutlery everywhere.

“What the devil?” Siddeley exclaimed, bending to peer underneath, right as the dog barreled forward.

Siddeley let out an *oomph* as Rudy catapulted himself onto his master’s lap. The chair went head over heels and so did both dog and man with a resounding crash.

That put an end to that.

thirteen

He'd disappeared. After Rudy had taken Siddeley down, things had been chaotic enough that only Tia had seen Henry slip away. Although her skin itched to go after him, she hadn't wanted to make his absence a big deal. So she'd bided her time, making excuses for him, and waited until the last spoon of trifle had vanished before shooting out of the room, tossing a "good-night" to everyone over her shoulder.

She faltered outside, the aged floorboards creaking under her hesitation as she swung her head from left to right.

A shadow moved ahead and Primm appeared, carrying a bundle of pine air fresheners in the shape of small Christmas trees. The fat white cat was on his heels, grumbling in its throat when it saw Tia. Surprise quickly gave way to inquiry and Primm halted. "May I help you, Lady Hightower?"

She eyed the growling cat. "Have you seen Henry—Lord Pearlmatter?"

He inclined his head behind him. "I think he wandered into the music room. Down the corridor, fifth door on your right."

"Thanks." She paused and looked at the air fresheners.

"For the rooms absent of a real Christmas tree. Lord Siddeley enjoys the scent."

Naturally. She didn't even know why she'd wondered.

Tia's heels clicked quietly as she skirted the cat and walked down the hall, her steps muffled by the carpet runner. The paintings on the walls were all landscapes, depressing gray and dark green made slightly cheerier by the silver tinsel decorating their ancient frames.

The door that Primm had indicated was ajar and she nudged it, peeking in. The room was bathed in shadows, only illuminated by the bay window opposite. She doubted the radiance was moonlight, more likely the millions of twinkle lights on the exterior, but it was enough to highlight the figure standing on the right of the window.

He looked so alone.

The thought was powerful enough to stop her breath for a stolen second.

She scowled in instinctive response, pushing the door open wider and sauntering in. "Thanks for leaving me alone."

Henry turned his head. Light slid over his nose, those sharp cheekbones, the mouth that curved so faintly, it barely counted. "Sorry."

Another spasm in her chest had her whistling out a long breath. Habit wanted her to strike; she hated feeling…well… feeling *anything* for him. But she said nothing as she made her way through the room to stand at the other side of the window. A piano, open to its keys, gleamed behind him, and comfortable couches were beyond, framing the expected Christmas tree glowing with intermittent lights.

She purposefully stared out at the view, same as him. The window faced the gardens but she saw more of her own reflection than the landscape. She watched herself as she noted, "She's something, huh?"

He chuffed a sound that might have been a laugh. "Mmm."

"Typical Higher society witch." Tia wished she could put her hands into pockets, but her green sweater dress was snug, and all she could do was brace them on the windowsill. "Where the rule is, if you don't have anything nice to say, say it anyway. I think Sawyer was just baiting her by the end. You shouldn't have missed dessert."

"I'm sorry," he said abruptly.

She flicked her eyes toward his reflection. "It was just trifle. It wasn't all that."

"No." He shifted his weight. "For being a stammering idiot in there."

"You're making this too easy," she joked. When he didn't reply, she angled her head.

His face was tight. Solemn.

Something inside her twisted. "You're serious." When he didn't look at her, she firmed her jaw. "It wasn't anything. I've done worse."

"Not that I'd know," he murmured, then combed a hand through his hair. "I screwed up, I know it."

"It was no big deal. Everyone started talking about the dog and then Siddeley harped on about the mulled wine tasting tomorrow."

He steadied his hands on the sill, close enough their pinkies could've touched. "You're depending on this. Everyone is." Out of the corner of her eye, she saw a piece of hair drift forward as he lowered his head. "I thought I'd anticipated everything."

"That's because you're arrogant as hell."

He didn't smile. "It was stupid. I should've known they'd ask. People always want to see my magic, but I… I didn't realize it had progressed to that level."

"I taught you." The admission was out before she'd thought it through and she kicked herself.

"I thought you were an alchemist."

She lifted a shoulder, cheeks hot under his careful scrutiny. "You wanted to learn something cool. So, I helped." She blinked away the memory of spinning on his shoulder, dizzy but safe in his hands. "You picked it up pretty quick. I can show you. If you want."

His hand inched closer to hers. "Yeah. Thanks. Except... Shit, Tia, I can barely light a candle."

"We'll work on it." She didn't like this feeling, a kind of fluttering, scraping sensation that made her extremely uncomfortable. And the more he worried, the worse the feeling got. "It's fine."

"You were right. I'm messing up." Her muscles locked as he added softly, "What if I can't do this?"

She had no idea what to say. This wasn't their thing; they weren't honest and open and vulnerable. She couldn't—couldn't do that. A stray red spark of magic burned under her fingers before she doused it.

Part of her, a part she struggled to drown, marveled that Henry *was* being honest and open and vulnerable. Even before everything, he didn't like to show that side of himself. He'd challenged her, provoked her, circled her. They'd fought and made up and danced their dance over and over, but this was new. She...

Tia cut the thought off, every atom in her driven to do *something*. It wasn't in her to be nice to him; it felt too weak to offer up compassion after only a little vulnerability. But it also wasn't in her to leave him twisting in midair alone. Because for all his smirks and bluster, that was how he must feel, stuck here with her, a stranger who barely tolerated him. Alone.

Fuck.

With her pulse tripping, she lifted her hand and, with only a small hesitation, curled it over his. She felt his surprise like a jolt.

When he turned his head, she mirrored him. Tension shivered in the air, building the longer they stared at each other. Her heartbeat picked up until it felt ridiculously fast.

Enough that she finally broke.

"You ready to head up?" She flicked up an eyebrow, hiding how unsteady she felt. "Or are you not done with your pity party?"

A faint smile lifted his lips. "Maybe I'm just hiding. I'm man enough to admit Lady Siddeley is damn unnerving."

Relieved the moment of *whatever* was already in their rear-view, Tia stepped back and headed for the door. "I'll play body-guard, tough guy. Come on."

"Okay. But just know I am one hundred percent behind you throwing your body onto mine if there's even a hint of danger."

Yeah. They were definitely back. She rolled her eyes as he caught up to her. "Noted."

Silence reigned for the next few seconds.

Then: "Thanks," he said as they turned the corner. His shoulder brushed hers and she felt it down to her toes.

She didn't acknowledge him.

But she didn't move away, either.

Henry sat on the bed and watched the bathroom door, flicking through the events of the night as he waited for Tia to come out. The sticky feeling of uncertainty still clung to his insides, triggering worst-case scenarios he couldn't help but play over and over.

A few seconds. That was how quick it could've all gone to shit tonight if Tia hadn't jumped in. And all because he'd been so arrogant to think he could get through this without a script or someone to prompt him.

He slowly exhaled, twisting his hands in the covers. He'd learned his lesson. Tia might hate being here with him, but even though he barely knew her, he couldn't think of anyone better to stop him fucking it all up. At least he could depend on her to be honest, unlike most of society, and tonight she'd made a choice to work with him, instead of against him. When Tia said they'd get through this, she'd meant *they*. Him and her.

It probably shouldn't have turned him on so much. But then everything about her did, a wisp of something forgotten tangling his insides. Strong urges and old aches he had no clue what to do with.

The sound of the doorknob turning interrupted that thought. He shouldn't look but he'd never known what was good for him. And it was painful, the heat that torched under his skin at the sight of silk and all that gorgeous leg. She'd pulled back her hair, softening her face as she approached the bed.

Fuck him. He needed a distraction.

"Mulled wine tasting," he blurted out, grimacing to himself as he stood up and flipped back the covers. He got into the bed, the intimacy of the moment shivering down his spine like a premonition. Or memory. "Tomorrow, right?"

"I hear it's all the rage." Tia switched on her lamp with a flick of one hand and the main lights off with the other. "Wonder if we can get Siddeley drunk and ply him with facts that'll amaze him enough to sign a deal."

"Tia..."

"I know, I know. I'm kidding. Mostly." She slid beneath the covers, making the mattress dip. His body screamed in awareness as his knuckles turned white on the duvet. "Fun and friendship, not facts and figures."

"You got it."

"And a united front." She checked her cell, then put it on the bedside table. "Griffith was showing way too much interest in us."

"He's a potions rival?" He frowned, searching his blank mind. "I've met him?"

She nodded, turning off the lamp and plunging the room into darkness. "Probably our biggest competition. He also has those golden bloodlines Lady Siddeley is so lusty for."

Fuck, he wished she hadn't mentioned lust. He knotted his hands on his flat belly and stared into nothing. "I'll do my research. He won't catch me off guard again."

"I know."

Her confidence made him smile. Especially considering Tia

was a bag of nerves covered with bluster. He wondered how everyone else didn't see it.

Silence passed a few comfortable moments and her breathing slowed.

"Tia," he said into the darkness, taking comfort from it. Confidence from it.

"Shh. Tia's asleep."

"Celestia."

He jolted, more from surprise, as her foot nudged his leg. "Don't call me that."

He shifted on his pillow to face her, only the outline of her profile visible. He wished he had enough control of his fire to light the room, but he'd probably torch her hair. Not the best way to keep on her good side. "Can I ask you something?"

"No."

"In the spirit of teamwork."

She grumbled under her breath. He caught the word *ass* and couldn't fight a grin. "What?"

He battled back the stupid nerves that rose. "Will you tell me how we met?"

Absolute stillness. And he meant absolute. There wasn't even a clock to break the silence.

"Why?" she finally asked. Wary.

"Research." True, but also a lie. "Tell me?"

More silence. So long he thought it was a no until—

"We've known *of* each other almost our whole lives." Fabric rustled as she rolled to her back. He kept his glee contained in case she could see his face. "Legacy families, Higher society parties, schooling and just...around."

"And you always had a crush on me," he teased.

She snorted. "Yeah, no. I had a crush on Allistair Peabody. Four years older, black hair, amber eyes and a smile that made my teenage heart go pitty-pat."

"And where's old Allistair now?"

"Married, sadly."

"All the good ones are taken."

"You got that right." She shifted, a small telling movement. "But we *met* when I accidentally threw a cat on your head."

He choked. "What?"

"The cat was fine."

"Why were you throwing it at all?" He squinted at her. "You're making this up."

"Swear to the Goddess." He heard the smile in her voice. "My boring as fuck cousin was in town and her familiar had wandered into a tree in Louis Armstrong Park. It was meowing and meowing and I couldn't stand it anymore, so I climbed up and nudged it out."

"Where it landed on me."

"I've never heard anyone yell so loud." Amusement rippled through the words, rich enough to tug an answering emotion from him. "The cat was pissed and dug its claws into your face as punishment."

He winced, even though he couldn't remember it.

"When I jumped down, you accused me of attempted murder—deathly assault with a cat. You were being such a baby, which I told you very diplomatically before taking you to clean your scratches."

"And you started crushing on me."

"Fuck off. I hated you," she informed him with a little too much relish, "and you were always around after that because our families developed little heart eyes." She muttered something he figured he was better not asking about. "We argued all the time. Until we didn't."

"Because you kissed me."

"*You* kissed *me*," she corrected with a haughty air. "And I decided to let you."

And the rest was history, he thought, not wanting to ruin the moment by saying it aloud. "Deathly assault by cat," he murmured, closing his eyes as he wracked his brain for any hint of it. "I wish I could remember."

She let out a breath, which was more of a sigh. And then, so quietly it was almost inaudible, "I wish I could forget."

fourteen

She woke to heat.

Tia stretched her legs lazily, nestling her cheek against the pillow. It was warm and smooth under her, and she was so comfortable, it took her a few seconds to realize it was moving. Breathing.

Her eyes flew open. Muscled pecs greeted her—or muscled *pec*, since she was currently occupying the other one. Her hand, dear sweet baby Goddess, her hand was on Henry's abs, fingers spread to touch as much surface area as possible. Her mind got a little sidetracked at the ribbed edges under her fingertips before she forced herself back to the point.

And the point was she was wrapped around Henry like a sloth on a branch.

She hardly dared breathe. It had been so long since she'd felt him against her like this, his arm looped around her waist in breathless intimacy. Her skin tingled every place they touched.

He was so warm. He'd always run hot, to the point where she'd used to complain about having a steam engine in bed with her. Then he'd tease her about liking it hot, wrestle her underneath him and prove how right he was.

But that was then. Way, way back then. And now she had

to get off him before he woke up and things turned extremely awkward. As if it wasn't already awkward that she felt all fizzy and faint. And that she throbbed. *Everywhere.*

Fuck.

One at a time, she lifted her fingers off his chiseled abs. Damn, he was cut. More than he'd been at twenty-one. Not that she should be thinking that. She hated him. Even if she'd made the choice last night to be less…*her*, that was temporary. Thinking about him like this was—

She squeaked as his arm tugged her closer. Close enough that her legs tangled with his and her shorts rode up dangerously high. He rolled just enough that their bodies bumped.

He was hard.

Lightning speared, melting her veins. His thumb tucked in the hollow of her waist and slipped down, hooking the material of her top so that skin met more skin.

Her toes curled as magic surged in her veins. She had to move. *Away,* she reminded herself sternly. *Not* closer.

With her breathing shallow, she braced her free hand on the mattress the other side of him and pushed up, intending to lean backward so his arm slid off her.

Except that was when the bastard chose to wake up.

His lids fluttered open to see her braced over him. His face lit with a hazy greeting before melting into confusion. Then realization dawned.

He swallowed. Hard. "Celestia."

Her name managed to be a statement and a question in one.

For once she didn't scold him. Instead, she wrapped the shredded coat of dignity around herself. "Could you let go of me?"

She watched his eyes go to where his arm was locked around her. A heady flush rose to his cheeks and he immediately pulled back. "Ah…sorry. I didn't mean to, you know…try anything."

Tia pushed off, sliding out the other side of the bed. She angled herself away, partly to shield her face but mostly so he wouldn't see how hard her nipples were. "Whatever," she said airily, heading for the bathroom. "But keep that shit for an audience, yeah?"

He stammered an agreement before she shut the door and promptly turned the shower on cold.

"Lady Tia," boomed Siddeley's voice right near her ear, startling her into dropping her iPad. It hit the couch cushions with a thump. "You're not doing work, are you?"

She winced. In her defense, she'd needed to catch up on some of the latest developments; plus, she was still emailing Lionel about Henry's potion antidote. She'd already done some tests with her travel kit, brewing different antidotes in four test tubes and watching the test solution for any reaction. Results had been disappointing—or they *should've* been to anyone with sense not to obsess over their ex.

Choosing avoidance over that fact, she'd given up and snuck off to this room to bury her discomfort in emails.

But she *was* meant to be playing, not working, so…

Sheepish, she angled her head to where Siddeley stood behind the couch. "Guilty. What's my punishment?"

He laughed as he came around to sit on the chair opposite, placing two steaming mugs on the coffee table. Rudolph coasters appeared beneath the mugs as he set them down. The fire in the grate flickered merrily, casting light onto the Christmas decorations in the small room.

Situating himself, Siddeley gestured to the space beside her. "Where's your partner?"

"Probably doing the same thing," she confessed, attempting to uncurl her legs without being obvious. She wasn't sure she was allowed to have her feet up on the sofa; it was probably a gajillion years old.

"Addicts to the office."

"Blame our parents." She said it with a smile and he replied in kind.

"At least you found each other," he pointed out, then added, "Again. I hear from my mother there was a split for a few years. But I'm a fan of second chances, too."

Bitterness bloomed on her tongue and she shifted her gaze down. She made a noncommittal noise.

"So, is it potion business or the bar you run with your friends in Chicago that has you sneaking away like a woman with a guilty secret?" he asked, picking up his mug and blowing on the steam.

Her skin prickled and she considered the balancing act she was about to play. "I thought you said no work," she joked, taking one step onto the tightrope. "Now you're encouraging me?"

His eyes were kind. "If that's what's important to you."

Her mom's voice in her ear demanded she go for it while he was asking, spit out all the facts and figures she'd brought along. Bend him to the business.

But.

She'd always had Knowings, impressions of people or places that would somehow be important. They were subtle and she could go for months or years without one. But as she considered how to answer, something inside her shivered like a plucked bow. This warlock was somehow important to her future in some indefinable way.

His words repeated on a loop. *What's important to you.*

She hesitated, then leaned forward to pick up the mug he'd brought her. The smell of hot cider wafted up her nose. "The company is important to me," she admitted, rolling her tense shoulders, "and so is the bar. Mostly because both are run with family."

"You consider your friends family?"

"I do." Emma's steady sass, Leah's teasing optimism. "When we opened the bar, we each wanted a project, an escape."

"I know the feeling well. Idle hands and all?"

"Something like that." *Idle mind*, her own supplied. She'd needed to keep busy. Stop obsessing over Henry and whether she'd made a mistake. Then he'd never come after her so she'd known she hadn't. Stomach plummeting at the reminder, she took a bracing sip of her cider. "But it's become as much about friendship and fun as anything else."

"People like us," Siddeley mused, "need to keep occupied. But good to slow down, eh? Appreciate life—appreciate that boy who watches you like the star on top of the tree." He gave her a sly wink.

"Oh. Well, he..." Flustered, she slammed the brakes on her instinctive denial. *Breathe. Play the role.* "I make sure to appreciate him every chance I get."

He chuckled and lifted his mug in a toast. "To second chances."

She forced a smile. "To learning from your mistakes."

It had been a good meeting, Tia figured, as she and Henry made their way to the dining room that night. She wouldn't say she and Siddeley were ready to inscribe their initials + BFF on a cauldron, but they'd chatted over their ciders easily enough. She'd choked down business every time it tried to spew out, concentrating instead on her friends, the holidays. By the time he'd left her to get ready for the mulled wine tasting, he'd definitely seemed more open. Excited, too. Apparently, he was portaling a winemaker in from Germany, one renowned for her knowledge.

"Don't be late, it starts at eight," he'd chided cheerfully when he'd left.

It was now five minutes to and she hurried along with Henry trailing. She blamed him for spending ages in the shower again. Seriously, the man took twice as long as she did, and her hair had a special care routine.

She'd gone with an appropriate color for her dress, dark red, the hem shorter than she'd like, but she figured Siddeley would enjoy the nod to Christmas. He was a man who appreciated tradition—probably because of his mom's obsession with bloodlines—but also whimsy. Since she couldn't conjure very well, she made a mental reminder to head into town to buy some Christmas accessories. No harm in sucking up at this point.

She was so preoccupied with the thought, it took her several steps before she realized Henry had stopped. She looked back, impatience riding her voice. "You forget something?"

He hesitated before blurting out, "I'm sorry about this morning."

Ridiculously, she felt her cheeks flame. "It's…whatever. I forgot to put up the energy wall, obviously."

His expression became as serious as she'd seen it since the amnesia. "I can sleep on the floor."

"Don't be stupid. More stupid."

"You shouldn't have to worry I'll attack you in your sleep."

How was she even meant to answer that? Especially when she had a sneaking suspicion who'd climbed on top of whom last night.

She settled for telekinetically flicking him on the forehead. "I said don't be stupid. You'd never hurt me. Well, not like that," she amended, gesturing forward. "Now, come on, we'll be late."

"I'm serious, Tia. Put up the energy wall tonight. I'd… I'd like to promise it won't happen again but…well." That hint of red appeared on his cheeks. He smiled ruefully. "I don't remember you but apparently my body does."

She hummed, gaze turning inward. "It'd have a lot to remember."

He blinked.

Shit. She'd said it aloud.

Tia made herself sneer before tension could touch the air. "Relax, pretty boy. It was a joke. And you didn't attack me. I woke up draped over you, okay? It was just as much me. Want *me* to promise I won't do it again?"

His snort was soft. "Maybelline didn't raise no fool."

She wet her lips, hiding her racing pulse. "Okay, so, can we go?"

He nodded, moving toward her. She told herself not to look, but apparently her self-control was shit tonight because her gaze dropped to the muscles she now knew hid beneath his sweater. She'd been able to kid herself before, that reality wouldn't measure up to a memory. Except they'd both been in their early twenties when they'd last been together.

He was a full-grown man now. Heavier, harder. Her face felt hot as he neared and she all but ran down the stairs ahead of him. Yes, definitely harder.

"Who's ready for some wine?" Siddeley was saying as she entered the dining room.

Her hand was the first to shoot up.

fifteen

Erika, their wine expert for the evening, didn't have a surname that went with a massive amount of wine. Tia knew this because every time she thought of it, a snigger bubbled up her throat. But seriously.

Erika *Koch.*

She inhaled the aroma of their next wine, dizzy in the head. After owning a bar for…more years than she could remember after six mulled wines, she'd assumed she was no lightweight. Ms. Koch proved her wrong.

She laughed softly as Erika moved in front of the group, talking about the depth of the mulled white wine.

"What's the joke?" Henry asked next to her, voice low and a touch slurred. He'd been as vigilant as her about using the bucket. Meaning, not at all.

"Hmm?"

"You laughed."

She leaned in, putting her lips to his ear. "Koch."

He turned his head, nose grazing hers. "I have one," he answered solemnly.

It made her giggle. She, Tia Hightower, giggled. If she could find her face, she'd slap it.

"Ahem." The pointed cough from their German expert had both turning guilty gazes her way.

Tia mumbled an apology. She tapped her glass. "Delicious."

"What do you taste?" Erika probed.

Wine. But Tia figured that wasn't the answer Erika was looking for. She took another gulp.

"Sip it!" Erika exclaimed, hands flying up. "Then spit it."

"Oh." Too late. "Sorry. I taste…" Her mind whirled.

Henry shifted, whispering.

"Elderflower!" she exclaimed.

Erika lifted an eyebrow as she crossed her arms. Her German accent clipped the words. "Correct. You should also taste cinnamon and vanilla, but perhaps Lord Henry hasn't had chance to whisper in your ear that information."

"I don't know what you mean." She batted her lashes too fast before slowing right down.

A hint of amusement shone in the German witch's face before Erika walked back to Annaliese. "And you, what is your favorite?"

The spellmaker's daughter deliberated but selected the amber wine with flaked almonds and raisins. "The Swedish glögg." She lifted her shoulder. "I like that they thought outside the box. That's how the best spells are created." She slid a look at Siddeley, who was fairly ruddy in the face himself. When he didn't comment, her shoulders slouched, but she still smiled at Erika. A slow signal of interest. "What's your favorite, Erika?"

Color formed in two blotches on the pretty blonde's white cheeks. She held Annaliese's gaze for more than two beats. "I like thinking outside the box, too."

"Oh, it's on," Tia whispered to Henry.

"On what? Me?" He batted at his sweater.

Tia swatted him on the arm. "No, the German and Annaliese."

"How can you tell?"

"It's all in a look." She let her head fall to the side, feeling like a puppet whose strings had been cut. "You can tell everything about a woman by the way she looks at you."

Henry's head was buzzing softly, a curtain of warmth blanketing him. It turned into a wall of flame as he took in Tia next to him, pressed up close enough so he could've angled his head into the crook of her neck and inhaled. He blinked, wondering what she'd do, if she'd welcome him. She seemed…

A hand grabbing at his hair, tugging his head back, lips colliding with his until he felt the mattress beneath him.

"Tia," he groaned, the weight of her breasts pushing into his chest. He was desperate to feel them, thought she might let him finally unbutton her shirt and slide his hands over them now they'd been dating for three months. Her hips writhed over his as a sexy noise hummed in her throat. His parents weren't home and he hoped she'd be louder, scream for him, if she'd agree to let him under her skirt. He'd never been this desperate for a girl before but with her, everything felt ten times brighter.

"Henry," she moaned against him. "Touch me."

Henry blinked, disoriented. As his gaze fell on Tia, an adult Tia, her words came back to him.

"You don't look at me like you hate me anymore," he said, vision sliding from his mind, lubricated by alcohol. He liked how she looked at him. He really liked how she'd looked at him that morning, sleepy and riled, with arousal swirling in those hazel eyes.

Tia pursed her lips, more thoughtful than irritated. He wanted to kiss her. "Because I don't," she said. "I don't know how I feel about you."

Triumph surged in his wine-sloshed brain. He'd known she'd made a choice last night to be "on his team," but that was a long way from liking him. This was one more step. He didn't know what the steps were leading to, only that he wanted her to…not hate him. It made his stomach twist every time he thought about it. Being the focus of Tia's attention was addictive, even more so when she smiled. He imagined being the center of her world would be a hard drug to give up, if you'd ever even want to.

Right now, he thought you'd have to be an idiot to give Tia up. Which meant eight years ago, somehow, someway, he'd been a fucking idiot.

Henry inched closer, ignoring Erika, who was talking to Sawyer about the wine he'd tried in Europe. "I can help," he informed Tia. "We can figure out how you feel. Close your eyes. Think about me." She ignored him, so he ignored that she didn't follow his instruction. "Do you get good feelings?"

Tia eyed him.

He frowned. "Bad feelings?"

She grazed her bottom lip with her teeth. "Define *bad*."

Shit. Heat bloomed, so quick and sudden that he started, staring at the fiery sparks flickering around his hands. When he looked back, Tia's pupils were blown, hazel eaten by the black. His mouth went dry and he leaned closer.

The little moth drawn to the fire warlock.

"I think we have lost our lovely couple again," Erika said wryly.

Henry dragged his gaze from Tia. His body felt flushed, tight. Familiar.

He cleared his throat. "Are we trying more wine?" He could use a liquid.

Erika considered him, moving to Tia and back. He wondered what she saw as a smile tugged at her lips. "Have you heard of a champagne kiss?"

"I have," Mina volunteered from next to Griffith, who was slumped in his chair, another victim of swallowing. "Traditionally done in France, right?"

Erika nodded. She gestured to the seventh glass in front of each of them, a bubbly white wine. "I am afraid that only the young couple in love can demonstrate the proper technique, if you both don't mind?"

Tia shrugged, draining her existing glass and placing it stem up like a shot glass. "Hit me, Teach."

"Traditionally, this might be done at a wedding, but one of you takes a sip of the wine." Erika waited until Tia picked up the glass. "Right and so. Next, Lady Tia will take a small sip of the mulled cocktail." She sent a stern look at her. "But do not swallow."

Tia did as ordered, turning inquiring eyes on the expert.

Who gestured at Henry. "And now you kiss."

Tia choked, wheezing as the wine went down the wrong way. Henry helpfully pounded her on the back, lingering to rub in slow circles as she caught her breath.

He couldn't catch his.

A kiss. Her lips. On his. Her taste. His mouth.

Excitement prickled, followed by nerves. Maybe it wouldn't match her memories. Maybe it was stupid to think he'd be in with a shot.

She blinked fast and furious and his heart plummeted.

Maybe kissing him was the last thing she wanted.

His breath whispered against her ear as he leaned in. "We don't have to… I mean, if you don't want."

Her body stilled, eyes swinging up to his. One heartbeat faded into two as they stared at each other. He heard each one in his ears as he waited for her to make the decision.

The awkwardness of the others watching faded as, still holding his stare, Tia slowly took another sip of wine. His pulse accelerated as she shifted closer, setting her hand on his shoulder to balance herself. That one touch sent a shiver through him as he braced.

Their lips brushed. Clung.

A second hung suspended for long beats of his heart. He inhaled as her tongue teased along his bottom lip.

He made a reciprocating noise, a small groan as recognition sparked. His hand curled around her nape, strong fingers gentle against her skin. She sank against him and opened her mouth.

The mulled champagne bubbled and fizzed, sliding along their tongues. The familiarity of this burned into him. Her taste—he knew it. It lived inside him, the feel of her body close to his, the same. Behind his closed eyelids, he *knew* he could shape her body with his hands. They *knew* this woman, this witch.

Tia.

She curled her fingers into his sweater, meeting him, slow kiss for slow kiss, her breathing ragged as the champagne disappeared and all that was left was them.

So fast it almost hurt, thousands of visions slapped into him, a million kisses in a million ways. Soft and shy, sweet and searching, hot and wild and angry and desperate. A roar drowned out everything as gaps in the invading memories cast out drops of her laughter, of her moans, of her voice calling his name.

"Henry," she murmured against his lips.

Yes. Just like that. Forever.

A ripple of laughter jerked him back. He breathed hard, keeping close to her as he stared at her face. Her mouth was damp, her eyes wide. Haunted. The memories swirled inside, rough and confused. He strained, needing to know more, remember more. But only slivers of kisses remained, settling like fractured pieces into a jigsaw with a multitude of gaps.

He felt it all, the echoes of that aching want, the clawing need. The adoration that underpinned everything.

It pulsed as he smoothed a thumb over her cheekbone.

"Well," Mina said wryly in the background. "Sign me up for a French wedding."

The next day, Henry braced himself against a decorated tree in Siddeley's woods and stared at the compact in his hands. The air was crisp, the sun out for once and near blinding against all of Siddeley's snow. He'd cried work after lunch, needing space to think. Tia had opted to head into town with Mina and Annaliese to shop, an unlikely trio. He doubted it was anything but tactical, but he could be surprised.

His eyes closed involuntarily. Holy hell, could he be surprised.

Last night, after that kiss, they'd both retreated to their corners. His head had pounded, brain disoriented from the memories dragged back from the veil. She'd seemed similarly struck, quiet and watchful. Who could blame her? One kiss and they'd gone up in flames. And now he knew, it'd always been that way between them.

Little moth.

He released a sigh as the nickname whispered through him, head already aching again. Putting that aside, he trained his eyes on the picturesque vista and pressed a thumb on the silver compact's lid, murmuring his mom's name. It was two p.m. in England, which made it early morning in New Orleans, but he knew his mom would be up. Gossip never slept, as she liked to say.

Sure enough, within seconds of opening the mirror… "Honey! It's wonderful to hear from you. How are you? How's Tia? You're calling with good news, I hope."

He looked down at the small mirror and the familiar blonde smiling widely in its reflection.

Guilt bloomed under his skin like a bruise. "Investment hasn't been secured yet. Timing's bad." Yeah, nothing to do with his tiny obsession with Tia. He coughed a little. "We're, ah, working on it."

Maybelline clicked her tongue. "Psh. Now, when have I ever cared about that above your happiness? I'm asking about you and Tia, honey. Are things…good?"

His eyebrows lowered. Mom-dar? "Why?" he asked warily.

"Because I am your mother, Henry Charles Pearlmatter, and I want to know what's happening in your life. And as much as your father grumbles about it, Tia is in your life right now. I for one would like to keep it that way. How're you getting along?"

Hot lips, soft skin. How her tongue had slipped into his mouth, rubbing against his.

Heat flashed down his spine and he gritted his teeth.

"Things with Tia are fine. Good. She doesn't hate me anymore." Though…maybe she was just biding her time until his memories returned. The idea made him frown.

His mom made a knowing noise. "I've got eyes, and I can see what you're thinking, plain as day. That woman has always been passionate about you, whether it's love…or the other thing. People don't lose that kind of feeling."

"It's the other thing that worries me," he muttered.

Maybelline gasped. "I knew it! I knew that if you spent some time together, things would fall into place."

Henry shook his head. "No, it's not… We're not together."

Her face fell.

He shifted against the tree, blinking when snow from the branches above sprinkled on his cheeks. "I just need some advice."

"Well, your mama gives the best advice in five counties. You want to know how to woo the woman, is that it?"

He cringed and rubbed the back of his neck. "I don't know. I just… I like her." It was freeing to admit it out loud. He did it again. "I like her, but things are complicated."

"Why?"

He gave the compact a look. "Off the top of my head? Amnesia, exes, investment to be won…"

"Details." She waved those away with an airy hand. "What I want to know is how *she's* feeling about this. Is the cold shoulder finally turning?"

His mind returned to that kiss. Her taste. But…she hadn't made a move. Should he? Was that weird?

Insecurity kicked hard. "She hasn't said she's forgiven me."

"Women are mysterious creatures," Maybelline said, sagely enough to make him grin. "We like our men to read between the lines. And we also like effort. Make some effort, Henry. Be bold. Be honest. Show her you want things to change."

He kicked his foot through the snow, dragging it back. "What if she can't separate the past from now? She's obviously hung up on it—not that anyone seems to know why we broke up." That had to be the key. He blew out a breath. "She's not exactly chatty."

His mom sighed, eyes fond even through the mirror. "I love that girl, but she can hold a grudge," she agreed. "Stubborn enough to only see trees, instead of the forest. But things have changed. Your…situation has forced her to remember the good stuff."

"But *I* don't," he pointed out. "What if without the mem—"

"Honey, memories shape our lives but we are who we are," she interrupted firmly. "You are still my boy and, underneath the anger, she's still your girl."

He grimaced, just a little, at the phrasing. He couldn't help it.

Her laugh sounded through the compact, loosening the knot in his belly. "You are so like your father. I had to knock some sense into his head, too. Still do. Speaking of which, he wants to say hello. Richard. Richard, talk to your son."

Henry's stomach knotted again, awkwardness stiffening his muscles. His dad's face appeared, just as uncomfortable. "Henry," he said to the mirror. Nodded.

"Dad."

"Things are good?"

Unlike with Maybelline, Henry knew what the older man was asking. "Siddeley hasn't picked an investment yet."

His dad paused. "Ah." Silence stretched. "Well, give him some time. Keep him away from Tia. That witch could blow the deal with her antics."

Henry frowned, bristling at the implication. "Actually, Siddeley seems to like her."

Richard blinked at the sharp tone. "Well. Good. Just keep

an eye is all. I know this is uncomfortable for you but you're, ah, doing your best, I'm sure."

"We are."

Richard nodded again.

"Sweet Goddess, you two are impossible," Maybelline shouted in the background. "Work, work, work. You know, he has other interests, Richard."

His dad's face twisted. "This is important, May."

"Maybe I should go," Henry interjected, seeing a window. "I've got to get back anyway."

"Yes. Fine. Keep checking in and anything we can help with, let us know."

"Sure."

"Bye, honey!" Maybelline hollered. "Think about what I said—be bold!"

He was under no illusions the past few days had wiped away years of resentment. If anything, Tia had only called a time-out on account of his memory loss. But Maybelline was right: this month was an opportunity. Maybe even a second chance.

Something to think about.

sixteen

Tia knew she was close to sulking. "It looks funny."

Henry glanced up from where he squatted on the snow. "We're not finished yet." He continued his task, gloved hands making short work of rolling snow into a ball. He hefted it with a grin. "It's all in the details."

Tia arched her eyebrows, doubtful. She examined their snowman, a classic structure of two balls, waiting for the third.

Then she looked at Mina's. The inventor had lived up to her name and found a way to magically harden the snow so it could be carved into a reindeer. She was now delicately chiseling a space to add the red bauble for its nose. Kiss-ass.

"I could tell her where she could stick that bauble," she muttered, smoothing the snow on their top ball for the head.

Her words lacked any real bite. Yeah, they were in competition, but Mina was pretty cool. She'd had Tia in stitches the couple hours they'd been in Westhollow, self-deprecating and sarcastic as they'd wandered the cute stores with a quieter Annaliese, who was still funny in her own way.

When they'd invited her, Tia had initially gone to suss out the competition, but she'd ended up having a good time. Pretty useless recon, though. She'd learned how Mina took her coffee and what season Annaliese considered herself but nothing about their game plans or skills.

Like the fact that both could fucking sculpt snow like Italian masters with stone.

"How fair is this?" she grumbled. "You have fire magic and I'm good with alchemy, both hopeless here. We've got an inventor over there with freaking Rudolph, and Annaliese, a walking Grimoire who can spit out any spell. And look, *three*? I mean, come on." She moved back as Henry placed the ball of snow in position, casting a sour look at Annaliese's three ice elves. "And Griffith volunteering to have tea with Lady Siddeley is such crap. That warlock's up to something. And if he wasn't, at least he'd be crap at this as well."

"You're going to melt our snowman."

"Huh?"

"All that hot air."

She rolled her eyes. "Can you focus?"

"Can you?" He waved a hand at their structure. "Ours has personality."

The head listed to the side as he spoke.

She lifted her eyebrows. "The personality of a drunk."

"Well, the holidays can be hard."

She wouldn't laugh. "You're an idiot."

"I'm not the one taking a snowman-building competition so seriously."

Tia glowered, folding her arms.

"Just watch the master work." Concentration lines dug into his forehead as he focused on his finger. A small tip of fire appeared, and with care he marked out a face.

"You're coming along," she said, quietly in case anyone was listening. That was, if they could hear anything besides the nonstop Christmas music blaring around the field they'd set up in an hour earlier. If she never heard "Rockin' Around the Christmas Tree" again, she'd die happy.

"Thanks to you." He added two holes for eyes, the tip of his tongue caught between his teeth as he concentrated. "Maybe I'll even be able to give Lady Siddeley her demo."

"Let's put that off as long as possible."

Due to a sudden problem with one of his investments, Siddeley had been AWOL the past couple of days. They'd wasted no time in sneaking off to a remote part of the estate, Tia casting a barrier between them and any snooping witch, and they'd got to work on Henry's magic. He could now call fire and conduct small displays, but he hadn't mastered anything close to what he was capable of.

Still, the sessions had been weirdly…fun. As much as he wanted to learn, Henry wasn't a serious student. He flirted shamelessly the whole time, using every opportunity to touch her while encouraging her to correct his position by putting her arms around him.

She'd like to say her willpower had held up, but she'd buckled like a cheap cauldron.

It was just so much like before. When she'd first shown him how to mold his fire, when he'd teased her and made her squeal, when the tension between their young bodies had made the air electric.

Then. And now.

A very loud, very insistent part of her wondered what the *hell* she was doing. How she could be weak enough to fall into this again.

The rest of her was deaf and blind to it—and yes, weak, sliding into familiar patterns with the shaky relief of a hot bath easing past aches and pains. Maybe she should've known this would happen, that it was inevitable they'd revert back to old habits. Things had never been settled, the past never put to bed. She'd ignored it, drowned it, coated it with anger, but she could never cut him out completely. And if she was honest, she knew the same was true for him. Even before this.

She'd seen it every time he'd looked at her from across their desks. Felt it in the spaces between their insults, the weight of his gaze cut with frustration and a deep and bitter longing she also struggled with.

She hated herself for it, even as her mind wandered to the same fact, again and again.

His kiss was the same.

Days later, the memory still had shivers dancing down her spine, curling her toes and sending a pulse right through her core. His taste, the grip of his hands, the feel of his strong body under her fingertips. It had felt so good, it hurt.

She wondered if everything would feel as good.

Siddeley's voice boomed and she startled, glancing over her shoulder as he approached.

All she could see was his eyes and nose above his thick red scarf. A matching cap covered his head as he nodded in greeting. "What a fine-looking snowman, Lady Tia and Lord Henry! Very, ah, distinguished."

Tia caught her expression before it curdled. "Thanks. We went with an homage to the classic snowman."

Henry snorted as he finished with the face. Tia glared at him in warning.

"Capital!" Siddeley said happily, hands on his hips as he surveyed the field. "I do so love a competition. It brings out everyone's best side. Why, look at Lady Mina's!" He laughed. "The spitting image of Rudy's namesake."

The Old English sheepdog woofed from beside him, trotting forward to sniff Tia's snowman. She didn't even shoo him away. At this point, adding a yellow tinge could only improve it.

She bared her teeth. "Yes, Lady Mina's is excellent. But don't write us off yet. We've still got a lot of details to add."

"That's the spirit!" Siddeley clapped her on the shoulder, making her stagger. He moved away, Rudy following, to Chrichton and Sawyer, who'd teamed up and built a similar "classic" snowman that, somehow, still looked better than theirs.

"This is stupid," she said to Henry. "How is making a snowman fun?"

"The problem," Henry said, wrapping his own scarf around their monstrosity, whose head was at even more of a slant now, "is you."

"Now you sound like your old self."

He bent to the ground and gathered more snow. "You're not getting your hands dirty."

"I see myself in more of a supervisory capacity. Giving orders."

His eyes flicked up, green against all the white. "You'll give a man ideas, Lady Tia." He gave her a lazy grin that shorted some circuits. "But," he continued as she stared at him, "the task is to have fun, remember? You're treating this as win or lose."

"Um…because it is?"

"And it really matters that you win here?"

"Duh. Yes."

He shook his head, laughing softly. "Why? Siddeley isn't going to choose his investment because of this."

"You don't know that," she argued.

"Any man who picks his investments based on snowman-building competitions wouldn't be as successful as he is."

"He's wearing a snowman sweater," she reminded him in a low voice. She gestured. "It sings if you press the snowman's nose. He showed me."

"Let the man have some fun. You could use some, too."

"I *am* fun. With a capital F."

He nodded seriously, hands smoothing over the ball he held. "Okay."

Then, faster than she could track, his wrist flicked and the ball—the fucking *snowball*—exploded on her chest. It drove a breath from her, more from shock and cold than anything else.

She gaped down at her sweater, ice-blue now covered in actual ice. Muddy ice. "Okay," she gasped, "that capital F stands for something else now. The other word being *you*."

He laughed, gathering more snow.

She took a step back. "Don't you dare."

His eyebrows rose.

"I mean it. You don't want to start something."

"I really think I do."

"Hen*ry*..." His name ended on a squeak as he flung another snowball at her. She threw up a hand and used telekinesis to toss it right back. In his face.

She hooted as he spluttered through the snow. "And everyone said I was the ice queen," she taunted.

His smile was dangerous. "Game on, Celestia."

"Bring it, Henry Charles."

Something sparked in his eyes, distracting her in the seconds before he lobbed a snowball he'd been hiding behind his back.

"Okay," Annaliese said, squatting back down from her scouting mission. The witch—whom Tia would've pegged as not saying boo to a ghost—took a stick and marked out the battlefield as seriously as if this was war. "The men are here, behind a trench Siddeley dug out with his magic. As far as I could see with my field glasses spell, all of them, except Lord Henry, are there."

Tia looked up, alarmed. "Why, where is Henry?"

Annaliese leaned on her stick. "Probably trying to sneak up on us."

"Agreed," Mina said, dusting off her gloves. "Is he good at that?" she directed to Tia.

The Henry she'd known the past few years? The stick up his butt wouldn't have let him.

The Henry she'd fallen for when they'd been young? AKA the Henry he currently, for all intents and purposes, was?

She nodded grimly. "We need a distraction."

The witches looked at each other and then sent wild grins her way.

Five minutes later, Tia cursed herself for choosing heeled boots as she picked her way through the woods.

The snowball fight had spread to the rest of the group after five shots. Within minutes, teams had formed, the men and women dividing and hunkering down wherever there was cover—which meant both had hauled ass to the forest since the field was open war ground.

The snow crunched beneath her as she slunk from tree to tree, heart racing as she listened for any sound other than her own breath and boots. The Christmas music got louder as she neared the field, this song screaming about Santa Claus coming to town.

She'd taken two more steps when a snowball hit the tree she'd been about to pass.

With an involuntary yelp, she darted to the side, sliding on the frost and almost ending up on her ass.

"Surrender," came Henry's deep voice, lined with amusement. "And I'll consider letting you live."

She scanned the trees. Bastard was invisible, not even a hint of platinum hair shining through the undergrowth. Crouching, she gathered snow into a quick and dirty ball. "In your dreams."

"Oh, nightly," he drawled, the sound coming from the right. She stood, facing that way, weapon raised. "My men have already taken your team hostage."

She squinted. Truth or lie? "I don't believe you."

"Look behind you."

She laughed. "If that's your best tactic, we're going to bury you."

"I mean it."

Damning her curiosity, Tia kept one eye on the woods and angled her head back enough to see the field. Where a rueful Annaliese and Mina stood between Chrichton and Sawyer. Siddeley was beaming with two snowballs in either hand, more guard puppy than henchman.

"Fuck," she muttered.

"Give up?"

She snapped back. "Never."

"Tia, Tia, Tia." His amusement was rich in the air. It made her snarl. "You need to learn when to give in."

"Compromise is for the weak."

"Not always."

She thought of her begging him to put her first. To choose her. Of him walking away. And thought how ironic it was for him to say that.

"How about this?" he suggested, unaware of the path her mind had taken. "The first to land the next snowball is the winner."

Oh, he was so confident. It set her teeth on edge and the past melted away, muddied by the present. The present where she was going to beat his ass.

An idea glimmered. She glanced again at the field, calculating. "All right."

A pause. One that went on so long her nerves shifted into high alert. She kept a wary eye on her surroundings, ready to throw up a barrier if he launched an attack.

Then: "And a side bet."

She hadn't had much luck with those.

"If I win," he said, a dark lilt to the words, "you have to kiss me."

Her breath stopped. Butterflies exploded into her stomach and she pressed a hand there as she tried to think of what to say.

So many things came to mind but all that came out was, "And if I win?"

His tone became even more wicked. "I have to kiss you."

She swallowed. "Seems a bit lose-lose to me," she rasped, fighting for control. Fighting to remember…why she shouldn't. Except she'd always loved doing things she shouldn't.

"Then you don't remember the other night."

His words were assured, as if he knew how explosive they could be together. Except he didn't. Only she knew. Remembered.

Craved.

His words came near her ear. "Do we have a deal?"

She didn't think. She reacted. "Deal."

She bolted into the portal she'd created, hearing the snowball he unleashed fizz against the sides. His curse made her smile as she closed it behind her.

She emerged next to their forlorn snowman, using it as a shield as she faced the woods. Under her breath, she murmured a seeking spell, sending it to find its target, right as Henry strolled out of the trees.

Her heart thudded harder at the look in his eyes.

When he reached her, he tutted. "Don't put poor Jack in the middle of this."

Jack Frost. Cute. "At least now he has a point to his existence."

"Shh. You'll hurt his feelings."

"He's ugly, Henry."

"But in a cute way."

"You're ridiculous."

"And you're mine." He lifted his last snowball and threw, aim perfect. Win secured.

He hadn't counted on Rudy.

Henry's eyes widened as the dog, called by her spell, leaped with a joyful bark into the middle of the fray. Tia flung herself out of the way of the excited dog, leaving him to sail past her and directly into the snowman, his weight too much for the sad creation. It tipped, then toppled, helped along by Tia's last shove of telekinesis.

Henry didn't stand a chance.

"Fu—" he swore, the rest buried as he went down in a heap of snow and sheepdog.

Tia collapsed in laughter, a foot away. "I win," she crowed, pumping the air. Pure delight flowed through her as she repeated the words over and over. None the worse for wear, Rudy moaned in delight, bouncing around and tugging playfully at the scarf lodged in the snow.

"You cheated," came the muffled response. "Assist by a non-team player."

"We never said another player couldn't assist." Grinning, Tia helped dig Henry out with her gloved hands, sitting back on her haunches as he eased up. He shook his hair, snow flying, the damp strands stuck to his face.

He looked young, young enough to be her Henry. And she felt like her old self as well, full of life, with no thought of what came next.

He grimaced at his wet jeans. "You won," he agreed. He looked under his lashes at her, those beautifully long, gold-tipped lashes. "Guess I'll have to kiss you."

Her belly fluttered. "Guess so."

More snow drifted off him as he leaned forward. This close, his scent wrapped around her, snaring her in place. She barely moved, couldn't, as he inched closer, closer, until his lips were at her cheek. He pressed them there, making her heart stop, then slam into a gallop as he slid them up, up, up toward her ear.

"Just a down payment," he murmured. A shiver that had nothing to do with the cold played down her spine. "I'll settle the debt later."

seventeen

"Did we ever have a one-night stand?"

Henry winced as the scissors slipped out of Tia's hand, telekinesis barely catching them before they punctured the parquet floor. Incredulous, she threw a pointed look at the group occupying the other end of the great room. Siddeley was a warlock in his element, beaming at the red berries Annaliese added to her wreath, commenting on the design of Griffith's even as he fiddled with his own creation. Next to him, Sawyer rolled his eyes and upturned a flask into his cocoa.

At their end of the room, Henry gave Tia a shrug. He doubted anyone was listening, partially because a good ten feet separated them but mostly because the soundtrack to the UK film *Nativity* provided loud cover. "Sparkle and Shine" blared in all corners as Siddeley continued the wreath-making task he'd declared the perfect afternoon activity for them all.

All...except for Tia, and him by default. Henry's lips twitched as she cast a sour glance at the wreath-makers before twisting back to the paper snowflakes Siddeley had tactfully suggested might be more her thing. Not hard to go wrong with a snowflake, though judging from the paper corpses littering the floor, maybe that was pushing it.

Henry didn't mind being relegated to the corner. At least he got to be alone with her.

They sat by the huge hearth, the fire low in the grate, on two plump pastel couches opposite each other. The carved wooden table between them held sheaves of paper and two mugs of cocoa, candy canes peeking over the rims.

His question also sat between them but she didn't make any move to acknowledge it. It'd probably been stupid to corner her here, in front of witnesses, but ever since the possibility occurred to him, it refused to budge.

"Well?" he prompted.

In front of the fire on the faded patterned rug, Rudy grumbled and rolled to his back, legs kicked up in the air. A hissing sound came from his back end.

Yeah, Henry could've waited for a more intimate atmosphere.

Tia's jaw clenched as she concentrated intently on the paper she was cutting. "No."

"Not even once?" he persisted. Past attempts at snowflakes crumpled under him as he shifted forward.

"I think I'd remember."

The fire in the grate crackled, calling to the magic under his skin, and he held out a finger absently, making the smallest flame dance in place. "Not once in all that time," he murmured, trying to wrap his mind around that. Around how someone could feel this much need and not act.

"It's not like we were drinking pals," she muttered, the long slide of the scissors accompanying the troubled words. "We've barely spoken. Or interacted."

Huh. "Did you want to?"

The paper split and the snowflake was ruined. Tia scoffed, shoving it away. "Jeez, cocky much?"

Hope rose like the flame he toyed with. She was always defensive when he got close to something.

He took the chance. "*I* wanted to, though. Right?"

Everything about her went still, except for her eyes, which flew to his. "You're remembering?"

Kisses and snippets of random conversations. Emotions in waves so strong they buckled his knees. More and more every day since that kiss.

But he couldn't tell her that. She'd already recoiled; what if this made her run? It made his heart beat faster, something cold and thick in the back of his throat.

So he shrugged. "Just feelings."

"And you feel..." She drew in a quick breath that lifted her breasts in the soft sweater she wore. "You feel something for me?"

The song ended and Siddeley's laugh fell into the gap like a roll of thunder, shaking the room.

Henry barely heard it as he slowly nodded.

She pressed her lips together and didn't speak. She was so hard to read; he wondered if she always had been or whether he'd once picked up her thoughts as easily as any book plucked from a shelf.

"You did." Her voice was quiet but the confirmation made his breath catch. She put down the scissors carefully, blades closed and at rest. "You never said outright. We always danced around it."

A memory surged, blinding him, his voice rough and her fingers touching his jaw.

If we could go back... Do you ever wish...?

"But we were inseparable once." Her eyes gleamed in the firelight, a hint of pleasure in the shadows. "I *know* you. And you still wanted me."

"Want," he said without much thought. "I still *want* you."

Her lips parted, color rising.

He should shut up but couldn't stop the words. "The man that knew you. The man that loved you. The man I am. It's all the same, Tia. The wanting never leaves. I think—no, I *know*. I know that I've always wanted you." He'd just needed her to confirm it so they could move forward. If that was what she wanted, too.

Silence replaced words, tension breathing into the air.

His nerves jittered, urging him to push her. Get her to admit she'd wanted him then, that she wanted him now. Their bullshit aside, it was clear to anyone they were still drawn to each other.

Little moth. Irony. He might've called her that but flip it around and it was just as true. Always had been. Always would be.

And still, he was goddamn nervous. His stomach tightened into a hard ball as he watched her silently freaking out, waiting in tense anticipation of her withdrawal. She was proud—fucking understatement. Whether it was memories he was regaining or if he was simply relearning her in the present, he was getting to know how she thought. She'd see admitting that she wanted him as a surrender. She needed to save face. She needed something simple.

Or he was full of crap and blinded by his own desire.

One way to find out.

Be bold.

He cleared the remaining nerves out of his throat. "You know," he said, making her start as he got to his feet. Paper tumbled from his lap. "I still owe you a kiss."

He held out his hand.

He had no plan, no real idea where this could go, but it was simple enough. If she wanted him. His heart beat a jagged rhythm, skin tight under his clothes as he willed her to take a chance.

For one moment, he thought she'd refuse and his stomach dropped. Then with a toss of her hair, Tia grasped his hand and pulled herself up, the heels she wore putting her closer to his mouth. Her own wore a half smile as she tugged. "C'mon, then."

They made it past the knowing looks, into the quiet hallway, up the stairs. They didn't speak but the air practically hummed.

His breath was coming in quick little pants, desire gripping him by the throat, until he couldn't imagine taking one more step without tasting her.

And then he saw it: the perfect excuse.

He pulled her to a stop. "Wait."

She turned, eyes questioning before they followed his to the small spiked green leaves and round white buds hanging above their heads. Mistletoe.

"Can't mess with tradition." He steered her back against the wall, watching carefully as he slid his hands to bracket her wrists before pinning them above her head.

Her pupils blew out, her breath shaky. "Play nice, Henry."

He leaned in so their bodies brushed. She felt new and yet familiar and so goddamn perfect, he could've licked her all up. "I don't think you like *nice*."

"Me? I'm sweet all over."

His cock jerked and he almost groaned. "Let's see, shall we?"

He knew she expected him to conquer. It was why he did the opposite.

The kiss was slow and it was soft and it was wicked as hell. This wasn't speed; this was seduction. He used his tongue in lazy caresses, his body settling into hers, teasing, until her hips rocked against him.

Her teeth sank into his bottom lip. He jerked, breathing roughly against her lips.

"I thought you said to play nice," he managed.

"And when have you ever done what I said?" She nipped his lip again. "I don't want romance and slow kisses."

He caught her chin in two fingers, holding her gaze equally firmly. "But you want me?"

Challenge sparked, defiance in every line of the spectacular body tight against him. Fighting herself more than him.

He took pity. "Shall I tell you what *I* want?"

He moved even closer, letting go of her chin so he could put his mouth to her ear. "I want to slide my tongue over every inch of your skin. Here." His hand barely touched her collarbones. "Here." He drifted to where shuddering breaths swelled her breasts. Then farther down, skating along her hip bones diagonally until a choked gasp met his triumphant ears. "Especially here," he said wickedly. His heartbeat thundered in his head and his cock hardened with every sharp inhale. "I want to watch you as I taste you," he murmured, teeth scraping her earlobe. Making her jerk. "I want to watch your face as I make you come."

"Fuck," she moaned, head falling back. Her hands clutched his hips so tight, he thought he might have bruises.

He swallowed hard, a slight edge sharpening the brutal desire. "So, the question is do you want the same?" *Do you want me?*

It took a century for her to lift her head, the hazy flush of lust sharpening her features. And she nodded.

Heat and triumph flashed down his spine as she caught his hand, walking backward to their room, flinging the door open with her telekinesis so hard, it banged off the wall. Neither of them gave it much of a glance as they pressed it shut behind them.

eighteen

Tia kept her gaze on Henry steady, even with the way her heart was trying to break her ribs. Shallow breaths lifted her chest with every second that passed. She had enough sense to activate the soundproof barrier but even that slipped away as her hand fell back to her side. She dragged her lower lip between her teeth and leaned heavily against the door. "Come here."

Henry's eyebrows arched. "That sounds like an order." His voice was deep, rough, acting like light sandpaper over her skin.

"So?"

He shrugged and sat on the side of the bed. His pants strained over his obvious bulge. "So," he said, a dark smile toying with his lips. Teasing. "Play nice, Celestia."

She narrowed her eyes, ignoring the way he caressed the syllables of her name. He was trying to get the upper hand. That was familiar; when had Henry ever not pushed back? Now he thought he could be in control? Now she'd decided that she could handle being intimate without being *intimate*?

She held back a wicked smile. Poor fool.

He didn't remember who he was dealing with.

In the end it had been simple. He was offering something they both wanted and it didn't need to be more than that.

Maybe they *should've* had a one-night stand years ago, but her pride wouldn't have let her, even though she knew Henry would've said yes in the flick of a wand if she'd ever suggested it. If they'd had a one-night stand, at least there wouldn't have been *years* of need humming under her skin, ready to explode.

He didn't get to win the upper hand here. She needed it.

She didn't move from her spot, instead lifting her hands above her head. The movement pushed her breasts out, outlined in her sweater. "A gentleman would come to me."

"A gentleman might," he agreed, leaning back on his elbows. The mattress dipped welcomingly. "You think I'm a gentleman?"

"I hope so."

Humor flashed. "No, you don't."

No, she didn't.

He watched her for a moment with heavy-lidded eyes. "This isn't going to be all your way, you know."

"I think it is." She trailed one hand down her neck, tracking how he watched. She traced a path to her breast, halting short of the hard point of her nipple. "I know you. I know what pushes all your buttons."

"Touch yourself," he ordered, raspy, glued to the inch between her stroking thumb and her nipple.

She held back. "Do it for me."

His smile was wry. "You're good."

"Baby, you don't even know." She moved her hand down, away from one ache to a deeper one. Toying with the button on her pants, she cocked her head. "Still don't want to come to me?"

"The show's too good from here."

Stubborn ass. It annoyed her how it aroused her, how he wouldn't give in. How he always gave as good as she did.

"You see," she continued, walking her fingers down her zipper, pressing against her clit. Her teeth sank into her lip as sensation overrode thought. When her eyes opened, his face was tight. "You see," she said again, breathless, "we've done this before. In beds, against walls, in gardens and once at a party where you covered my mouth and I had to bite your hand to keep my screams in."

His throat bobbed.

She throbbed in response, the memories crystal in her mind. Her magic bubbled inside her, adding to the ache. "I remember how you go wild if I bite a certain part of your neck," she said throatily, gaze latching there. Imagining herself straddling him and nipping at it until he tossed her on the mattress. "I remember how you swear if I drag my nipples down your chest. Your thighs are sensitive to touch, especially my nails." She touched the seam of her pants, feeling how wet she was through the fabric. Her chest was lifting and falling rapidly. "And how you break if I take you into my mouth."

His hands on the bed caught fire and he jerked, immediately moving to throw a pillow on the flames before it could spread.

Tia tutted softly. "Premature eruption? How disappointing."

Fire out, he stalked toward her and every atom trembled in victory as he braced his hands on either side of her body. "Touch yourself," he gritted out.

"Not until you say I win."

Genuine humor shone in his eyes. "Brat."

Her breath caught. She shored the gap in her defenses up, desperate to make sure her battered heart survived. Fucking, not feelings. That was what this was, for both of them. They didn't need her tangling emotion into it.

Of course he saw anyway, but he didn't comment. Instead, he took her hand in his. And said, "If you won't do it, then show me. Show me how to touch you." He dipped his head, brushing a kiss across her lips.

Her heart hitched. It was too much and not enough, the way he was looking at her, the affectionate nickname from the past, his words. He'd always been good at words. *Just* words.

She couldn't handle it. So she handled him instead, cupping

his cock in one decisive motion. He swore, a harsh word that fell between them like a flash potion. His fingers clenched on the door as she took him firmly in hand.

She didn't waste time with more words. Instead, she rubbed him exactly how she knew he liked, pressing closer and kissing his neck. He shuddered violently, a scraping sound telling her he was digging his nails against the door.

"You're not…going…to…win," he managed, groaning on the last word as she squeezed at the root. His back arched and he bit his lip hard. She recognized him fighting the pleasure, loved the dark torture on his face. He shuddered again and scowled. "Every time," he finished, and fell on her.

She didn't have time for victory, too busy with feeling everything else. How his hands, familiar and not, moved roughly down her body. He cupped her breasts possessively and she moaned as his thumbs caught her nipples. He was gentle to begin with but when she only moved restlessly, he caught them harder between finger and thumb. He tweaked and her hips jerked.

"Yes," she moaned. Her panties grew wetter.

He leaned back enough to strip her sweater away, then the cami under it. His gaze was hot as he dragged it over her yellow satin bra, before he reached for her pants, tugging them off. She helped, kicking them into the corner and standing in front of him in matching panties.

"You're perfect," he growled, shaping her curves with his hands. He clutched her hips, smoothing his fingertips under the flimsy barrier of her underwear. "I need to touch you."

She read the intention and something flared under her breastbone. He wanted to go slow, take his time. She wasn't having that.

She hadn't been lying when she'd said she knew this man. He might not know her secrets, but she sure as fuck knew his. And nothing hit Henry's detonate button like seeing her on her knees.

She dropped to the carpet, the plushness cushioning her as she unzipped his jeans, tugging them lower in one quick motion. His boxer-briefs barely contained his erection and she wasted no time before wrapping her lips around the shape of him.

He roared, one hand slapping the door. "*Tia.*"

She barely had time to savor it before he was hauling her to her feet and shoving her toward the bed.

She landed with a small bounce and a victorious laugh. He stalked toward her, pushing off his underwear as he stopped at his suitcase. His cock bobbed, large, hard, as he opened a box of condoms, tearing one off. He never moved his eyes from her as he took himself in hand, giving his cock a rough stroke.

She was soaked now, pulse a racing blur in her ears, and her fingers went between her thighs. He watched as she touched her clit, her back arching as lightning speared down it.

But she wanted it to be him. She let her legs fall open as she played with herself, panting as he stretched the condom over his cock.

That done, he prowled forward, not stopping when he hit the bed, instead crawling over her. He caught her lips in a hard kiss, mastering her with his tongue as he let his weight rest against her. Her breath hitched at the pressure, the pleasure of it. Her hips came up and rubbed, again and again, frantic with the pulsing need. An orgasm hovered and all she needed was a push.

Then his broad fingers were there, pushing aside her panties and spearing into her. One at first, then another as he pumped, her own wetness making it an easy glide. He crooked his fingers and she cried out, her body surging at the sensation. Her gasps fell against his skin, sweat gleaming over her, over him, as she reached her peak and came.

He waited until she stopped quivering, until her eyes opened and his blurry figure came into focus. For a moment, she swore she saw something like relief cross his face.

"You ready?" he asked gruffly, need stretching his expression tight.

For an answer, she lifted her hips so he could slide her panties off. He positioned himself and began pushing in. He was thick and hard and even though she was wet, it had been a while. She felt every inch of him going in and clutched at him, at the cover, breathing hard as he bottomed out.

His eyes were brighter than she'd seen them and he stroked a hand up her thigh. "This good?"

He wanted to *talk*. *Now?*

She grabbed him by the back of the neck and yanked him close enough to bite his bottom lip. When he jerked, she glared at him. "Do me already."

He grinned fiercely and, for once, did as she'd ordered. He started slow but was quickly powering into her, the wet sound of flesh meeting flesh overriding the noises both of them made as they charged toward climax. Something crashed around her and she couldn't even care.

"It's so good," he groaned, holding her tightly. She moaned in response. "It can't have been this good before."

She didn't remember him being this chatty but sex between them had always been hot and fast. They'd been young and so greedy for each other.

"I don't believe it," he was saying, voice strained as he swiveled his hips and hit a spot inside her so pleasurable that she dug her nails into him and gasped. "If it was this good…how did I…let you…*go*?" He snarled the last as she began to come, her body writhing, everything inside her ripping to shreds.

The next moments became a blur of speed and sound and sensation, her orgasm hitting every nerve in her body until she felt wrung out.

He grunted her name, stiffening, his cock shallowly thrusting as if he couldn't help it as he groaned harshly through his own climax.

When he collapsed, his head tucked into the crook of her

neck. Exhausted as she was, her heart pinched at the familiarity. Hesitantly, her hand came up and cradled the back of his head, fingers sifting through his hair.

She allowed it for one minute before shoving at him. "You're sticky."

He lifted his head, every line deepened into laziness. Even his grin was slumberous as he dropped a kiss on her nose. "You were amazing."

"I know." She shivered as the cold touched her heated skin.

He watched her, something creeping into his expression. "And…it was good for you?"

"You want a performance review?" She snorted, before catching the flicker in his eyes. Was he actually worried?

She remembered the music room, his lack of confidence masked by swagger.

She softened. Just enough to lift her head and kiss him, lushly. A thank-you.

"You're sticky," she murmured again, an idea coming to her that had her smirking up at him. "So am I. We should shower."

Only when he grinned did the pinching around her heart ease. At least until she noticed the room in disarray and the burnt carpet in the shape of feet.

Tia yawned, resting her head against the headboard. It was a late start, made later by Henry's wandering hands. The man might have felt some insecurity last night but that had vanished by their next round. And their next.

She swallowed as the memories of the long, hot night made her squirm. It had been perfect. Mostly because every time he'd tried to slow it down, she'd sped it back up. Contrary to his big talk about her not winning every time, so far it was Tia 3, Henry 0. Or maybe 2.5 since the last round had been strictly oral for both of them.

She'd convinced him to go to breakfast, to put in some time with Siddeley. They needed to keep the warlock sweet, especially since she couldn't imagine explaining the burnt carpeting in a way that didn't make her or the proper English warlock blush.

Maybe she'd get some practice now.

She'd talked herself in and out of this call for twenty minutes, getting more and more agitated. Not a big deal, no big thing. She forced her thumb to press the call button before she could be any more ridiculous.

Emma's face popped up, extremely uncomfortable. "You know I hate looking at myself when we do this. Why're we FaceTiming?"

"Duh, because I like looking at *my* face." Tia made her voice casual. No big deal. Not a big thing. "Is Leah with you?"

"She had to run to the shelter, but it's slow so I told her I'd be fine."

That tracked. Ever since Gabriel and Leah had taken over the animal shelter Leah loved, it'd been busier than ever.

Tia couldn't decide if her friend's absence was better or worse. "Okay. I'll catch her later."

"For what?"

She'd practiced this. "Breaking the news" felt like what she had to say was too important, so she just dropped it in like—phrase of the day—it was no big deal. "I figured I'd let you guys know that Henry's with me and we had sex. You know, before you hear anything on the grapevine."

Emma's face froze. "Wait, what?"

Tia directed some telekinesis into the covers, lifting the corner up and down, up and down. She kept her expression nonchalant. "Henry came with me on the work trip. It's boring as fuck so we figured why the hell not."

"Why the hell not," Emma echoed. "Are you kidding?"

"It'd be a weird joke."

"You. Slept with Henry. Pearlmatter?" she clarified. Disbelief rode her voice. "Like insert part A into part B?"

Tia had to grin. "That, and part C, part D, part E…"

Emma slapped a hand over one ear as if that'd help. "No, no, no. Why do people keep telling me these things?"

"You're acting like this is big news," Tia told her, curling her toes under the covers. "It's not."

"You had sex with your nemesis—the man whose dick you've threatened to hex multiple times—and it's not big news?"

"No." She pulled her legs up to her chest. "It was stress relief. *You* told me to."

A choking noise came from Emma. "I didn't tell you to sleep with Henry!" A beat. "Was it good?"

"Attagirl."

"I hate you. Just tell me."

"It was…" No big deal, she reminded herself. "Good."

"That's it? Good?" Emma sounded doubtful. "You guys steamed up every room when we were younger. I walked in on you once and my hair practically caught on fire—thanks for that therapy bill, by the way. You're not telling me after eight years of buildup that the sex was just *good.*" Emma searched her face. "You're hiding something."

Sometimes she hated how well her friend knew her.

Tia rolled her eyes to disguise it. "Geez. Okay, look, it was fucking amazing. But it's casual. We're casual."

"Nothing about you and Henry is casual."

Except they weren't *them*. Special circumstances meant they were living in the moment and Tia wanted to keep it that way. But she couldn't tell Emma that without telling her the actual secret, the one her mom had made her swear to keep. If she broke that promise after her string of screwups… She swallowed.

"Don't make this what it's not, Emma," she told her, shifting under the weight of guilt, torn between her two worlds. "Just because you're in love and seeing hearts everywhere doesn't mean everyone is. Sometimes hot sex is just hot sex."

"Uh-huh." Emma snorted. "Gingerbread man incoming."

"What's that supposed to mean?"

"You can't catch me," Emma recited in a singsong voice. "Run while you can, Tia. Henry's always been good at catching you."

Something sharp and cold sliced her. "Not this time," she insisted. "It's not the same."

Emma smiled but backed off. "Fine. You want me to tell Leah?"

She couldn't deal with another version of this call. "I'll text her."

"That text is sure to go down well." Emma smirked.

Tia smirked back. "Just like Henry."

"Gah. I'm hanging up now."

nineteen

They got through the caroling, just about. Tia's singing...well, Tia's singing was as good as her baking and acting. Unable to help it, Henry spent half the time laughing at her, which she made clear she didn't appreciate. Afterward, he apologized by dragging her into an alcove and using his fingers to make her come. She forgave him pretty quickly.

He couldn't keep his hands off her. Which wouldn't have been an issue since, you know, they were faking being in a relationship, but the unfortunate side effect when he got too hot for her was that he got, well, too hot. And he tended to burn... stuff. But at least she seemed to like it. Liked his hands on her.

If he had one complaint, it was that she wouldn't let him take his time. He wanted to learn her body's secrets again, inch by inch, but whenever he started to savor her, she flipped the switch and used every wile she had to make his brains blow out.

There were worse problems to have.

Like the fact that more memories had floated to the surface— and he still hadn't told her.

It wasn't like he was hiding any major revelations. He remembered the encounters she'd teased him with the afternoon they'd first had sex: a night in the gardens, in her childhood bedroom, at a party when she'd had to brew a healing salve for his hand after she'd bitten too hard when he'd covered her mouth.

She liked the excitement of that, almost being caught. It was a gut-deep certainty, a fact to add to the others creating a clearer picture of Tia Hightower.

There'd been a few non-sex-related memories, too. A meeting in Jackson Square, an impression of being young, trying desperately to look cool when he'd seen her approach, delighted with how she'd blushed when he'd tucked her hair behind her ear.

Another random day when they'd been reading in his parents' library, her head in his lap, one of his hands holding his book, the other softly sifting through her hair. Peace.

An argument about his being late and her having sat alone in a restaurant for thirty minutes, his pointing out anyone could be a little late, her declaring anything over fifteen minutes without messaging the other person was shitty. She'd been right, but he never did like backing down, holding his corner even when he knew he was being dumb.

There were a couple more memories that made him frown, ones he tucked away to examine, where he'd been late or canceled and she'd been—as he'd thought back then—unreasonable. It made his stomach twist, when he replayed the instances, seeing the unhappiness in her eyes.

It was shitty not to tell her he was remembering things; he knew that, but she was so quick to throw up walls. And if he kept quiet and paid attention, he might actually understand why they'd ever broken up. Because right now, being with her, he couldn't.

He needed a little more time to learn how to fix them. Just a little more time.

It was better to focus on the present, on walking behind Siddeley, Tia and Annaliese as the group headed into the village for the Starlight carnival. On what he could do instead of what he had done.

Siddeley was bundled up in a Christmas scarf, eyes bright with excitement as he expounded on something to the witches on either arm. Annaliese was smiling, much more relaxed than at the beginning of the house party, and Tia…

He couldn't look at Tia without his blood catching fire. It was stupid and distracting and he needed to get a hold of himself—not her—if they were going to secure this investment. People were counting on him…yet all he saw was her.

At least Siddeley seemed to be responding to this looser Tia, happy now that he wasn't getting statistics shoved down his throat. Behold the benefits of sex.

Pondering that, Henry sensed more than saw Griffith sidle up to him. His muscles instinctively locked, but he strove not to show it.

They walked together in silence for a couple of houses before the warlock spoke. "Never thought I'd see you and Tia together again."

Despite the faintly sardonic tone, Henry didn't break his stride. "Stranger things."

Griffith matched his pace, hands in his cashmere coat pockets. They passed more cute cookie-cutter houses, nearing the town square. "Convenient, though. Just when an international investor comes along, one who's known to prefer family-owned companies, you two fall back into a relationship."

Henry forced a polite smile. "If you know Tia at all, you know nothing about her is convenient."

"Doesn't seem to stop you from being with her."

"I never wanted easy. And no offense, but it's weird you're this interested in us."

"Just saying what I see."

"And what's that?"

"Two corner pieces."

Henry frowned, sending a questioning look at Griffith.

"Both integral, but they're never going to fit together."

Henry turned to him then, peering through the twilight. "Seriously? What's your problem? Are you into Tia or something? Because in case we haven't made it clear, she's with me."

A faint smile. "The possessiveness is a nice touch. But c'mon. Tia Hightower isn't built for a relationship. You found that out years ago. So, this? Who're you fooling?"

He was looking for a reaction and Henry refused to give him one. Even if the words sparked nerves never deeply buried. "People change," was all he said, refusing to rub the ache under his breastbone.

"Hmm." The other warlock aimed a pitying look at him before drifting away.

Tia immediately fell back from Siddeley. "What was that about?"

Henry glanced once in Griffith's direction before wrapping an arm around her shoulders. "Nothing."

Tia.

Tia.

Tia.

Help, I've been kidnapped.

Okay, if I had been, you'd have felt like a shitty friend for not messaging back.

I'm not going away.

I can do this for hours. Gabriel is with his sister this afternoon so I have all the time in the world.

This is cruel and unusual punishment.

Do you not like me anymore? Are you embarrassed?

Is he that bad in bed?

Tia pursed her lips at Leah's last desperate message. She was standing near the ten-foot Christmas tree in Westhollow's town square, the scent of pine and fried food hovering in her nose. Children squealed and laughed with their parents as they walked past, the glittering lights and decorations woven amongst the different stalls for food and games.

Henry had gone to get them a drink, and she'd made the mistake of checking her phone. Her brief message to Leah had, as predicted, dropped like a hex grenade.

To be fair, she'd known her simple *I had sex with Henry. Nothing serious but it was fun. Thought you should know* would kill Leah, whose curiosity was like a sixth sense.

Time difference aside, it hadn't taken Leah twenty minutes before she was blowing up Tia's phone.

With a small laugh at the running monologue, Tia typed back: Yes.

Ten seconds passed before her cell buzzed. Liar. Call me. Need to hear every detail.

No. Pervert.

Yup. But also what does this mean?? Can we go on triple dates now??

Tia grimaced and sent the middle finger emoji.

Leah sent a crying-laughing emoji. Then an eggplant.

You're a teenager.

And you're avoiding, Miss Avoider Avoidstein. A pause and then, How come Gabriel didn't tell me? Has Henry not told him? Why? He should be shouting it from the rooftops.

Her friend switched from teasing to indignant on her behalf faster than it took most people to pull on pants.

Tia hesitated, fingers hovering over her cell's touchscreen. She hadn't thought of that, that Henry's friends would be bugging him for answers. She knew he'd been getting messages from them and had been faking it pretty well. If Gabriel wasn't so circumspect himself, Henry's oldest friend would've definitely been a problem. She never thought she'd be glad for Gabriel Goodnight's lack of social skills, but it was a funny old world.

Finally, she typed I asked Henry not to spread it around.

Just to spread it? *wink face*

Think he'd be telling ME that.

Seriously, WHAT'S HAPPENING? Are you guys a couple now?

NO.

All caps. Nerves. In-ter-esting. Dude must be crazy good in bed.

Tia scowled at her phone. Her friends sucked.

"What's up?"

She looked up at Henry's question and immediately tucked her phone away. Leah deserved no response. "Just my friends ragging on me. What's in the cups?"

"Apparently, Baileys and hot cocoa—or chocolate—is big here. Figured we'd give it a try."

She accepted the steaming takeout cup and sniffed. Chocolate and liqueur rolled over her. "Thanks."

“So, this is a Starlight carnival,” he said, angling so he stood next to her, looking out at the array. “Subtle.”

Tia snorted a laugh. Thousands of twinkle lights hung above them in an elaborate net of stars, suspended with magic, though the humans would believe it was down to clever engineering. She had to admit it was pretty, if dramatic.

“What do you want to do first?” The heat of alcohol tinged with dark chocolate teased her tongue as she sipped, her gaze going to the stalls.

“Happy to do whatever. It’s our first carnival.”

She paused. “Actually, it’s not.”

He raised his eyebrows and lifted his drink to his lips, grimacing the next second. “That’s not for me.” He looked around and placed the cup on the bench to the right of them. Tucking his thumbs into his jean loops, he studied her. “So? What do we do at carnivals?”

She rubbed a hand along her thigh, uncomfortable. “What anyone likes to do, I guess. Play games, eat too much junk food, people-watch.”

“All right.” He offered his arm. When she only stared, he waggled it. “Come on. Show me how we carnival. You know, since I lost my memories and all.” He affected a sad expression.

Even though she knew he was joking, guilt made a fist and squeezed. Hiding it, she rolled her eyes and slid her hand around his biceps. “Lead the way.”

He was as terrible at the games as she remembered, and she tried to hide her laughter as he missed shot after shot at the milk-bottle toss. He’d joked about winning her the giant red bear but ten minutes later, several pounds down, his face had gone hard with competition.

She leaned her hip on the stall and exchanged a humorous look with the middle-aged human operating the game. “Give it up,” she advised Henry. “That bear’s going back in her car at the end of the night.”

"Nope." He rolled his shoulder like a baseball pitcher. "This next one is the one. I can feel it."

Tia's lips twitched. She watched as he threw the ball, hard and fast. And missed.

"You haven't improved with age," she commented, raising her voice over the burst of noise from a ride.

He threw her a look. "I'm warming up."

"Uh-huh." Taking pity, she added her own bill to the ones already on the stall. "Give him some balls. Man needs them."

The woman snorted and plonked a case on the top. "Good luck, handsome."

"You hear that? She appreciates me."

"Maybe you should leave with her and the bear, then." Tia shook her head at his next throw, clucking her tongue. "You're not aiming right."

"Stop backseat throwing."

She ignored that. "Here." Tia moved behind him, tucking her body in close enough to feel his heat. From the way he inhaled, she figured he could feel hers, too. She slid a hand down his arm, over his muscled biceps to his forearm and angled his wrist. She wasn't tall enough to whisper in his ear, so stroked a finger down his back as she murmured, "It's all in the wrist."

"You have a lot of experience?"

"Oh, I've had many compliments on my wrist action." She grinned, pressing her breasts into his back.

The small tremor went through his body into hers. "From me?"

She squeezed his wrist and stepped away. "Throw the ball."

Color flushed his cheeks as he glanced at her before focusing on the bottles again. "So, tell me," he said, winding up. "When did we go to a carnival?"

"Not often. A few times when we were teenagers."

"Did I ever win anything for you?"

Tia thought of the tatty purple cat buried in the back of her closet. "With your skills?" she evaded. "It's just getting embarrassing."

He swore when he missed. "All right, hotshot," he said, turning with a hand flourish. "Show me what you got."

"You've already seen what I got."

His eyes glinted. "The memory's fuzzy. I'll need to have another look."

She snorted and took the ball he offered, rolling its weight in her hand. "What'll you give me if I knock the bottles over?"

"You've got to be the most competitive person I've ever met, Celestia."

"I take that as a compliment." She cocked her head as a drunk man nearby belted out a Christmas song. Neither of them blinked. "Ante up, Henry Charles."

His grin was fast. "I like when you call me that."

Her light mood filled with shadow. "You always did."

"I guess some things don't change."

"Right," she said, an ache forming in the pit of her stomach. "Right."

He touched her nose and she batted at him out of habit.

"Sometimes they do," he told her, lips curved but eyes solemn. He leaned down. "How about a kiss? For the bet," he clarified.

"Lame," she told him, relieved he wasn't going to push. She didn't want to think about the heavy topics. She was still just… in the moment.

Challenge rose into his expression. For all his talk, he was competitive, too. He moved in, so close his words whispered across the sensitive shell of her ear. "How about an orgasm?"

Her pulse spiked. "Right here?"

"Maybe not this exact spot." He brushed his lips over her earlobe, sending thousands of tiny sparks over her skin. "But somewhere close."

It was dark, sure, but still. Excitement shivered over her as she stared up at him, before twisting to suspicion. But—no, she'd told him about the party they'd almost been caught at, she realized, relief easing the tightness in her chest. He was guessing.

Still, she recognized the dare in his eyes as the one he used to give her. When he'd been reckless and free, before expectations had buried that part of him.

Choosing to play along, she shot him a cocky smile. "How many chances do I get?"

"Three."

"You had about fifty."

"Not my problem."

She huffed but stuck out her hand. "Deal."

Instead of shaking it, Henry lifted her palm to his mouth. He nipped the soft skin between her thumb and forefinger. "Deal."

Lust sizzled through her as he released her hand and leaned casually on the stall. His hair fell messily, longer than ever, the green of his eyes shocking against those thick lashes.

He lifted his eyebrows in question. "Nervous?"

She released a breath. With complete nonchalance, she adjusted her grip on the ball in her hand, faced the milk bottles and threw. The trick here was that one of the milk bottles was always heavier than the others. Since the carnival operators were cheating, she figured it was only fair to even the odds. Using a nudge of telekinesis, she toppled the bottles on her first try.

Henry's mouth fell open as she crowed in victory and pointed to the pink unicorn.

She offered it to him with a flourish.

With a laugh, he took it. "You cheated."

"Prove it." She tilted her head back, hooking her fingers into his belt loops. "Now, about that orgasm."

twenty

Henry linked his fingers with Tia's as he walked them through the crowd toward the abandoned town hall at the side of the square. His cock was already hard, making him damn uncomfortable as they passed the other revelers. He suspected they knew what he'd already figured out, like he had a big sign above his head confirming *this witch can lead me around by my dick.*

Tia's eyes were bright, color in her cheeks most would think was from the cold but he knew was from arousal. He knew from *memory.*

He savored that even as he wished she'd tell him more. How was he going to learn where they'd gone wrong if she pulled back every time he brought up their past?

He was so lost in thought, he didn't see Siddeley and Lady Mildred until they'd almost collided with them.

Siddeley lit up like a Christmas tree. "Lord Henry! Lady Tia!" He wore a thick tweed coat and a flat cap decorated with stitched snowflakes. "Are you having a good time?"

"Uh," Henry said inelegantly, hiding impatience under a smile. He had the sinking feeling now they'd run into the warlock, Tia would set her sights on bigger prey. The investment was everything to her.

"I haven't been to a carnival in years," Tia was saying, grinning at the pair. "Will I sound old if I say it's so noisy?"

"Quite right, Lady Tia," Mildred piped up, wrinkling her nose at the roar of laughter from near the drinks stand. "However, the tree-lighting is at midnight, so we always stay for that. And Archie does love to watch everybody enjoying themselves." She smiled at him dotingly.

"The noise is part of it," Siddeley countered, grinning down at her. "You love it really, Mother."

She sniffed. "Are you enjoying your stay in England, Lady Tia?" she asked instead of answering. "I seem to recall your mother enjoying her time out here."

"My mom came here?" Tia asked, surprise flickering across her expression.

Mildred nodded. "A few years back now, maybe twenty, thirty years ago. Stayed with some of her wilder friends, I believe." Disdain traced the words.

It wasn't hard to conclude that *wilder* probably meant *not Higher society*.

Tia looked more surprised than ever. "My mom? Gloria Hightower?"

"Mmm. I'm happy to see the next generation hasn't any of those same unseemly impulses." She nodded in approval.

Henry coughed. Tia's hand squeezed his in warning.

"We were heading over there." Siddeley motioned in the direction of a makeshift stage. "Some of the locals have put together a Christmas choir."

"That sounds great," Tia enthused.

Henry's disappointment ballooned. Not only was he not getting his hands on Tia in the next five minutes, he'd also have to listen to carols with a hard-on. Fan-fucking-tastic.

"Can I escort you?" Siddeley offered his other arm.

Henry watched as Tia beamed at the other man. "We were actually about to get something to drink. How about you save us some seats and we'll catch up?"

His heart began to beat harder, faster, blood rushing south.

Siddeley agreed and he and his mother headed off toward the stage.

Tia tugged his hand. "You'll have to work fast."

Five minutes later, he had her pushed against a wall in the town hall, his cock buried in her from behind. He covered her mouth with his hand to muffle her moans, his other hand supporting them both as their hips rolled into each other.

"Fuck," he hissed, sweat dripping into his eyes. The fire raged inside him and a red glow appeared around his fingers on the wall. Smoke wafted around his hand.

"Yes," she moaned, her voice muffled, and she bit him as she came.

Neither Siddeley nor Mildred commented on the fresh bite mark on his palm when they found their seats, but he made sure to keep Tia's hand in his to hide it. Just in case.

Tia's compact chimed loudly from her suitcase.

She capped her mascara, musing on every person it might be as she dropped the tube into her makeup bag. Her friends typically used their phones, but it could be business. Maybe Xia. Or Lionel?

"Want me to get it?" Henry called from the bedroom.

"Why would I?" she retorted, walking in from the bathroom.

He was sprawled on the bed, eyes closed, one arm behind his head. The picture of contentment and a temptation to sin. She wanted to climb on top of him and also run fast in the opposite direction.

His eyes cracked, reading her. He patted his thighs once.

She gave him a vulgar gesture, prompting a laugh, and only when she'd turned to get her compact did she let herself smile, too.

After fishing out the engraved gold piece, she flipped open the lid and her pulse tripped. "Mom."

Gloria's lips curved in the mirror. "You sound surprised. Can a mom not call to say hi to her daughter?"

"She could." Tia lifted a warning finger to Henry as he sat up so her mom didn't see him. The last thing they needed was more matchmaking. "She could also be wanting a progress report."

"Guilty."

"Give me two secs to get private."

"Oh." Surprise made Gloria blink. "Aren't you in your room? I thought that was a bed."

Shit. Tia shifted the compact farther to the left. "I am. It's just, uh, Henry and I were going through some…stuff. Strategy."

A gleam sifted into her mom's dark eyes.

Tia scowled. "Don't even," she warned quietly.

"Let me at least say hello to the boy."

Tia let out a short sigh as Henry rolled off the bed immediately. His hands rested on his hips, then he crossed his arms, before finally he leaned on the night table.

She held back a laugh, pivoting the mirror to him. *Smooth*, she mouthed.

Henry's smile stayed polite. "Lady Hightower."

"None of that, now, it's Gloria. How are things?"

"They're going well."

"And your memory?"

He shifted, the movement awkward. "Yeah. Okay. Mom says the potion master thinks he's getting closer."

Tia's heart fluttered. She hadn't known.

"Yes," Gloria confirmed, making the fluttering worse. "I met with Lionel yesterday. He's having some trouble eliminating the side effects, but as you say, believes he's getting close. He had hoped, though, since you took such a small dose, they'd be coming back on their own."

Henry shrugged, broad shoulders moving under the sweater in discomfort. "A few feelings, here and there," he evaded.

"Tia, I hope you're also working on it."

She had been. She had…and then it had been less of a priority.

Tia fought to keep her unease beneath her skin and turned the compact back to her. "No luck so far," she sidestepped. "I'm going to go somewhere private, Mom. I'll call you back."

"All right."

Tia clicked the compact closed. Heavy, beating silence followed. "So," she said, forcing a casual tone, "chances are you'll get your memories back soon if Lionel keeps going. He's obviously having better luck than me."

Henry nodded. He didn't look happy or unhappy, just… weird. Like he didn't know what to think, either.

"I guess I'll have to get used to arguing with you again," she pushed out in a lame attempt at humor. "It's been…well, strange, but also nice? I guess. Not being wands at dawn with you." Immediately, she felt like she'd exposed her throat and backstepped. "But whatever, not like I can't deal with brooding Henry."

His careful gaze stripped her of her armor and she clutched the mirror until her fingers went white.

"Maybe nothing will change," he said, voice as careful as the way he was looking at her. Like she was a step from shattering.

She jutted up her chin, her only defense to attack. "You're forgetting that we broke up for a reason. This is just…a Christmas vacation from reality."

"Does it have to be?"

His question made her heart catch, then race, so fast she felt her breath shorten. Her fingers tingled as magic pulsed under her skin.

There was no real answer. He was Henry, but without the memories of what stood between them, he couldn't possibly understand how complicated things were. How they always seemed to end up hurting each other. And when it came down to it, when he got those memories back, that fact would drive them apart again.

She held up the compact, forcing her hand steady. "I'm gonna go call her back."

Obvious frustration crumpled his expression before he sighed. "Stay. I need some air."

His tone was brusque enough that she caught his arm as he passed. As his chin angled down, fear lifted her onto her toes. Stupid after what she'd just said, but if she could only have this time with him, she didn't want to ruin it with talk of feelings. Heat was easy and she showed him how by planting a hot one on his mouth.

He caught her waist and held her close as he answered the invitation with a soft, thorough kiss. His hands spread across her rib cage, big and tight enough to cause loops of lazy desire in her system.

"I'll miss you, too," he teased as he pulled away. Sounding more like himself.

She dropped back on her heels, relief buried behind layers of scorn. "Go, if you can get your giant ego out the door."

"Not my ego that's giant, Celestia." He stole another kiss as she tried to smack him, and was out the door on a laugh.

It held in the air for a couple of seconds, fading as she stared after him. Then she got herself together and used the mirror to call her mom back.

twenty-one

The conversation had gone very differently once Henry was out of sight.

Tia didn't see him when she left their room. She could've asked the locator cloud hovering in the hall, but instead she headed outside. She realized her mistake when she hit snow and her nipples froze.

Summoning a thin heat barrier, she wrapped her arms around herself and stood on the terrace, looking out to the woods where the snowball fight had happened days ago. The memory prompted a small smile but it didn't last long.

Act like a Hightower.

Her jaw firmed and she squeezed her arms tighter.

A woof of delight from behind brought a weird relief, and she managed to half turn before Rudy bulleted into her legs. She staggered one step, swearing under her breath, but couldn't find the heart to scold him. Wearing a red Santa bandanna, his hair flopping into his eyes, the dog panted, wriggled and danced around her feet.

Nobody could look at the giant baby and not smile. She did so, bending to fuss over him for a few seconds.

He licked her hand over and over before running in a circle, then to the end of the terrace. He paused, looking back at her, wagging his tail.

"What the hell."

They walked without much direction, the dog gamboling ahead. Footprints marked the snow and crisscrossed hers, leading off to the right. She deliberately went left, heading into virgin snow. She wasn't in the mood to "people" right now. Her boots left fresh tracks as she trudged on, her gaze watching each mark she left behind.

If only it was that easy to leave her mark in business.

She and Rudy crossed into the gardens, where bushes wore their frost like jewelry, and trees extended bare branches covered with twinkle lights and tiny silver bells. The bells blew in the breeze, a soothing lullaby for her jangled nerves.

She wiped off a bench under one tree and sat, ignoring the cold under her butt, and stared broodingly at a figure of a nutcracker.

Her mom wasn't happy with the progress. Specifically, *her* progress.

"Spending time baking and drinking wine and singing carols isn't the way a Hightower does business," Gloria had scolded. "Don't forget this debacle is of *your* making, Tia. You need to be the one to fix it if you're ever going to win back the company's trust. *Our* trust. We can't afford another mistake. Stop fooling around and for once act like a Hightower."

She wasn't sure why she was brooding; she'd long ago accepted her role as the family disappointment. It was different when she could be in Chicago with her girls, at the bar where she could relax and feel part of a strong team.

Staying so close to home these past few months, dealing with the constant suggestions and tiny criticisms, had been wearing her down, like a pencil shaved to a nub. She knew her mom loved her but she'd already been left once for not being enough. She'd tried and failed. Rebelled, and that hadn't made it better. At this point, she had to wonder if she'd ever win in her mom's eyes.

Not to sound like a kid, but it was unfair. All her mom saw was Tia doing her own thing, playing around. Well, Tia had tried it the Hightower way and Siddeley had fled in the opposite direction. But Gloria didn't want to hear that, always thinking she knew best.

Tia's lips curved in an unamused smile. Apple, tree, she supposed.

Footsteps heralded someone's approach and Rudy lifted his nose from where he'd been snuffling. He barked in greeting, charging forward into Henry as he appeared from a copse of trees.

He caught the dog's head inches from his crotch. "Sorry, boy," he greeted him, ruffling Rudy's fur. "Tia's going to need that in working order."

She didn't laugh. "Can't I get any peace from you?" The words bit harder than the frost as she banded her arms around her body.

The smile slid off his face. "Want me to go?"

Fuck. Why did he have to be nice?

She let her head fall back, blowing out the annoyance. "You might want to," she admitted, dropping her arms. "I'm in a mood."

"So, what else is new?" He unzipped his coat and shrugged out of it, coming forward to slip it around her shoulders.

It was warm and smelled like him, and she hated that the gesture melted her. "Big, strong man needs to remember I can heat the air around myself. You need this more than I do."

He shrugged. "I could use the practice. And you looked like you needed it."

She let it slide, especially since the coat smelled good. "Whatever," she muttered, aware she sounded about fifteen. "Thanks."

He propped himself against a tree opposite her, crossing his arms. Trying to hide his shivers, probably. Stupid man.

Kind man.

"So, what's got you in a mood?" he asked to the tune of twenty silver bells.

She kicked her legs out, eyeing the toes of her patent leather boots and their skinny heels. "Things."

"Like?"

She didn't want to get into it. Honestly, she wasn't even sure why she'd told him. That was asking for questions. For concern.

"Your mom?" he guessed. He patted Rudy when the dog shoved his head against his hand. "She's not happy we haven't got the investment yet."

Tia shrugged.

"My dad isn't, either. But he probably can't complain as easily as your mom. Bad manners to scold the amnesiac."

She made a noncommittal noise.

He concentrated on Rudy. "Me and my dad… I get the sense things haven't changed much in the past few years. Our relationship, I mean. Not exactly watching football and drinking beer every Sunday?"

She rolled her neck irritably, trying to loosen the tension locking her muscles. "I don't know. You always seemed like you got on well enough to me." Words, snide ones, trembled on her tongue, barely held back.

He noticed. "What?"

"Nothing. Just…nothing."

Irritation formed a line between his eyebrows. "Don't do that. Make a pointed comment and then not explain. It's annoying."

"I can do what I want. Just because we're fucking doesn't mean you're entitled to my private thoughts."

He stared at her for a full five seconds. "You *are* in a mood."

Her skin was too tight and she rolled her shoulders now, trying to ease it. Under his stare, she hissed out a breath. "Look, your dad is just a touchy subject for me. All right?"

She could see the questions in his eyes but to his credit, he swallowed them. "All right." He settled harder on the tree, shivering a little. "So, Gloria's pissed we haven't got the money. Is that all that's put you in this charming mood?"

"Have I ever told you that you ask too many questions?"

"I wouldn't know."

Ah, damn it. She was killing it today. "Sorry."

He lifted a shoulder, easy to forgive. "Without memories, questions are all I have. C'mon, help a poor amnesiac out. You know, since you're the one responsible." He paused, curiosity tilting his expression. "You never told me how that happened."

Tia was absolutely not going into the competition. Which she'd *lost*. "Mom was reminding me not to say anything to my friends about this whole thing," she said instead, pulling a different string to steer him away from the topic. "Sore subject, old ground, since she doesn't really approve of them."

"What's wrong with your friends?"

"Nothing. They're perfect. But," Tia relented with a sigh, watching her breath drift in the frosty air, "Emma's family is barely scraping Higher status and Leah's a human. She has permission from the High Family to know about magic and witchkind, but still, not exactly *Legacy* friendship material." Tia scrunched up her nose. "Mom's always had a thing about behaving like a Hightower, so in her mind, my status could be lowered by hanging out with them. Crap, but that's society, I guess."

He hummed. "She liked me, though, right? I mean, what's not to like?"

If looks could skewer, he'd have been on a barbecue.

"Anyway," she continued as he only grinned. "I hate lying to them and she knows it. I get it. I screwed up and it's my responsibility to fix it. I agreed not to tell them in case it leaked. But I hate it. I hate lying. I never see the point."

"Nobody would accuse you of being anything but direct," he agreed. He crossed his ankles, propping more of his upper body on the tree. "You think they'd tell anyone?"

"No. But I promised and your word should mean something." Ironic that she'd say that to him when he'd once made her all kinds of vows. She ran her tongue along her teeth. "It just feels like there's this distance now."

"Because of a half-truth?"

"Maybe it was there already?" She shook her head, slumping. "It doesn't matter."

"Tell me."

"It's fine."

For a second, frustration beat in his jaw. She thought he might push, was already annoyed about it, but instead he asked, "How long have you been friends?"

She wanted to be alone with her mood but clearly, that wasn't happening. "Since childhood with Emma. Leah, it must be six, seven years. And yes," she said, anticipating his question, "they've met you."

"Did they like me?"

"No," she lied.

He grinned. "So much for being honest. Of course they liked me. I won *you* over."

"I was bored."

"Did I like them?" he asked, ignoring her.

She played with the zipper on his coat. "Nobody hates Leah. It'd be like hating a puppy. And Emma…" Her sentence soured. "You said you did."

There was nothing but the sound of Rudy snuffling in the snow, a cheerful bark of discovery, then him rolling in something.

Henry straightened in slow increments, like he was trying not to startle a wounded animal. "Something happened between us. Emma and me."

Tia sent telekinesis into a strand of twinkle lights, twisting them around. "Leave it alone, Henry."

"Is it why we broke up?" he persisted. "Tell me. I want to know."

"I don't want to talk about it."

"But why—?"

The lights whipped off the branch as she leaped to her feet. "*I don't want to talk about it.*"

The sound of her quick breaths fell into the sudden hush. Her heart rabbited in her chest, so fast she felt dizzy. "Just… leave it alone. Please."

Avoiding his stare, she bent to the lights haphazardly lost in the snow. With fingers that betrayed her unsteadiness, she reached to wrap them back around the branch, fighting the hot wave of humiliation.

She stilled when his strong hands slid over hers. Without saying a word, he took over until the lights were back where they belonged. Like the outburst had never happened.

"Okay," he murmured into her hair. Tension crackled, a lightning storm of fury and fear under her skin she struggled to contain.

He inched around to face her. She didn't look him in the eye, staring past him as she waited for his questions. No point in running. She'd already made herself look stupid, the explosion overly dramatic. She should've just deflected.

The wind stirred the bells in a soft jingle as Rudy sneezed three times. She heard Henry breathing, solid and sure, and she tried to match him. In and out. In. And out. In—

"Tell me a good memory."

His words knocked her off balance. "What?"

"A good memory," he repeated. "Of us. Please?"

She worked her jaw, tempted to refuse. But he watched her, green eyes warm and kind, just like when he'd been seventeen and found her curled up miserable after one of her mom's lectures. He'd pulled her into a hug, whispering she was perfect as the brat she was. She'd breathed in smoke and spice and known he would always be her safe space.

Pain made her throat raw as she continued to breathe. In. Out.

He could only hurt her again if she let him, she reminded

herself. She was safe behind the boundaries she'd set. Everything had been fine between them before they'd started a relationship. Friends, or friends with benefits, couldn't do her harm.

Besides, refusing made the memories a bigger deal than they had to be.

So she shrugged. "Fine." She tucked his jacket tighter, casting her mind back. Something fun. Sexy. Not fraught with messy emotion.

It hit her and she smiled, unbidden, rubbing the back of her neck. "I tricked you into our first kiss."

His laugh was short, surprised. "What?"

The cramp in her belly eased, warmth blooming instead. "Yeah. I was seventeen, you were eighteen. We'd been hanging out for a while, just friends—if you can even call it that. You annoyed me as much back then as you do now."

He snorted.

"Anyway, we'd been hanging out in Jackson Square, arguing, insulting each other, the usual. It was past curfew and I knew my mom was going to be pissed but I didn't want to leave."

"Because you were so into me."

She scoffed, even though he was right. "You were being insufferable because these girls were mooning over you, like always, and I was sick of it. I blurted out how I was ready to kiss the guy I liked." She remembered the moment so clearly, how his head had snapped around, a fierce scowl quickly melting into his usual sardonic expression.

"You said I was making him up, argued how you'd never heard about him before. I mean, you were right, but you were always talking about other girls and I wanted to be the one winning for a change."

"Let me guess. You told me all about the fictional guy." Amused, Henry shook his head. "I bet I took that well. I've never liked to share."

"You got more annoyed the more I told you," she confirmed.

And her stomach had fizzed with excitement, the obvious jealousy, the meaning behind it. "Then I went in for the kill."

Henry lifted his eyebrows.

"I asked you to tell me if I was a good kisser." Tia huffed an affectionate breath at the ridiculousness of her teenaged self's plan. "You refused pretty passionately, but I kept after you." It made her cringe now, but at the time, she'd only seen the dark glitter in his eyes, how they'd dropped to her lips. "Finally, I said if you wouldn't, I'd go find Gabriel—your best friend—and ask him." The forgotten memory tickled her. Leah would probably find it hysterical since both Tia and Gabriel would sooner kiss a toad before each other.

"And?" Henry prompted.

"*And.* You kissed me."

It had been the start of it all, clumsy passion and teenage desire, all 200 percent and raging like wildfire. They'd kissed for minutes, hours, his young, strong body pressed to hers against the railings. Even when they'd stopped, breathless, wide-eyed, they hadn't pretended it had been a joke. After that night, they'd been inseparable. Kissing, touching, laughing, challenging each other, arguing, making up over and over. A wild ride with no brakes. No wonder it had all crashed.

She shrugged now, swallowing against the bittersweetness of it all. "I always wondered if you knew I'd tricked you. Only an idiot would've fallen for such an obvious bluff."

Henry's hand came to her chin, tilting it. His lips caught hers, a lush kiss that spun out into long seconds. Her hands tangled into his sweater when he drew back, something odd she couldn't name in his eyes.

"Only an idiot," he informed her with a grin that scrambled her pulse, "would've passed that opportunity up."

The rush of something old, something new, made her stomach drop away as she stared at him.

And weakly reminded herself only an idiot made the same mistakes twice.

twenty-two

Two weeks before Christmas, Siddeley turned the festive dial to an eleven.

Every room Tia walked into looked like it belonged in Who-ville, the impact so dazzling she joked to Henry about going blind. Every member of staff wore a nod to the season in their hair or on their clothes, even Primm, who seemed desperate to pretend he wasn't wearing a bright green tie that played "Silent Night."

She'd never admit it, but Tia was getting into all this Christmas stuff. It was cheesy as anything but it was sort of nice to see everyone laughing, all the lights and the snow. And if she had to be stuck with someone, it might as well be Henry.

She was in such a good mood she didn't even mind their latest group activity, Westhollow's annual Christmas light competition. Siddeley had shown them the website that morning where they could vote after the walkthrough, encouraging them to get involved. Tia had scoffed but was secretly enjoying the hell out of judging each display.

The group stopped at the fifth business in the town square, a florist, where twenty red-and-green bouquets hung at varying lengths out the front window, lights sparkling in each one. Glittering silver reindeer lined the street under the window with a sleigh carrying a poinsettia centerpiece at the end.

It was her favorite so far. She slid her cell out, snapping a photo before quickly putting it back in her coat pocket before anyone saw. After all, Tia Hightower didn't do sentimental.

She snuck a look behind her and cursed as Henry winked. Yeah, he'd noticed, and he'd rag on her later for it. Good thing she could take it out on his body and shut him up.

A sacrifice she was willing to endure. Again and again and again.

As if he heard her thoughts, his cheeks creased with a knowing smile. He kept talking to Sawyer but his eyes dragged down her body, lingering and intent. Her breath hitched, mind flying back two hours to when he'd found her in their bathroom, lifted her onto the vanity and buried his head between her thighs as she panted and moaned and clutched blindly at him.

The things that man could do with his tongue…

Flushing, she used her middle finger to scratch her nose and turned her back before she overheated.

Mina made a noise next to her. "You're so into each other," she drawled in her lyrical accent. "It's kind of sickening."

Bashing her first instinct—complete, passionate denial—Tia formed an embarrassed smile. "Sorry. He's…not shy."

"Hey, if I had a man look at me like that, I'd never leave the bedroom." Mina tucked her hands into her suede jacket, dark hair tumbling over her shoulders. "Sorry to be blunt but the man oozes sex. He's good, right?"

Tia choked. Refusing to fan herself in December, she brazened it out. "Let's just say he's a great multitasker."

"Ay." Mina boldly checked Henry out. "No wonder you found your way back together."

Tia's nerves pinched. "What about you?" she said, flipping the tables. "Sawyer seems to know you well. Have you two ever…?"

"Once." Mina shrugged, angling a look at the handsome

warlock cracking a joke. "But he's a boy in man's clothing. Peter Pan," she explained at Tia's frown. "I need a man who's grown."

Tia thought of Henry and his dad, a cloud on her horizon. "Amen to that." She nudged her chin to the only building on the block that sneered at the very idea of tinsel. "What about Damon? Gorgeous, owns his own business."

Amusement stamped Mina's features. "Maybe for a holiday fling. I can't imagine dealing with that attitude on a daily basis."

"Maybe he just needs some multitasking."

They both laughed.

"Ladies!" Siddeley came over, Annaliese in tow. The spell-weaver looked as shiny-eyed as the English warlock, probably more to do with the flask she'd been passing around than her love of Christmas. "What do you think of our little competition?"

Tia let out a breath as her gaze moved over the square. "It's pretty cool. Awesome, really. They go all out. Well, most of them."

Siddeley's grin faltered at the undecorated bakery, a black spot in a sea of glitter. "Yes, Damon resists the tradition for reasons of his own. Won't even put up a Christmas tree." He shook his head, mystified. "But live and let live, I say. We are all cogs in this great clock of life."

Clearly, someone else had had a nip or three from Annaliese's flask.

Annaliese sighed, the American dressed like a ski bunny. "I loved the mechanic's, with the car turned into a sleigh and all the lights and figurines."

Considering the town mechanic was a tatted giant of a ginger, that had been one of the night's biggest surprises.

"Yes, Jenkins did superbly, didn't he?" Siddeley rubbed his hands together. "Well, before we go around the residents, how about I try to convince Damon to make some of his famous candy cane coffee?"

"That sounds amazing," Annaliese breathed, clutching the flask and spinning until she had to reach out to Mina for balance.

Tia took one look at Siddeley's face—a face that said, *honey, kiss me, I'm headed to war*—and said, "I'll come with. I could use the, uh, break from walking."

He jumped on her offer like it was the last Christmas tree on the farm.

They left the group behind, Tia waggling her eyebrows at Henry when he tilted his head in question. Matching her steps to Siddeley's, Tia sent out a breath and watched it plume white. A week ago, she'd have dove down this warlock's throat, data crystals first, at this opportunity. Her mom would've opened his mouth for her, insisting she use this to her advantage.

But Tia kept quiet, appreciating the hum of Christmas music in the background and the clean, crisp air. The now. Reality would hit soon enough.

Siddeley paused at the doorway, clutching the handle. "He, ah, might be a tad grumpy so best leave the talking to me."

Tia nodded, something like affection taking root as Siddeley heaved in a breath and opened the door.

Damon glanced up from the counter where he was leaning over an open book, a steaming mug by his elbow. He didn't smile.

"Good evening, Damon!" Siddeley ambled to the younger warlock, kitted out in green and red, the bell on his bobble hat chiming.

Damon's eyes lingered on it. "We're closed."

"Then why do you keep the door unlocked?" Tia asked, leaning against one of the stools.

"Hadn't got around to locking it."

"We were hoping to convince you to make some of your scrumptious candy cane coffee." Siddeley sent him a winning smile.

It was lost on Damon. "Should've come earlier."

Tia glanced at the book, the words upside down. "Good book?"

"Yes."

"You want to get back to it?"

"Yes."

She leaned in. "Then make us eight candy cane coffees."

A fleeting impression of amusement lit his dark eyes before he grunted. He conjured a small bookmark, sliding it between the pages and closing the cover.

"You're a peach," she called out, smiling, settling onto the stool to wait. "He's fun," she told Siddeley, who was blinking at her like she'd turned water into wine. Which wasn't that hard; she had a cousin who could transmogrify. "Doesn't really fit with the rest of the town, though."

"He's not as bad as you think." Siddeley dropped onto one of the stools. He picked up a plastic menu, smoothing his hands over it. "He has his story, much like everyone does." Before she could pry, he changed the subject. "Are you enjoying yourself?"

"It's great," she said truthfully. "My family doesn't do any of this kind of stuff so it's cool to see everyone go mad for it."

"Your parents don't decorate for Christmas?" The question shivered with absolute horror.

She hid a smile. "They put up a tree," she reassured him, "but that's about it. We don't even really go big on presents. My mom says you should show the people you love that you appreciate them all year round, not because a holiday dictates it."

Siddeley sat back, pursing his lips. His bell tinkled. "I don't argue with the sentiment," he agreed, "but there's something special about committing to a big celebration once a year."

"My friend Leah loves it." And now that Leah had Gabriel's house to decorate, she'd go nuts. The staid warlock would let her do it, too. Gabriel would dress up in a sequined Santa suit if it made Leah happy. "I usually spend Christmases with her and our other friend, Emma."

"Not this year?"

"They both have plans."

"Will you be with Henry?"

Tia faltered. She attempted a smile. "Yes."

"Well, at least you have him for Christmas."

He'd probably have his memories back by then. No playing with potions all morning to create the best cocktail or watching him roast chestnuts with his magic. No drinking mulled wine until their kisses turned tipsy. No unwrapping each other. Their issues would build brick by brick between them until they were on opposite sides. She couldn't forgive him and he couldn't understand her.

Instead, she'd be with her parents for a casual dinner and holiday movie before going back to her apartment. Leah would be with Gabriel and his sister; Emma would likely be whisked off by Bastian for another amazing trip. And she'd be alone again.

She shoved that down, deep inside where she didn't have to face it.

"My parents don't hate the holidays," she elaborated, twisting the subject away from her and Henry. "They broke up once around this time of year for a few months. I think it's a bit touchy for them. The memories."

"Then they should replace them with great ones! Second chances are what this season is all about! Take you and Lord Henry. You'd never know the two of you had a day apart with how in love you are."

She wanted to cringe. No, she wanted to bolt out the door and stick her face in the snow, since a cooling potion wasn't in range.

"I guess," she sidestepped, the first hint of peppermint uncurling in the air from the kitchen, "we have the business to thank for that."

"Potions research. I admit, it's an area that fascinates me."

No doubt why he'd also brought Griffith here, she realized, as he leaned an arm on the counter to face her. His smile was easy and wide. "Tell me more about it."

Her heart leaped. Shit. Fuck. She wasn't prepared.

"Uh...o-okay," she stammered, trying to organize her thoughts into business lines. A red spark tickled her palm, magic reacting to her emotions, and she closed her hand around it. She swore she felt each individual sweat bead form at her hairline.

She could so easily ruin this. It was her thing.

Keep it casual, Henry's voice whispered. *Talk to him one-on-one.*

A steadying breath helped. She stumbled at first, picking her way through giving too many facts and not enough, finding a rhythm.

Damon brought out the coffees two minutes in and complained ten minutes later when they went cold, but neither moved for half an hour.

"I'm not saying you're not trying." His dad's voice droned through the cell phone pressed tightly to Henry's ear. "But the house party breaks up end of next week and what have we got to show for it? You haven't had any one-on-one discussions with him about bottom lines, stocks and shares, projections..."

"Siddeley doesn't do business like that," Henry reiterated, wrapping his free arm around his middle as he stared at the fountain. He'd come out front to return his dad's call, figuring the gushing water would give him some privacy. It said everything that his mom used the compact, his dad the cell.

He didn't linger on that as he added, "Tia said the other night went well. He actually listened to her about how we plan to run the business, where we want to go."

"Exactly. *Tia* said."

Henry felt his forehead furrow. "Yeah. So?"

A sigh. "Henry, where's your competitive spirit? You've never been one to lie down and surrender."

"That's not what I'm doing." He didn't know what his dad was smoking, but whatever it was, they shouldn't offer it for sale. "We're meant to be a team? As in, I do my bit, she does hers and we all go home happy."

"You and Tia are both in line for inheriting the company. I know you don't remember much about the merger, working together, but you want CEO. You want it more than anything."

Henry doubted that. With each day that passed in a haze of twinkle lights, more memories of his past with Tia slipped in.

Claws sinking into his neck and a howl of laughter from above at their first meeting.

The taste of her lip gloss when he'd first caught her mouth with his.

Sweat dampening his hair after a solid hour of carnival games to victoriously hand her a purple cat.

Staring at her at a party as she spoke to another warlock, overwhelmed by possession. Need.

Arguing with her again and again, the same frustration, the same results, the way they'd collided, sex the only way they could win with each other.

A few pieces of the jigsaw remained lost, the breakup, the years after, but he knew enough. He'd adored Tia with every beat of his heart. He couldn't give a shit what'd happened between them since then. There was no fucking way he was about to cheat her out of her win, and he couldn't believe things had tipped so sideways he ever would've.

An unpleasant taste coated his throat. "We're a team," he repeated. "I'm not screwing her over for a job."

"You don't understand now, but trust me. You'll want justice."

"You don't know me."

"I know you better than most."

"Do you?" Henry wondered. For weeks, all he and his dad had been able to talk about was work. For years, maybe. They'd never been close and no new memories had contradicted that. It was work. Responsibility. Duty. *And what did he have to show for that decade of dedication?* "If you knew me, you'd know I'd never hurt Tia. Memories or not."

His dad let out a noisy breath. "That woman has always screwed things up for you. A stain on your life."

Henry's hackles rose. "Careful," he warned softly.

"I'm not trying to be cruel. It's… This could be a chance to prove yourself, what you've been working so hard for. Everything you've ever wanted."

Tia's eyes laughed up at him in his mind. "You don't know what I want."

"I'm your father."

"And when was the last time you acted like one instead of my boss?"

The other end of the line went silent.

Henry dragged a hand down his face, frustrated with himself and his dad.

"It's not just about the investment," Richard said after a beat. "Henry—Tia isn't good for you."

He snorted. "So, this is parental concern?"

"I'm not going to pretend I don't want you to secure Sideley," his dad said tightly. "But I also… Well, I don't want you hurt by her. Again." The words were gruff, if blunt. Henry almost believed he meant them.

They ended the call not long after.

He kicked at a pebble lying on the snow, driving it deeper. Stupid, that was what it was. People changed, no matter what his dad thought. She'd given him a second chance, even with their past.

The past she wouldn't talk about. She didn't answer his questions unless pushed and she never entertained the future. Stirrings of unease lit his magic and he breathed through the simmer of fire, directing the heat into the snow beneath him.

He took the unsettled feeling to their bedroom. Steam and vanilla hung heavy in the air from her bath, but she was—sadly—out of the tub, wrapped in a long-sleeved red dress that clung to every curve and flattered her brown skin. She was carefully blow-drying her hair when he walked in.

She smiled in greeting, absent affection that twisted something in his chest.

He echoed it with his own, bending to kiss her shoulder, easing the material out of the way. She hummed as he pressed two more kisses up her neck.

"Hi," he murmured into her skin, inhaling her scent. Trying to settle.

"Hi yourself." She angled her head in silent invitation and he complied, taking her mouth in a drugging kiss. She nipped his lip and drew back. "How was the call?"

He shrugged, moving to the mirror, staring at his own reflection. He watched his face as he said, "Same old, same old."

He saw her sneer as she finished her hair and set the tool aside. "He's got to be happy we're making some progress. Or is the stick in his butt blocking that emotion?"

"He…said a few things."

"About me?" she guessed. She dropped onto the bed, hair a sleek curtain as she tilted her neck. "Let me guess. He doesn't want me talking to Siddeley. He wants you to."

He shouldn't be surprised she'd guessed. "Wants me to win it all by myself."

"Ass."

Henry kept his eyes on her in the mirror. "We win as a team or lose as a team, right?"

"I don't lose, but sure."

"You wouldn't claim the win for yourself?"

She pressed her lips together. "I thought about it at the beginning, but I'd be a dick if I did that. It's my fault we're in this mess."

His smile was genuine as he turned and propped his hips against the dresser. "Such a way with words, Celestia."

"I know, right?"

Humor danced in his chest. On impulse, he said, "Tell me a memory."

Even though he'd gotten their past before the breakup back,

it wasn't enough. He wanted to know it all from her side. Her view. How it led to them separating. If she opened up, talked about it, maybe this time things could be different. It was why he continued to keep the truth to himself. For them. For a chance.

He knew better than to push, but with his dad's words pulsing like a warning, Henry couldn't help it. "Come on. Give me one of your memories."

"Why?"

"I want to know you. Us."

It was obvious the second the shutters came down. Disappointment crushed him as she patted the bed next to her with a sinful smile. "Then come here. I got clean just so you could get me dirty."

He ignored the way his cock leaped. It would be so easy to give in, go to her. "Why do you do that?"

"Do what?"

"You change the subject any time I want to talk."

She glared, sitting up. "Because I *don't*."

"And I do."

"Well, that sounds like a you problem."

"It's an us problem," he countered, frustration tipping into bubbling annoyance. It was a repeat of his memories, one of them always pulling away. Using sex as a band-aid. This time had to be different.

He dragged his hands through his hair, pushing back the rising tide of magic that surged with his irritation. "Why did we break up? Is that why you're so stubborn about keeping distance between us?"

"Distance?" she scoffed, looking at him like he'd lost the battle with a mind hex. "I don't even know what you mean. We're having sex."

"According to you, we're fucking. Fucking," he repeated harshly, pleased when she shot daggers at him from her eyes. "Like two strangers. I don't want that. Talk to me."

"About what?"

"Anything. Everything. Besides what position to do you in."

She stood, throwing her hands up. "You're being ridiculous. I'm leaving."

"What a surprise. Tia runs away," he mocked as she strode around the bed to pass him. The sentence knocked something inside his mind, an impression of familiarity that almost shivered something loose.

She swiveled and stalked up to him, brandishing a finger. "It's not me who runs around here."

"Oh, no?" He caught hold of her finger, straining to unlock why. The veil over those memories held and he made a sound of frustration. "Then tell me why."

She breathed harshly through her nose. Every hot thought rolled through those hazel eyes, sank into the angry flush that burned her cheeks. For one second, maybe two, he thought she would. That she'd cross the line she'd drawn between them.

Then she scoffed again, tugged her finger out of his grip and stormed out of the room.

twenty-three

Men were unreasonable, Tia thought an hour later, playing with the paper that covered her milkshake straw. Warlocks were even worse.

She sat in Pie Hard, brooding over a chocolate Oreo milkshake since she couldn't get hammered the way she wanted. One drunk episode where everybody indulged: fine. Two drunk episodes, Siddeley would start asking questions. And he was supposed to think she and Henry were in capital LOVE.

She crumpled the paper and tossed it on the counter.

She had no idea what had crawled up Henry's ass to make him come at her that way. Demanding to know why they'd broken up, accusing her of keeping distance, of not talking to him. Excuse him, she talked. Maybe not about hopes and dreams and all that gushy crap, but they weren't *actually* in a relationship. Maybe his memory problem was worse than they'd thought and he'd forgotten that, too.

"Men suck," she directed at Damon, who was fixing drinks for a family of four in a corner booth. The steam from the coffee machine didn't mask his sardonic look.

"You do," she insisted as he shook the canister. "You all say you want sex and fun, but when we don't start clinging like dog hair, it riles your male pride."

He didn't say anything, concentrating on filling the mug to the brim. She felt like his back said a lot, though, considering he turned it deliberately.

"Sure, side with the rest of your sorry gender," she mocked, flicking the paper farther away with telekinesis, then glancing around guiltily when she remembered the humans. "I'm just saying, what do you want from us?"

He placed both mugs on a tray and retrieved two glasses from the shelf. From a tub in the chiller underneath the counter, he poured fruit, milk and ice cream into a blender.

"All I'm saying is—" she began, but with a pointed look, Damon switched the blender on, drowning out her voice.

She scowled at him. Typical.

If this was any other situation, she'd call Emma and Leah, but she knew what side of the line they'd fall on. Especially with that Gingerbread Man comment from Emma. Which, by the way, was totally unfair. Just because she preferred to keep things casual didn't mean she ran from men.

The trouble was Henry didn't remember their history. And yes, she got that he was asking to understand, but even eight years was too short to rehash their past. Any amount of time was.

She plonked her elbows on either side of her milkshake and sucked the thick mixture up the straw. Her back teeth hurt from the cold but she didn't blink.

She didn't know what to do.

Option A: stop fucking him.

Every nerve in her body was opposed to that. Besides, time would do that job for her when he got his memory back.

She sucked up more milkshake, choosing one pain against the other, deeper, infinitely more troubling one.

It wasn't like she wanted a relationship with him, not really. Not with the Henry who had chosen to follow his dad and leave her behind. Who had abandoned her because she wasn't worth staying for.

That Henry held too much pain. And this Henry was a mirage. The "before" when she knew there was an "after" hovering on the horizon. This Henry hadn't made the choice to devastate her, which was why it was so damn hard not to get sucked back into his orbit.

The plain fact was that she and Henry would always want each other. Arguments, breaking up, time—hell, even memory loss hadn't wiped that truth away. But a battlefield lay between them, hexed and scarred and impossible to navigate.

Maybe it was stupid living in the past. Maybe it was, but she didn't, couldn't, give it up yet.

She concentrated on her milkshake.

So option A was out.

Which left option B.

What the fuck was option B?

"You've been working on that milkshake for an hour," Damon informed her, crossing his arms as he stood, legs braced. He wore a black sweater and jeans, hair rumpled and shadow growing in on his jaw. Not a speck of festive cheer on him.

"So?" she said.

"So, buy something else or get gone."

"You should run business seminars," she told him. "I'm savoring it."

"You're pouting. What's worse, you're trying to drag me into a conversation."

"So?" she repeated.

He tilted his chin. "Does this look like a bar, sweet cheeks? Do I look like a bartender waiting for you to spill your shot and your troubles?"

"If I said yes, would you listen?"

He pointed toward the door. "Finish the damn milkshake and take your pouting face with you."

"See, you're the kind of man I should be with."

He blinked, eyes widening at the corners. "'Scuse me?"

"Rude. Argumentative. Clearly doesn't want to be all lovey-dovey with a woman. You're me with a dick."

"Just to be clear, you were nuts *before* you had your milk-shake."

"That's rude to people with mental health issues."

"Ask me if I give a damn."

She pursed her lips. "One bit of advice," she bartered. "And then I'll go."

He regarded her with deep suspicion. "Fine."

"Okay, so, I'm guessing you hook up a lot."

He arched one eyebrow.

"Taking that as a yes. And I'm also guessing you don't want it to go any deeper than...well, insert obvious joke."

A smile ghosted across his lips.

"How do you do it?"

"Do what?"

"Keep things on one level without anyone's feelings getting hurt."

He shrugged. "Up front about it from the beginning. Can't moan if I've already said I'm not looking for anything serious."

She nibbled her fingernail. She hadn't done that, she realized. She hadn't wanted to talk it all out, make it a bigger deal than it was. Just sex. Except...apparently, it could never be *just sex* with her and Henry.

Fucking Emma had been right.

"I thought keeping a line between us was working," she muttered, tracing the condensation on her glass. "What's so wrong with that? As soon as you start talking, you start feeling." The stupid things were like a snowball and she was already rolling down the hill. Not that she could tell Henry that. Easier to attack than to be vulnerable. Cue her dramatic exit.

Damon sighed irritably. "Look, if you don't want what he wants, shut it down. Easy."

"Not easy."

He ignored her. "Either break it off or give him something."

"Give in to him?" Open herself up just to get shot down? Distaste rose up over her like a shadow. "No."

"Up to you. Now—" Damon pointed behind her "—finish. And go."

"Your advice sucked. I want a refund."

"Good luck with that." He walked off, leaving her irritated.

Which only deepened when, minutes later, Griffith slid onto the stool next to her.

"Tia," he greeted her, picking up one of the plastic menus on the counter, fixing his eyes on it. "I was walking through town and saw you in here. Looked lonely without your other half."

"So, you thought you'd make my mood worse?"

He flashed the grin that had all the society witches swooning. "Where is the old ball and chain anyway?"

"Working, probably. We're not attached at the hip."

"Could've fooled me. Siddeley, too," he added laconically, making her hackles rise. "You play the couple well."

"What do you want, Griffith?" she asked directly, not in the mood.

He set down the menu and turned so his knee bumped hers. She immediately shifted backward. "We know Siddeley's only going to go with one potion company, even if he invests in multiple projects," he said, dropping the casual act. His eyes glinted. "It was clever to try for the generational family angle, hats off to you. But it's just us. Realistically, how long are you going to be able to keep it up if Siddeley does invest?"

A nugget of unease poked Tia's ribs and she wrapped her arms around them, fixing a sneer on her face. "Are you officially president of our fan club, Griffith? Do you want us to sign a napkin for you?"

He smirked. "Isn't it tiring keeping up the act? It'd be better if you just came clean now, stopped pretending and let Siddeley make his decision based on business."

She smiled sweetly around the temper he'd thrown gasoline on. "We're not pretending," she lied, or...didn't. Or did. Who the fuck knew at this point? "And if Siddeley was solely looking at business, you'd still have to bend over because we spank your ass every time. Maybe you should concentrate on your own company and stop poking around in me and Henry's relationship."

"Relationship," he scoffed. "You? The queen of fucking and ducking?"

It grated too closely to her exposed nerves and she flinched.

"You." Damon strode over, scowl fixed in place. "*Out.*"

Tia's mouth fell open. "Men *suck*," she exclaimed, pushing away her milkshake. "Fine, I'm going."

"Not you. Him."

Griffith blinked. "What?"

"Out."

"But I'm a customer."

Damon jabbed a thumb to a plaque on the wall. It read: *We reserve the right to refuse service to assholes.*

Griffith's face darkened. "I was only telling the truth. Nothing wrong with that."

Damon just stared. A static shock of power rippled in warning.

Griffith pursed his lips before shrugging. "I wasn't going to stay anyway. Just think about what I said, Tia. Better if you back off now."

Tia's mood blackened as Griffith sauntered away. She let out a breath that took air from every crevice. "Maybe he's right," she said glumly. "Maybe I should just end it now."

Damon snorted. "*I'm* right. *He's* an asshole."

Give him something.

After another hour at Pie Hard testing both Damon's pie and patience, she headed back to the Hall. She chose to walk, preferring to turn the surly baker's so-called advice over and over, rather than portal in quickly and have to make a decision.

It was late afternoon, sun already sinking into its bed, by the time she reached her destination. And she still wasn't sure what to do.

"Lady Tia," Primm greeted her as she strode in the front door, a pile of wrapped presents in his arms, the smallest obscuring his nose.

"Primm." She nodded at the boxes. "You need some help?"

"I'm fine, thank you. May I help you with anything?"

She hesitated. "Do you know where Henry is?"

"I believe he's in your room."

"Thanks." She walked far more confidently than she felt up the stairs, the route so familiar now that she was on autopilot, there at their bedroom before she knew it.

She stared at the door.

Give him something.

But what if something led to everything, like last time? She'd sworn…

Enough. She let out a breath and opened the door.

He was on the bed, lying with an arm behind his head, a book in his hand. His gaze came to her, held.

Nerves pushed and shoved for prime position as she shut the door behind her. It clicked in the quiet. "Hi."

"Hi."

She'd forgotten this tense silence, she realized, staring at the man on the bed. This fraught empty air filled with words she couldn't say.

She hated it.

"Look," she said, drifting to the foot of the bed. He didn't move. Magic twisted under her skin. "I know you're pissed, but trust me, I've got reasons why I keep stuff to myself."

"That's not why I'm pissed at you," he said, deep and neutral. Older. Like the one who'd left her.

The corner of the curtains folded under her unease. "Sounded like it earlier."

He scooted up to sit, putting the book facedown, pages

splayed. One arm wrapped around his updrawn knee, where his fingers tapped. "I'm pissed because I actually like you, and you're treating me like any old hookup."

"That's not true," she protested, ignoring the first half of that sentence for her mental health. The curtain curled under her telekinesis, pulling at its hooks. "We're...friends."

"Friends share things." He dragged a hand down his neck. "I can't believe I'm saying this, but I don't want it to be all about sex. I don't want to be—" outrageous pink bloomed on his cheeks and he cut a glare down at the book, which she realized was one of her romances "—just anyone to you," he mumbled. "Or worse, someone you want to hate-fuck."

She froze in place, the curtain barely hanging on at this point. *Same, curtain, same.*

Her throat hurt as she swallowed. "I don't hate you." Her voice sounded papery to her own ears. Nervous.

"But you don't trust me."

She didn't want to do this, have the big conversation that cracked her open and scooped out her emotions for him to peer at. She couldn't handle him remembering their issues, remembering that he'd left her, and worse, feeling *sorry* for her. But the hurt in his face made her chest ache.

Give him something.

A glimmer of an idea had her straightening. Something didn't have to mean everything. She could keep things casual and sexy and not catch feelings if she was clever. Compromised.

"How about a trade?"

"A trade?"

Tia leaned against the dresser opposite the bed, crossing her heels. Her hem slithered up. "Twenty questions. For twenty kisses."

His eyebrows winged up. "Who asks?"

"You. You have free rein to ask me twenty questions and in return, I get twenty kisses."

"Hmm." He tapped two fingers on his thigh as she held her

breath. Then he smirked, all traces of vulnerability erased as he made a slow inspection of her body. "Where?"

Relief surged as she felt the change in him, in the atmosphere. Her smile was probably too big, too brilliant. "Wherever I want. So? What do you say?"

twenty-four

"Name the terms."

Henry's mouth was dry but he forced the words out. His cock was already hard, pushing against his zipper as Tia shrugged one shoulder. That red dress was sinful—and she knew it, judging by how she adjusted her body so the hem inched up farther.

"One question, one kiss." She slid her hands down her sides, trailing her nails. "And I get one veto."

"Then so do I," he countered, which was pure shit and they both knew it. Like he'd refuse to kiss her anywhere.

Laughter lit her eyes. "Sounds fair."

"And I don't want just yes and no. Full answers for a full kiss."

She hesitated. He waited her out, watching for any hint of what she was thinking. Finally, she gave a clipped nod.

He knew what this was; he remembered it. This was signature Tia Hightower—stubborn as fuck but reaching out through physical touch. This was her way of compromising.

It meant there was a chance. She didn't hate him. She *cared.*

Warmth and something like hope burst in his veins and he flashed her a smile lazier than he was feeling. "Deal, Celestia."

When she'd first entered the room, the air had been tense. Now it was electric, every tiny movement razing his skin. His heart pounded as he edged back so he could rest against the headboard. He considered her.

She didn't break. Just stared back with that haughty, naughty look of hers that drove him wild. That always had.

He knew he was a dick for picking a fight about her holding back when he was doing the same thing. She should know that he remembered their first meeting, their first kiss, their first everything. But he couldn't tell her. He'd stared at her sleeping next to him in bed the night before, tasting panic at the idea. She'd pull away so fast, there'd be skid marks.

He just needed a little more time.

"Let's start with an easy one," he mused, tapping his knee. "Do you like working for the family business?"

Surprise flickered. Maybe a bit of relief. "Yeah." At his pointed cough, she rolled her eyes and expanded. "I don't like being away from the bar as much as I have been, but I like dealing with potions. Cocktails aren't really the same."

"If you were named the heir, you'd have even less time for the bar."

Her lips curved. "That wasn't a question."

He chuckled, dark amusement washing their argument into the past. "All right, are you sure you'd like managing the company if it took you away from the bar completely?"

She shifted her weight, face tipping up to the ceiling in contemplation. "You and I, we both grew up knowing we'd take over," she said slowly. "I had to fit into the mold of a Hightower. You had to fill the role of Richard Pearlmatter's heir. The bar..." The tip of her tongue touched her lip. "It's somewhere to go when it all gets to be too much."

"An escape." He purposely didn't make it a question. "Our parents have high expectations." Understatement.

The noise she made was dry, as if she'd heard his silent addition. "And we'll keep trying to meet them, no matter what."

No matter what...

His lips pursed. It felt like that sentence was half-finished.

Like she'd meant to say more. No matter what…she had to do? What he'd had to do?

"Screw 'em," he offered, wanting to rub away the ache in his chest. "And their expectations."

Words hovered in her eyes, unsaid, as she aimed an unreadable glance at him. "You think so, huh?" She didn't let him answer, moving quickly on. "Anyway, I like working at the bar. I'm just me there and that's enough. But weight of my name aside, I love potions. I love creating them, fine-tuning them. The feeling you get when it's right." A glow lit her skin and he stared, dry-mouthed again. "I'm proud of our name, the legacy we built. I want my chance to show I can be worthy of it all. So, yeah, I want to do both, even if it's hard. Nothing worth having is easy."

"Truer words," he murmured, somewhat troubled, though he couldn't say why. He crooked a finger. "I think I owe you two kisses."

"You'll have to come here to collect."

"Your way again?"

She tilted her head. "Compromise."

He didn't want to argue, not when his skin hummed with the urge to be close to her.

He raised his hands in surrender and shifted off the bed, sauntering to where she stood. His hands came down on either side of her hips and his nose skimmed her neck. He felt her shiver and smiled.

"My mouth," she ordered before he could ask, and he lifted his head on command, taking her in a kiss that was all greedy heat. She rolled her hips, shuddering as he sucked her tongue, took it even deeper.

When he lifted his head, they were both breathing hard.

"I think that was two kisses' worth," he told her. "Next question. Were you happy to be working with me again?"

"No." She fisted a hand in his sweater, tugging him toward her. He resisted until she cursed. "I didn't want to be around you," she pushed out through her teeth. "I didn't want to have to look at you or talk to you. I didn't want to share the same air."

"Liar," he breathed and showed her how true that was. Somewhere during the kiss, he boosted her onto the dresser. Bottles wobbled and fell, some rolling onto the carpet with dull thuds as she stole his soul through his mouth. He trembled as her hands dipped, shaping him through his jeans. He caught her wrists.

She glowered.

He took his time torturing both of them, thinking of his next question. "Have you ever pictured me back in your bed?" She'd told him that he'd wanted her all along. Would she admit the same?

Her mouth fell open. She spluttered. "What...? You...arrogant...dick!"

"Not an answer," he taunted, letting go to smooth his hands over her hips, inching her dress higher.

Hazel boiled and his fire magic mirrored it, crackling under his skin.

Her jaw worked, resistance pushing against honor. She'd made the game, she'd play by its rules and her own personality dictated that she tell the truth.

Lazily, he rubbed his thumbs against fabric. "You want to use your veto?"

"No," she bit out. "And you owe me a kiss."

He opened his mouth, then snapped it closed with a grin. "Fuck. But before you collect, I get my answer."

Tension crackled in her body as she finally spat, "Yes."

He waited. Not just yes or no answers, he'd specified. And he was enjoying the hell out of that clause.

She dragged her nails down his chest, on the line of pain. "You know we're good in bed. Anyone would think back during periods of drought for some...inspiration." She smirked.

His groan caught the air. "I want to see that," he rasped, stroking up her rib cage. "You picturing me to get yourself off."

She caught his sweater and lifted it to scrape her nails against his belly. He shuddered. "Like you didn't do the same."

"I never said I didn't." He dove for the kiss, taking her hotter, faster, breathing her in as his hands rose and cupped her breasts. His thumbs flicked her hard nipples and she moaned into his mouth.

When he lifted from her lips, it took all his will not to just hike up her dress, tear off his jeans and drive himself inside her. Long game, he reminded himself, tweaking her nipples through the material, unable to tear his eyes from the hard points as she wriggled under his touch.

"Were there a lot of them? Droughts?" he asked, the words out before he knew they were there. Unreasonable jealousy reared up, squeezing at the image of a nameless man handling her, bringing her to climax, sharing her vulnerability in the aftermath.

"You're not the only man I've been with, Henry," she said softly. Warning flared in her face. "And I'm not the only woman you've been with."

He could've pushed, but she was right, and that didn't matter now. He let it go.

His next kiss was an apology, gentle and teasing.

He made sure to think through his next question. "Did you ever miss me?"

"Sure, but I have bad aim."

He pinched her nipples and she gasped, arching.

Her fingers, clutching the top of his jeans, tugged him closer. She didn't look at him, instead bowing her head, focused on her hands. "Sometimes. Not how you acted with me after we broke up. But the boy I grew up with? The…the man you are now. Yeah. Sometimes I missed him."

He stared at her as she pressed her mouth to his neck. Hiding her face. An ache, long felt, throbbed at the admission and he swallowed hard.

A memory swirled at the edges of his vision: glass walls,

desks, rows of people watching them covertly. Staring at her as he pretended to read a report and missing her so much, he couldn't breathe. Recent. But the feeling of longing had always been there.

His voice sounded like crushed rocks as he said, "Let me kiss you."

When she did, when he went for her lips, she lifted a hand to press against his. She shook her head. "Not there."

Fire roared in his veins as she cupped his hand at her breast.

He bent his knees and did as his woman ordered, closing his mouth around her nipple. It was hard against his tongue as he lapped, as he grazed his teeth warningly around it. As she panted, he switched to the other, his hand plumping the abandoned one in tandem. Her legs moved restlessly and if he wasn't mistaken, the bottles on the floor were rolling again, thanks to her escaping magic.

His cock was in agony when he forced himself to stop. She swore, wrapping her leg around his hip and yanking him into her. He trembled, dropping his head to her neck as he caught his breath. Then he ran his hand down her bare leg, closing it around her ankle. And removed it.

"Only so much temptation," he rasped. He returned to his stance, an arm on either side of her. Her face was flushed, pupils blown. She was so fucking beautiful.

"What did you miss about me? The me I was before we broke up," he managed.

"Definitely not the teasing," she answered, arousal heavy in her impatient voice. "You used to bait me all the time and laugh when I exploded. Said it was a good thing you were born with fire magic so you could tame me. Then I'd tackle you and we'd end up naked."

He laughed.

Her lashes fluttered as she skimmed her hands under his sweater, making the muscles there suck in.

"I missed the quiet," she told him, so softly it was practically a whisper. A confession. "Even when you challenged me, you—I thought you accepted me. My mom has always pushed me to be better, to try harder. With you, I could be me. I didn't have to be a Hightower. I could be…quiet."

Words stuck in his throat. Big words. Meaningful words. Ones he shouldn't say yet.

Before he could break, she uttered a self-deprecating sound. "But then that went to shit," she said in her normal voice, walls slamming back into place. She gave him an arch look. "And then I didn't miss you at all."

Just a little more time, he told himself. He'd fix this.

So he made his lips curve. "Not even when I did this?" He used his hands to push her dress up, encouraging her to lift her hips so it was above her waist. Red panties against soft brown skin. The image was enough to make him come in his pants. He closed his eyes, breathed in. And dropped to his knees.

She didn't protest, instead eagerly submitting when he yanked her to the front of the dresser. Her panties were roughly stripped and dropped to the floor.

No, this was the sight that was going to make him blow his load. He hissed out a breath and pressed a hand to his cock, throbbing with need. "You're fucking perfect, Celestia."

She leaned back on her elbows, watching him with heavy eyes. "Words, Henry Charles. Always just words."

It was a taunt, but he sensed more. Maybe when all his blood wasn't in his cock, he'd be able to decipher it. For now, he forced her legs wider with his shoulders. His hands eased up the tender skin of her inner thighs, making her quiver.

"Words are important," he told her, skimming a finger closer and closer to her heat.

"Not when action doesn't back them up," she hissed. "Kiss me."

"As my lady witch commands."

Tia was nervous to go slow, which was why he took his time, teasing her shallowly with his tongue as she groaned before thrusting deep, using his fingers to work her in tandem. Her hips rocked under him, moans increasing, wilder and louder, almost nonsensical…until he backed off.

Her eyes flew open, half-crazed. "*Don't. Stop.*"

He felt drunk as he grinned, lopsided. "My turn to ask a question."

Her head fell back against the mirror. "*Fuck.*" Her hand went to herself, fingers playing with her clit. He stared, transfixed, roaring in his ears before reason forced through. He clamped his hand on hers.

"Ah ah ah," he warned, the Southern in his voice thicker. "Remember the rules."

"That's not the rules."

"My rules."

She bucked her hips uselessly and then scowled. "Ask your damn question."

He bent and kissed her inner thigh. Licked it and felt her shudder under his tongue. "Do you like me?"

Tia stared at him with half-lidded eyes. "Your head is between my thighs. What does that tell you?"

"Evasion won't get you off, Tia." He summoned heat to his fingertips and carefully traced a line down her inner thigh.

She sucked in a breath, body clenching. "W-what…? How did you learn to do that?"

"Fire is my magic," he reminded her, dodging that his control had come back with his memories. "And we've been practicing." Enough heat to tingle the sensitive flesh but not hurt. Never hurt.

As she watched, he circled his fingers to her clit, summoning flame again. Her fingers fastened around his wrist, her back bowing and her head falling back, hair skimming the dresser.

"Goddess," she panted, breasts heaving. "Yes."

"Answer the question," he reminded her, his control at breaking point at the sight of her undone.

Her eyes squeezed closed. "Yes, damn you. I like you. I didn't want to. I hate that I do."

"Why?"

"Henry, please." Her plea was broken as her whole body shuddered.

It was that shudder that tipped him over. He dipped down and clamped his lips around her clit, sucking hard the way she liked. In the next breath, he sank two hot fingers into her. She was slick and tight and he groaned around her clit, driving her to the edge and beyond.

Her fingers clenched his hair and her head hit the mirror as she came, a strangled moan spilling from her throat.

As her body trembled in the aftermath, Henry lazily continued to pump his burning fingers in her channel, crooking them slightly, enough to make her jerk.

She altered her grip on his hair. "Because," she said breathlessly, "I refuse to give you power over me again."

His mind wasn't at its sharpest but he didn't think that answer made sense. He put it aside to think about, when a naked Tia wasn't above him like the Goddess made sinful flesh. He pulled his fingers out of her, getting to his feet. He gritted his teeth against the ache in his throbbing cock.

Tia noticed. "Regretting the game?" she cooed, flushed and panting.

"Not even a little." He slid his hands up her thighs, skimming higher and taking her dress with them. He pulled it over her head and arms with her help, tossing it behind him. All she wore now was a red lace bra, basically transparent.

"I love red," he said absently. "I love you in red."

"I know." She looped her arms around his neck with that soft admission. "You're wearing too many clothes."

The second his came off, question time would be over. But his cock was an insistent scream, balls tightening with every brush of her fingers against his nape. He couldn't hold out any longer.

One more question. For now.

He pulled Tia off the dresser, spinning her until she clutched its edge, meeting her startled gaze in the mirror. He breathed her in, skimming his nose along her jaw, hands splayed at her hips.

"Unzip me," he ordered into her skin.

Tia's smile was slow. She didn't move her hands, instead using magic to tug down his zipper.

He used one hand to urge her flatter, the other to shove his jeans and underwear to the floor. Retrieving a condom from the dresser drawer, he made short work of rolling it on. He was so fucking hot, he had to squeeze himself at the base to keep from coming.

"Watch," he gritted out as he sank in, driving himself into her snug channel as she panted hard, fingers curling against the wooden top. She rippled around him and he shuddered, sweat beading his forehead as he bottomed out.

He caught her gaze in the mirror. Her eyes were wide, blurred, her mouth a perfect O.

Still keeping her stare, he pulled his hips back torturously slowly, dragging his length against her. Her breath caught and she clenched as he lifted almost out before pushing in again.

"Watch *us*," he breathed, chest rising and falling rapidly, heart a riot in his chest. His fingers dug into her hips as he picked up the rhythm, unable to keep the slow pace.

She didn't take her eyes off him, bending farther so he hit new places inside her. Places that made her gasp, that made her squeeze his cock until his vision went hazy. He moved faster, faster still, bending over her, rattling the dresser with every downward stroke. He swore he smelled smoke and couldn't give a shit.

"See me," he said, barely hearing his own words. "See *me*."

"Yes," she moaned, biting her lip hard as she rose onto her toes to thrust back against him. "Henry...yes." Her hazel eyes softened in the mirror.

“Do you regret leaving me?” he rasped, needing to know. Needing her answer as she was looking. Seeing.

He saw the truth reflected in the glass for one heart-stopping moment before she shot into climax, clamping so hard around him that he cursed violently, pumping into her as she cried out and reached back for him.

He caught her hand, threaded his fingers through hers as he thrust home and exploded, black stars behind his eyes.

He had no idea how long they stayed slumped over like that, his rapid heart beating out a rhythm some might call a heart attack. But he wasn’t fully relaxed, and it had nothing to do with the fact he smelled burning fabric.

She might not have said it aloud, but her answer had been there.

Did she regret leaving him?

No.

twenty-five

The game had been a stroke of genius. Air cleared, situation back on track, and Henry had gotten to ask his questions in a way Tia was, mostly, fine with. She didn't think about her answers, or how he'd watched her as she'd said them. It made her feel edgy and she didn't want that. Things were fine.

Or they would be if he'd drop this conversation.

"You had your shot," she muttered as he followed her to their seats at the dinner table. She speared him with a look. "Not my fault if you didn't ask all twenty questions."

"We never specified a time frame," he countered, wiggling his eyebrows and looking stupidly adorable. "Therefore, the game's still running. Don't look so pissy," he added, lifting a hand to touch her nose and grinning as she batted him away. "You'll get your payment. In full."

Her skin heated and she turned her nose up on his laugh. She couldn't help huffing in amusement as he pulled her chair out with an exaggerated air.

"A gentleman when Lady Mildred is here," she murmured.

"Always." He leaned in as she sat, his whisper warm against the shell of her ear. "Didn't I prove earlier the lady always comes first?"

A shiver tickled her skin.

"What are you whispering about down there, Lord Henry?" Mildred demanded from the head of the table. She lifted her wineglass and a staff member in a snowman tie came forward to fill it.

Henry dropped into the chair next to Tia's. "I was complimenting your table arrangements, Lady Mildred."

She nodded at him in approval. "A good arrangement sets the tone of the evening, much as the music does."

Considering the instrumental version of "Silent Night" was playing, Tia hoped not.

"You may want to take notes," Mildred directed to Sawyer, who sat on Tia's left. Condescension dripped like melting ice. "In case you ever host a dinner for your...clients."

The confectionary warlock tilted his already empty wineglass at her. "Top tip," he said, his accent making it hard to tell if he was knocking on the door of sarcasm or already had a foot inside.

Mildred harrumphed and shifted to Mina on her right.

Tia chuckled under her breath. "No headway with her, then?" she asked the Brit.

"Other than our countryland, the only thing I have in common with that witch is our lack of tolerance for bullshit." His eyes slid lazily to Henry. "Table arrangements?"

Henry shrugged. "Better than what we were actually talking about."

Tia dug a telekinetic finger into his ribs and he jumped.

Sawyer's lips curled. "You know, Griffith doesn't believe you two. You want to watch him."

"You're not worried about losing?"

"Archie and me go way back. He's already invested capital with me. Besides, I'm not a potion maker." He looked at Griffith across the table, talking quietly with Annaliese. "He's feeling the heat."

"Good."

As Sawyer snorted, Tia glanced around. Siddeley was noticeably absent, as was his dog and familiar. "Where is our festive host?"

Sawyer shrugged.

They waited another ten minutes before Siddeley's voice boomed through from the hall.

"There he is," Mildred announced, as if they'd all gone collectively deaf. "Archie, you're late and our guests are already seated."

"Apologies, Mother." Siddeley appeared, bundled in tan pants, a white sweater with a reindeer nose that flashed and a tan gilet. Excitement made him bounce. "I wanted to wait outside for our guest."

Tia slanted Henry a questioning look. He squeezed her knee, slipping his thumb behind to stroke the soft skin there. She squirmed, warning him with a harder telekinetic poke.

Devilry made the pale green of his eyes dance.

She tugged his hand away, sighing when he only threaded his fingers through hers, nipping at the knuckles. She refused to smile at his antics.

"We're so happy you extended the invitation," crooned a familiar feminine voice that made Tia's blood freeze before it rushed straight to her head. Black spots twirled around her vision.

There was no way. No. Way.

But there she was. Isabella Castello, bright-eyed, bushy-tailed and about to fuck Tia and Henry over.

The High daughter was dressed in teal, a pretty A-line dress with a black patent belt and matching shoes. Oblivious to the snow outside, she carried only a black purse tucked under her arm. Her white hair curled softly around her shoulders as she nodded at the guests.

When she reached Tia and Henry, her smile was slow and feline. "My, my, if it isn't my friend Tia," she greeted her, flicking her amber gaze to Henry. Then their joined hands. "And her arch nemesis."

Tia flinched. She didn't bother letting go of Henry's hand; shit was already sprayed around the room by the fan. Damage control was all she had left.

"Isabella," she returned, voice strained.

"You don't look happy to see me," Isabella teased, hands linking behind her back.

"I'm just surprised."

"Don't you love surprises?" Isabella tucked an arm into Siddeley's, who flushed red. "Dear Archie here knew I was coming into town to talk to the English High Family about boring politics and invited me to dinner. Isn't he a lamb?"

"Such a lamb," Tia echoed. Henry's hand tightened on hers.

Isabella's smile deepened. "You'll have to sit by me. We have *so* much to catch up on."

"Lady Isabella," Mildred intoned from up the table. "What do you mean by 'archnemesis'?"

Griffith smirked in his seat. Asshole.

To Tia's surprise, Isabella waved that away. "Just teasing, Lady Mildred. Referring to their past locking horns." Isabella's pretty face didn't show a flicker of her lie, but she *was* raised in a cradle of them.

Her next words landed like a well-aimed hex bag. "Sometimes it feels like only last month they hated each other." Before Tia could even think of a reply, Isabella was sauntering up the table. She stopped by Sawyer. "If you'd be so kind, handsome gentleman?"

Sawyer grinned in appreciation as he rose. "For a pretty girl, always."

"She's far more than a girl, *Mister* Sawyer," Mildred barked. The sapphire collar around her throat quivered with her noble indignation. "This is Isabella Castello, daughter of the American High Family."

Sawyer tipped two fingers to his forehead in a salute.

Far from insulted, Isabella inclined her head. "And you are…?"

"Theodore Sawyer."

She offered her hand and he took it, brushing a kiss over her knuckles. "Yes, I believe my butler enjoys your death-by-dark chocolate."

"Orgasmic, some say," he said, winking.

"*Mr. Sawyer.*"

He just laughed and took the seat next to his original. Isabella held up a hand to the fuming Mildred. "It's fine, Lady Mildred. I recognize a scoundrel when I see one."

"Archie invited him. And this one." Poor Chrichton stiffened as a thumb jerked his way. "Please be assured we don't usually have such a…mix. Only for his business would I be welcoming them to my table."

Isabella tilted her head, never letting the sweet smile slip. "Of course. I never imagined you any differently, Lady Mildred."

Her words were polite, soothing, but Tia swore there was a jab underneath. Of course, this *was* Isabella. Every word she spoke should be weighed, measured and sifted to understand its true meaning.

Isabella gracefully took Sawyer's abandoned seat and angled her face to Tia. Although her lips barely moved, the words projected right into Tia's ear.

"My friend, you have some explaining to do."

Friend, Tia thought later, when she and Isabella were out under the cloudy night sky. A net of tiny glowing orbs Isabella had conjured drifted over their heads as they walked, illuminating the snow crunching under their shoes. Isabella had swapped her patent heels for boots, motoring over Tia's lame excuses to herd her into the chilled air.

They walked in silence broken only by Rudy, who'd followed as soon as he'd clocked they were headed outdoors. But inside Tia's head, Isabella's voice kept repeating.

Friend. *Friend.* Friend? Were they, in Isabella's mind, friends? She had no idea what to think about that. How could they be friends when Isabella had so much power over her? It wasn't like the afternoon teas were optional.

"What do you think of Archie?" Isabella asked as they started into the part of the garden where the copse of trees grew and the bushes sparkled with lights.

Tia burrowed her hands into her pockets. "I like him."

"He's a character."

"That's why I like him."

Isabella's smile was soft as she brushed bare fingertips over a frosted branch. "He's honest. Possibly one of the only people I know who always means what he says or does."

Tia would argue, but her fake-relationship act kind of kicked that in the teeth.

Isabella's gaze turned sly as she released the branch. "And his mother?"

She hesitated only a moment. "She's pretty much every society witch I don't like in one being."

Rudy looked over at the bright sound of Isabella's laugh, wagging his tail furiously. Isabella touched a finger to his nose affectionately, steering him back onto his path.

"Indeed," was all she said. She let the silence spin out another few seconds. "Things have changed between you and Lord Henry."

Tia wrapped her arms around her middle, staring ahead. She fought to keep her breath even, her shoulders low, her muscles loose. She'd known this was coming and still, she had no answer. There wasn't a way to win here; Isabella loved playing games.

Friends.

She rolled her lips. "Are we friends?' she asked bluntly. "I mean, do you feel like we're friends?"

Isabella clasped her hands, her face a perfect mask of contemplation. "I talk to you more than most witches of my acquaintance."

That was kind of…sad. But she guessed in Isabella's world, everyone wore two faces. How could you trust anyone to have your back?

She liked Isabella, at least, in the way you liked a Pallas cat—you admired its beauty and watched for the claws. She liked that the witch could be compassionate, that she didn't hold herself too high, even with her name and power. And she was kind of funny. Maybe they *could* be friends, or at least start on that path. They just needed a step.

She set a bauble in a tree swinging and braced herself. "Then as a friend, can we not talk about it?"

Isabella stopped. Tia did, too. The bauble was the only thing that moved for the next ten seconds.

"Why?"

"It's…complicated."

Being under Isabella's keen gaze was like being under a spotlight. Tia didn't underestimate the witch's sharpness for a minute and tried not to drop all her cards face up. Her magic didn't help, roiling in response to her nerves.

She almost leaped out of her skin when Isabella made a noise.

Of surrender, she realized, as the witch lifted an easy shoulder. "Fine. But for the record, I really hate being out of the loop."

It was like winning an impossible bet. Victory roared through her, leaving her to sag in relief. She surreptitiously wiped her clammy hands on her sides. "I'm the same."

"Mmm." Isabella glanced upward at the starry net she'd cast. "I could demand you tell me."

Tia wet her lips. "But you won't."

Isabella's chin ducked sharply. A laugh briefly lit her eyes. "So, this is friendship? I can't say I like it."

"It has its moments."

Isabella hummed again. "If you're not going to spill secrets, maybe we'd better get back before Mildred skewers what's left of the men's pride."

They didn't go three feet before Isabella halted again. The pause had every worst-case scenario flying through Tia's mind.

"I'll be around for a few days," she eventually said, a trace of...*something* in her voice. "Most of my time will be spent dealing with the English High Family, but...maybe you'd want to...get a drink?"

Uncertainty. It had been uncertainty in her voice.

A step from Tia. A step from Isabella. And all the while praying to the Goddess none of these steps sucked her into quicksand.

"Uh...sure." Her voice came out a pitch higher than normal and she breathed out, adjusting. "That'd be cool. Henry has his moments but he can't girl talk worth a damn."

Isabella's eyebrows arched. "What kind of moments?"

Well, she'd stepped into that one. "I'll save that for the girl talk."

twenty-six

"Okay, but you're not giving me details." Leah tapped the mirror glass, her frustration obvious. "I tell *you* everything."

Tia smirked as she sat cross-legged on the bed the next day. With help from Annaliese, she'd cast a linking spell between her compact and the large mirror that sat opposite. It was easier to speak to both her friends this way, especially when this wouldn't be a quick call. She'd been dodging them for a few days, procrastinated all morning, but she knew she couldn't avoid them any longer.

She'd survived the morning, just about, no thanks to Isabella. Her revenge had been subtle, innocently pleading for Tia to entertain them all with a cocktail masterclass after dinner. Yeah, it sounded great until you considered that this party wasn't known for sipping their drinks. They'd been trashed even before Mina had begun inventing drinks like a bartending alchemist. The last one had mixed three different spirits and a shot of espresso to boot.

Henry had fetched her bacon and ingredients for a hangover potion, securing himself a spot on her hero list.

It had been fun, at least. With Isabella and Mina leading her astray, she'd let go of the weight of her mom's expectations. She knew Gloria would hate that she'd swung the High daughter in a jig and drunkenly agreed with Mina that they could go into trade, brewing new cocktails for the masses. Not Hightower behavior, but Tia couldn't bring herself to care. Apart from Griffith, who could bite her, they'd all let loose. The last time she'd seen Siddeley, he'd had his ascot tied around his forehead and was swaying with Sawyer, who'd pleaded with her to help him. She liked them all.

A smile touched her lips. Who knew? Maybe she'd end up getting more out of this than she'd expected.

"Um, *hello*?" Leah demanded, bringing Tia back. "Spill!"

Her friends were in the bar's office, and considering it was early morning in Chicago, they must be at Toil and Trouble to accept deliveries. Both were dressed in jeans and bulky sweaters, Leah's ever-present Cubs cap perched on her ponytail. Both looked much too interested in her sex life.

"Spill what?" Tia sidestepped, even though it was pointless. Leah was a human whetstone and wore everyone down eventually. "I already told you me and Henry were having sex."

"Having sex, she says, as if that isn't blowing my mind right now." Leah turned to Emma with a *can-you-believe-this-witch?* expression. "You never even said how that started."

"I think he put Marvin Gaye on."

Emma laughed and then shrugged at Leah's look. "What? It was funny."

"Don't encourage her."

"You're a little pervert," Tia told her. "Why do you need to know who touched whose bits first? Gabriel not satisfying you?"

"Yeah, that's the problem," Leah deadpanned. "My super-hot, super-intense magical boyfriend suddenly lost the ability to give me multiple orgasms. Now I'm forced to live vicariously through you."

Emma eyed her. "I think she's avoiding because this isn't just sex."

"Ooooh." Leah's smile widened. "I like that."

"No," Tia protested. Ignoring the way her toes curled. "I just know what you two lovesick fools are gonna do."

Both stared at her.

"Make this into more than it is," she elaborated.

"Which is?"

Tia sighed. "Just. Sex."

"I call bullshit," Leah sang.

"Yeah, I'm gonna second that." Emma pointed at her. "You have a look on your face."

Shit. "Is it annoyance?"

"Maybe." Emma grinned. "But that's not all."

"Just tell me this," Leah interrupted, holding up a hand like a traffic cop. "Are you going to keep having hot, nasty sex when you come home?"

Her stomach twisted. "No."

"So just boring missionary, then?"

"Funny. It's vacation sex. It's not real."

"But it's Henry."

"Shut the fuck up, it is? I know it's Henry." Tia made sure her voice was exasperated and not at all conflicted. "That's why it's ending after we leave here. It's too complicated."

"Aha!" Triumph lit Leah's face. "That means it's not just sex."

"T, just be real for a sec," Emma said, dialing back the teasing before Tia threw a shoe at the mirror. "Seriously, why did you go back down that road? What changed?"

Like that was an easy question.

Obviously, Henry's amnesia temporarily putting their issues on hold helped—not like she could hold a choice he didn't remember making against him—but it wasn't just that. Being here with him, away from everyone, everything, that made them the Legacy witch and warlock at odds, it was easier somehow to…well, to be just *them.*

Just Tia and Henry.

But she couldn't tell Emma and Leah that.

She hated lying, even by omission. The guilt fell like a slick layer of slime on her skin as her feet shifted on the duvet. "I told you. We were both horny and hate sex is hot. And then, we were stuck here so we figured...why not keep doing it?"

"So, there's no possibility of exploring this back home at all?" Leah pressed.

"Why're you so invested in this?"

"For one, because you didn't keep your nose out of my business with Gabriel." Leah smirked as Tia flipped her off. "Second, Gabe told me he thought Henry had a different vibe when he talked to him."

Tia's whole body froze, from muscles to heartbeat to lungs. It wasn't until she felt pain from the lack of breath that she inhaled. "What? He said what?"

"Well, he didn't say *vibe*. You know Gabriel." Leah's smile was affectionate as she toyed with the ends of her ponytail. "He'd have no clue what that meant. But he said Henry 'gave the impression' that it was more than sex."

"When...ah, when did he speak to him?"

"Gabriel called him yesterday. Why? You look worried."

Double shit. She eased the creases out of her face until it was smooth and unconcerned. "Not worried. Weirded out, maybe, if Henry's thinking it's more than a holiday hookup."

Her mind picked at that like a sore. No, not true. Couldn't be. Not that they'd talked it to death but he knew where she stood on this. They were temporary; Lionel got closer to perfecting that potion every day. They were friendly now but everything would go back to normal soon.

"Do you still hate him?" Emma asked as if seeing the sharp ache the thought had created. She shook her head when Leah went to speak. For once, the human obeyed.

There was no one word for how she felt about Henry. He was exasperating, maddening, arrogant, even a little brutal sometimes. He put his own ambition and his dad before everything. She didn't trust him.

But she'd forgotten how funny he could be. How he could

tease and charm her out of any mood. How he listened. How he fucked, intense and playful and all consuming. How when he smiled, just for her, only for her, she felt absolutely electric. No matter if he was frustrating her or seducing her, she never felt more alive than when she was with him.

And it scared the crap out of her.

Ducking that truth, she shrugged. "It's too exhausting to hate him. But that doesn't mean anything else has changed."

Emma's gaze flickered. She said nothing, even as Leah sighed.

"Now," Tia said, uncomfortable with the way her oldest friend watched her. "Can we drop it?"

"One detail," Leah bargained, prompting a reluctant snort from Tia. She held up her hands like a dog begging. "Come on. I told you about Gabe ripping my dress at the charity dinner. One little dirty detail about you and the hot warlock. Please. Let me live vicariously."

"I'm telling Gabriel you said that," Emma noted.

Tia blew out a breath. "One," she agreed. "And then we drop it."

"Dropped," Leah confirmed. "Just like your panties."

Emma grumbled and put a hand to her forehead.

"Tell me the best date we ever had."

Tia let out a snort, rolling her head on the pillow. "What, so I can pump your ego?"

"Feel free to pump something else." Henry laughed as she shoved him in the side. He caught her hand, bringing it to his lips so he could nip the knuckles. "C'mon. Tell me."

Honestly, she'd *rather* pump something else than go back to the past. Her conversation yesterday with her friends had left a stain behind, one that could spread if she wasn't careful. She'd much rather bury that, live in the now and enjoy the time she had left until his memories returned. And things changed.

"You know," he mused, threading his fingers with hers. "You kind of have to tell me."

"Enlighten me."

"It's one of my questions. I have eight left, remember?"

"Seven now."

"That was rhetorical."

"And the game is over."

He bit the heel of her palm gently. "Nope."

"Yep."

"We never negotiated an end date. Ergo, I get my twenty questions."

"Ergo?" She found her lips curling in amusement. "It's too early for ergo."

"It's almost nine."

"Maybe my body's still on American time."

"Come on." His gold-tipped lashes swept down over his eyes as he gave her a pleading look. "Please?"

Better sense whispered in her ear but under his puppy-dog look, Tia let out a groan. "Ugh. Fine. Whatever."

His grin lit his face up like a child on Christmas morning.

She took a moment, staring up at the ceiling. Not for the memory; the answer was always with her, but she needed time for the right words. "My eighteenth," she said, not looking as he shifted beside her. "Our best date was my eighteenth birthday. We... My parents insisted on throwing one of those soul-sucking society parties. You know, same people, same canapes, same shit. Except at eighteen, an adult, I got twice the lecture as usual about being a proper Hightower."

"*That's* our best date?"

Tia nudged his shin with her bare foot, then kept it there, sliding along the crisp hairs. "We hadn't been official that long, a few months maybe, but you said we could spend the day together, do the duty thing at night. Except...for your dad."

She didn't look at him but felt his gaze boring into her.

"I don't know if it was on purpose, or if he just didn't know, but he took you on a work trip. You were starting to learn the business and he was adamant you put that first. You messaged me, promising you'd make it back in time. So, I waited all day and nothing. Zip."

His hand brushed her skin, almost petting her. Soothing her?

"Finally, I gave up and dressed for my mom's thing, this red dress I bought for… To make me feel good. I'd literally stepped into my shoes and you portaled in. Before I could even start, you grabbed me, kissed me and told me to come with you." Emotion washed over her, surprisingly strong, enough that Tia took a steadying breath. "We portaled to a beach in Cabo. You'd set up a blanket, candles, sodas, snacks. Man, your dad was *so* pissed," she said on a laugh, remembering. "You'd pretended to go to the bathroom in a business meeting and never came back. And my mom was furious that the guest of honor never showed. But we didn't care. We drank and ate hot Cheetos—my favorite—and we laughed and we kissed. And…more." Telekinesis released from her, unbidden, into the clothes she'd left on a chair. She turned to see Henry watching her with an unreadable expression. "It was our first time."

Henry squeezed her hand but said nothing. His expression was troubled, eyebrows drawn low.

She didn't want to face the questions in his eyes so dropped her gaze to his chest. "So, yeah, it turned out pretty great. You, ah, gave me a glass rose as a birthday present. Made it out of the beach's sand and your fire, said it would be a reminder that you'd always show up for me, no matter what. Eighteen-year-old me swooned." She laughed so she didn't feel the weird burn in her throat. "But we were kids. Work and your dad took you away more and more, and you stopped being able to show up." She should've stopped there. But the words slipped free from their locks. "I stopped being the person you wanted to show up for."

"I doubt that's true," Henry said, the words rough.

She cleared her throat, trying to remove the emotion clogging it. "Yeah, well. Past is past, right?"

He didn't say anything for a long moment, too long, so long

that she battled the urge to vault out of the bed, run to the bathroom and lock the door behind her.

As if sensing it, he tightened his grip on her hand. He moved closer, bending to trace his free hand down her cheek. "No wonder I love you in red," he murmured. And kissed her.

She took the outlet gladly, spearing a hand through his hair and yanking him down. The bittersweet memory beat like a pulse, bleeding into her chest, and she licked her tongue along his, desperate to feel the burn of lust, the vibration of his groan as he settled more weight on her. She shaped his erection through his loose pajama pants.

"Wait," he gasped with a half-strangled groan. "Slow down."

"No," she countered, locking her mouth to his and squeezing him firmly. She didn't want to think. Only feel.

His skin heated against hers, almost burning as he took the kiss deeper, as he slid his own hand down to cup her. She arched, relieved he was going with it.

Her toes curled as he toyed with the line of her panties, knuckling the dampening center.

And the door flew open.

Tia grunted as Henry bit her lip in surprise.

"Whad the thuck?" she lisped, touching her throbbing mouth and peering over his shoulder.

Isabella, clad in pastel pink pants and a white cashmere sweater, beamed at her. "I'm ready for our drink."

Henry muttered something, pained as he slumped onto the mattress, facedown.

Tia tried to calm her racing heart, unfulfilled lust fueling her glare at Bianca, who leaned in the doorway. "Seriously?"

Bianca shrugged.

Tia looked back at Isabella. "First rule of friends," she said tightly, hiking the covers up so her nipples weren't on display. "*Boundaries.*"

twenty-seven

Because of the magic concentration in Isabella's blood, she gave off a constant, low-level hum of power that buzzed against the skin. It wasn't bad, not really, but combined with a sour-faced butler staring daggers at her back, Tia couldn't help but feel on edge as she and Isabella made their way down Westhollow's main street.

"Does Bianca come with you everywhere?" she asked, sneaking another look behind them.

Bianca's expression didn't shift.

"A High Family member must have a companion at all times." Isabella glanced back with obvious affection. "B and I have been together since I was five."

"You're friends."

"I suppose, of a sort. Except I pay Bianca for her friendship." She traced a finger along the thin hammered silver ring she wore and chuckled. "And she heavily disapproves of some of the things I do."

"Trust me, friends can disapprove of each other," Tia said wryly, thinking back on *her* friends' recent decisions. She shrugged. "It's more of a test to tell each other the truth."

"Friendship is truth?" Isabella mused, walking directly over a puddle without touching the water. The magic was so smooth, Tia wouldn't have noticed if she hadn't been looking. "I like that. It must be relaxing to count on someone always being honest."

"Sometimes." *Unless you didn't want to hear it.* Tia gestured at Pie Hard. "Hungry?"

"I always have room for cake." Isabella patted her belly and smiled brilliantly at a human man walking past. He stuttered and then grinned back, his expression shifting to stunned when Bianca body-blocked him.

Tia snickered. "You must make a great third wheel on a date," she informed the butler, who stared at her stone-faced.

Isabella tilted her face up to the weak sun, unfazed by the cold wind. "So," she said, ignoring the crestfallen man, "tell me of your trip here. How're you liking England?"

"It's fine. Cold. I like the accents."

"British men are delicious...but I suspect you're partial to a hint of Southern twang." Mischief bloomed in Isabella's expression.

It made her pulse trip. She tried to ease the instant battle mode her muscles locked into. "Uh..."

"Friendship is truth."

Well, dammit. Swallowing her desire to deny, Tia rolled her lips. "Maybe. Some."

Isabella clapped like a toddler presented with a magic trick. "I wondered if there was something still between you."

News to Tia. "Why?"

"You've always been so passionate about him. Hate is the other side of the coin to love. Indifference is the real tell. And, of course, there was Henry's ban on you."

Tia stopped dead. "His what?"

"I'm not one to gossip..."

Bianca snorted and Isabella narrowed her eyes at her companion. "But from what I've heard there's an unspoken rule that no warlock should approach you."

Tia's mouth fell open. Shock and fury collided in a storm and exploded outward in a shower of red sparks, angry fireflies of magic. "*WHAT?*"

"Apparently, you didn't know." Isabella batted away the sparks, extinguishing them with her touch. She didn't reprimand Tia for losing control where humans could see. Probably was hiding it anyway with some super-fine magic invisible to the naked eye.

Tia didn't really give a shit. Instead, she tried to find her footing, hard to do when your body is molten lava and about to melt through the sidewalk.

"That arrogant, insufferable *dickhead*. He thinks he can *ban* other warlocks from dating me? Like I'm his possession?" She actually felt a little dizzy as she seethed.

"I don't think he *strictly* put a ban on you," Isabella offered. "It's just sort of...unspoken that he wouldn't like it. And you know how Legacy warlocks are. They always get what they want. More likely it was his friends who put it about."

Tia didn't care if he *or* his asshole friends instigated it. This was why she'd been alone for the past eight years? Not that she particularly liked any of the Higher warlocks but still. Eight. Fucking. Years. Because his Higher-ness might not like another man touching her?

"I'm going to kill him," she said matter-of-factly. "I'm going to get three hex bags and he's not going to know what hit him."

Isabella's forehead crimped. "Is that a joke or would you actually like me to make him disappear?"

The roaring in Tia's ears popped and she blinked at the High daughter, who shrugged. "I'm just saying I could."

And that was one freaky reminder of whom she was walking with.

Tia breathed out a steady stream of air, focusing on her center. Aggravation ground behind her closed eyelids, emotional nails on an old chalkboard, but she resolutely pushed back until she had her magic under control.

When she opened her eyes, she was steady, if still pissed. Fucking Henry. Unbelievable. When he got his memories back, she was going to toy with him like a black cat and her prey. Real slow.

Isabella interrupted her dark thoughts, gesturing for Tia to walk with her. "It doesn't matter now, surely. You're back together."

Tia hesitated briefly before she fell into step. She'd promised not to tell anyone the truth about Henry's amnesia. A promise should mean something. But… Goddess, she was a dehydrated man ten feet from a river and Isabella was cool, impartial water. She'd kept all her words, all her doubts, all her feelings bottled and each passing day eased the cork out. If she didn't relieve the pressure herself, she had a sneaking suspicion she'd pop at the worst time. Isabella understood politics. She might be the best option. If Tia could trust her.

Tia paused again, barely having gone a foot. "Friendship also means loyalty." Her heart shoved into her throat, fluttering there as she took the next step. "If I tell you something and ask you not to repeat it…"

"I know what loyalty is, Tia." Isabella's eyebrows winged up. "You have me intrigued."

Tia raked her teeth over her lip, folding her arms around her stomach. "Henry's…different. Not himself. Being away from our world, he's kind of…gone back to how he was when we first started dating. More carefree, less asshole."

Isabella waited.

Tia looked past the expectant white-haired witch to Bianca.

"B will take it to the grave," Isabella assured her.

That didn't mean Tia wanted to bare her guts to the witch.

Clearly sensing that, Isabella shifted to look over her shoulder.

Bianca's scowl was resolute. "No."

Isabella didn't budge.

A muscle feathered in the other witch's jaw but after thirty seconds, she grudgingly clipped a nod.

Instantly, Isabella twirled a finger around the pair of them. Light burst up and down, there and gone before anyone would notice. A thin shimmer settled, soundproofing them. "Will that suffice?"

"You probably think it's dumb."

"No," Isabella surprised her by saying. "I don't like letting my guard down for people, either."

Grateful, Tia threaded a hand through her hair. Tugged. "It's not like it's a big secret or anything. It's just..." *Embarrassing to admit.* She exhaled. "You know when you go on vacation, nothing counts? Calories, men, drinks."

Isabella tilted her head.

"Right, forgot who I was talking to." Tia sank her jittery hands into her back pockets. "It's out of time. Not real. And then life goes back to normal."

A couple walked by them, hand in hand, one man laughing down at another with obvious affection. The smaller of the two lifted their hands to kiss.

Tia dropped her gaze.

"So, you think," Isabella said slowly, as if running the words through a gauntlet in her head, "all your previous problems will come back when you return to New Orleans and Henry will become an asshole again?"

"I never thought I'd hear a High daughter say 'asshole.'"

"I can say 'fuck,' too, if the occasion calls for it."

Tia barked a laugh.

Isabella smiled prettily, nothing but a sugared Southern lady who'd never dream of soiling her mouth with curse words. Her body swayed in the breeze, responding to it unconsciously as she hummed. "Why *did* you break up? Nobody seems to know for sure."

"Probably because I don't like talking about it."

"Even to a friend?"

Tia looked away, scuffing her heel on the sidewalk. A gum

wrapper blew past, touching her toe briefly before whispering on.

"You know, not many witches talk to me," Isabella said, bald as anything. She avoided Tia's startled gaze by examining her unpolished nails. "Sometimes being a High daughter can feel lonely."

A pang of solidarity caught Tia square in the chest.

Isabella once again touched her ring, smoothing over the precious metal. "I think that's why I like our monthly teas so much. I like being around Leah and you and Emma. It makes me feel…part of something normal." She inclined her head to Tia with an almost shy smile. "Like friends."

Shit. Now Tia would feel like a dick if she didn't answer.

Okay, she could do this. Stick to the headlines, move on.

"It's nothing dramatic," she started, reluctance dragging the words out. "Not like he cheated on me or one of us wanted someone else. It was…slow. A missed dinner here, an unreturned call there. Dates forgotten. We argued a lot, more than our usual bickering. His dad didn't help." Tia produced a thin smile. "He doesn't think I'm good enough for his son."

Isabella didn't blink.

Tia sucked air in through her nose, hating how often she'd had to revisit this ground over the past month. It didn't get any easier. "Emma's situation made it all come to a head. I demanded he finally show up for me, choose me over his work. He didn't, so I left."

"And," Isabella said quietly, understanding, "he didn't come after you."

The reminder of how little he'd cared made her feel raw inside, scraped over a rough surface. She chafed her arms.

"Has he said sorry?"

"He doesn't think he was wrong." He hadn't understood, the only time she'd deigned to hash it out, six months later at a party she got dragged to. If she hadn't been there, she doubted he'd have sought her out, and when she'd thrown the truth in his face, he'd thrown it right back.

"And you do."

"He was."

Isabella hummed again.

Tia cut her a look. "Is that meant to mean something?"

"Oh, no. Just making noise." Isabella's dimples flashed but Tia didn't believe a word. "I'm surprised you took him back."

Tia faltered, dread mixing with the old grief. "Because it's weak?"

For a second, Isabella looked surprised. "You feel weak for taking him back?"

"I *am* weak." Tia twisted to the florist window, to the display of poinsettias in pretty red pots. She avoided her reflection. "But it's only for now. When we go home, we're breaking up again."

"He wants that, too?"

"He will."

Isabella hummed a third time.

"You know that's annoying, right?"

"I think I like how disrespectful you're being." The delight in Isabella's tone made Tia wince in realization. "And I was only thinking it sounds like you're worried he's going to drop you so you're preparing to attack first."

"I'm not *worried*. And don't you fucking hum again."

Isabella's grin was genuine in the semireflective window. "Why don't you ask him if he wants to keep dating?"

"We're not dating. We're having good sex." She snorted. "That's something I can count on him for at least."

"Maybe he's changed."

"He hasn't." She wouldn't let herself forget it. "He still jumps when his dad asks him. The perfect Higher son. Hell, maybe he did me a favor banning the others. All warlocks are the same, looking down on anyone who makes mistakes."

"Not always." Isabella's forehead wrinkled, before she offered, "I know some warlocks who don't judge."

Tia scoffed.

"Horatio Mikito makes a point of escorting a warlock not in society to every party." Isabella's gaze turned inward as she thought it through. "Tobias Rowntree took back his wife after she was found in the coat closet with someone at last year's celestial ball."

"Neither of them are Legacies," Tia pointed out, not even sure why she was arguing this when she wanted done with this whole conversation. "You know what Legacy parents are like. Everything has to be perfect in every way. Trust me, I know." As if her mom would ever let her forget.

Isabella's face brightened. "Well, if you want a Legacy example, there's always your father."

"My father?" Something whispered down her neck in warning and she suddenly wanted to take back the question.

Not that Isabella took any notice. "Yes," she confirmed. "If his forgiving your mother when she came to him pregnant with someone else's child isn't a perfect example, I don't know what is."

twenty-eight

For a moment, the world stilled. Every blade of grass, every wrapper on the street, every person going about their normal day. The silence shushed in Tia's ears like water.

"What?" she heard herself say.

"I know it's a secret," Isabella assured her, one hand out as if to soothe. "I wouldn't normally speak of it, but I think it proves my case, right?"

Glass shards ripped up her throat, ensuring her next words were raw. "She was pregnant."

"Right, during their breakup. And he hasn't treated her or you any differently, even with your not being his natural child."

She might actually be sick.

Isabella peered at her. "Are you okay? Did you— Oh, fuck." Under normal circumstances, that word from Isabella's perfect pink mouth might have Tia laughing. Now her eyes were wide in the window reflection. "You knew, yes? Please tell me you knew."

She wasn't Peter Hightower's daughter.

She wasn't a Hightower.

Who the hell was she?

Tia swallowed the oncoming meltdown and concentrated on

the facts. She didn't want to have it out now in front of Isabella Castello. In front of anyone.

"Yeah." She forced a smile, the curve feeling odd, and finally turned away from her reflection, mask in place. "I just don't like being reminded."

Relief stained Isabella's cheeks a normal color. "Of course. I only meant if your father was different, maybe Henry could be, too."

She couldn't think about that right now. She just nodded.

Isabella hesitated. "Should I apologize for bringing it up?"

"No, it's fine. I just...didn't know you knew."

"We're privy to all matches and births. But it goes no further." Isabella frowned, setting a hand on Tia's arm, sending a shock wave of power across her skin. Tia barely felt it. "You look ill. Do you want something to eat?"

She leaped for the excuse. "Yeah. Yes, let's get something."

The sooner they ate, the sooner she could run back to the Hall, lock herself away. Try to make sense of things.

Funny. Like that would be possible. Even now, her gaze bounced around, thoughts sliding through her head so fast they didn't make sense.

Like the man across the street that looked familiar. Damn familiar.

She focused on him, an anchor in the tsunami.

He moved like he was on the hunt, head down, shoulders back, dressed in a tan jacket, faded jeans and boots. And definitely familiar.

"Kole?" After a beat, she recalled the soundproof bubble and gestured at Isabella to break it. Immediately after the witch complied, she yelled his name. "*Kole!*"

Emma's brother's head jerked up. A moment of *oh shit* crossed his face. "Tia?" His gaze moved from her to Isabella, eyes bugging out. "Your Excellency?"

"Lord Bluewater," Isabella purred, linking her hands behind her back. Her dimples made a showing, any trace of a real person hidden behind the façade. She lifted her voice. "How handsome you look today."

He was handsome, Tia supposed, not that she'd ever really concentrated on that. Kole had never had a problem finding willing witches in his bed, despite the fact he was gone most of the time overseas, researching water magic or something with scientists. He shared Emma's coloring, dark brown hair and dark brown eyes, ruggedly handsome in an aww-shucks-ma'am kind of way. They'd never been especially close, even though she'd been best friends with Emma for years. Still, that didn't stop her from charging right up to him, suspicious as hell about his coincidental appearance.

"Was it Emma or Leah?" she demanded as soon as she stopped in his path. Relief soothed her hollowed-out gut, relief that she could focus on this, locking the other thing away. Relief that she could be angry instead of in pain.

Kole scratched the back of his head. "What're you talking about?"

"Oh, please." Tia crossed her arms as Isabella fell in behind her, and Bianca behind *her.* "I can't believe they sent you to look in on me."

Kole flicked his eyes to the High daughter. "Maybe you need someone to look in on you."

"Unbelievable." It took skill, but Tia sidestepped all the times she'd meddled in Emma's and Leah's lives. She fisted her hands. "Well, you can portal your ass back home."

"But I just got here."

"Exactly." Isabella preened, a picture of a Southern belle. "He can accompany us to the bakery."

"He's a spy," Tia hissed between her teeth.

Isabella's smile widened. "A spy, Lord Bluewater? Surely not."

He rolled his eyes. "A friend can't look in on another friend?"

"Uh-huh." Tia pointed in the opposite direction. "Go home."

"But I so rarely get such a handsome escort." Isabella slid her hand around Kole's arm, ignoring how he tensed. "Stay. You can tell us how Emmaline is doing. And dear Leah, of course."

A muscle in his jaw jumped. Maybe because of the power coming off Isabella, or maybe because Tia knew—like the whole world knew, except the woman in question—that Leah was a sensitive subject for him.

"I'm sure nothing I can say would be news to you, Your Excellency," he said smoothly, though his eyes hardened into cold brown disks.

"I don't know about that," she mused, tapping her fingers lightly on his biceps. "I'm sure you have many secrets just dying to be whispered into someone's ear."

Isabella was playing again, Tia thought, part exasperated, part relieved, maybe even a touch entertained since Kole looked ready to flee.

She took pity on her oldest friend's brother. "She's just teasing, Kole."

Kole glanced slowly between them.

Isabella smiled brightly. And hummed.

It wasn't until Kole and Isabella retreated into their respective portals that Tia let herself think about the secret again.

The secret. As if something that brought her entire reality crashing down could be summed up in two simple words.

She didn't return to Silkwood Hall. Way too many prying ears, eyes and magic. Instead, she followed her feet to the town gazebo and ran a hand from the floor to the ceiling. The soundproofing spell shimmered pale white before fading. Only then did she pull out her compact. Her heart was thumping wildly, each beat painful, as she rubbed her thumb across the mirror and said her mom's name.

The mirror flickered for a few seconds. Then a few more.

Tia hadn't even considered she might not pick up. She couldn't wait; she had to know. *Now.* Her toes scrunched in her heels as she paced the confines of the gazebo, refusing to hang up.

After a solid minute, Gloria's face appeared, looking harried. "Tia, I'm in a meeting," she said, voice clipped. "I have to get back. We'll talk later."

"Is my dad really my dad?" Tia blurted out before Gloria could disconnect.

Her mom's expression blanked. And Tia knew.

Her breath hitched as she pressed her lips together, struggling to keep the grief in, to hide it so nobody would see. Her fingers spasmed around the compact. She wanted to crush it under her boot. She wanted to smash it until it was silver and shards, until it was dust and floated away, far away from her. Fuck. She couldn't breathe.

The wind chimes that hung in the gazebo rafters tore off their hook in a jangle of discordant notes, hurled to the floor. Tia stared at them as she focused on drawing a breath through the band around her ribs, ignoring her mom's progressively loud demands from the mirror.

Only when she felt like she wouldn't scream did she lift the compact again.

"Why?" she rasped. "How?"

The background had changed, her mom clearly having moved to her office. Gloria's eyes were pinched. "Are you secure? How did you find out?"

"Does that fucking matter?"

"Please don't swear at me."

Anger crawled like ants over her skin, making it impossible to sit, to be calm. She paced, the click of her heels too polite when she wanted to rage.

"I know you're upset—"

Tia cracked a laugh.

"Please. Just answer me. Are you secure?"

"Yes," Tia bit out. "Nobody's around to hear your precious secret."

"It was for your own good."

Tia didn't even bother acknowledging that crap. "Isabella told me."

"Isabella who?"

"Castello."

Gloria's eyes widened. "She's there?"

"She turned up a couple days ago. Does it matter how I found out? What the hell, Mom? That's still true, right? You are my mother?" Tia wiped her free hand down her face, hardly caring if her mascara streaked.

"Your dad and I discussed it—"

"You mean Peter?"

"I mean your dad," Gloria said, stern. "It takes more than sperm to make a father."

Tia dug her nails into her palms. "Who's my—who got you pregnant?"

Gloria hesitated, exhaling on a sigh. "He was a warlock I met in London, when your dad and I broke up for a few months. It was casual. I was hurting and didn't want another relationship. It wasn't until after Peter and I resumed that I realized I was pregnant."

Tia continued to eat up the ground, back and forth, again and again, the background a blur of fading twilight. "Who is he?"

Gloria paused. "Are you sure you want to know?"

No. Yes. No. She sent telekinesis into the loose stones around the bench. They scattered like gunfire. "Does *he* know?"

"Yes."

Tia read everything in that one answer. "He didn't want to be a dad," she said flatly.

"We were young. And he had responsibilities."

Goddess, she was so *sick* of that being used as an excuse.

"He married shortly after," Gloria continued, only a hint of nerves in her eyes betraying her feelings. "All he asked was that I never tell anyone. His wife wouldn't take it well."

Rejected before she was born. One more person finding her

a disappointment. Tia sent more stones scattering, her throat burning with that knowledge. "So you decided to raise me as a Hightower?"

"Peter wanted you to be one. He thought we could raise you together."

It clicked. "That's why you got married so quickly after the breakup."

"Among other reasons. It was a good match. And you know I love him."

Her childhood passed before her in a long row of lectures, the endless string of admonishments and expectations that forced her to chase approval and never find it.

"That's why you always told me to act more like a Hightower." The realization tasted bitter. "You were scared someone would see that I'm not one."

"Yes, you are," her mom snapped, sharp enough to cut. "Blood isn't everything."

"Tell that to Higher society," Tia muttered.

She slumped against the wall, stretched to the point of pain. Everything she'd ever been told—how she was a leader in society, how what she did mattered because of her position—all of it sugar spun out of pretty lies.

She wasn't a real Hightower. She wasn't a real Legacy.

Which meant she wasn't a match for any warlock who was.

Her throat burned hotter and she trembled. Hating herself for even thinking of that right now.

Her mom cleared her throat. "I know this is a shock, and we can talk about it when you get home. But I need you to think of the company, Tia. You can't let anyone know."

The noise Tia let out wasn't audible.

Her mom wasn't completely unmoved, even Tia could see that, but Gloria Hightower was practical, first and foremost. "Mildred Siddeley is a stickler for bloodlines. If anything, this is where you and Henry have the advantage."

His name was like a hot poker to the heart.

"You come back next week, anyway, so you only have to hold it together until then."

How was she going to act normal with this hanging over her head? She was already fake dating and real sleeping with her ex-not-ex. It was practically a Shakespearean comedy. All they needed was for a long-lost twin to show up. Honestly, she wouldn't even be surprised.

She needed to talk to someone. She needed to scream. To sink her magic into something and watch it explode. She wished she had fire magic; a giant blaze would feel so cathartic.

"I know this seems cruel but it's for the best." Gloria softened, adding, "I am sorry, darling."

Her mom's sympathy made it worse. Tia bore down on the tears that sank tiny daggers into the backs of her eyes. She managed a nod.

"I promise we'll sit down with your dad and talk when this is over." She paused. "This doesn't really change anything. You are who you are."

When Tia closed the compact seconds later, the words rang in her head, hollow.

You are who you are.

The trouble was she wasn't sure who that was anymore.

twenty-nine

She knew she couldn't avoid people forever. There was still a week to go on the house party and she was finally gaining ground with Siddeley. The finish was in sight and all she had to do was stay the course. Be a fucking Hightower.

The thought jabbed straight into her chest.

Still, it took all her energy not to flinch as Siddeley called her name from the sitting room. Out in the corridor, she took a moment, one moment to pretend she wasn't holding everything together with glitter glue, before she walked in with a smile.

Most of the party was there on the two couches, marshmallows bobbing in mugs of hot cocoa on the coffee tables.

"Lady Tia, we haven't seen you all day," Siddeley exclaimed from his wingback chair, a jaunty tartan that complemented his pants. "Sit, catch up."

A red mug appeared for her on the coffee table as she eased down next to Henry. He gave her a lopsided grin, dropping an arm around her shoulders.

She stiffened.

He frowned. He shifted his arm to the back of the couch, respecting her boundaries but still there for support. She reached for her mug, staring in at the marshmallows masquerading as tiny snowmen and tried to ignore the burning in her gut.

A fire crackled in the hearth and Rudy sprawled in front of it, his tail thumping in greeting. Siddeley's enormous cat lay next to him, head cocked and tail upright, two seconds away from sinking its claws into the blissfully unaware dog.

Enjoy the ignorance while you can, she thought, steeling herself as she turned her attention to their host.

He settled back, glancing at the doorway. "Lady Isabella didn't come with you?"

"She portaled back to London, but she wanted me to pass on her well wishes." Tia blew on her drink to avoid Henry's questioning stare. He'd always been able to read her if he'd bothered to look and lately, he hadn't stopped. Like she was all he wanted to look at.

It stuck in her throat. They were both fools.

Siddeley beamed. "Capital, capital. A joy that one, so sweet and amiable."

Right. That was Isabella. "I took her to Pie Hard."

"You...took her to Pie Hard?"

Sawyer snorted from where he lounged, a glass of something amber in hand. "Ten pounds says Damon didn't give a fuck who she was."

Siddeley's neck descended into his shoulders as if his mother would hear, relaxing when she didn't burst in. Probably organizing stuff for the Snowflake Ball that was only days away, or maybe off in London. She seemed to spend a lot of time there.

Next to Sawyer, Mina crossed her legs in consideration. "I'll take that bet. Even being in the same room with her for an hour left me unsettled half the night."

"You could've come to my door," Sawyer offered with a lazy grin.

"I needed comfort for more than five minutes, darling."

Annaliese's laughter and Chrichton's snort didn't faze Sawyer. He shrugged easily.

Henry grinned. "I'll put my money on Damon being his usual charming self."

They all looked to her. Tia's skin itched under the scrutiny and she watched the marshmallows in her mug dance. "He told her she might be a High daughter in America, but he was the High baker in Pie Hard and she could damn well wait her turn."

Siddeley murmured something, practically making the sign of the Goddess.

Everyone else laughed.

Henry settled back, thumb grazing her shoulder. "Told you. We are who we are."

Tia's breath hitched.

Luckily, the conversation managed without her input, most of it focusing on the Snowflake Ball, an annual tradition the whole town was invited to. It was relaxed, casual, like everyone had given up trying to win points with Siddeley and was enjoying the lack of pressure. Tia wished she could say the same. She was just glad Griffith hadn't put in an appearance. He'd have spotted her weakness and leaped on it, predator tearing apart prey.

She waited thirty minutes before making her escape. "I'm a bit tired," she said with a strained smile, setting her mug down. "Think I'll go have a nap."

She barely waited for Siddeley's, "Of course, of course," before scurrying off as fast as her high heels could carry her.

She hadn't even made it halfway up the staircase before Henry's tread sounded below.

The vulnerable parts of her, the shadowy places she didn't want exposed to the light, cringed. She took the valuable seconds before he caught up to buckle on her armor. It was harder than she remembered, not a perfect fit now she'd left it off for so long.

"Hey." His hand cupped her elbow as he drew her around. She didn't resist. That would be too obvious. "You okay?"

She produced a thin smile. "Just tired. You know Isabella, like boxing with a rosebush. Gotta watch for thorns."

His expression didn't change. So casually open, so concerned for her, so different from the warlock she'd had to guard her heart against for years. And now would again.

Pain stretched its claws inside her and she cleared her throat, skirting around him.

She didn't make it two steps. "Something's wrong."

She couldn't stop. If she did, she was scared it'd be over. "No."

"That wasn't a question." He jogged to catch up, sliding in front of her. "Talk to me."

The burning in her throat was back and she kept her head down as she veered around him. "I'm in a mood. Don't push."

"Like that's going to work."

Fire burst into her path and she squeaked, throwing herself backward, tripping on her heels into a painting that wobbled precariously. A wave of embarrassment crashed with flickering bolts of wrath, both fueling her as she whirled on him. "What the *hell*?"

"I'd never have hurt you." He strode to her, too fucking relaxed for her liking.

"You don't have full control yet," she hissed. She let the anger flow, relieved to welcome it. "Just because I want some space doesn't mean you should give me third-degree burns."

"I'd never hurt you," he repeated, insistent.

"Well, that's not true, is it?"

He visibly drew back.

She swallowed the urge to apologize and turned on her heel. "Just leave me alone."

He didn't. "What happened in town?"

"Nothing."

"You're lying." He kept pace with her, refusing to budge even when she shot him a deadly look. "Something's upset you."

"No."

"I want to help."

"And I want you to leave me alone."

"Do you?"

"Yes."

"*Do you?*"

"Yes!" she shouted, turning on him so fast, his back bumped the wall. "That's what your dad wants, right? Do what you did before and leave. Stop pretending you're going to choose differently. Stop acting like this."

His jaw firmed. "Like what?"

"Like you were before...*before.* Like..." Her chest was heaving and she realized with horror that the burning in her throat had moved to the backs of her eyes. "Like you...like you..."

"Like I care?" he challenged. He stepped off the wall, into her. His hands came up to cup her shoulders. She shoved them off. "I do."

"No."

"Stop being a brat."

"I can't do this. Not now."

His voice thundered down the hall as she took off. "Celestia, don't walk away from me."

Her laugh cracked through the air, broken as she felt. "Might as well do it first."

He cursed. "You know, I used to think you were hard to read but this, what you're doing, it's textbook Tia. You're feeling vulnerable, so you lash out."

Panic surged up her throat. "What, you're some kind of shrink now?" she mocked, trying to hide the hitch in her breath. "You don't know jack about me."

"I know more than you think."

"Says the amnesiac," she returned, hating herself.

"Why can't you talk to me? What do you think's going to happen?"

It was a question she didn't want to answer. So she marched instead. He followed, catching up to walk beside her.

They went to their room in the kind of silence that weighed

down every step. Worse was the look in his eyes—like she'd hurt him. Before, that would've made her happy.

Now it just made her feel like peeling off her own skin.

Her entire focus was getting into the bathroom, into the shower, turning on the jets and washing everything away.

She was halfway to the bathroom when he said softly, stubbornly, "I'm not going anywhere."

She braced a hand on the doorjamb, staring blindly forward. The words stamped on her skin, sank beneath it. Words, she told herself. Just words.

"I can't," she heard herself say, those words falling almost desperately into the air. She didn't look back.

His steps sounded over the carpet until she knew he stood behind her. "I could ask a question."

She shook her head, mute.

His hands braced on the jamb above her, so close she felt his heat through the thin material of her dress. "At least tell me you're okay. I need to know you're okay."

It broke her. Resistance crumbling, she angled her head up. He watched her, concern etched into his brow. Concern even after she'd been such a bitch.

He hadn't walked away.

Hope glimmered before she immediately shut it down. Like a small fire, too dangerous not to snuff right out.

Still, she couldn't bring herself to walk away again. "Distract me."

"From what?"

She stayed silent.

"Tia..."

"Please." Her voice sounded foreign to her. "I... Not now."

He stared down, lifting one hand from the jamb to cup her cheek. "Later." It was more demand than question.

She couldn't promise that. Because as stupid as it was, as reckless and as idiotic and as fucking foolish as it was, part of her couldn't snuff the flame all the way out.

"Just distract me," she whispered. Begged.

Now his other hand cradled her cheek and he lowered his head so his breath brushed her lips. "One day," he murmured, "you'll let me in. And I won't fuck it up this time."

Before she could think of a response, he kissed her.

thirty

Tia gripped onto Henry like he was a life preserver, sinking her hands into his shirt and holding tight as his lips moved over hers. It was lazy, intense, tasting instead of devouring.

She tugged harder, trying to dial up the speed.

"Not this time," he said against her lips. "This time we do things my way."

She opened her eyes and glared. "No."

"You wanted a distraction." He dipped his head, laid his mouth on her skipping pulse. His tongue flicked out and she gasped. "You didn't say what kind."

"Well, I want fast."

"Sorry, negotiation window closed thirty seconds ago." He kissed up her neck, pausing at the spot behind her ear that made her shivery. He released the doorjamb and clasped her hips, backing up to the bed before spinning her to face it. "Take off your dress," he whispered in her ear, sending more shivers across her skin.

Fine. No man could go slow once a woman was naked. Sending a hot look over her shoulder, she crossed her arms at her hem and slowly pulled the dress over her head. Her heart pounded at the way his gaze blurred, his hands tracing bare skin as he brought her back against him.

His body was hard and hot, achingly familiar, and she battled back the feelings that tried to overwhelm her. Instead, she moved her body in a teasing figure eight, brushing deliberately against every sensitive part until she heard his breathing go uneven.

"Get on the bed," was his next order.

"But I'm happy here." She yelped as his teeth closed gently over her shoulder.

"You don't get to be in charge this time, Celestia," he murmured against her skin. "Get on the fucking bed."

Her legs trembled at the silken order. Maybe it was weak, maybe it was wrong, but she slowly did as she was told, crawling onto the mattress before twisting around.

His face was tight with desire, pupils blown as he watched her.

"Good girl," he rasped. "Open for me."

She waited a few seconds until he sent her a warning look.

His hands clenched at his sides as she let her legs fall open, her panties already damp.

"Fuck," he swore. "You're so beautiful."

His praise sank into her and she tried to ignore the warmth that filled the emptiness. "Are you going to join me?" she prompted.

His chuckle surprised her. He stuffed his hands into his pockets and leaned against one of the bedposts. "You can't help yourself, can you?" He trailed his eyes over her, the only sign of his arousal his flushed face and the bulge no jeans could hide. "I see you, Tia."

"What the fuck does that mean?"

He moved faster than she'd anticipated, circling her ankle with a hand and jerking her effortlessly to the edge of the mattress so her legs were dangling. The careless show of strength sent an explosion of butterflies into her belly.

He leaned down, bracing himself on one hand. With the other, he tapped her nose, smiling darkly at her resulting frown. "It means you're going to have to get used to compliments, baby. Because I plan on worshipping you for a while."

"Big words," she scoffed, hiding how they'd made her toes curl. "Always words."

A small pinch between his eyebrows was his only reaction. "I want you to agree to three things."

"Tell me what they are and—"

"Scratch that," he spoke over her. "You're *going* to agree to three things."

Her eyebrows winged up. "I am?"

He trailed his free hand down her neck, her collarbone, to the curve of her breast. He never took his eyes off hers and she fought not to react. It was impossible when he pinched her nipple through the lace, her back bowing in a physical gasp.

"One," he said with a dark laugh, "you will do everything I say." He rubbed her nipple between his fingers, watching as she tried to argue through the haze of pleasure. "Two, you won't try and rush me."

She bit her lip as he left her nipple to trace a path down her stomach. He toyed with the hem of her panties.

"And three?" she questioned breathlessly.

"Three." He dipped under the hem, eyes intent on every ripple and shudder as he toyed with her clit. "You're going to love every fucking moment of how I make you come apart."

She could barely breathe, gripping his forearm as he expertly worked her until her body was thrumming.

"I'm waiting," he challenged as one strangled moan left her lips.

"Henry."

"Give me the words."

She hated him. And she loved it. "Fine, you bastard. *Yes.*"

He left her then to her cry of outrage, only to work her panties off her legs, lowering in front of her.

"Look at me," he murmured, smoothing his hands up her thighs as she watched. As she trembled. "I'm on my knees for you, Tia."

She shuddered. Her hand twisted in the covers and magic rippled out to play with the rug, both results of his head lowering to her center.

He started teasing, tasting, annoying the hell out of her as she shifted, trying to get him to move faster. He stopped, lips shiny when he peered up. He pinched her inner thigh gently. "Rule two."

"Fuck," she spat and flopped onto the mattress.

"Good," he praised, before settling back between her thighs.

He was rougher this time in reward, sinking his tongue deeper and squeezing her clit, just as she liked. The pressure built, twisting so tightly it hurt, sweat pooling at the base of her spine. Her feet moved restlessly on the carpet, her hands tightened and twisted in the covers, but it wasn't until he lightly closed his teeth on her clit and shoved two fingers into her channel that she bucked against his mouth and came.

He snarled and crooked his fingers, both of them heating against her inner muscles. She shuddered as her pleasure fired with them, lost to the glittering, spinning dark.

When she went limp, he slowly removed his fingers and circled her swollen clit. When he tapped it, electricity launched up her spine.

"I don't think I could ever forget your taste," he rasped. Before she could point out he had, he brought his fingers to his mouth and sucked them clean.

The sight made her clench on nothing.

He rose to his feet. His erection must have been painful by now, the bulge almost obscene.

A little sweaty, Tia went up on her elbows as she looked at it. "Regretting your game yet?"

"Nope."

"You sure?" she crooned. Sitting up, she cupped him, pleased when he quivered, when he gripped her wrist. She looked up through her lashes. "My mouth would make you feel so good, Henry."

"I know," he agreed, pressing her hand harder against him. His shoulders trembled before he peeled her away. "You'd like that, wouldn't you? But I told you, you can't rush me."

"Maybe I *would* like it," she said, ignoring the last bit. "Maybe I'd love it."

"Maybe I'll let you. Later. When you beg."

She rolled her eyes, amused and aroused at the same time. "I don't beg."

He leaned down and took her mouth. She tasted herself on his tongue, an erotic intimacy. When he lifted away, her pulse was pounding. "Sounds like a challenge to me."

Oh. Fuck. The words echoed through her entire body as he pressed her back with one hand between her breasts.

Time spun out in a haze of deep kisses and hot touches. Literally burning, his fingers trailing what felt like flames over sensitive skin, followed by his equally hot mouth. He left no part of her untouched, like he was making a new memory for every one he'd lost. And he whispered praise as he went, not letting her fully escape into the void.

"So gorgeous," he groaned against her breast. "So responsive."

And she was. She had no idea how exciting this would be, giving up control to him just this once, but her body trembled and bucked under every new exploration.

It didn't take long until his chest was heaving, breaths rough and raw as he sank three fingers into her. She was so wet, he slid in easily and they both groaned. He teased her clit as he worked her roughly, pressing a soft kiss to her belly as it quivered on the verge of orgasm.

And he paused.

Her eyes flew open. "Don't *stop*."

His face was drawn tight, eyes glittering, sweat dampening the hair at his temples. "You can take it."

"Fuck you."

"Soon. When you beg."

"Fuck." It was all she had to say as she sent her own hand down.

He caught her wrist. "Ah ah ah. Only my fingers will get you off tonight. Only me."

"Bastard." She squirmed, aching for friction. "I need to come."

"Soon."

"I'll make *you* come if you let me."

His throat bobbed and he blew out a breath. "Nice try."

Her magic coiled, thrashing. She let out a strangled shriek and felt her heart thudding against her ribs as he stroked her wrist. Only when her breathing calmed, did he start again.

And again.

And again.

By the fourth time, she needed to come so bad, her nipples were on fire and her center was knotted tight. "Henry," she gasped as she quivered everywhere. "Fucking hell, I need…"

"Ask me," he ground out, sounding an inch from losing it. His fingers worked her faster, harder, and she let out a groan of pleasure. "Beg me."

Still, she hesitated.

His eyes flashed to hers, the pale green intense against the blow of black pupil. "*Trust me.*"

She couldn't think, not when his fingers were inside her and thrusting, his thumb squeezing her clit, his eyes, *Henry's eyes*, watching her.

Her heart trembled at the emotion she thought she saw.

She curled her fingers into her palms, nails biting deep as she took the chance. "*Please.*"

The noise he made was part relief, part something she couldn't describe. He removed his hand and she made a sound of protest, cut off when he practically ripped his jeans open and shoved them off with his boxers. His cock sprang out and he picked up a condom he'd retrieved who knew when, palming it and rolling it on.

He covered her to claim her mouth, one hard, deep kiss, before he spun them both so she was on top.

"Take me," he commanded, hands grasping her hips.

She thought he might have done it as a concession, a way to make her feel more in control after all, but she didn't focus on that. Instead, she maneuvered backward, lifting up onto her knees and positioning herself above him. She didn't want gentle. Didn't want slow.

But he did.

So fighting the urge to slam down, she took her time, sinking onto his cock, feeling every inch of him stretching her. She was gasping by the time he bottomed out, hands flat on his tight abdomen, which rippled as he battled to control his breathing.

Like this, he felt bigger, more swollen, or maybe she was. Whatever, it felt un-*fucking*-believable.

She let her head tip back as she rode a slow rhythm, heart bashing around her ribs. Pleasure screamed inside her veins like the rush of her own blood.

"Fucking hell," he gritted out. His hands dug bruises into her hips. "You're going to kill me."

"You're the one—" she shuddered, biting her lip as he hit a spot inside her that made the curtains shake "—who said to go slow."

"I'm a fucking idiot." He pinned her with a feral stare. "Move. Faster. Now."

"Wouldn't want…to not follow the…rules of play."

"*Fuck.*"

Before she registered what was happening, he'd sat up, using his abs in a distracting way. He gripped her nape and hauled her in for a kiss, ending with a harsh nip. "Fine," he snapped. "On your knees, then."

Either she moved or he moved her, but suddenly he was slamming into her from behind. She cried out; maybe she screamed as she went to her elbows. He didn't let up, only pounded into her again and again. She sank her nails into the covers, had to push her face into them before she let the entire Hall know what they were doing, since they hadn't reactivated the soundproofing spell.

Her orgasm powered down on her, denied too long, and the sheets barely contained her noises as her inner muscles clamped onto him. She came on a black wave of pleasure and magic that swept out in a chorus of thumps and broken glass.

He grunted his satisfaction, one strong forearm wrapping around her to keep her upright as he continued to thrust, again and again, until finally he came, too.

They were both sticky, sweaty, when he padded to the bathroom. When he came back, she still lay facedown, boneless.

She felt too good to move.

"Tia?"

She made a noise of acknowledgment.

"You can go down on me now."

"Fuck off," she slurred.

His chuckle was warm and she startled when his hand slipped into hers. Her heart, just back in its normal rhythm, kicked. But she didn't pull away.

Instead, her fingers curled around his.

thirty-one

There'd been some knowing looks at the dinner table that night. Tia had clearly been embarrassed but Henry felt like strutting like a warlock asshole and giving everyone a high five. She'd trusted him to please her, to be in control. And the result had been in-fucking-credible. Even with the burnt curtains.

But with the haze of sex dissipating like morning mist, his mind kept returning to the why behind it all. Tia had been distraught when she'd come back from town, enough that she'd settled into her default mode and attacked. He'd made her a promise, so he wouldn't ask why, but the idea of her hurting made him furious enough to burn down Siddeley's woods.

And then there was the other thing.

Leave. That's what your dad wants, right? Do what you did before and leave. Stop pretending you're going to choose differently.

He'd lain next to her after she'd fallen asleep, the words turning over in his head, an itch he couldn't satisfy. He needed to know what she'd meant. He needed to know what choice he'd made.

Dinner was the usual, Lady Mildred insulting Chrichton and Sawyer, the former miserable and the latter cracking wise. Siddeley shifting in sheer embarrassment. Mina and Annaliese discussing dresses for the Snowflake thing. He'd played his role, affectionate and charming, all the while buzzing with impatience to get Tia alone.

His chance came after dinner, when he volunteered them to walk Rudy. Now snow churned up in the Old English sheepdog's wake as he bounded ahead, Henry and Tia following across Snowman field.

"This afternoon," he said into the quiet, as they reached the halfway point. He felt her tense, her steps stutter. He didn't stop, figuring she'd be more comfortable if they kept walking. "What you said about my dad. About me. Making a choice." A small indrawn breath from her and suddenly his heart was racing. "What did you mean?"

"Henry..."

"Please." The same word she'd used. The same desperation. "I feel like I'm going crazy. I've got to know."

The sky was a sweep of indigo pockmarked by stars. One blinked at him as he stared up, hands tight in his coat pockets. "Why did we break up?"

Instead of answering, she twisted to the right, heading toward the snowman corpses. Rudy barreled into one with a delighted woof, scattering chunks of snow. She watched it rain down, tugging her bottom lip with her teeth.

He didn't dare say anything as he waited.

"Your dad's never liked me," she finally said, softer than the breath that plumed white before disappearing. "He's always had someone else in mind for you. More...I don't know...biddable."

"Biddable?"

Her smile was sad. "You might've noticed I'm not a typical Higher society witch." Pain flashed over her face before she cleared her throat. "He wanted you to focus on the company, on him. I divided your attention. Demanded it, really."

He knew this. Memories of him and her going around and around on it, never agreeing.

"You didn't care. Not at first, but slowly it got to you. You started to change. Just a little, bits and pieces, but you started to put his opinions first. Started to put the work first."

Something dark moved through his chest. "So, I worked more. How does that lead to a breakup?"

She hunched her shoulders, refusing to look at him. "It wasn't about work. It was about him. Your need to prove something—and that meant choosing him over me."

"No."

"You don't even remember that night."

"*What* night?"

Her jaw worked. "The night in the gardens when you finally chose him over me."

He remembered enough. She was the most important person in his life. How could she even think that he'd—

The memory reared up and swallowed him.

She faced him in his parents' gardens, all storm-fried fury and determination.

"You have to help," she demanded, jabbing a finger at him. "We need you to help, Henry."

Night fell around them like a warm cloak, perfumed with his mom's roses. He held back a sigh, irritated that she'd dragged him out for this. He loved how passionate Tia was but it also made her way too dramatic. She was twenty-one now; she needed to grow up.

"Emma'll be fine," he said with all the patience he could. "It's just gossip."

Her eyes flashed. "You know what gossip can do."

"It's just words." He checked his watch and winced. His dad had said he'd be back from the office at seven and it was five to. He'd expect to see the reports he'd entrusted Henry with. He couldn't let him down, not when he was finally being treated like a partner. He glanced up to see Tia glaring at him. An answering emotion sizzled into life. "What now?"

"I'm sorry," she said sweetly, too sweetly, and he felt his temples begin to pound. "Am I distracting you? Is my life not important enough?"

"Of course it is," he said between his teeth. "But you're exaggerating everything. Yeah, it sucks Bastian left but he'll probably be back in a couple weeks. Maybe he needed some space."

She drew back, looking like he'd punched her. "Like you do, you mean?"

For fuck's sake. He hardened his jaw. "Tia, I don't have time for this. My dad—"

"Of course, the great Dick has to come first. What was I thinking?"

His temper simmered and he dropped the patience. "C'mon, Tia. You know how hard he's been riding me."

"Then tell him to shove it."

"I don't want to."

She laughed, the sound bitter. "Right. It's only me you're happy to disappoint."

He dragged his hands down his face, much too stressed for this. "I don't know what you want from me."

Something sparked in her face and she stepped forward, reaching for his hand. "I want you to stand up for Emma at the next party, and all the parties after. Tell the haters to shut the fuck up. Then you can work for two weeks straight, I won't say a word about it, but please. Be there for her, me, for once."

He had no idea what she was talking about. "I've always been there for you."

She gave him a look that called him a liar. "When was the last date we went on where you weren't late or didn't have your head buried in a data crystal? Hell, when was our last date?"

"It's a difficult time," he deflected, irritated as he tried to remember when he'd last arranged something for her. More irritated that she had a point. "Why can't you think of me for a change?"

It was old ground and they kept wearing the same paths through it. He didn't get why. A year ago, they'd been happy. Now all they seemed to do was hurt each other. He hated it and he was so fucking tired of it. But he could never let her go. She was it for him.

"Look," he said, because of that simple truth, reaching for her hand. He stared at features he'd grown up loving, softening. "I know I've

been busy working on this project for my dad. But I can't cause any scandal right now."

Her face hardened and she pulled at her hands.

He held on. "Give me a little more time and then I swear I'll back you and Emma up. I'll be there for you."

"You keep saying that." She bit her lip, looking away. When she turned back, his heart kicked at the sight of tears. "Please, Henry. Please. Do this for me."

It fucking killed him to see her cry. He wanted to gather her close, promise the world to her. But...his dad, the project. He was so close.

He knuckled a tear away. "Just give me a little more time," he repeated. Frustration bloomed in his chest as she knocked him away, something darker, more painful, in her eyes. Something like panic stirred, an urge to take back his words, but he refused. She had to be reasonable. His reassurances fell on deaf ears as she shook her head and stalked off into the night...

Henry opened his eyes, blinking. His chest was cracked open, heart sore. She'd never come back. She'd walked away and left him, them, in the dust.

His breathing was labored as she looked back at him in a field of white snow. No idea his memories had all locked back into place.

He cleared his throat. "You're saying," he managed, drinking her in with the dizzying perspective of eight years longing for her, confused and angry and bitter. "You're saying my dad broke us up?"

How did a person look the same and yet completely different? He cataloged everything, the slight wrinkle of her nose, the flattening of her lips. Lips he'd kissed again like he'd yearned to every night, even when he'd tried the first few years to forget about her with other witches. Nothing had worked; it had only made him feel hollow, and he'd stopped trying.

Remembering their breakup, the years after, didn't change much, but it sharpened his view. Before, he'd wanted her, felt the ache, the joy of those simple early memories. Now, living so long without her, he burned to touch her. Hold her. And never let her go.

He watched as she struggled for words. "Do you know what it's like to be the other person in a relationship? Because that's what it felt like. Dates got canceled, calls ended, I got left alone at parties because there were more important people you needed to speak to." He opened his mouth and she interrupted, somewhat pointed. "You canceled on me my last birthday before we ended. For a business trip. And no, you didn't portal back with another pointless glass rose."

He froze. He…had. He'd reasoned it away with his work being important, that she should understand. Her words from the other day lingered. *I stopped being the one you wanted to show up for.*

He'd made her feel that. Just like her parents.

Sickness congested in his throat.

"It came to a head when I begged you to help me with something that was important to me. You kept saying you would but work took priority. Again and again. And again. Finally, I got it."

He blinked, almost scared to ask. "Got what?"

She held herself very still. "I wasn't important enough."

Only Rudy made any sound for the next thirty seconds.

Henry ducked his head, staring at his boots. The snow was melting around him, revealing the hint of grass. "Did you ever talk to me about this back then?"

"What does that matter?"

Fire flashed in his veins, pushing against his skin, and the snow steamed. "Just answer," he said tightly.

"Yeah, I did."

She was lying. If she'd tried, he'd have listened. He would have. His teeth ground together. "Really? Or did you start arguments and throw insults around?"

She backed up. "Uh, what the hell is that meant to mean?"

"It's just a question."

"An insulting one. Of course I tried. Not that you were bothered." She stared at him, defiant. Just like in that garden. "It's not like you came after me."

A muscle in his jaw flexed but he couldn't deny it. Call it pride, call it stubbornness. He'd tried to talk to her at a party after giving her some time to cool down and it had gone so badly, he'd realized she was closing herself off to any possibility of their getting back together. He'd figured he'd wait, let her come to him…and they'd never recovered.

He took a breath in and let it out. He had a lot to think about. He wasn't blameless—but neither was she.

He ruffled his hair, searching for words. "Thanks. For telling me."

"Sure." She folded her arms, saying sarcastically, "You asked a question. You want a kiss?"

He recognized she was baiting him, but his mama didn't raise a fool. "Sure."

Growling, she pointed at her ass. "Kiss this."

Swiveling on her inappropriate heels that made that ass look incredible, she stalked toward the house. He knew the amusement tangling with annoyance probably made him sick, but it was why they were perfect for each other.

She didn't make it a foot before he tackled her. He turned them in midair so she landed on him, both grunting as they hit snow. Rudy woofed from nearby and sprinted over to throw his body on top of Tia's. Henry lost his breath.

"Get…off…Rudy," she wheezed, pushing at his bulk. He gave her a happy lick then bounded off again.

She levered up to stare at Henry. He wrapped around her, preventing her from standing. "What. The. Hell?" she spaced out.

"I need you to do something," he said, very seriously. His ass was going numb in the snow but he could take it. What he couldn't take was not finishing this.

"You tackled me." A tickle of mania ran through her words, as if she couldn't believe it.

"Celestia."

"*What*? You need me to do what?"

He leveled her with a look. "Stop walking away."

She quit struggling.

"People fight," he said, their argument still echoing in his ears. "That doesn't matter. What matters is that they stick. If..." For a moment, he faltered, hesitant.

Her face was the same. "If?" she prompted.

"If we want another shot at this," he said carefully, making her hands slacken on his chest, "we need to do things differently. I'll listen. And you stick."

Her mouth parted. "I..." she began, seeming clueless what to say. "I don't..."

He shifted under her, letting go with one hand to press hers to his lips. "Just think about it."

She stared dumbly down at him. Wide eyes, parted lips. So fucking adorable.

With Tia, it was all about keeping her off balance so she couldn't find solid ground to shove him away. Which meant... he still had to keep his memories to himself.

This was more progress than he'd ever made. In the past, every time he'd stepped a foot over the line she'd marked, she'd shot at it. No way would she have let him kiss her, hold her, try to understand why she'd shut him out. He was so close. And when he knew they were solid again, he could tell her everything.

Brushing aside any unease at how she'd take it, he shifted his other hand down to her ass and tapped it. "Now," he said, with a wicked smile, "I'll claim that kiss you offered."

Tia yelped as he spun her into the snow. He hiked her dress up and smoothed a hand over her cheeks before proving he was a warlock as good as his word.

And when they walked up to the house an hour later, he tangled his hand in hers, idly hoping nobody commented on the giant patch of grass where the snow had mysteriously melted.

Tia offered Siddeley the falayla root, explaining how all the tiny grounds needed to stay level in the jar. "So," she said, guiding him to the glass bowl they'd set up on the dining table, "the next step is to add a pinch of this to the mixture."

Standing next to her in the room they'd commandeered for potion making, Siddeley took the jar as carefully as a newborn. He unscrewed the lid and set that aside, reaching in to grasp some of the pink sand.

Tia smiled encouragingly as he glanced at her. "Yep, straight in."

On the opposite side, she saw Henry hide his grin as Siddeley, exuberant as a kid, did as ordered. The liquid in their bowl shivered and turned pink.

Siddeley exclaimed in astonishment. "Capital, Lady Tia! What's next?"

Sunlight streamed through the French doors where Siddeley's familiar lay sprawled, barely blinking as Tia added a dash of sugar-spun agent from her own supplies. Their mixture hissed and bubbled frantically for ten seconds before calming.

She leaned back, gesturing. "Now we stir three times clockwise, and once counterclockwise with a brass spoon."

Henry handed over the correct spoon from the other side of the table. "The brass is important because it adds positivity to the mix."

"Fascinating." Siddeley's brow furrowed as he concentrated on his task. "Would you use different spoons for different mixes?"

"Depends on the potion master." Tia watched him, eagle-eyed to intervene if he went over his strokes. "Some religiously stick to the precious metals, while others imbue a spoon with their magic and think that's enough. Every master has their secrets." She grinned.

He completed his four circles and withdrew the spoon. "And now?"

"Now we wait for thirty-six minutes." Tia tapped a crystal on the side of the pot and placed it on the table. "When the quartz turns pink, it's ready."

Siddeley hummed in his throat, eyes bright. "It's rather fun, isn't it?"

"Best part of the job," Tia agreed, reaching around for her bottle of water. Uncapping it, she swallowed half, peeking over at Henry. He winked and she felt herself flush like a moron.

It was early afternoon, only a few days before the Snowflake Ball and the official end of their time at Silkwood Hall. Rather than stewing over that, she'd suggested to Henry a final power play to get Siddeley on their side. It was Tia who'd come up with Potion Making 101, while Henry had posed the idea of brewing something to add to the champagne, should guests want it. Siddeley had leaped at the chance and if his grin was anything to go by, their afternoon had been a success.

They were luring him in one pinch and one stir at a time. Not that the investment seemed as all consuming as it had almost a month ago.

This doesn't really change anything. You are who you are.

I'll listen. You stick.

"Do you think your guests will try it?" the warlock who'd strongly indicated he wanted a second chance asked. Still reeling from that, Tia awkwardly offered him the bottle of water and he passed with a shake of his head, giving her a quick smile in thanks. It made her heart flutter. She should really smack herself for being such a girl.

Siddeley's cheeks creased. "I jolly well do. Who doesn't love a good cheer around Christmas?" Thankfully, he didn't pause for an answer. "I thought you heated potions," he added, studying the glass bowl.

Tia set the bottle down. "Some. Depends on the result you're trying to get. This is a pretty beginner potion."

"Didn't trust me with an expert level, eh?" He boomed a laugh as her face froze. "I'm pulling your leg, Lady Tia. *I* wouldn't trust me with an expert-level potion. I could blow us all sky-high."

"Potions can have serious consequences," she confirmed wryly, flicking her eyes in Henry's direction. He wiggled his eyebrows. "But," she continued, burying her laugh, "in the right hands, it's very safe."

"You have to wonder why people buy potions ready-made when they can brew something in their own kitchen."

Tia's ears perked up, recognizing the shift in his mindset. "Well," she said, keeping her body relaxed, "there's the convenience. People buy store-bought cakes and cookies all the time, even though they could make their own."

Siddeley nodded thoughtfully. "That's true."

"And some people are too scared to mess around with certain ingredients," Henry put in. "So you get assured safety as well. Of course, more time and ingredients and magic spent on a potion equals a higher price tag, so you have to market accordingly."

Tia picked up the thread, sliding into a rhythm with him that was as natural as breathing. "A teenage witch isn't going to drop hundreds of dollars on a Time-Turner potion, for example—it softens wrinkles for twenty-four hours," she explained at Siddeley's blank look.

"And some are marketed as fun extras for bachelor or bachelorette parties, corporate retreats, even teenage sleepovers." Henry shrugged. "The possibilities are endless, from business to personal."

"Indeed, it seems so." Siddeley studied their potion before looking between them. "May I say, it's delightful to see people passionate about their jobs. Not enough of that going around."

"Yes, we're very passionate," Henry said with a straight face.

"We are," Tia returned with a warning jab of telekinesis

that made his eyes warm with laughter. "I don't believe in half measures in anything. Neither of us does."

"I see that." Siddeley leaned his weight on the table, mirroring them. "It's sometimes hard to find that honest enjoyment in business these days—people have the drive but they lack soul. Words are just words at the end of the day."

"Actions speak louder." She didn't dare look at Henry but felt his gaze on the side of her face.

"Precisely," Siddeley agreed. "Take the pair of you for instance. When you first arrived, you were both very rigid, so keen on hooking the big fish." He winked broadly and she cracked a weak smile. "Now look at you both, relaxed, smiling, passionate again instead of desperate."

She winced.

"I do beg your pardon," Siddeley rushed to add, holding his hands up. "I wasn't trying to be insulting. It's just that being too invested in business at your age can be such a bad idea."

Tia blinked slowly. Okay, that was…not what she'd expected a potential investor to say.

Siddeley bent to pick up the chubby white cat as it prowled over and wrapped around his legs. Her purr rumbled in the room as he stroked a hand down her back. "Passion is wonderful but work will always be there. Now is the time to devote yourselves to each other. Trust me." His hand faltered. "You don't want to wake up one day and find you have nobody but employees around you."

A knot formed in Tia's chest, tied double tight.

You listen. I'll stick.

But would he? Would he still mean it when he remembered their past? Would he even want to try? Wanting someone was different from wanting to put in the effort to make it work. He'd already decided she wasn't worth it once. She wasn't sure her heart would survive a second shattering.

And she didn't know why she was even thinking about this

when she wasn't sure what she wanted. It was too much, too soon. And yet, it felt like it had taken them years to get here.

After a long—too long—pause, Henry said, "We're happy in the work."

"I'm sure, but a little Christmas magic and time off certainly seems to have done you a world of good." Siddeley shook his head before they could say anything else, chuckling. "Forgive me. I'm coming off as a patronizing fool. It's the season. Always gets me reflective."

While Siddeley easily shifted topics to the upcoming ball, Tia gathered her courage and slowly lifted her gaze. Green eyes locked on her, intense. Sorrowful. Determined. Her stomach dropped to her feet.

But for once, she didn't throw up her barriers. She didn't smirk or make a face or look away. And when he smiled, her heart pulsed wildly. From fear, yes—but also with a little bit of hope.

thirty-two

Tia paced the length of the bedroom to the bathroom door and back, staring at the cell on the dresser.

After the fifth pass, she muttered a curse and snatched it up, pulling up her contacts.

When Emma answered, Tia said, "I'm in trouble."

"Okay." The background noise faded. A door shut on her side. "Where do I portal and do I need to bring a shovel?"

A half laugh, half groan came out of Tia's mouth. "I'm serious."

"So am I. Though if we're really talking body, I feel like Bastian might be good—telekinetic skills and all. Plus, he'll know the best place to hide a corpse with all the digs he's done."

"There isn't a body." Nervous energy rolled through her. "Is Leah there?"

"No, she's at Gabriel's."

"Is there—could you portal to her?"

"Okay, now I'm actually worried. What did you do?"

"Be a complete ass, that's what."

"Because I'm genuinely concerned you've got a loaded wand at your head or something, I'm gonna portal to her. Hang on."

Emma paused and the line fizzed with static for a few seconds as magic interfered with the signal.

Then Tia heard an annoyed British voice demand, "Don't you knock?"

Followed by Leah's worried, "Emma? What's wrong?"

"Tia needs us."

"Bye, babe."

"May I be of assistance?"

Emma came back on the cell. "You need Goodnight?"

"*No*," Tia said emphatically.

"We're good, thanks. Leah, move your butt."

"I'm coming, I'm coming."

Another bark of static. "Okay, T, you've got both of us. What's wrong?"

Tia sank her magic into the curtains, watching them twitch open and closed. *So much*, she wanted to say but couldn't. "I'm in trouble," she repeated.

"Animal, vegetable or mineral?" Leah demanded.

"What would a vegetable disaster even look like?" Emma asked.

"I'm sure people have been impaled on carrots before."

"Pretty sure that's in your head."

"Let's Google it. After," Leah added belatedly. "Tia, use your code phrase if you've been kidnapped."

"I haven't been kidnapped," she said, lost between despair and humor. "I'm... It's Henry."

She could just imagine the shared expressions on the other end of the phone. She pressed a hand to her head, rubbing at the tension there. "He's... I'm..." She trailed off, heart thudding harder at the thoughts that came into her head.

For once, her friends didn't tease.

"You've fallen for him again," Emma said softly.

Tia gritted her teeth. "Asshole," she muttered.

"Me?"

"Him. And myself." Tia thought about it. "Mostly him."

She thought it might have been Leah who chuckled. It was definitely her voice. "I'm sure you'll get used to it."

"I don't want to." Tia plopped onto the bed, running her bare toes along the carpet. "I don't even know how he feels." Not with his memories.

"Yes, you do." Emma's voice was pointed, though she didn't know the whole situation. "You're both as hardheaded as quartz, but you know he's never gotten over you."

"Multiple orgasms give that kind of thing away," Leah added.

"That's just sex."

Another beat. "She's serious," Leah said, sounding awed.

Tia covered her face with her hand and flopped backward onto the mattress. She stared up at the ceiling, listening to the curtains swish. "I don't know what I want."

"Yes, you do. You want him. You've always wanted him."

She did. Had. She'd hated that fact, despised it, tried to burn it, lock it out, tear it up by its roots, but no use. He'd carved his name into her heart all those years ago when she'd dropped a cat from a tree and looked down into annoyed green eyes.

"I can't let him hurt me again," she whispered, real fear twisting her insides at the idea.

"Tia." Leah's sympathy bled down the phone like a hug. "He's going to."

That stopped her cold. "What?"

"Yeah, I second that," Emma echoed in a what-the-fuck voice.

Leah huffed. "I'm not saying in the way you think, but you can't protect yourself forever. Once you let someone in, they always have the power to hurt you. You just have to decide if he's worth that risk."

How did anyone know if someone was worth it? Especially when Henry had already weighed that decision once before. The Henry that might come back when Lionel finally mastered the antidote.

It was so fucking complicated.

"I don't know what to do," she admitted, low and pained.

Her friends paused.

Tia curled her fingers around the cell so tightly they hurt.

Emma cleared her throat. "You've been running a long time, T. Maybe...maybe it's time to trust him to catch you."

It was the night of the Snowflake Ball before she knew it. Time had proven to be a bitch again and raced past, the seconds and minutes like a blurred watercolor.

She'd painted baubles, fed a reindeer (real name Blitzen), taught a few more potions to Siddeley, suffered through a lineage lecture from Mildred when she hadn't moved quick enough at breakfast, gone Christmas shopping with Annaliese and Mina and mocked Damon mercilessly until he'd threatened to put her in an oven. And in amongst those moments of tinsel and twilight was Henry, grinning with her over a renewed attempt at a snowman (failure), walking Rudy with her in the snow and rescuing him when he went into the pond, looming over her in the hall, warning her to be quiet as his fingers wandered, kissing her under mistletoe that suddenly hung all over the house...

And now this was it. The final event before everyone headed home. Siddeley hadn't made any announcement; she didn't even know if he would. Her parents weren't happy about that—not that her mom had been able to lecture her, considering everything. She doubted Richard was happy, either, but Henry didn't say anything and she really didn't want to bring up his dad again.

She'd like to say that was what she was obsessing over as she readied herself in the bathroom. But it was pure crap.

The last night. *Their* last night.

It actually caused a pang, an ache that cracked her heart in two.

Only if you're too chicken shit to ask for what you want, her inner badass retorted.

Unfortunately, her inner *lameass* was running the show and one second away from whimpering in the shower.

At least she was a damn fine-looking lameass. She turned this way and that, examining her reflection critically.

The dress was long and followed her curves, as was her style. Because of Mildred, she'd gone for a demure collarbone neckline with tiny spaghetti straps, but the back was a different story, with the entirety cut out and scooped so low she'd had to leave her panties in the drawer.

And it was red. Bright, bold, brilliantly red.

She'd gone for diamonds, at her ears and in her hair, a clip that appeared to be the only thing keeping her hair up (such a lie when about sixteen thousand pins and a bit of telekinesis were involved). Her shoes were the highest she'd worn all trip, open-toed silver to show off toenails painted to match the dress.

The woman in the mirror looked ready to slay. Until she saw her eyes.

"Tia?"

Henry's voice made her pulse trip. She tapped her fingers on the vanity, then smoothed her hands down her thighs.

"Yeah?" she called back.

"You almost ready?"

Was she?

The answer lost in a tornado of nerves, Tia walked to the door and opened it.

Henry was facing the mirror, head tilted as he slid in a cuff link, muttering something as he fought the clasp. A white-blond lock fell over his forehead, drawing her eyes down.

Because of the breakup, she'd never allowed herself to stare during the many parties they'd both been forced to attend. Now she drank him in, and damn if he hadn't been made for a tuxedo, the crisp angles of the bow tie, the snappy lines of the suspenders overlaid on a white shirt. He'd done something to his hair that made him look sleek and sophisticated, minus the rebellious lock. She liked it.

"I think he wanted us there by eight," he said when she didn't speak.

"Sure," she answered, relieved her voice didn't wobble. "Ready whenever you are."

"I figure we get some drinks first, then do the rounds. Maybe—" He glanced up and stopped dead. His gaze dipped, slowly returned. His lips tipped up. "You're wearing my color."

She wasn't sure why that sentence made her heart turn over. So she scoffed, folding her arms. "Please. I happen to like red. That's all."

"Uh-huh." He finished with his cuff link, keeping his gaze on her. Then he moved, gliding across the carpet to meet her. He skimmed two fingers down her bare arm until he took her hand in his and brought it to his lips. When he kissed her palm, she felt weak in the knees.

Then he said, "You're beautiful, Tia."

No teasing. No heat. No smoke screens.

She trembled.

"You're already guaranteed to get lucky." She tried to mask it, even though she didn't pull away. "No need to dust off the compliments."

He shook his head, nothing but sincere. "You're always beautiful to me."

She couldn't think of a word to say. Literally. All she could do was stare at him.

As if sensing she was at a loss, he flashed her a smile and tapped her gently on the nose. "One day you won't feel so awkward when I tell you that."

One day. Energy exploded in her veins, and her mouth parted on a breath.

He moved away to pick up something from the dresser but she was rooted to the floor. Fear twisted inside her, wringing itself out until it hurt. But hope, that bitch, fluttered in her chest.

"It's our last night," she blurted out.

The muscles in his back tightened. When he faced her, his expression was a study of neutral. "That's what you want?"

"It's what it is."

"Only if you want it to be."

"Do you?" she challenged. Sweat dampened every pulse point.

He slid one hand into his pocket, casual while she was ten seconds from a nervous breakdown. "I think I've made it clear what I want." When she opened her mouth to contradict that, he simply stated, "You."

Breath burst from her lungs in a wheeze. She blindly reached for the bedpost, relieved to have something to prop her up.

"You might regret saying that when you get your memories back," she managed.

"No, I'll mean it the same."

He seemed so confident and maybe he was. Henry always had been decisive. Known what he wanted and never faltered. But…even if it was true, he couldn't be with anyone who had a scandal waiting in the closet. His dad, maybe even Maybelline for all her kindness, would have a fit.

Always obstacles between them.

A fractured laugh slipped free as she slumped. "Henry…"

"Don't tell me you don't feel the same." His stance shifted as if preparing for a fight. "I know you, Tia. You can't hide it."

"I'm not saying that." Although her hackles rose from the arrogant statement. "I'm saying there are things you don't know."

He rolled his eyes upward. "You're being ridiculous."

And that just pissed her off. "You really have a way with women," she retorted. "We love being told what we think and that we're being dramatic."

"I said *ridiculous*. Because there's nothing that could change how I feel about you."

She longed for that to be true. It surprised her how much. "Henry…"

"Fuck's sake," he exclaimed. "Then tell me these *things*. Tell me the dark, twisted secrets that will stop me from…caring about you."

She was too busy freaking out to obsess over the small pause. "You see?" She changed tack, desperate now. "This is why we could never be more than a vacation hookup. We can't have one conversation without arguing."

"That's because you frustrate the hell out of me!"

"And you're a dick!"

"And this *isn't* a vacation hookup." Real anger shone through those words. "You can try and hide all you want, but we both know this, us, never went away. It was always waiting."

Her heart beat faster.

"You need me to say it first?" Challenge gleamed in his eyes.

Actual panic pushed her into action. "I told you, there are things—"

"Then what are they? Because I thought we'd finally found some middle ground the last few weeks. What aren't you telling me?" He faltered and some of the anger drifted away, replaced by realization. "That day, the day you got back from Westhollow…"

She shook her head. "Don't."

"Something happened. Tell me."

"Henry."

He ignored her weak protest and walked right up to her. He didn't touch her; he didn't need to. Being this close to him was enough. "*Trust me*," he pleaded.

She closed her eyes. Her heart pounded so hard it felt like she shook from it. But she forced the words out. "I'm not really a Hightower. Peter Hightower isn't my dad."

The pause was excruciating. The rush of blood in her ears was overwhelming, even as she strained to hear anything. Regret. Condemnation. Him walking away from her again.

Which was why she knew it had to be a mistake when she heard him say in his deep voice: "I know."

thirty-three

Tia's eyes flew open. None of the shock or horror she'd thought she'd find in Henry's face was there. Instead, she saw ruefulness.

It made her want to punch him but that was her issue.

She drew back. "What do you mean you know?"

"Research. From when the companies joined. I was thorough."

She shook her head, dazed, focusing on the question she needed to ask. "You get what that means, right? I'm not a true Legacy."

He made an "ah" noise, rocking back on his heels. "You mean, you're beneath me."

Now she *really* wanted to punch him. "It's not funny."

He lost some of the humor. "I know." His gaze was excruciatingly tender as he watched her carefully. "How're you doing with it all?"

"Fan-fucking-tastic, thanks." She put her hand to her head, massaged her temple. "I've been lied to by people I trusted, who insisted I be the perfect Hightower, and now I have no clue who I am."

"C'mon." His eyes flickered but he nudged her chin up. "You know who you are. Who you've always been."

"Don't give me that crap. This changes things."

"No," he challenged. "Not you. We are who we are. What does finding out you have a different sperm donor change? You're still the defensive, arrogant, prickly witch you've always been."

She glared at him. "Thanks."

"And when you peel all that back," he continued, lifting her hand and nipping at the soft skin. "The kindest, most loyal, most generous woman."

She didn't like the weakening happening in her body, like a toughened clifftop crumbling away. "Henry—"

"And sexy," he added with a growl. "Especially in red."

"Your dad won't like it."

He hummed. "My woman in my color."

She shouldn't like that as much as she did. She snapped her fingers in his face. "Pay attention. We won't be allowed to be together. When you remember that you want your dad's approval, you'll be forced to choose." She lifted her chin. "And I'm not waiting around to *not* be picked. Again."

His forehead creased. "I don't— That's not..." His frown lingered as he said forcefully, "I don't care what he thinks."

"You say that now." She slipped past him, unable to stand still. "But when you—" She stopped when he let out a deep groan and spun back. "What?"

His eyes were on fire as he traced her body. "What happened to the back of your dress?"

"Focus."

"I'm trying."

When he moved forward, she moved back, heart in her throat. "I'm serious."

"So am I." He caged her against the dresser, dipping his nose to her neck and inhaling. "I don't care what made you, Celestia Hightower. I know what you are. What you've always been."

"And what's that?"

He lifted his gaze. "Mine."

She couldn't breathe, couldn't find her balance. She found herself gripping his arms for it. The fucked-up thing was, even with everything, he did that for her. Grounded her. Her safe space.

She tried to find her arguments. His memories, his dad…

But they paled when she saw the resolve in his face.

"You won't change your mind?" she whispered, naked, truly naked for the first time in front of him. And terrified.

He feathered a touch along her cheek, visibly softening. "We're inevitable, little moth. I wouldn't change it if I could."

She was scared to hope, scared to believe, but maybe…

The blood drained from her head. "What did you call me?"

He was quick to hide it but she saw when he knew he'd slipped up. Her hands slid off his arms and she braced heavily against the dresser. A hollow ache spread through her until she felt numb. "You remember."

When his lips pursed, she knew. And that quickly, rage burned through the nothingness. Ready to incinerate him.

Shit. Shit. Shit.

The word echoed around his mind, rebounding with greater force with every second that passed. He hadn't meant for it to come out this way. He'd needed this final night. One more night to lock everything down and he'd have told her everything.

Now she was pale with anger, the green-and-brown flecks in her eyes incandescent with it.

"Tia," he began, not having one fucking clue what would come next. "I can—"

"Get away from me," she hissed between her teeth. "That's the first thing you can do."

He wanted to argue. He wanted to hold her tight, sensing her slipping through his fingers like sand. But nobody could hold what didn't want to be held.

He let his arms fall and took several steps away.

She was every inch a queen in that red dress she'd worn for him, her chin tipping up as if to take a punch. "How long?"

"Can I just—"

"*How. Long*?"

He flexed his hands, feeling useless. "It started after we kissed. Gradually at first and then—then everything, the other night in the snowman field."

She nodded. As he braced, she turned to the mirror and slid a strand of hair back into place. Then she picked up her clutch from the dresser and walked to the door.

It chilled him to the bone. Tia didn't take things quietly. She raged, she stormed, she threw every speck of herself into an argument. She was passion unleashed.

Real panic galloped through him and he acted without thinking, locking the door with a band of fire. "Wait."

"We're late for Siddeley's ball," she answered evenly.

"We have to talk."

"Why?"

He swallowed. "Because… I have to explain."

"I don't want to hear it. It doesn't make any difference."

"Don't say that." Flustered, he dragged his hands through his hair. "Just…let me explain why."

"I get it. You win."

He frowned, confused.

"You wanted to get one over on me and you did. Well done. Now, we need to go."

He reared back. "I wouldn't do that to you. It's not like that."

She still refused to look at him.

"Tia, I would never hurt you."

The beautifully exposed line of her back stiffened. "I wouldn't let you hurt me."

But he knew it was a lie and so did she. She'd all but admitted it not even two minutes ago when she'd asked him not to break her heart.

Shit. He licked his dry lips. "At first, it was confusing," he told her, determined to have it out, "like the memories were resettling and I had to wait for the dust to clear. Then, I don't know, it was like getting a free pass to…figure stuff out without the pressure." Someone who didn't always have to be wands at dawn with her. Someone who didn't have to deal with all the bullshit that'd haunted them for eight years.

"Let me out."

He pushed. "We've never talked, not really, not since that night."

"Henry." The warning couldn't have been clearer, but her voice brimmed with heat. He was ridiculously, knee-weakeningly glad to hear it.

"I never knew why you'd walked away."

She rounded on him then, a flush staining her cheeks. "If you don't stop talking, I'm going to portal out."

But she hadn't yet. "I needed to know," he pressed. "I needed to know so we could fix it. So we could have a second chance."

"You don't get to say that." She stalked toward him, silky material rustling around her legs. "You don't get to pretend you weren't a lying asshole these past few weeks. You don't get to pretend you haven't been manipulating me this whole time for your own amusement."

"I have never manipulated you."

"*Why did we break up?*" she asked, affecting his voice. "*Tell me a good memory. Tell me if you've ever thought about me, dreamed of me, wanted to fuck me again.*" Her voice went shrill and magic sparked into existence, flecks of red around her hands.

He winced at the echo of his questions. "I was trying to understand."

"To humiliate me."

"*No.*" He struggled for words. "You always accused me of walking away but to me, it was you who walked. I needed to see it from your side. If we were going to have a chance—"

"We don't," she hissed, slicing a hand down. "Because the Henry I thought you've been this past month, the Henry I *thought* I knew, he's just an illusion. You've been playing me this whole time."

"Everything's been real. Everything I said, everything you felt."

"Don't flatter yourself. We were supposed to fake it and I did."

"Celestia."

The curtains ripped off the wall in a violent clatter. "*You don't get to call me that.*"

"Don't you get it?" he said, urgency tearing through him. "This is what always happens when we try to talk about it. We fight, we walk away. You never let me in."

"Why should I?" She shook her head. "You want to know why we broke up? Why I don't regret it? Because you can't be trusted."

His jaw set. "That's bullshit."

Her laugh was bitter and so sharp, it should've left him bleeding. "You've *lied* to me for weeks. What part of that screams *trust*?"

"I told you, that was so—"

"And *I* never let *you* in? When I begged you to stay that night?" Her breath came in ragged bursts. "When I made myself *weak* for you and you—*you*, Henry—walked away?"

He came forward to meet her. "You gave me a bullshit ultimatum about choosing you or my dad. You know I'd have been there for Emma. My dad just asked me to wait a week."

"Well, if Richard asked."

"Don't be a brat. It's not as simple as that." Her voice when she'd recounted her memory of it made him falter but he shored up his resolve. "The truth is you can't let yourself forgive."

Her voice went deathly quiet. "Don't you put this on me."

A rush of fear and determination and anger seared his veins, his magic reacting. He talked faster. "You're too hard on people who make mistakes. You don't accept weakness in yourself so you don't accept it in others. Well, we make mistakes, Tia. We fuck up. It doesn't mean you get to kick us out of your life."

"I'm done with this."

"I know you. I know you better than anyone. You push people away so you don't have to be vulnerable and I make you want to be. Me. You're scared of what I make you feel."

"You arrogant, condescending, conceited—"

"But when you thought I was safe, when you thought you might not have to deal long-term, you made a hole in the wall. You let me in. But now, now that I'm me and I'm asking for a real chance, you're shoving me out again. That's all you. Not me."

"How convenient I'm the bad guy." She looked stricken, lines around her eyes, her mouth. It made him sick. "That even though you're the liar, I'm the one who's messed up."

"Fuck, do you even hear yourself? Putting up the bricks so fast you can't hear me. I'm trying to *tell* you something."

"What? What are you trying to tell me?" she yelled.

"*That I love you*!" he shouted back, immediately regretting it as her face went slack with fear. It blanked out a second later and she shook her head.

It made bitterness swell in his chest. "Of course," he retorted, feeling utterly exposed. He swept a hand mockingly. "Shouldn't have said that. We don't say what we're really feeling. We just fight and pretend we don't care about each other. We don't forgive."

She smoothed a hand down her dress. He thought he saw it tremble but her face was rock steady when she turned it to him. "No," she said, heading for the door. "We don't."

thirty-four

Betrayal. It simmered in her blood, powering her tense smile as she moved through Siddeley's guests, pretending a bomb hadn't gone off in her personal life.

Again. He'd fooled her *again.* Fooled her into thinking…

Well. It didn't matter. She just had to get through this one event and then she could go home.

What home?

She ignored that whisper, just as she ignored the male specter shadowing her every step, grim-faced and making poor attempts at small talk.

They were supposed to be a couple, the next generation love affair that would clinch the investment. Except her stomach roiled every time she looked at him.

Siddeley hadn't appeared yet but Mildred was holding court from an ornate chair tucked in the corner of the decorated ballroom. The theme was in the title, the walls iced over thinly so they formed frost, while overhead, snowflakes blew in a night sky. The humans would think it an optical illusion and pretend. She got it. Simpler sometimes to bury your head in the sand.

A band played from the raised platform they'd erected on one side of the rectangular ballroom, all classical music with contemporary numbers mixed in. The guests mingled in their party dresses and tuxes, people from the town mostly, along with a few Tia would bet were English witches. The expressions of boredom gave them away.

The ballroom opened up to a balcony that stretched its width and they'd offset the chill by using a more powerful than usual heating system around the doors—Annaliese's efforts. Food was served in some of the smaller rooms that adjoined the ballroom, but Tia thought she might throw up if she even tried. Same for the champagne that circulated. Less inhibition wouldn't be good for this party. She might push Henry off the balcony. He was just lucky she'd left her hex bag supplies at home.

It was almost ten when she felt him stir. "Siddeley's coming."

When his hand cupped her elbow, she jerked it away and didn't care if anyone saw. "Don't touch me."

Out of the corner of her eye, she saw his lips press tight together but he didn't reprimand her. How could he?

Like her, Siddeley was dressed in Christmas colors, a velvet green tuxedo with a white bow tie. It shouldn't have worked, but on him, he looked…spiffy.

Which was what she told him when he got close enough.

He didn't smile or offer any compliments in return. Instead, he fiddled with his sleeve, addressing the floor at their feet. "Lady Tia, Lord Henry. Would you accompany me to the drawing room?"

Tia didn't frown but a sliver of concern worked its way into her chest as she nodded.

She didn't look back at Henry—they were *not* on the same team—but he stayed close as all three wove their way through the throng and exited out the far right door. Their steps were muffled by the runner as they passed a few partygoers, Siddeley only polite and reserved each time.

Her concern mounted as Siddeley shut the drawing room door behind them. Mildred stood in front of the lit fireplace, one hand perched on the mantel. She'd worn silver, looking every bit the ice queen as she speared a frosty look their way. "Sit."

In silence, both Tia and Henry took up positions on the low-backed antique couch. Tia clasped her hands in her lap to keep them from fidgeting.

Siddeley stopped behind an armchair opposite to them, face unusually drawn. He said nothing.

"It has come to our attention," Mildred said with no preamble, "that we have been harboring snakes in our midst these past weeks."

A chill swept through Tia like a warning. "Lady Mildred?"

The older witch ignored her. "Earlier tonight, someone came forward with information about the two of you. Ironclad information that cannot be refuted."

Tia's throat went dry as she stared, searching for something to say.

"Is it true?" Siddeley's weak question made her pulse skip. His face was cast into sorrow as she turned helplessly to him. "Were you really faking a relationship to manipulate me?"

She swallowed, the truth harsh as he laid it bare. Beside her, Henry stiffened.

"Of course, it's true," Mildred hissed, spinning from the fire toward her son. "He presented us with recordings."

"Lord Siddeley," Henry appealed, obviously ruffled. His hands curled into his palms. "If you let us explain..."

She felt like she'd hexed a puppy as Siddeley's expression fell. "I can't be in business with people who'd lie to me for weeks." His voice was low. Pained. "Who I can't trust."

The echo of her own words ripped into her. She winced.

Mildred sneered, sweeping a dismissive hand at Tia. "But what else could we expect from a lesser witch masquerading as a Legacy?"

Everything went quiet. Cold.

Henry's hands flattened with great care. "With all respect," he said neutrally, though she heard the tremor of fire beneath, "watch your words very carefully."

"I speak as I find." Diamonds quivered at Mildred's throat as she hiked her nose into the air. "Not only did you lie to my Archie, to me, about your relationship, but about who you are. I think it's disgraceful. You should be ashamed."

Each word dug into Tia like spiked thorns curling toward her rapidly beating heart. Every staggered breath caused her pain. Because she was right. They'd lied. For weeks. For profit. To someone who'd only ever been kind.

She was just as bad as Henry.

She was dimly aware that Siddeley had shifted, uncomfortably saying, "Mother;" that Henry had surged to his feet, hotly chastising Mildred for her bald words.

If anything, that spurred her on. "Forget the investment," she declared in a shrill voice. "I will personally ensure that every witch across the world knows of this lie you've been perpetuating. Soon, everyone will know who you really are, Tia Hightower—a surname you have no right to."

"She has every right to it," Henry ground out, the flames in the grate dancing higher with his anger. "I'm sorry we lied, I really am, but you don't have any right to talk to her like that."

"I can speak to liars however I choose. This is my house, my land and I'll thank you to remove yourselves from both within the next half hour or I'm calling our High Family to remove you for us."

Henry muttered something rude and held out his hand for Tia. She didn't take it, staring down at the carpet as she rose to leave. When she got to the door, she hesitated, flattening a hand on the handle. "I'm sorry," she whispered, the apology rough and raw. "I'm so—" She pressed her lips together tight and left.

Henry snapped something else she didn't hear before his hand was cupping her elbow. "Tia."

She didn't want to hear it. The investment was dead.

Worse, they *knew*. And soon the world would.

You should be ashamed.

She hated the creeping feeling of cobwebs, binding her ribs, slipping over her skin until it prickled. Her mind went over everything, weighing, measuring, trying to figure out how she'd failed, where she'd messed up.

Her foot froze in its next step as Mildred's words came back to her.

He presented us with recordings.

Anger blossomed, unfurling until she saw red.

He.

"Griffith," she swore. She didn't give Henry a second look, bolting toward the main ballroom. An arrow in search of a target.

When she spotted him in the corner with Chrichton and Annaliese, she didn't hesitate.

"Feeling smug?" she launched at him as she got close. Her fingers pulsed with magic she didn't hide. "Celebrate all you want but you're still an asshole."

Griffith, elegant in a tux, spared her a bored look. "And what're you babbling about tonight?"

"Don't even. Siddeley kicked us out, you'll be happy to hear." Conscience twanged and she added, "We shouldn't have lied to him, but you didn't have to tell him about *me*."

"Seriously, no idea what you're on about. Pearlmatter, maybe you need to keep a closer eye on your date, huh? Too much champagne can go straight to a witch's head."

She pushed into his face, ignoring Annaliese's confused expression. "How long have you been spying on us? Are you some kind of pervert, getting off on recording people having sex?"

His face flushed. "I have better things to do with my time than concern myself with you."

"Right. So I'm supposed to believe the warlock who's always in our business wasn't the one who told the Siddeleys we were faking it?"

She saw it, the flash of surprise, before his sneer returned.

It knocked her back a step. "You weren't?"

Griffith passed a disdainful glance over both her and Henry. "I don't need to sink to those tactics to win an investment. Besides, anyone with eyes could see what was fake clearly turned real."

She didn't want to hear that. "And you didn't tell him about...me?"

"What *about* you?" Exasperation colored his tone. "I haven't told anyone a fucking thing."

"I did."

Tia's lips parted. Her gaze slid slowly away from Griffith, past Annaliese...to Chrichton. Quiet Chrichton, whom nobody paid much attention to. Non-Higher witch Chrichton, who wanted the investment and whose efforts to win Mildred over had always failed.

"You?" she echoed stupidly.

He nodded, something close to apology on his face. "I knew something was going on, so I'm afraid I've been keeping tabs."

"Keeping tabs?" Henry echoed from behind her, his anger warming the air until her face felt hot. "You've been fucking spying. How did you even get recordings?"

Annaliese made a noise. Paler than she'd been a second ago, she put a hand to her belly. "You asked me about my spells." She shook her head, color circling her cheeks as she rounded on him. "Made out like you were interested."

"I was interested," he confirmed, smoothing down his lapel. "Interested to know how to break through a soundproofing spell. Not very inconspicuous of you, by the way," he threw at Henry and Tia. "It made it fairly plain you were hiding something. Admittedly, the other fact about your lineage was a surprise, if fortuitous."

Fortuitous. Like her parentage was just another nail in their investment coffin.

"You shut your fucking mouth," Henry growled, stepping forward like he'd make him.

Tia's head was throbbing. "Why now?" she asked faintly.

He shrugged. "I heard Siddeley was going to make an announcement, and after your little confession earlier, I knew it was my one shot. You've been the clear favorites for a while."

Annaliese shook her head in disgust. "That's the way you do business?"

"Whatever gets the job done, Annaliese. Surely, you understand that."

She screwed up her face and turned to Tia. "Can I help?"

Surprised and not a little touched, Tia shook her head numbly. "It's done. We've been told to leave."

"Well, look me up when we're on the other side of the Atlantic. Maybe Mina and I can visit your bar."

Tia wondered if she'd still be saying that after she learned the truth. "Sure."

"And you." The demure, ladylike Annaliese rounded on Chrichton. "You can eat shit."

As she sailed off, Tia stared Chrichton down. Everything inside her quivered, longing to rage, to scream, but what would be the point?

In the end, all she did was back away, pausing at Griffith's side. "Sorry."

He inclined his head, unruffled. "Be seeing you, Hightower."

She didn't respond, much too aware of the warlock that followed her out of the ballroom.

Luckily, because it was the last night, most of their stuff was already packed. She threw the rest into a bag as Henry brooded by the bed.

"She was wrong, Tia," he said as she zipped up the suitcase.

"Was she?" Tia pushed hair out of her eyes as she created a portal to her apartment and began shoving suitcases through. "As far as I can tell, we screwed them over like you did me."

His lips thinned. "It's complicated."

"It's really not." She hefted the last suitcase and forced herself to meet his eyes. "And now that the investment is dead, so are we."

Something broke at that, deep inside where she could no longer shield it. The investment. Her parents. Henry. She had nothing left. She'd failed on every count. And if she wasn't a real Hightower and couldn't even do this right, what did she have to offer?

Henry's nostrils flared and he took a step. "Tia."

She drew on the anger, let it make her strong. "I'm serious, Henry. And not in a trading snipes, making-pig-curses way." She stalked to the portal. "*Done.*"

If he responded, she missed it as she left him behind.

thirty-five

The secret crossed the Atlantic quicker than any portal.

Tia barely had an hour before her cell started chiming with text after text, call after call. She didn't bother to look, just let her dress drop to the floor and crawled into bed. Her head ached but worse was her heart. She refused to let a single tear fall.

She lay staring up at the ceiling for who knew how long, going over everything. When she thought back, she felt like she should've seen the subtle shift in Henry. How he was less embarrassed around her. More purposeful, challenging. Confident. No more hiding in the music room, worried he'd let her down.

Everything hurt and she burrowed under the covers into the dark. But that didn't help because now she saw his mouth quirk as he teased her, how his eyes shone with appreciation. How he'd made her feel valued.

He'd really known how to work her. And she was a damned idiot for believing anything that came out of his mouth. Even...

Because I love you!

Another manipulation. Another pretty set of words.

Time passed. She moved from Henry to her parents, who'd

resorted to sending mirror messages she ignored. She felt wrung dry, and worse, now everyone knew she was a fraud.

She dozed a bit. When she woke, it was to pounding on her door. For a second, her heart jumped to her throat. She left her bedroom, drifting across the hardwood toward the door. She'd told him they were done but maybe…maybe this time he'd ignored that and come for her.

She wasn't sure if she was disappointed or relieved when Leah settled that. "Tia, it's us. Open up."

Tia marshaled her voice. "I'm fine."

"Yeah," Leah scoffed, just as Emma said, "C'mon. We'll break it down if we have to."

Tia sighed. She knew her friends; they'd change their address to her hallway before they left.

Leah was through first, barreling into her like a quarterback. Her arms went around Tia's waist and squeezed. "Why didn't you tell us?"

Emma shut the door behind them, gaze serious and soft. "How are you?"

Tia avoided their questions with her own. "How did you find out?" She wandered to the couch, where she dropped, pulling her knees up to wrap her arms around them.

Leah followed and sat next to her, bright and festive in her pink gingerbread man sweater. "Gabriel. For a man who doesn't gossip, he gets it quick enough."

"And what're they saying?" Tia wasn't sure what her friends knew, even though it barely mattered. She'd tell them everything anyway. It wasn't like she could kill the investment twice.

Cupboards clanked in Tia's small kitchen as Emma got out cups. "I'm making tea," she announced. "Any preferences?"

"Not tea?" Leah made a face.

Tia shrugged listlessly. "What're they saying?" she repeated.

Emma hesitated over the box of tea bags, angling her head around. "That you're not…" She stopped. "That your dad isn't…your dad."

Tia pressed her lips together.

"It's true." With a small sound, Emma abandoned the tea, hurrying over and kneeling at Tia's feet. "T, why didn't you tell us? When did you find out?"

"Is that it? Is that everything they're saying?"

Leah glanced at Emma. "Is there more?"

Tia laughed, dry and humorless, and told them everything. They barely moved, barely spoke, except for a lot of blinking and silent curses.

When she got to the part about Henry's lie, Emma put a hand to her forehead. Tia swore she heard the words, "*Damn it, Henry,*" under her breath.

When Tia finished, Leah exhaled noisily. "Well, hell."

Emma rocked back on her heels. "I don't know what to tackle first," she said finally.

Tia felt hollowed out. She rested her head on the back of the couch. "You and me both."

"So, you haven't seen your parents?"

Tia shook her head.

"And Henry…?" Emma stopped herself.

Leah put a hand on Tia's knee. "You've told us the facts," she said, jostling her. "Now tell us how you're feeling."

"What's the point? Bad. It's all around shitty and I'm giving serious thought to becoming a hermit witch who talks only to her dog."

"You don't have a dog."

"Maybe I'll get one." She thought of Rudy and for some ridiculous reason, the image of that sweet face made her throat burn. She hadn't gotten to say goodbye.

"C'mon. The Tia I know doesn't hide from her problems."

She looked at Leah, tired. So tired. "Maybe it's time I start."

Leah's face pinched.

Emma was more direct. "Okay." She stood, moving back to the kitchen to fill the kettle. Once it was set to boil, she turned, hands on her hips. "You need to talk to your mom."

"No."

"Yes." Emma's tone was brusque. "You need to face this like the big witch you are. It's already out there. Might as well know the whole story."

"She lied to me." She hunkered down, brushing away a stray hair that fell over her lip. "A lot of that going around."

"And you need to talk to Henry, too."

Tia scoffed. "Fuck that. He lied, manipulated, all to screw me over."

Leah gave her a castigating look. "Really? That's what he said?"

Her jaw clenched. "Aren't you meant to be on my side?"

"Hey, I can go grab my Tia pompoms from my closet but I don't think that's what you need." Leah poked her. "What did he say when you asked him why?"

"Why does it matter?"

"Because Henry isn't the villain you make him out to be." Leah held firm under Tia's glare. "And nobody plays the role of cute amnesiac without a reason."

"I agree," Emma called from the kitchen as she poured boiling water over the tea bags.

Tia shifted, pulling away from Leah. "I don't care why he did it."

"Tia."

Her lips twisted into a snarl. "Fine. He said he did it to *understand* or some bullshit."

"Understand what?" Emma put a mug down in front of her and kept her own. Steam circled the questioning look on her face.

"The breakup. Whatever, he was lying through his teeth."

"Did he want to get back together?"

Her cheeks felt hot. She blamed the tea sitting a foot away. "He said so. He said…" *I love you.* Like it would change what he'd done. If he'd meant it…well, his absence said everything.

"He said a lot of things," she finished, picking up one of the decorative cushions and squeezing. "Like accusing *me* of being to blame for our breakup. Saying how I didn't try to talk to him, that I don't accept weakness in people. As if he wasn't the one who threw us away."

Her friends said nothing for a moment. Then Emma put her mug carefully down on an end table. "Okay, don't hex bag me, but I'm going to cross the line you've drawn all these years."

Tia frowned, tightening her hold on the cushion. "Okay…"

Emma licked her lips. "It *was* kind of your fault, too."

"What?"

Her friend visibly braced herself. "He didn't come for you and that sucks, but you also never gave him a chance."

"I *begged* him," Tia hissed, Henry's similar accusation pounding in her skull. "Why would I give an asshole who just walks away—who made me feel like I wasn't worth *choosing*—" The words jammed in her throat.

"Because he was young. Arrogant. And just as stubborn as you. Neither of you was willing to admit you were wrong or talk through your issues. Really *talk*, Tia. And how did that work out for you? Lonely. For years." Emma's voice was firm. "Enough is enough."

"She's right," Leah added, their betrayal stinging like salt on a thousand open wounds. "From everything I've heard from you and Gabriel—"

"He's Henry's friend! Of course he's not going to blame him."

"Tia. Be honest. You could've relented a bit instead of throwing everything away."

Her jaw locked.

Emma muttered something. "I'm not going to apologize," she said defiantly. "It needed to be said, if only to show you that second chances don't make you weak. If I'd been as stubborn as you, I wouldn't be about to marry the love of my life."

Tia bit down on words she wouldn't be able to take back.

Especially as she knew her friend was right—under her circumstances. It didn't mean… It didn't mean that Tia was wrong now.

"I did let him back in," she pointed out with savage relish. "And it was a mistake."

"He lied and that's crap," Leah confirmed, squeezing her knee. "But it sounds like he tried to explain himself and you didn't listen. You ran away."

"Again," Emma added.

"Are you *trying* to hurt me?"

"I'm trying to do what you did for me—knock you out of your own stupid fears. You don't like feeling weak, T. That's just you, whether it's how your mom kept after you to be the perfect Hightower all your life or what, but you hate letting people in, in case they hurt you. And Henry, he's your red button. He makes it impossible for you to hide."

Hearing Emma echo so closely what Henry had accused her of made Tia flinch.

But her friend wasn't done. "Think about it. You could've used a TARDIS spell at any point on that bedroom so you didn't have to share a bed. You're the one who compromised, kept it going. You're the one who was considering a future—and then used the first opportunity to bail."

Tia breathed raggedly, the raw ache worsening with every word. She couldn't speak.

Seeing that, Emma knelt again, taking Tia's hand. "We love you. We want you to be happy, really happy, but that kind of happiness only comes from letting yourself be utterly open to someone. Of fighting through the fear. And I think you know it's always been him."

Tia squeezed her eyes shut as she felt a tear trickle down her cheek.

"I know it's scary," Leah picked up, pressing her knee. "Trust me. I know. We both do. Handing over your heart to someone who's already hurt you isn't for the weak."

He'd lied. He'd manipulated.

He'd asked questions. He'd wanted to hear it from her side. Because she'd never told him.

"You need to talk to him," Emma repeated as Tia sat there, sick to her stomach. "You need to listen. And decide once and for all if he's worth the risk."

Tia dragged in a breath that hurt her lungs, the cushion in her lap forgotten as she hunched forward. Her hair swung.

Leah reached out, tucking a strand behind her ear. "So, I guess the question is," she challenged softly, "is Tia Hightower a coward?"

There was too much swirling in her head to even think about talking to Henry. So Tia pulled on her boss panties and portaled to her mom's office instead. As she'd suspected, even on Christmas Eve, Gloria was at her desk. Except…she wasn't working, she was staring at a photo frame. At Tia's entrance, her gaze jerked up and her body followed suit, sending the chair spinning.

"Where have you been?" her mom demanded, the stern note wobbling like a three-legged cauldron. "You haven't been picking up any messages, the investment is dead and everyone knows the truth."

Tia kept her hands in her pockets so her mom wouldn't see them tremble. "Sorry it's caused you embarrassment."

This would normally be where her mom would chide her. Instead, what looked like real pain darkened her eyes. Tia's eyes.

No wonder she looked more like her mom and not her dad.

"They found out about me," she said, voice flat, disinterested, any trace of pain buried. "That's why they killed the investment. Well, that and the fake relationship you made up and I went along with. So, I guess it's both our faults."

"Will you sit?"

"No."

Her mom pursed her lips. "I know you're angry," she said quietly, "but nothing has to change."

The office was so silent, Tia heard every fast jerk of her heart as she tried not to laugh. She had a horrible feeling if she started, she wouldn't stop.

Gloria sighed, coming around her desk. She leaned her hips back against it, clasping the wooden lip until her knuckles showed. "Tia," she repeated, "nothing has changed."

"That's bullshit," Tia shot back, half of her waiting for the castigation that never came. "You know what'll happen to us."

"Nothing. Because we're Hightowers and they wouldn't dare."

"You might be, but since Dad isn't…mine—"

Gloria flung up a hand. "Yes, he is. And it'd kill him to hear you say otherwise."

A thousand regrets pricked her skin and she glanced away. "You know what I mean. Society isn't going to be kind."

"You never showed any interest in society. Why should it matter now?"

Henry's face floated into her subconscious. "The company," Tia answered, shoving him back out. "They're not going to like it."

"Fuck the company."

For a minute, Tia thought she'd cracked. Because no way had her respectable mom just cursed like a seawitch.

"The company can wait," Gloria continued, compounding Tia's confusion. "Society can go fuck themselves, too. You're more important."

The words hammered into her, nails into a wooden pole. She *felt* wooden, numb as she blinked at her mom. *You're more important.* Than a company. Than being a Hightower.

She'd never heard those words. Hadn't realized how much she'd needed to. "You didn't say that when I called."

"It was still a secret then. And I thought… I thought having a purpose would help you. You're always so much better with a goal than dealing with emotions." Gloria's smile was small. "A true Hightower."

Was she, though? "So, everyone knows," she said tonelessly. "What now?"

"Your nana is on the warpath against anyone daring to whisper about it in her presence. Your father and I had to confiscate several hex bags. You know what she's like."

Yep. Tia had learned from the best.

"We were waiting for you to discuss what to do next."

A bitter laugh escaped her. "*Now* you're willing to let me in on a discussion about my life?"

"Tia."

"No. You should've told me. Unless…am I…" The words were difficult to shove out. "Are you ashamed of me?"

Sincere horror engulfed her mom's face and her fingers twitched as if she wanted to throw herself off the desk. But they'd never been demonstrative. "*No,*" she breathed, sinking utter conviction into each letter. "Never. Peter—your dad and I, we always wanted you."

"But only as a Hightower."

"You *are* a Hightower," her mom stubbornly insisted. "In all the ways that matter."

Tia shrugged. "He must sometimes wonder."

"Who?"

"Dad." The word felt foreign. "Sometimes he's so disappointed in me. He must wonder if he made the right choice. Maybe even regrets calling me his."

Her mom moved then, years of tradition crumbling as she strode forward to grip Tia's shoulders. "No," she said firmly. "We've never regretted our decision to raise you as his. He's *never* thought of you as anything *but* his."

"But sometimes…"

"Never, Tia. If he's disappointed, if he's mad, if he's sick with worry, it's *because* he's your father. Not because he isn't."

"He might regret it now." Her stomach twisted; burning turned to nausea. "With everyone throwing it in his face."

"You think anyone will dare?" Gloria raised an eyebrow.

Tia stopped. Her mom was right. Her dad was quiet, but he wasn't a pushover. Otherwise, his personality would've been crushed under the weight of his mother and his wife, not to mention…

His daughter. If that was who she was.

A pained, soft noise escaped its chains. "I don't know who I am anymore."

Gloria lifted a hand to her chin, pinching it. "You are, and always have been, Celestia Hightower. Nothing in this world has the power to change you. Finding out you and your father don't share DNA. That Higher society knows. Even when some small-minded witches—and there will be some—point it out. Nothing can ever take away who you are."

She let her eyes flutter closed. "Why not just tell me if you believe that?"

Gloria hesitated, letting go. "We thought it best not to."

"You lied to me."

"Yes."

Bitterness rushed in, forcing itself down her throat. Out through her words. "Everyone lies because they know what's best for me."

"Better a harmless lie than a painful, pointless truth."

"That's such crap, Mom." Tia paced away, jumbled up inside, a junk drawer with no hope of a fix. "It's my life. I should know the truth."

"Maybe. But we'll always be your parents. We didn't want to hurt you."

From the stubborn tilt of her chin, Tia knew her mom wasn't about to back down. And part of her could almost understand the reasoning. The rest of her was too sad and mad to want to be anything other than a screaming vortex of hurt.

"If I am who I am," she challenged, fisting her hands on her hips, "why have you always pushed me to be better? To 'be a Hightower'?"

Now her mom winced. She ran an unsteady hand through

her hair, something that made Tia stare. Her mom was always composed.

"You were so different to other society witches when you were young. So wild and carefree. I was terrified the secret would come out when you were little and you wouldn't understand why everyone was being cruel." Gloria licked her lips. "It's not an excuse, but I guess it became habit. A way to make you strive to be the best. I had no idea you ever felt you were a disappointment. To us, you could never be anything but our bold and brilliant daughter."

She soaked that up, letting it fill the cracks. But there was one more thing. "And Henry?" Even saying his name aloud stung. "Did you push him on me to hide the truth?"

A weak smile tugged at Gloria's lips. "No. That's nothing more than a mother's wish for a good match for her daughter. Especially with how compatible you are."

"We argue all the time."

"You like that."

The statement set her back with its simple truth. She powered through. "Well, say goodbye to that dream because no way will Richard approve of me now."

"Do you care? Wait." Her mom's instincts kicked in and she straightened. "Did… Did something happen in England?"

"We're not talking about this." She couldn't.

She saw the struggle it took for her mom not to pry, appreciated it when she swallowed the questions. "Okay. Then what?"

She had no idea. She'd come here for answers, for some kind of resolution, but she wasn't sure how anyone was supposed to brush something like this under the rug.

They'd lied to her. She struggled with that, unsure what to do. How to move forward. How to let go when she'd always hung on—to regrets, to old pain, to grudges.

"Tia."

Her whole body stiffened at the masculine voice from the doorway. One that evoked memories of big hands mending skinned knees, of learning her first potion between strong arms, of grinning with him like a conspirator when her mom lost her temper.

She turned on wobbly legs. "Dad?" It was more breath than word.

He stood framed in the door, tall and solid and silent. A constant, calm presence in her life.

She hesitated, nerves binding her insides together, twisting and twisting.

Until he opened his arms.

A sob tore from her and she stumbled forward, sinking into them.

"My Tia," Peter murmured into her hair as he rocked her slowly. "Forgive us."

And as her dad—her *dad*—squeezed her tightly, Tia felt the grudge lodged under her breastbone slowly give way. And for the first time in her life, she let go.

thirty-six

"Well, this is pathetic."

Henry jerked his head up from where he'd rested it on the back of his office chair. Bastian and Gabriel stood in front of him, one golden in jeans and a leather jacket, the other dark in a cashmere coat and leather gloves.

He frowned, swinging the chair toward the door. "What?"

Emma's fiancé touched a finger to the frame on Tia's desk, lifting it up to look at. "You, working on Christmas Eve." He put the photo of Tia and her friends down, then picked up the lipstick she'd left, uncapping it to reveal the deep red.

Henry's fingers itched to burn Bastian's so he'd quit touching Tia's things. "Mom and Dad are at some party. Didn't feel like joining."

Especially when Henry hadn't bothered to see them since he got back. He didn't feel like listening to his dad count the ways he'd failed. The investment, the company. Tia.

We're done.

He purposely glanced away from Bastian and his sticky fingers to his oldest friend, who remained in the doorway like a silent specter. Bastian and he had been friendly all those years ago, but Gabriel had been there through it all. His friend had a reputation for being aloof but Henry knew personally the warlock would go to the mat for the ones he cared about.

Speaking of… "Aren't you meant to be with Leah and Melly?" The reindeer sweater he wore had to be for them. That or the warlock, who normally preferred suits, had lost his damn mind.

Gabriel followed his gaze and his pale cheeks flushed. "I will be. After."

"After?"

"After we knock some sense into you." Bastian at last turned from Tia's desk. "What the hell were you thinking?"

A deep scowl slashed Henry's face. "I don't need this."

"Seriously," Bastian continued, ignoring him, pacing up and down. "You masqueraded as an amnesiac to—what? Humiliate your ex?"

"No," Henry denied, bracing his hands on the reports he'd been pretending to read. "And it's none of your business."

"Leah is very upset by it," Gabriel put in. "*Leah* is my business."

Henry stared at him. "You're meant to be on my side," he said finally, wincing at how the words made him sound about ten. "You don't even know why."

Gabriel arched one perfect brow, his green eyes vivid and sharp. "You've never got over her so you decided to find out why she broke things off. That way, you could win her back."

"And to do that," Bastian added, his pretty face twisted in disbelief, "you decided to airbrush the past for a few weeks to get close without her cursing your junk."

Henry slouched. "Okay, so you do know. But I really did lose my memories. For a bit."

"I just want to know how you thought it was going to go down when you told her the truth." Bastian glanced at him, his navy gaze dark against his tan. "You *were* going to tell her the truth?"

"*Yes.* When the time was right."

"Never. It's never the time to tell Tia you lied to her for weeks."

Henry longed to argue but he couldn't pretend. He uttered a curse and pushed his hands into his hair. "I fucked up," he muttered.

"Yes," Gabriel agreed, earning a glare as well. His British accent clipped the next words. "What *I* want to know is why on earth you let Tia walk out on you a second time."

Anger kindled in Henry's chest and he shoved up out of his chair, leaning his weight on his hands. "It's not that simple. She said we were done."

"And what about when you've talked to her since?"

A muscle ticked in Henry's jaw.

Bastian groaned.

Gabriel sighed.

Heat hummed in Henry's blood as he fought not to set his friends on fire. "I can't chase after her all the time," he gritted out. "She has to fight as well."

Bastian wagged a hand at the chair they'd found Henry in. "This is you fighting?"

"I tried to explain and she wasn't hearing it."

"So you explain again. When she's cooled down and a good twenty feet from any hex bags."

"You tried to explain," Gabriel smoothly intercepted before Henry snapped. "Did you apologize?"

Henry glowered. "I did it for us. So we could have a chance."

Both warlocks stared at him.

He tried again. "If she'd only listen, she'd see that, but she's always too stubborn. Too stubborn to look at a different side and admit she might be wrong."

They kept staring. Pointedly.

His skin began to steam. "That's not—it's not the same."

Gabriel said a lot with a second sigh. "Did you at least learn anything through your masquerade?"

Yes.

She thought he'd stopped putting her first in any situation. And he had.

She thought he didn't listen. And he didn't. Because if he did, he wouldn't have fallen back into old patterns, yelling at her as she yelled at him. Trying to *win* instead of losing ground for the longer battle.

Hell, he'd yelled that he'd loved her like it would help him win. Using those words like a sword instead of the unshakeable fact it'd always been.

The sun would always rise in the east. The tide would always roll in. And Henry Pearlmatter would *always* love Tia Hightower.

When she'd told him they were done, he could've argued. He could've chased after her. He could've done anything.

Instead, he'd done nothing. Again.

What had she said?

Words. Always just words.

"Fucking hell," he said aloud and dropped back into his chair.

Bastian rubbed his hands. "We have about thirty minutes before Emma and Sloane realize I'm not still in The Louvre. Let's talk Operation Hightower."

Christmas Day came and went, and this year, the Hightowers celebrated.

Tia never went back to her apartment, instead heading with her dad to the family manor to talk. After a lot of tears and tissues, her dad had sworn he'd answer anything she asked, even about her biological father. That he'd even go with her to meet him—if that was what she wanted.

She wasn't sure it was. Why should she chase after some dick who'd abandoned her?

The echo of her bitter thoughts about Henry had her flinching. Uneasy, she'd said she'd think about it. No rush to make that choice. She already knew who her real dad was.

She slept in her childhood room, redecorated in calming

blues, and woke up to a tree, presents and beignets. They exchanged presents, ate turkey, discussed new potions—once a Hightower, always a Hightower—and when her nana turned up, instead of heeding Tia's hesitation, she prodded her granddaughter with her cane and demanded who she should kneecap. Wisely, Tia kept Chrichton's name to herself.

By the time Boxing Day rolled around, any residual awkwardness between her and her family had cleared like the sky after a storm. She wasn't sure if she'd completely forgiven them, but not holding on to her pain with a death grip made her feel less tight inside. Like there was more space somehow. And one day, she figured this would be just another fact, like her nana's penchant for grits or the way her mom always groaned when her dad brought out his antique potion books.

It wouldn't be accurate to say she'd never thought of Henry, but she'd given it the old college try. It was hard being so confused about him. About everything. The threads surrounding the whole messy situation were too tangled together, and she had no clue where to start picking it apart. For all she knew, he was fine with the way things were, even with his final declaration.

Because I love you!

She had a shift at Toil and Trouble, so left her parents' house with enough time to jump into the shower at home. His words followed her into it, whispering in circles as she ran conditioner through her hair. Maybe he did love her, but love hadn't been enough last time. Not for him. Not for his dad.

Thank fuck for the bar shift. She hadn't had near enough time there lately, and with all the revelers, it'd be too busy to do things like *think*.

She was halfway out the door when she noticed the small wrapped gift on the hall table. Emma, she thought with a smile, grabbing the gold package the size of her hand. Living it up in Paris but still remembered to send gifts. Just like her.

Time zipped by for the next few hours as she laughed with

repeat patrons, pouring unlimited glasses of wine, mixing up Christmas-themed cocktails, lining up shots and even doing one with a favorite regular. She was rushed off her feet, even with the temporary bartender they'd hired over the holidays.

Finally, somewhere around three, she declared an official lull and sent the poor twenty-two-year-old off to recover some sensation in her feet. Tia's own hummed in her heels, but used to that, she instead drained half a bottle of water from the under-counter fridge.

The little gold package caught her eye.

She'd untied the red bow and lifted the lid, revealing red tissue paper, when the door opened again. Intense power slid down the back of her neck, frying the tiny hairs there.

Isabella sauntered in, all swaying hips and confidence, like she visited bars all the time. Bianca followed at her heels, a perpetual thundercloud glaring at any of the single men who dared sully Isabella with their commoner eyes.

Tia's mouth parted as the High daughter stopped at the bar. "Uh. Hi."

"Hello." Isabella glanced around, sliding off berry-pink cashmere gloves. Her hair was a mass of white curls threaded with a pink hair ribbon, lips the same shade as the coat she unbuttoned, revealing a modest ivory dress that left her shoulders bare. "So, this is your bar." Interested, she surveyed the room, missing the few men who eyed her back. Or they did until they saw Bianca.

"Yeah." Tia tried to look at it through her eyes. It was no ballroom, but it was a decent-size space, outfitted with wine leather booths, a giant TV on an exposed brick wall, dozens of wooden tables and chairs and a small stage where they hosted local bands or karaoke nights. It was cozy, comfortable, a place that invited you to relax.

Something Tia reminded herself to do as the High witch settled on a worn bar stool.

"It's nice." Isabella folded her hands in her lap as she crossed her legs. Her shoes matched her coat and were gorgeous peep-toes. "I like the colors," she added. "What would you recommend to drink?"

"Ah…" This was surreal, like two worlds crashing into one. Not to mention, the last time she'd seen Isabella had been in England—when she'd let slip a secret that had, in many ways, been the first domino.

But that hadn't been the High daughter's fault. And they *had* been making moves to be friends…

Tia cut the shit. "Isabella," she said, leaning on her elbows, ignoring the slight stickiness their temp staff hadn't wiped yet. "What're you doing here?"

"Chicago?" Isabella shrugged as a roar of laughter sounded from one of the groups. "Who knows? Maybe an art show, a jewelry heist, a little murderous mayhem. Followed by a baseball game. I do love those tight little uniforms."

"Baseball season finished months ago."

"Another sporting event, then."

"I meant this bar. *Any* bar."

"I can't go to bars?"

"You're wearing white."

Isabella looked down. "So?"

"It won't be that color when you leave."

She looked unconcerned. "I'm expanding my horizons and catching up with a friend." She smiled brightly. "What do you recommend?"

Tia briefly met Bianca's dark stare but gave up. It wasn't like Isabella shouldn't come to a bar just because she was, in their society, royal of sorts.

"We've got some gingerbread gin that'll spice up any tonic."

"Sounds perfect."

Tia busied herself getting a glass. "Rocks?"

"Please."

They didn't speak again until Isabella took a tentative sip. Surprise was chased by pleasure. "It's good. I like the kick."

"Uh-huh. Why're you here, Isabella?"

Isabella lost some of the Southern belle sugar and something real came and went in her eyes. "I heard about what happened. Your parentage and...with Henry."

Tia didn't doubt it; intelligence probably whispered in Isabella's ear, even when she was sleeping. She firmed her jaw. "So?"

"So..." Isabella looked a bit lost, hand curling around the glass. "I wanted to make sure that you weren't too distressed." Obviously new to the witch.

Because of that, Tia didn't lash out. "I'm fine."

Isabella's look called her a liar. "And Henry?"

"Nothing." Tia's lips curled up without humor. "Just like I thought."

Life at the bar continued around them, men laughing and women flirting, drinks being toasted and tapped together. But in their bubble, neither Tia nor Isabella moved.

Isabella's glass made a ringing sound as she traced its rim. "Are you sure—?"

Tia focused on the package on the counter to hide the prickling behind her eyes. "I don't know why I thought things might be different this time," she said, hating the wobble in the words. She fiddled with the tissue paper. "I don't even know if I want them to be. He lied. He—"

She stopped. For no reason, her heart began to hammer against her ribs, fast and heady, as she lifted the small cat figurine from its box. It was made from fine glass, the quality sparkling as she turned it over in her hands.

"What?" she murmured, the next second fumbling to catch the ornament as a spark whipped up from the tissue. And then another, and another.

Isabella's hand came up, wrist turning twice clockwise. A shimmering veil settled into place, hiding more and more sparks—embers, Tia realized with a flipping sensation in her stomach—until, with a flash, a piece of paper exploded into existence.

Smoke notes. Someone had written a note, ripped it up and burned it to reassemble the other side.

She knew only one warlock that talented with fire.

She ignored the quiver in her hands as she grasped the waiting note, unfolding it so the lines of text shimmered up from the paper.

Tia. You gave me your memories so now I'll give you mine, right from the beginning.

I was pissed about that damn cat for about two seconds until I looked into eyes I knew would be my forever. I wasn't ready for what I felt. I didn't deserve it. And I never lost it.

I lied because I needed to know where we broke down, how to fix it. But I also lied because I was scared. Scared you'd push me away when we were getting close, scared you wouldn't give me another chance if you knew I was still the clueless man who made you feel inferior. And each day that passed, it was easy to justify how I needed more time. It was easier to lie than be vulnerable. I think you know what that's like. And I'm sorry.

I was an idiot to let you walk away last time. This time, I'm not going quietly. This time, I'm going to show up for you. Again and again, I'm going to show up for the most important person in my life.

Because fighting with you is better than peace with anyone else.

Tia let the note drift to the counter. She felt weightless, adrift, *unsure*. Henry had made a move.

He'd *done* something.

She watched hands that didn't feel like hers lift the glass cat again. Now she looked at it, it resembled the rose she'd kept hidden, glass only a fire warlock could create. She thought about how long it must have taken to carve the lines, the details of the cat's features.

Her heart shivered.

Isabella, after blatantly reading the note without any thought to privacy, pressed her lips together. "Are you going to talk to him?"

Tia blinked. "I..."

A wave of panic almost tugged her under and her hand instinctively tightened on the cat. She forced herself to let go before she broke it. "It's not that simple."

"It's not?" Isabella looked skeptical as she tapped the note. "He's fighting for you."

"With words." Tia put a hand to her head to try to stop it swirling.

"You thought his father would dissuade him. That clearly isn't the case."

"It's easy to say things." Tia wanted to believe; fuck, did she want to believe. Even now, it took everything not to reread the note, not to hoard it like the treasure it was. "He's always been good at promises."

Isabella's expression turned understanding. "But not follow-through."

Tia bit her lip, trying to steady herself. "I just… I need some time." Time to decide if this, he, was serious or if it was just another move in their chess game. One that neither of them ever seemed to win.

Isabella lifted her glass, contemplating the liquid inside. "You need to see if he's serious," she murmured.

Tia nodded. It was strange but she knew Isabella got it. She had the same guards Tia did.

Sure enough, Isabella nodded back, sipping her drink. And hummed.

thirty-seven

For the next four days, a gift appeared on her hall table. Each one with a memory.

The first time I knew I loved you, we were arguing in my parents' gardens. I can't even remember about what. But you lifted your chin, insulting me and looking so damn beautiful doing it, and I knew. I suddenly realized this was where I wanted to be. Forever. You probably don't remember, but I cut you off by kissing you, taking you to the ground as if by holding you to the earth, I could hold you to me. I was so damn happy and terrified at the same time, like I knew there was never any going back.

I think our best date was when you were nineteen and we snuck out to Bourbon Street and pretended to be human (with our magical fake IDs). We drank our way down the bars, kissing in corners and making friends with everyone. It wasn't anything special, except it was the first time I'd felt normal. Just a normal guy with his girl. But there are so many more. Like the moment you tried whiskey for the first time, spraying it in my face and threatening to kill me because I'd told you it tasted like molasses. Or our first adult event where you cornered me in a cloakroom and we did bad things on a pile of Higher witch coats. Or the day you dared me to eat as many beignets as I could in a minute. I still can't stomach beignets, you know.

You know how you said you tricked me into kissing you that first night? Well, I tricked you into saying "I love you" first. I was nervous you didn't feel it, too, but at the same time, I was sure you must. I knew if I could get you mad, you might admit it, so I took you out to the fair. I made you play all the games and beat you every single time. Your eye started twitching and it was so adorable, I almost blurted out the truth. I goaded you over and over, until I dared you. I fucking dared you like I was twelve. But I can't regret it because hearing those words from you, even at a volume that would shatter most windows, was one of the sweetest moments of my life.

I've always regretted not coming after you. That last fight, our worst one, and I quit us. I just accepted that was it. Didn't push back. Didn't try. Every night for the first six months, I lay awake going over it, wishing I could replay it and talk you down, but I was so fucking stubborn. Always wanting to win, both of us. I was just as brash, just as sure I was right. I've thought about that moment over and over, but it wasn't until England, when I heard you tell it that I realized. You needed to see me fight for us again. If you can't forgive me, I'll at least know that this time, I had the guts to fight, even if I lose. Because you're worth that. You're worth everything.

With each memory, a glass memento. A small gazebo from the Pearlmatter gardens, beads from Bourbon Street, a cuddly toy that was a life-size replica of the one hidden in her closet. And a rose, a twin to the one he'd given her when he'd promised he'd always show up for her.

He hadn't kept that promise.

Maybe it was that that made her stomach twist as she stared at the objects she'd carefully placed on her dresser. The reminder that they'd been here before.

Except…this time he was trying. He was fighting. For *her.* His memories were just as precious as the glass art, just as fragile. She'd felt exposed, giving him her memories. Now he was doing the same. He was trying.

She just couldn't work out if it was enough.

And then the next day, the invitation arrived through the mirror.

The High Family invites Tia Hightower to a New Year's Gathering at High House, it read on embossed font, with the details below. And one extra line that had her teeth sinking into her bottom lip:

A New Year for new beginnings.

Henry would be invited, too. Everyone who was a Higher witch would. Ready to gossip and sneer.

She swept a thumb over the font, drifting back to sit on the edge of her bed. She could choose *not* to go, she reasoned, as spikes of anxiety drilled into her spine. But when had she ever let society dictate her actions?

Of course, that was when she'd been sure of her place as a Hightower.

Hearing her own thoughts, she exhaled an annoyed breath. She was Tia Hightower. She cowered before nobody, and fuck it; she wasn't about to be scared off by some snobs in overpriced dresses who couldn't even say what was in a Sleep potion.

But if she went, she'd have to face them. Him.

I'll at least know that this time, I had the guts to fight.

Did she?

She mustered a weak smile as she let the invitation drop. Well, she always had loved a party.

They lined up out front. Emma and Bastian flanked Tia on one side, Leah and Gabriel on the other.

It was chilly but her skin burned as she stared at the open doors. Music swirled out alongside polite laughter and chatter.

Stray sparks of magic from portals opening and closing drifted by. The same as any other society event.

Except this wasn't any other event.

As if summoned by the thought, two witches a couple years older than Tia walked out of the doors and stopped dead as they caught sight of her. They whispered behind their fans as they slowly began to walk again, eyes flitting to her and away. A giggle floated on the air.

Leah glowered. She took one step before Gabriel caught her arm.

"Let me go," she growled. "I'm about to cut a witch."

"Let's at least wait until we're inside before assaulting the guests," he suggested. But the one who'd giggled at Tia suddenly stumbled into her friend, sloshing wine down their gowns with a cry of dismay.

Uptight Goodnight was defending her. The world really had turned upside down.

She let out a breath and felt her friends crowd closer.

"You sure about this?" Emma murmured. "We can leave."

"I'm sure." If she said it firmly enough, maybe she'd believe it. Her hands found theirs. "Thanks for coming with. I know there are other things you could be doing."

"Our date with whipped cream can wait," Leah chirped. On cue, pink scored Gabriel's cheeks. He shifted in place.

Bastian snorted. "Didn't know you had it in you, Goodnight. Tell me, does she hold the can or…?"

Emma elbowed him. "Behave."

"You sure?" he teased, tucking her hair behind her ear and then whispering something that made equally fiery color sweep down her face.

Tia might've groaned aloud if she hadn't been seized with envy. That was what she wanted, what she'd had with Henry. Well, that, but less sickening. Tonight could make or break it.

She smoothed a hand down her dress. It wasn't red; she felt that was too telling. Instead, the gown was deep purple, with a corset-style waist that hiked her boobs up to display the glass beads Henry had created. Wearing them made her feel naked. Exposed.

What if…?

She cut off the thought before it could poison her mind. No. She'd made the decision, and she was Tia fucking Hightower. She didn't second-guess.

Chin high, she started forward. Each step was easier than the last, her friends falling in behind her like security. She might have teased them if she could have drawn enough breath.

Intellectually, she knew it wasn't a big deal when she entered High House. For one, they came into the foyer where only a few witches gathered, most already wandering to the hall leading to the ballroom. For another, it wasn't like the music stopped, trumpets sounded, or she was announced on a PA system.

And yet, it felt like the air shivered as she crossed the threshold. Like everyone who used to kiss her ass now turned to stare at her. And gawk.

Nothing has changed, she repeated to herself as she moved through the quiet murmurs, shoulders back, gaze level. Her heart galloped, wild and frenetic, but she kept her face serene, holding herself so tightly, her muscles ached.

When she walked into the ballroom, a dozen or so heads swiveled to face her. She'd never been more thankful for her friends as they stepped up next to her. Even Emma, whose social anxiety would always make her awkward in crowded settings, frowned fiercely at one warlock whispering to his companion.

She scanned the faces, searching for a familiar platinum head, when she spotted two women arrowing straight for her.

"Do I need to run interference?" Leah asked under her breath, the pint-size blonde ready to shuck her stunning gold dress and wrestle both witches to the ground.

"I…ah," Tia began but stopped as Mina and Annaliese arrived in their circle.

"Tia," Mina said, her lightly accented voice louder than necessary. "It feels like it's been an age." She leaned in and kissed Tia's cheek, whispering, "We figured you might need backup with the sharks."

An ache squeezed Tia's heart and she smiled shakily at Mina, accepting Annaliese's kiss on the cheek next. Both were Higher witches; both carried weight in society. And both had shown up to throw that weight behind Tia.

Not only them, she realized, as Sawyer swaggered up behind Mina and Annaliese. When she caught his eye, he shrugged. "Figured us mongrels better stick together." He winked, softening the words with a squeeze of her shoulder.

Tia introduced her friends and let the conversation flow, long enough for the worst of the gossip to subside. The dancing started, couples whirling before the orchestra and the chairs where some of the High Family sat, bored out of their minds. Isabella was nowhere to be seen.

Magic crafted to resemble fireflies danced in rhythm above their heads, sometimes as a swarm, sometimes individually. It was beautiful, but she couldn't fully appreciate it. It was edging toward midnight and she still hadn't seen Henry.

Maybe his dad had forbidden him from coming. Except refusing an invite from the High Family wasn't a great move, socially or financially. Maybe it was a statement. Maybe he'd been joking. Maybe…

Maybe she should calm the fuck down and get out of her head.

So she waited. And waited. And the glass beads became heavier around her throat.

Henry paced the foyer of his parents' house, pausing to holler up the stairs. "If you're not done in two minutes, I'm going alone."

"You hold your horses, Henry Charles," came his mom's tart reply.

He might have grinned if the idea of Tia waiting alone at the party didn't make him crazy. He knew what society was like. They'd scent blood in the water and attack. A rush of urgency descended like fog. He wasn't leaving her to face that without him.

Finally, his mom appeared, wrapped in dark green silk cut low enough he wasn't sure where to look.

"I know," she said, sticking her chest out. "I've still got it."

"Goddess," he muttered, conjuring her cape and holding it out for her. "Let's go."

"What about your father?"

"He's at the office. He can meet us."

Maybelline put a hand on his arm, slowing him. Her eyes searched his. "Are you sure?"

He knew what she meant. "Never been more sure of anything."

Her smile was radiant and she tweaked his cheek like he was a child. "All right, then. Let's—"

She was cut off when the front door flung open.

The temperature dropped ten degrees as his dad stormed in. His face was clouded, skin stretched over his cheeks as he took them in.

"No," was all he said.

Henry's stomach jittered but he kept his gaze level. "Yes."

"Son, this is a mistake."

"You've never liked her, have you?" he challenged, ignoring the way his bones ached at the disapproval in Richard's eyes.

He hadn't wanted to admit it. Blind stubbornness or ignorance, he hadn't wanted to see that Tia had been right—he'd become a doormat for his dad. He hadn't meant to be; hadn't started out that way. Yet somehow, over the years, for one approving nod, for every office conversation where his dad patted him on the back, he'd sacrificed everything else. It had taken a month of being an outsider to his life to see it. And make some changes.

"It's not about her." His dad's jaw looked equally tight, hair mussed as though he'd been running his hands through it.

Henry snorted. "Right."

"It's about you. She's hurt you before. She's not serious enough."

"Richard," Maybelline cautioned as Henry all but snarled at his dad's words. She slid in between them, one hand on his chest.

He pressed his own hand to his wife's but didn't take his gaze off Henry. "It's a mistake," he repeated softly.

"No." Henry shook his head. "The mistake was thinking I'd ever be good enough for you."

Something like shock passed through Richard's eyes. He took a stuttered step back.

Because he'd said it aloud, Henry thought. Finally, no more games.

"I'm done trying to play the perfect son for you. It's never won me anything, but I lost someone vital because of it." He angled his jaw up and felt the last ties wither and fall away as he echoed Tia's words. "I'm done."

He created a portal in the few seconds of silence, his footfalls determined as he strode toward it. He cast a silent apology at his mom, pale under the foyer lights.

"Henry," his dad suddenly said, stricken. "Wait. I've never thought—"

The rest was stolen as the portal snapped closed. He took a moment for regret, a bittersweet ache that things between him and his dad would never be the same. Then he stashed it to confront later. He had bigger potions to uncork.

He appeared in one of the private meeting rooms of High House, one he'd become familiar with a few days ago when a certain High daughter had summoned him. He'd have been pissed if he hadn't been so desperate for news. Tia hadn't reached out about his gifts. He'd thought she might have destroyed them, refusing to give him another chance. Instead, Isabella had offered hope.

He quietly exited the room and strode along the upper level, examining the scene below. Society whispered, their poison slipping through the air like fumes.

Scandal, their eyes sang.

Hold on to your brooms, he thought with a curl of his lip.

He was about to give them a better one.

thirty-eight

It was almost midnight and he hadn't shown.

She wasn't sure why she was surprised. Tia fingered the glass beads, listening to the notes of music as they soared and dipped like the couples on the dance floor. Above, the fireflies had retired, candles in their place, flames capped so no sparks drifted down to burn.

Too late for that, she wanted to say, even if it was melodramatic. Because she had been burned, yet again. By him.

Heart and head put up their fists and duked it out as she watched Emma laugh into Bastian's face as he spun her in circles. As Gabriel held Leah at a precise distance even as her friend's hand slid to his ass, making his lips twitch.

Head said he'd been all talk again, trying to lure her back with pretty words and clever phrases.

Heart said this time was different. She couldn't even say why, but it was why she'd accepted the invitation, why she'd dressed up, why she'd worn his glass beads. She was on a precipice, the wind a song in her ears that threatened to tumble her over if she just let go.

She'd taken one step.

Where was he?

A commotion by the doors drew her eyes from the dancing couples to where a crowd had gathered. Some kind of entertainment, maybe, though she was mildly surprised it wasn't being unveiled at the witching hour for maximum effect.

Gasps and shocked titters got louder as the crowd thickened, some couples halting on the dance floor. A few witches headed in that direction, craning their necks, hands over their mouths.

Then the crowd parted. And her brain flatlined.

Because it was Henry. Henry striding into the ballroom wearing a determined expression, a pair of black boxer briefs—and that was it.

That was fucking *it.*

She blinked. Blinked again. How much had she had to drink? Was she dreaming?

But she heard Bastian choke out a laugh, watched Gabriel blink even faster than she had. He was real. This was happening.

Henry saw her then, eyes alight with ferocity that turned pale green into shimmering pools of color. His lips curled into a smirk and he spread his arms wide, putting himself on display. For her.

She could only stare.

She'd expected him to make his way to her; instead, he angled toward the stage, ignoring the shocked glances—and fluttering fans. Tia had enough mind to scowl at those witches.

He jumped up, crossing to the musicians, who nodded like this was planned. The music stopped, leaving only the titters and murmurings of the crowd. Above them, Henry stood as relaxed as if he were in full armor. Or, you know, any clothes at all.

"Evening, everyone," he said, and his voice was everywhere, that smooth baritone with a nudge of Southern, deeper than anyone might expect. She had no idea how he was projecting but she drifted forward as if pulled by it.

"I'd say I'm sorry to disrupt it," he continued, surveilling the crowd. "But that'd be bullshit. Especially since the reason you're all here is to gossip and spread rumors about the Hightowers."

Tia stiffened as gazes slid her way.

"Personally, I don't get it," he said conversationally. "Tearing someone down to make yourselves feel better is something children do. You're all grown-ass adults. Fucking act like it."

Expressions around her soured. Tia's hands came together and she squeezed. His dad would shit wands when he heard about this.

"Anyway, I came here tonight for one reason. One person. And that's Celestia Hightower." She swore even across this distance, his eyes glowed as he arrowed in on her. "The witch y'all are delighting in tearing to shreds, because you know she's superior to you in every way. Just gossip, right? Wrong. Gossip hurts people. We've learned that."

Out of the corner of her eye, Tia saw Emma wince. Bastian slid his arm around her waist.

Henry rocked onto one bare foot. "It's funny. I've always put a lot into words, the power of them. Hell, society twists words into games that cut and stab and bleed. Words can hurt." He nodded slowly. "But they can also mean everything. Like, when I say I love you, Tia—" Gasps exploded around the room and Tia swayed. Henry never moved his gaze off her. "—it means I *love* you. That I adore every disagreeable, prickly, passionate part of you. That I will be your rock, your safe space. Your *quiet.*" He swallowed, memory flickering over his face. "It means I will stand by your side, behind you when you need backup, in front of you when you need checking. It means I'll probably screw up and hurt you because an idiot in love isn't logical. And I am so fucking sorry for every moment I've ever hurt you."

A tear dashed down Tia's cheek and she couldn't move to hide it. She couldn't breathe.

Henry watched her, his face taut with emotion. "You own me, Tia. My heart, my soul, my magic, body and bone. All of me. No matter how we fight and rage and make mistakes, no matter how much we push each other away. Just know I'll always come back. Because all I want, all I've ever wanted, is you." His smile was crooked, rueful. "Just words, though, huh? You don't believe in words alone. So. I'm baring it all for you." He glanced down, an eyebrow raised. "Literally. I've quit PH Inc."

Tia barely heard the crowd's murmurs as her stomach dropped to her feet. He...*what*?

He cleared his throat. "Turned in my resignation today. Unemployed. No longer shackled to the chains of my family's company. I'm done with making it a priority. It's not worth the effort. *You* are. And you always will be."

It was official. She was going to faint.

Henry tore his gaze off her and examined the crowd. "Thanks for listening. I'm here all night—try the champagne." He began to walk away and stopped, snapping his fingers. "Oh, I almost forgot. Anyone who thinks they can talk shit about Tia or her family will find themselves on the wrong side of the Pearlmatters, so if I were you, I'd be very fucking careful before I start getting fire-happy."

"That goes for the Truenotes, too," Bastian called out, grinning foolishly.

Emma glanced at Tia, shy but sure. "And the Bluewaters."

"And the Goodnights." Gabriel nodded at her, stern with soft eyes.

Leah danced on the spot, clapping her hands, tears spilling over her cheeks. "And the Turners!"

"Uh... Leah..."

She rolled her eyes at Gabriel. "Whatever. We'd still bring it hard."

Tia's chest felt too full, pressure building behind her eyes at them all standing up for her, even Leah, whose human status wasn't worth anything to these people but everything to her.

Back on the stage, Henry arched a single eyebrow at the shocked audience. "You've been warned. Happy New Year, y'all."

He jumped off stage to a few stray claps. The crowd parted

as he came for her, all bemused at what to do. One of its leading sons had told them to fuck off. Did they snub him? Did they pretend it never happened?

They were nothing more than ghosts as Henry stopped in front of her. This close, there was so much skin on show it was distracting, muscles under taut flesh and a smoky scent that sank into her lungs.

They stared at each other for a solid thirty seconds before he finally spoke. "Hi."

"Hi?" she repeated, voice strangled. She tried to form words. "Henry. What. How. You."

The corners of his mouth twitched. "I've finally made you speechless."

A noise left her. "What the hell?"

"What?"

"You're naked."

"Not really." He looked down as if to confirm. "This was the original consequence of the bet, right?"

Loser has to attend a society ball in their underwear.

Her jaw literally dropped. Then she shut it with a snap. She'd forgotten about the bet; it felt like a thousand years ago. "You didn't lose the bet."

"No." Emotion moved in his face, dark, anguished. "I lost something much more important."

Her breath stuttered.

He hesitated before reaching out and lifting her hand. His touch sparked embers under her skin, spreading heat where she'd felt only cold for days.

"Did you get my gifts?" he asked softly. "My notes?"

She nodded.

"I meant every word in them. And I meant every word up there, too." His thumb brushed her knuckles, unlocking feelings she'd tried to bury since the night of the Snowflake Ball. "I'm fighting for you, Tia. And now I'll have a lot of free time to show you I couldn't give two shits what last name you have. Just as long as I can call you mine."

She would not cry. She would not fucking cry.

Her voice was thick, more breathless than angry as she concentrated on the part of his sentence she had issue with. "Over my dead body are you quitting the company."

"It's done." He nipped his way down her knuckles.

"No," she denied stubbornly, warning her knees to hold their ground as they softened like butter.

"Yes," he countered. "I told my dad. Twice, in fact. Once when I resigned and once at the house when he came after me."

She hesitated. "Are you...okay?"

"It's weird," he answered after a pause. "Like I feel like I should be doing something. Conditioned, I guess. But I'll be okay."

He'd quit. Told his dad. She dragged in a breath. "You stood up to your dad. For me?"

"For you. And for me." He squeezed her hand. "It was time."

"I can't believe you quit." She shook her head. Gripped him. "Take it back."

Humor lightened his face. "No."

"Yes," she hissed. "You love working. You're the heir."

"Now I'm not."

"Henry Charles."

His eyes gained a deep cast. "I love when you call me that."

She felt panic pinch her insides as he tugged her, drawing her close. "You didn't have to quit. I don't want that."

"I know. But you needed to know that I'll always choose you. That you're worth that." He cupped her cheek, thumb brushing her cheekbone. "I'm all in, little moth. I'll wait as long as it takes for you to trust me again."

If she could've swooned without ruining her badass reputation, Tia thought she'd already be on the floor. He'd taken his step. Actually, he'd taken several. Now, her turn. "Henry, look at me."

"I am."

"What am I wearing?"

His gaze slid down admiringly. "A dress."

Save her from men. "And?"

"And…"

He finally saw the beads. She knew because his whole body stiffened. Hope warmed his face, the sun peeking from under a dark cloud.

She smiled through the suspicious water in her eyes. "You were right," she said, willing her husky voice to steady. "I should've talked to you instead of hiding behind arguments. I felt you pulling away and it terrified me how much it hurt. Better to quit you before you realized I wasn't worth the hassle."

"Tia."

She touched her hand to his lips. "Both of us hate losing. It's why we fight so much, I guess, never wanting the other to have the upper hand. Love…gives the other person the power, makes us vulnerable, and neither of us is comfortable with that. But if we're going to win, we have to stop fighting with each other and start fighting *for* each other. Every day. Even if it means risking everything. Even if it means trusting the other person won't let go or hurt us. We've both made mistakes." She licked her dry lips under Henry's stare, against the building heat as his fire magic flared. "We both let go, stayed away, because it was easier to protect ourselves. I don't want to take the easy way. I want to be better than that."

Behind Henry, Emma caught her eye. Her friend nodded at her, tearfully.

Tia swallowed, heart in her throat as she went over the precipice. "I choose to love you, Henry Charles Pearlmatter. Even with our past, our mistakes, our history. Because choosing to forgive, choosing to love you every day and giving you that power again, doesn't make me weak. It makes me *strong*."

Henry's smile was brilliant in its joy. "Say it again."

It was instinct to make a joke, that she wasn't about to stroke his ego by saying he was right a second time.

But instead, she breathed out shakily and held on to him. "I'm so fucking sorry. And I love you, too."

His mouth crashed onto hers and she threaded her hands through his hair, reveling in the feel of him, the beloved taste, everything pure Henry. Her Henry.

Even when his mouth became desperate, when his hands clutched at her, when heat collected under her skin and desire clenched in her belly, they clung to each other.

Finally, she broke away, gasping as she turned her cheek for air. His mouth skimmed it, toward her ear. "Want to get out of here?"

"Fuck, yes," she groaned and felt his laugh like it came from her own soul.

When they drew back, all the tension had melted from him. From her, too. Instead, she finally felt light. Almost a decade of regret sloughed off like old skin.

He grinned at her, boyish. "Admit it. The nudity won you over."

"Please." She rolled her eyes like getting him against a flat surface was the farthest thing from her mind. "Put some clothes on, you egomaniac."

Something lit his gaze, something she didn't trust. "Right," he purred. "I should do that."

She frowned as he swiveled, searching for someone. When he gestured, it was Isabella who walked toward them, a bundle of fabric in her arms.

Tia's eyes darted from the High daughter dressed in emerald satin to Henry. Light dawned as Isabella reached them.

"You knew about this?" she accused her quasi-friend.

Isabella's smile was serene. "I know everything." She handed the bundle off to Henry. "But I may dabble in areas when I know I can help."

Tia narrowed her gaze. "What did you…?" She cut herself off. "Next tea, you're spilling it all."

Isabella's smile took on a shade of soft delight. "Of course." Then, in front of society, she took Henry's hand in one of hers and Tia's in the other. "Better entertainment than I could've hoped for," she simpered. She squeezed once, glanced around at the gaping witches and left them to it.

"She gave us her seal of approval," Tia murmured, watching Isabella's white curls bob away into the crowd.

"Well, you're friends, right?" Henry unfolded one T-shirt, slipping it over his head.

Tia's smile was soft as she watched Isabella disappear into her role. Whoever she ended up with would need to be light on his feet to keep up. "Yeah," she agreed. "We are."

Really freaking happy, she turned back to Henry—and stopped dead. Bold text stretched over Henry's chest, black on white.

DADDY.

"What the…?" Sudden comprehension gripped her. She stepped back. "No."

Henry waggled the other T-shirt. "A bet's a bet, Celestia. Or are you a welsher?"

Damn it all to hell.

Henry watched with obvious amusement as she ripped the T-shirt out of his hand and yanked it over her head. She smoothed out the words as if they didn't make her spine tingle with embarrassment.

Henry was pure male satisfaction as he examined her. "Daddy's girl," he read, deep and on the edge of laughter. "I like it."

Ugh. "I'm on top when we get home," she grumbled, trying to save face.

"Whatever your fragile female ego needs."

He grabbed her, narrowly avoiding her fist, and kissed her. She threw her arms around his neck, kissing him back, ignoring that all of society was watching her give in to him. They gave in to each other.

She had Henry and he had her. That was all that mattered.

epilogue

Tia carefully secured the small tiara in Emma's hair, adjusting the folds of teal gauze around her friend's face. Tears pushed at the backs of her eyes but she refused, she absolutely refused, to cry.

"All done," she said, with a voice much too thick for her liking. She took a moment to just look and couldn't help sighing. "You're beautiful, Em."

"Let me see." Leah nudged Tia aside, holding her hands to her cheeks. "Oh, Emma."

Color scored Emma's cheekbones. "You guys are going to make me cry."

With a short breath, she turned to the mirror in the suite of High House. Isabella had offered it to them as a wedding venue and only a fool turned that down.

Emma had always been the shy witch, the one who thought of herself as brown and boring. Imperfect. But Tia had watched the past two years as Emma had blossomed, finding new confidence, and she saw it culminate now, here, in this one moment. When Emma looked in the mirror at herself.

And smiled.

Bastian was going to swallow his tongue, Tia thought as she,

Emma and Leah hugged it out before she slipped out to fetch Sloane for Emma…and to check on a few things. The wedding had been months in planning but she couldn't help it. Everything had to be perfect.

A wolf whistle pierced the air as she ducked under a flower arch, and she whirled to see Henry leaning against the brick wall of the guesthouse where Emma was getting ready. Dressed in gray with a teal bow tie, platinum hair mussed, he was utterly gorgeous, but it was his grin that drew her in.

"Spies aren't welcome," she scolded, unable to help walking toward him. Maybe swaying her hips just a little in the bridesmaid dress Emma had chosen—dove gray, to her displeasure, but hey, it wasn't her getting married. And judging from the way Henry's eyes heated as they dipped over the satin mermaid gown, she pulled it off.

He put an innocent hand to his chest. "No recon," he promised. Then grinned. "Okay, Bastian wants to make sure Emma's okay."

"She's fine. She's more than fine. And he's a lucky bastard."

"He knows it." Henry caught her hand, tangling their fingers together. "So am I."

"I know." She squeaked as he spanked her.

"Less of the lip unless you want me to ask another question."

Exasperation filled her. "Those questions have expired."

"We never negotiated a time limit." He dipped his head and whispered in her ear. "What are you wearing under there?"

She smiled slowly. "Moisturizer."

He looked pained as he leaned back. "Fuck. I have to stand up in front of three hundred people in forty minutes."

"Shouldn't play games you can't win."

His eye took on a gleam. "Forty minutes…we could do a lot in forty minutes."

A laugh caught in her throat as he advanced. "Henry Charles, I do not have…ah…time for…oh, *fuck*…"

Twenty minutes later, she slumped against him, breathing

hard. They'd found an unused greenhouse and within minutes, he'd had her balanced on one of the tables, dress around her waist. She wished she could be angry about the mess he'd no doubt made her into, but it was so damn hard when she'd had a breath-stealing orgasm. Besides, that was what magic was for.

She laughed when she saw the state of the pots behind him. "Lose control there, sparky?"

He lazily looked up from where he'd buried his head in her neck, glancing back at the incinerated pots. "I'll transfer some money." He kissed her, lingering. "Worth it."

They pulled themselves together and walked back to where the ceremony was being held. If they'd been honest, Emma and Bastian would've preferred eloping, but both their parents had been all for a ceremony. Tia figured Emma had gone along for Bastian's parents more than for her own mom, who was being watched by Kole for now, seated next to her in a tailored navy suit, alongside Emma's other sour-faced brothers.

It was sunset, which meant the moon would be rising soon, paving the way for the ceremony. Tia checked with the wedding planner—who informed her icily that this was *her* job—and with the priestess who was performing the rites, ignoring Henry's obvious amusement at her inability to relax.

He was one to talk, considering he'd been back at PH Inc. after a month.

He and his dad had talked it out a few days after the New Year's party. Richard was a dick but at least he could apologize. According to Henry, his dad had fumbled through an explanation about the way he'd been raised and how focusing on work had been a way to show affection and connection with his son. Something they could have in common.

Tia could buy that, but she was less convinced that Richard's disdain of her had been founded on his belief she'd break his son's heart. Apparently, she was *hard to read*, which he'd interpreted as selfish and spoiled. He hadn't wanted Henry to be hurt again.

She knew she had her own issues to work through about fathers, though. She'd been thinking more and more about a conversation with her biological dad to see if it would help, though she still wasn't sure if it was something she wanted or if it felt like an obligation. She knew whatever she decided, Henry would be there. He deserved the same from her with his dad.

With the air clear and them meeting up to *bro bond*, as she called it, he'd given in to her demands to come back to work very quickly. She loved it. Not only did she have him in her office as a sounding board and sparring partner, she got to say she told him so every day. And she couldn't deny office quickies had their appeal. Two days. They'd lasted two days before they changed their office walls to opaque glass. It didn't suck to be the boss.

Even she and Richard had come to some new understanding, slow and tentative as it was. They both loved Henry, after all, and both had fucked-up ways of communicating it. They were trying. As for Maybelline and Gloria, those two were so delighted by the renewal, someone might think they'd had a hand in it all. She pitied Henry because soon enough whispers of proposals would start.

They weren't there yet. Eventually, maybe, but they were still learning to talk things through instead of withdraw. They had a long way to go but both were willing to put the effort in. And that was what mattered.

With one more apology to make, they'd portaled back to England a few weeks after New Year's to talk to Siddeley. Mildred had demanded they be thrown out, but surprisingly, Siddeley had walked with them down to Westhollow, where they'd told him the whole truth over coffee and doughnuts in Pie Hard. Maybe it was because Tia hadn't hidden her delight at seeing Rudy again, and the feeling was entirely mutual. Maybe it was because they'd stripped themselves embarrassingly bare by admitting everything. Maybe it was because they were obviously so happy with each other now.

Whatever it was, he'd listened to it all. He'd yet to make an investment, but he had reached out last week and invited them to dinner. So who knew what would happen in the future. Business wasn't everything.

Tia caught Henry's eye as she made her way back to the guesthouse. Progress was a thousand little steps. Sometimes it was a sincere apology. Sometimes it was a glass cat. Sometimes it was reaching out instead of playing safe.

Emma and Leah had taught her that. And Henry.

And when Bastian turned to see Emma walking down the aisle with Kole, dressed in the teal silk gown she'd worn for him, when he blinked back furious tears and walked to meet her as if he couldn't stop himself, Tia's heart sang. Leah didn't even try to hold back her tears, Gabriel kissing her temple and conjuring tissue after tissue.

But it was later, when they'd vowed under the Goddess' moon to love each other for forever and a day, when they'd cut the cake Emma had baked with Bastian's assistance, when they'd danced their first of many under the veil of stars, that Tia sank back into Henry's arms.

"Today was a good day," she murmured as they danced. His hand flexed on her back as he hummed in agreement.

Her eyes followed the line of dancers to Melly, Gabriel's little sister, and Sloane, the teenagers giggling at something. Sloane had insisted she come face the monsters once and for all, and under her half sister's plea, Emma hadn't had the heart to refuse. She'd worried about her mom, but the little half-human, half-witch had everyone in her corner. Sloane was as safe as a witch in her own coven.

Oh, she'd been nervous; that had been as plain as the gray dress she'd worn. In a strange twist, it hadn't been until Gabriel had walked over, offered her his hand and whirled her around the dance floor that she'd lost her anxious expression.

The girls spun crazily now, squealing loudly and almost knocking into an elder couple. Emma called out, chastising, which only prompted Bastian to spin his bride around until she shrieked with her own laughter.

Business as usual.

To her right, Gabriel and Leah swayed, his arms tight like he knew he held something precious. In an unguarded moment as he listened to her talk, everything he felt for her friend reflected in his face, naked for the world to see. Unashamed.

It made Tia smile. At least until she caught sight of Kole at the edge of the dance floor. Even from her vantage point, the air of regret surrounding him was obvious. She hurt for him, but at the same time, she couldn't deny Gabriel had done what Kole hadn't. He'd moved mountains for Leah. He hadn't settled. He'd fought, his fears and the world, for her. She deserved that. Everyone did.

Still, it wasn't nice to see anyone hurting and she was about to pull away from Henry when someone else appeared at his side. His shoulders stiffened as Isabella spoke to him, luminous in silver lace that hugged her curves and set off her light brown skin.

Well, at least it was a distraction.

"I have a question," came Henry's voice at her ear.

Tia sighed, attention returning to him. Glowing orbs above the dance floor mingled, mirroring the stars, floating between the dancers. She flicked one away from her hand, a light buzz on her skin, before looking up into Henry's eyes.

He toyed with her nape. "Are you happy?"

She couldn't restrain the smile that slid over her lips like silk. "Yes," she answered softly. "Are you?"

He hummed. "I have very few complaints." He laughed when she hit him, drawing her in.

She let him kiss her, drifting in that space between reality and dreams. When he lifted his head, she waited one more blissful second. Then, narrowing her eyes, she poked him in the chest. "Now, about that dating ban you put on me..."

★ ★ ★ ★ ★

acknowledgments

Guys. I finally got to write a book at Christmas. Pause for happy dance. I love everything about Christmas, from the lights to the movies to family time, and all those hours between the day itself and New Year's, where it's okay—nay, encouraged—to do nothing but chill (and in my case, read all the books I stored up like a squirrel with her nuts). I wouldn't define this as a "Christmas book" but I got to play with the elements and I couldn't have been happier in my sandbox.

My thanks, in no particular order!

Thanks to my editor, Stephanie Doig, who loved the idea of a witch romance set at Christmastime enough to let me run with it. You always take the rough stone I give you and in turn, give me the tools to make it shine. I appreciate you!

To Cole, the best and most reassuring agent, who has been known to email me when I've been quiet to "check in" (i.e., not gone into a panic spiral) and always has time for me and my ideas.

To my bookstagrammer friends online, there are so many I am appreciative for, but particularly Ashley, Temma and the indomitable Kristen, who never fail to get their pompoms out their closets for me and my books. I wish I could name everyone but in the interests of keeping the page count down, know I'm so grateful for all of you!

To my friends IRL—I'm sorry and I don't know how you put up with me. Particular applause goes to Siân, Steph, Raisa and Donna, who know just how to coax me off the cliff. Life would be less fun without you in it (and far more tense).

To the author friends I've made since this incredible journey began, thank you for your support, your sympathy, your sufferance. I'm incredibly privileged to be able to slide into your DMs and have you not only talk back, but also give me blurbs for my babies. You'll never get rid of me now…

To every single bookshop and librarian who continue to support my trio of witches—there are no words except thank you!

To my readers, old and new, who spend your valuable time reading, loving and sharing my books with your friends, you'll all definitely be on the nice list (or the naughty one, depending on your preference).

To my family, who make Christmas magical, then and now.

To Molly, who, on the day I wrote these acknowledgments, got into the last box of savory Christmas crackers and demolished them. What an angel.

And to me, who will always believe.